THE ART OF GREED

THE ART OF GREED

A NOVEL OF THE RISE AND FALL OF THE ASIAN GREAT GATSBY

HANS PETER BRUNNER

GREENLEAF
BOOK GROUP PRESS

This is a work of fiction. Although most of the characters, organizations, and events portrayed in the novel are based on actual historical counterparts, the dialogue and thoughts of these characters are products of the author's imagination.

Published by Greenleaf Book Group Press
Austin, Texas
www.gbgpress.com

Copyright © 2025 Hans Peter Brunner

All rights reserved.

Thank you for purchasing an authorized edition of this book and for complying with copyright law. No part of this book may be reproduced, stored in a retrieval system, or transmitted by any means, electronic, mechanical, photocopying, recording, or otherwise, without written permission from the copyright holder.

Distributed by Greenleaf Book Group

For ordering information or special discounts for bulk purchases, please contact Greenleaf Book Group at PO Box 91869, Austin, TX 78709, 512.891.6100.

Design and composition by Greenleaf Book Group
Cover design by Greenleaf Book Group
Cover images used under license from ©adobestock.com

Publisher's Cataloging-in-Publication data is available.

Print ISBN: 979-8-88645-254-9

eBook ISBN: 979-8-88645-255-6

To offset the number of trees consumed in the printing of our books, Greenleaf donates a portion of the proceeds from each printing to the Arbor Day Foundation. Greenleaf Book Group has replaced over 50,000 trees since 2007.

Printed in the United States of America on acid-free paper

25 26 27 28 29 30 31 32   10 9 8 7 6 5 4 3 2 1

First Edition

To my wife, Katharina, who always stood by me through the most difficult times, and to Raphael and Gabriel, my two sons, who never doubted me

The question isn't who is going to let me;
the question is who is going to stop me.

—Attributed to Ayn Rand

Preface

When the 1Malaysia Development Berhad (1MDB) scandal erupted in 2015, authorities in Switzerland, Singapore, Malaysia, and the United States had no clear understanding of what had happened; nor could they even imagine the sheer enormity of the scale of the fraud that had just started to unfold. Thus, caught off guard, they reacted by adopting a frantic scorched-earth approach of charging and arresting numerous individuals up and down the chains of command at several prominent international banks, many of them only alleged to have any connections to the dealings of 1MDB.

At that time, as I became aware that something was seriously wrong, I began my own internal investigation as the head of BSI Bank's Asia operations. However, before I could get to the bottom of the problem, all hell broke loose. In Singapore, five senior officers from BSI were charged with fraud, allegedly for not reporting suspicious transactions and other offenses, by the Singapore regulator and prosecutor. Eventually, some were fined, some were forced to return illegally obtained money, some were banned from working in the banking industry for ten or more years, and a few received stiff prison sentences.

In May 2016, I was placed under a publicly announced criminal investigation in Singapore. After five and a half years of intense scrutiny by the authorities, a mountain of legal paperwork, and enormous financial cost, I was completely exonerated when the investigation against me was finally closed in 2021 without any charges being filed.

But the damage had been done: My outstanding reputation, built over forty-five years in banking, had been destroyed virtually overnight. The investigation forced my retirement from BSI in 2016 and, needless to say, changed my life forever.

Through the duration of my ordeal, I became absolutely determined to uncover all the facts underlying the 1MDB scandal and its worldwide ramifications. Over the ensuing nine years since the scandal broke in 2015, I have collected and read voraciously just about everything that has been written, reported, or video-recorded about the scandal. My sources include U.S. Department of Justice papers and court filings, government and private bank regulators' announcements, newspapers, TV, Internet blogs and postings, and three books written about the 1MDB affair, as well as other sources that must remain confidential. As a result, I have become one of the world's leading experts on what actually happened and just who were the people chiefly responsible for the massive fraud. And I decided to write about it.

Amid all this research, three important themes or aspects emerge from the saga of 1MDB.

The first is something of a psychological question: What manner of cognitive hubris drives the sheer personal arrogance, fearless tolerance for risk, and utter disregard for international law as that breathtakingly exhibited by the mastermind Low Taek Jho, now known to most of the world as Jho Low?

The second theme centers on the staggeringly extensive list of people who, in their own way, and often within the particular niche of their own professional expertise, willingly served to facilitate one key facet or another of the broad and intricate complexities of the 1MDB affair. Incredibly, many of these participants managed to stay within a hair's width of the limits of the law.

The third aspect is perhaps the most incredible of all, and the one that remains a serious cause for alarm: A scandal in many if not all aspects like 1MDB could happen again. In short, nothing has been done to effect meaningful legal reform or to enhance global regulatory diligence that would prevent an operator from engaging in the very same fraudulent activities that enabled the theft of over $10 billion and the misdirection of billions more.

Written from the perspective of the mastermind, *The Art of Greed* imagines the provocative mindset, the complex personality traits, the flawed genius, and the sheer unflinching bravado of the man who today in self-imposed exile nevertheless sits atop the massive fraud that was 1MDB, while revealing, perhaps, some of the underlying sociocultural prerogatives that may have motivated him. And while this book is a work of fiction, it reveals many lesser-known facts about the people, places, and institutions that played a significant role—sometimes without even realizing it but mostly, it must be said, by simply looking the other way—in perhaps the greatest financial fraud in history.

—*H. P. Brunner*

Acknowledgments

I acknowledge and thank my real friends, the ones who gave me unflinching support and reassurance, as well as Art Lizza, my editorial consultant. Without his hard work, persistence, research, patience, and good humor, this book would never have happened.

Prologue

When I turned twenty, I threw a birthday party for myself. I was then a student at the renowned Wharton School of Business of the University of Pennsylvania. In fact, I was still a sophomore, not even an upperclassman, when I plunked down $40,000 to rent Shampoo, one of Philadelphia's poshest nightclubs, exclusively for one uproarious night. The fee included a full bar, with an exquisite selection of hors d'oeuvres and plenty of Cristal champagne to go around, as well as a five-piece band and a number of other choice entertainments to wow my fellow collegians, like, for instance, a gorgeous model who sauntered across the dance floor wearing only a scant bikini made of lettuce leaves and then reclined on top of one of the bars, where the chefs covered her body with sushi for my guests to eat with chopsticks. Or whatever way they liked, if they had the nerve.

I'll say the whole affair was a shock—even to the few close friends I had accumulated on campus to that point. To everyone else, the under- and upperclassmen, I was one of those geeky, awkward, seemingly nervous newbies shuttling silently from class to class, never talking to anyone. I was regarded by some, perhaps, as a good target for the reigning senior class students to prank if they possessed a mean streak. I can only presume this is how I must have appeared.

That perception was only exacerbated by my unmistakable Chinese-Malaysian appearance. My squat body and moon-shaped face were features that marked me as having a vastly different heritage from the majority of my student peers. Self-consciously, that heritage weighed on me more heavily than any of the majority white American and European matriculants could possibly understand, because I am my father's second son. In my culture, for thousands of years, it is the first son that is exalted and lavished with favor and praise and adoration, given the lion's share of inheritance and favorable life-affirming opportunity. Such is the inescapable power of one's cultural milieu that subconsciously and insidiously convinces a man that he has so much to prove and that he must do it all by himself, all the while additionally burdened with the task of bringing up the rear within the family's ancient and archaic hierarchy. Anyway, that was how I felt, although it was by no means how I acted. Little did my dear father know how I was spending the education money he was persistently sending me, which I acknowledge was received in wire transfers for as much as $10,000 at a time. Okay, so it wasn't like I was a total outcast, spurned and financially abandoned.

This is why my twentieth birthday was no typical college party with sloppy local draft beer and chips and dips flying around the room. No, my invitations read, "Fashionable attire is a must; no jeans or sneakers," and I issued two classes of invites—a standard, general admission one plus a special VIP invitation that entitled the holder to a complimentary "premium open bar" and special access to Shampoo's private rooftop atrium. The VIP invitations, I admit, went to the wealthiest students, or the ones with the highest connections that I could discern. In some cases, they went to a few guys and girls with such drop-dead good looks that I simply could not bring myself to exclude them from the VIP delegation. You want to have as many pretty bodies and faces—male and female—as you can at these kinds of events. In fact, I personally called the social directors of the top sororities to make sure the party would be well attended by the hottest and the most sought-after women. And I even arranged shuttle buses for my partygoers, from campus to the club and back.

THE ART OF GREED

Why would I do all of this?

Many of the kids I met at Wharton, as well as those I had met at Harrow, in Great Britain, where I had previously attended prep school, came from some of the richest and most powerful families around the world, not to mention the ruling families of some of the wealthiest nations on Earth. Many were fantastically wealthy beyond anyone's imagination. When you reach a certain stratospheric plane, money becomes almost meaningless—in and of itself, that is. Yet such ungodly wealth dictates—it demands, in fact—a whole different lifestyle milieu far and above and incomprehensibly alien to the common man. An altogether separate existence wherein one is thrust, often along with one's entire family, whether willingly or unwillingly, into the upper, rarefied orbit of political leaders and governmental statesmen (who often seek your advice foolishly, simply because you are so wealthy!), as well as that of the captains of global industry and business, the moguls of finance and international investment. In America, I would soon learn, such prodigious wealth also provides open and almost inevitable access to the high-wire world of entertainment, of Hollywood and the movies and the upper echelons of the most famous and most attractive and most desirable stage and screen celebrities in the universe.

Of course, if you ask me, many of the kids at Wharton—those from the most eternally moneyed families—were old before their time. Talking to them often felt like talking to my grandfather. Such stuff-shirts, I'm telling you! And I thought, *These guys could really use a good party!*

But in all seriousness, what I really wanted was for all of these fellow students to feel special, like the elite members of an exclusive club. It wasn't much of a stretch! The truth of the matter is that I wanted them to know precisely who I was. That's why I made sure to have my name—in big gold lettering—emblazoned across the invitations and right next to the sorority names. That way, no one could fail to see who the host of the party was. It certainly seemed to work; someone at the party that night referred to me loudly as "the Asian Great Gatsby," and as the label seemed to spread gleefully around the room like fans doing the wave at a football game, I was quite pleased and certainly did nothing to stop it. I wanted them to remember me, especially should I come to them somewhere down the line—after they'd graduated and become key executives at J.P. Morgan or Goldman Sachs or UBS—with a complex, majorly lucrative deal I wanted to make. Or for them to remember me when *they* had a deal *they* wanted to make, and they needed a get-it-done player like myself to make it happen with both flair and efficiency. It's funny, but Gatsby, Asian or otherwise, suited my purposes abundantly well.

One of the few people at Wharton whom I was able to relate to with any familiar intensity was a classmate named Seet Li Lin. It stood to reason, naturally enough, because Seet was from Singapore and from a prosperous family. And just as naturally, of course, he had received one of the exclusive VIP invitations, despite—let's just say—his lack of pedigree. In the early morning hours, as the party was winding down and after most of the guests had drifted away, he and I were sitting down together at a private table, Seet's tie undone and hanging on either side of the collars of his open shirt, my tux in rumpled disarray. (Of course I was wearing a tuxedo! Would you think anything less?) We were both exhausted.

"You know, Jho," Seet observed, "you had some pretty important kids here at this little shindig." He took a drag on the cigar he was smoking, exhaled a stream of white smoke, and then continued, "Sons and daughters of prominent and powerful families in business and industry, even government and politics, here and around the world."

I shrugged, lounging back in the soft leather of my chair as I swirled my glass of Macallan twenty-five-year-old single-malt scotch. "The stock-in-trade of Wharton," I sighed, trying to sound nonchalant about it, even a little deliberately cynical for effect. But, in fact, I was keenly interested in where Seet was going with this line of thought.

"Yes, of course," he replied, "but what I'm thinking is that they're the kind of movers and shakers that could help you move up in the world, maybe land you a great position with a Fortune 100 company anywhere in the world where you might choose to work and reside."

Abruptly, I shot upright and looked Seet squarely in the eyes as I clacked my scotch glass down on the glass tabletop.

"You mean employment?" I exclaimed.

Taken somewhat aback, Seet said nothing, only shook his head in a manner as if to say, *Yes, but what did I say?*

"I don't want to work for these people," I declared emphatically. "All these brilliant kids you see walking around and coming from their elite, old-money aristocrat families, they're all just stepping stones. They're just the keyholders to wealth and power and true greatness, and I don't think half of them even realize what they represent, the doors they can open. No, Seet, *they're going to work for me!* Or more precisely, they're going to partner with me—under my direction, of course, but using their influence—doing the international investment deals that I'm going to design, direct, orchestrate, and execute. Do you understand?"

Seet looked at me silently for a long moment, as if reading my intensity.

"Okay," he said finally.

"Just watch me," I said firmly, in the manner of laying down a challenge. "Just watch me go."

I mean, what ambitious kid halfway through business school doesn't insanely desire to become an instant world-beater?

Chapter 1

They say that the most successful people are the ones who learn from their mistakes. I'd have to say I found that out in a big way when my own odyssey began with the Iskandar land deal, or as it was formally known in Malaysia, the Iskandar Development Region. To state it flatly, I never felt that I was duly recognized for all of the hard yet mostly behind-the-scenes work I did in connection with those negotiations; nor did I ever feel that I was particularly well remunerated for my efforts. Yet that experience was where I began to learn the ropes of international financial deal-making, and it's where I got my first glimpse of the enormous amounts of money involved—and that, moreover, could be had—at that level, within the global interface of government leaders and multinational corporations, powered by an elite collection of banking monoliths.

And it was through the Iskandar development experience that I came to the conclusion that somehow, one way or another, I absolutely had to gain control of the funds in a national investment trust fund, like the ones I saw among the oil-rich Middle Eastern sheikhdoms, and which were just beginning to be formed among some emerging nations in Southeast Asia. Nations that, as late as the turn of the twenty-first century, were just beginning to gain—and leverage—the kind of sophisticated, Westernized capitalization of the natural resources they possessed—coal and crude oil or forest products and palm oil production on a grand scale. Nations that were just beginning to flex the powerful muscles of the financial wealth that lay on or beneath their sovereign soil, virtually stockpiled there and just waiting for the taking. Nations that were just beginning to have their eyes opened to how that wealth could catapult them as key players onto the stage of rapidly emerging globalization in financial investment and business development far beyond their borders.

Naturally, my prime target became my own country of Malaysia.

When I graduated from the Wharton School in 2005, I was ready to take on the world. More specifically, I was ready to take on the world of international finance, where I was determined to be a dealmaker operating only at the highest echelons, where multinational banks and corporations and governments do business and politics in an almost incomprehensible, ethereal realm of billions of dollars; that's billions with a B rather than the chicken feed of paltry millions. You could say I was incredibly brash, I suppose; some people would even have said that I was monstrously arrogant. Yet to know me now, even after all that has happened in the ensuing years, you might be surprised if I told you that, back then, I was also incredibly idealistic. I thought I could do good things for the world, and if I possessed the ambition to do that on the grandest of all possible scales, what could possibly be the harm in that?

In particular, I wanted to do good things for the people of Malaysia. I mean, why not? As long as I could make a ton of money for myself and my friends along the way.

In addition to providing a world-class education, my days at Wharton—as also my preparatory education at the Harrow School in Great Britain—had fortuitously provided me with introductions to well-connected and powerful people whose access to virtually unlimited capital wealth was nothing short of breathtaking.

I did not covet their inconceivably staggering wealth, and that's the truth—at least, not for the sake of wealth alone. Because, at the time, all I could think about was what I could do with all of that capital, which was to say, the massive deals I could make, the international capital investment mountains I could move. Although in truth, I knew that once I gained that sort of access, I would also have as much money for myself as I might desire or imagine.

That's really the thing about it. When you move in circles of people and organizations that essentially swim in virtual oceans brimming with endlessly flowing cash, the sheer volume of it becomes almost meaningless; the value of that capital becomes downright trivial. As the old cliché goes, "There's always more where that came from." Or so it seemed. And yet all the while, in the most incorrigibly subversive of ways, the deep, subconscious, insatiable urge to have and create even more of it becomes as diabolically addictive and all-consuming as any opioid you can imagine. So, for me, it became a rhetorical question: *Just how much money can one person possibly generate or accumulate?*

I would eventually come to the conclusion that the possibilities were simply limitless, but far more intriguing to me was that this meant there always would be the opportunity for making an even bigger deal with that ever-accumulating capital and a bigger deal after that.

You take the countries in the Middle East, for example, an economic region of the world that has fascinated me since—I don't know—as long as I can remember. Perhaps since the day I learned that the Middle East sits on eighty percent of the world's known oil reserves. It seemed to me that capital poured out of the ground like the crude oil itself, continuously, never-ending, the gift that keeps on giving.

Yet the more I learned about the members of the sheikh families that I would come to know, the more I realized that the money wasn't the thing driving them. It was power and prestige, the ability to shape the globalization of the international financial world to suit their specific interests while having the oldest and most historically storied financial institutions kowtowing to their every whim. And I wanted that. Or maybe I wanted their ability to dictate to their own sovereign governments the prescribed social and political policy of the land, both foreign and domestic, rather than having to knuckle under to the prevailing regime. From what I was able to discern about the wealthiest—and, for that reason, the most intriguingly attractive—nations in the Middle East, the wealth and the governments were essentially one and the same. The families that owned the wealth also ran the governments. I thought, *What a great platform for doing business!*

At the same time, I sensed a great deal of promise in developing nations that were just beginning to discover their own fantastic sovereign wealth, whether that happened to be in the form of oil reserves beneath their own soil or in more heavily commodity-based resources like timber and minerals and the right climate conditions for palm oil production and on and on—including and especially my own homeland of Malaysia.

And I was absolutely convinced that what they desperately needed was a guy with the ability and the skills—and the sheer bravado—to connect them with other movers and shakers, who could help them put the pieces of financially complex, multinational deals together, someone who could turn millions into billions and billions into trillions. The way I looked at it, the powers that be in Malaysia—not to mention the Middle East—had more money than they knew what to do with, and I was determined to be the guy who could solve that problem for them. The only question that remained was *How do I get access to that enormous wealth?*

In order to find an answer to that question, and while I was still a student at Wharton, I traveled to the Middle East, where I took a grand tour of the region. The year was 2003, and basically, I wanted to learn how things worked there, in a place where so much of the world's wealth was so delightfully concentrated. Ultimately, my quest led me to Abu Dhabi, the capital city of the United Arab Emirates, and I was downright blown away speechless by what I saw there.

If I were to even pretend to be poetic, I might describe the approach to Dubai airport as *descending below a veil of clouds to reveal* this magnificent city. But there are no clouds over Abu Dhabi—almost never. The city shimmers to rival the eye-tearing brightness of the sun, as if all of the buildings everywhere are inlaid with cut diamonds.

At that time, the city was in the early days of one of the famously greatest construction booms of all time, which would turn Abu Dhabi into one of the most modern, most vibrant, and most visually iconic metropolises outside of the Emerald City of Oz. Even seeing it from the air, the vision of this treeless ultra-modern city rising out of the desert was mesmerizing.

Once on the ground, riding in my limo to the hotel, I felt invigorated in both body and mind by the energy that seemed to be generated there, seemingly out of thin air. In the middle of the city, work was proceeding furiously on the three-billion-dollar Emirates Palace, destined to become one of the world's glitziest and most exclusive hotels. All of this frenzied development was being financed through the staggering profits derived from the steadily rising oil prices of the day, and this epic transformation was being directly overseen by Abu Dhabi's royal ruling family itself. I marveled just trying to imagine the enormous amounts of capital that must have been driving the capital's wholesale transformation, almost overnight, into a world-class city.

Difficult as it was through all of that lustrous distraction, I was determined to keep focused on what was really my central mission. Specifically, I wanted to make connections among the people who controlled all that wealth, and it was in Abu Dhabi that I managed through a great deal of wrangling to arrange to have lunch with Ambassador Yousef Al Otaiba. Otaiba is the son of a former Abu Dhabi oil minister who, at age twenty-six—three years prior to when I met with him—had become a key advisor to none other than Abu Dhabi's crown prince, Mohammed bin Zayed Al Nahyan, for whom he also became the chief national security liaison coordinating with foreign governments. He was exactly the kind of rising star, with access and influence over the wealth and power of Abu Dhabi that I wanted to connect with.

And, truth be told, I had absolutely no standing to even be in the same room with him. But I didn't let that stop me. Even before my arrival in the Middle East, I had begun pestering Ambassador Otaiba with emails and texts, including one text that I sent as soon as I got to my hotel, in which I announced my arrival and formal request for an *audience*. I used that term deliberately, like someone reverently seeking to speak with the pope.

Finally, a terse text response came back: "Who are you?" And I knew I was in.

"I am a student from Wharton, in America," I texted back, "touring Middle Eastern nations to learn about international finance and wealth management from the very best."

Otaiba seemed amused but curious. "Why?" he replied.

I responded that I was from Malaysia, my home country about to emerge into its own wealth development boom from oil and forest products, and I made up some fantastic things about my father's political connections back home.

I got my audience. And I must say, Ambassador Otaiba was remarkably more than gracious with this "simple student" from Wharton, patiently answering my questions about international investment.

That was all to the good. But, as these things often do, the real breakthrough came only a short time later, when Otaiba introduced me to Khaldoon Khalifa Al Mubarak, from whom I would first learn about sovereign wealth funds and how they operate.

I had already done my homework on Mubarak, and I knew that, quite tragically, his father had been working as an Emirati ambassador when he was murdered in the streets of Paris by Palestinian terrorists in 1984. That, however, had not stopped the son from rising to a position of power and influence in Abu Dhabi, where, just as Otaiba had done, Mubarak had also made himself into a trusted advisor to Crown Prince Mohammed bin Zayed Al Nahyan. Of even greater interest to me was the fact that Mubarak was in charge of running an Abu Dhabi sovereign investment fund called Mubadala. I'm sure that my eyes widened as Mubarak explained to me how such funds work.

"Sovereign wealth funds have been around since the 1950s," Mubarak said, "when countries like Saudi Arabia and Kuwait needed to create entities through which they could invest the prodigious oil wealth they began to acquire in the postwar decade—wealth that I'm sure you know only grew exponentially in the decades after that, right up to today."

This was the cash that was gushing out of the ground that I talked about earlier.

"Like, for example, the wealth that is building this city right now," I offered.

"Correct," Mubarak said. "The original idea had been to establish these instruments as a means of securing national stability while also promoting growth through government investment in domestic infrastructure improvements, business and real estate development designed to support and boost the national economy. For the good of the people, you see."

I could see immediately that, as nice a civic gesture as all that might have been, coming from the government in question, this was a way, way too conservative approach to exploiting the potentialities for all of that money! To my way of thinking, these countries began by very timidly using all that massive capital like some sort of rainy day fund or piggy bank, when there were such fabulously larger opportunities at hand—and on a much grander and more influential global scale. And to some extent, I was right.

"You said that was the 'original' idea?" I asked. "What happened after that?"

"A couple of things," he explained. "For one, gradually, these oil-rich nations became less and less content with simply using their sovereign trust funds to invest oil profits for the modest purpose of securing capital for future generations, as commendable as that might have been."

At this, Mubarak paused, and a faint smile came over his face that I can only describe as salacious. "After all, when you have billions of dollars coming out of your ears—"

"You want to play with it," I attempted, perhaps too brashly, to finish his sentence.

Mubarak seemed to stifle a laugh and then became serious again. "Let's just say that when you have such an overwhelming abundance of cash, you need—in fact, you have a fiscal responsibility—to invest that money wisely. You can only build so much infrastructure, and you don't want to leave ridiculous capital in what amounts to a low-yield money market account, so you need to diversify. You want to make that capital work for you."

"Of course," I acknowledged.

"Yes, but that's more important than you might realize," Mubarak counseled, "because another thing that happened, as the new millennium approached, was that the paradigm oil-producing countries around the world began to learn some lessons about the economic precariousness of relying almost exclusively on a single-commodity national industry."

I knew very well what Mubarak was talking about. The discovery of new oil reserves outside the Middle East and the implementation of new oil production technologies like fracking in the United States and elsewhere could wreak havoc on the economies of Middle Eastern nations, for whom oil exportation was their lifeblood. They could no longer depend on a steady, uninterrupted escalation of the per-barrel price for oil from one year to the next—or even from one month to the next. Even more worrisome, those other emerging oil and gas resources served, to a significant extent, to weaken the monopoly that the traditional exporting countries once held and had taken advantage of most notably—and most diabolically—during the infamous oil embargo of 1973.

"So," Mubarak summed up, "the leading oil-producing countries began investing their sovereign fund capital more broadly across global markets—aggressively seeking to diversify their economies. They wanted to promote greater national economic resiliency, and a greater role within the broader universe of international investment and finance would give them that. To become investment partners with the other nations of the world, if you will."

"And you manage that investment portfolio for Mubadala?" I queried.

"Of course," Mubarak replied with a broad smile of satisfaction.

"As we speak, Mubadala has significant investments in over forty of the leading economic nations of the world."

Well, so much for the history lesson. But by now you can probably surmise what it was that I really liked about the fundamental concept of the sovereign investment fund. It was simply this: Just imagine being in control of all that money, all the while having the government's blessing to invest it any way you wanted. This, for me, was rapture.

Now, certainly, one didn't need to go to Wharton to understand that it was utterly senseless to keep enormous wealth languishing in a piggy bank, even at interest. But that didn't mean you spent it recklessly—at least, not right away. Quite to the contrary, I seem, even from my youth, to have always believed that whenever you came into a windfall of money, there were only two things to do with it. The first was to leverage an even bigger deal to capture an even greater amount of capital, and the second was to spend it lavishly. I don't know where exactly I got such notions; perhaps they are in my DNA. In any case, I did quite a lot of both, as you will learn in these pages, and frankly, it didn't matter to me whether it was my money or someone else's. In fact, as far as I was concerned, it was much better when it was somebody else's money! My conversation with Mubarak had only served to ratify that conclusion.

When I looked toward my homeland of Malaysia, I discovered that it too had a nascent sovereign wealth fund called Khazanah Nasional, founded in 1993, although it was nowhere near the size and stature of Mubadala. I was nevertheless intrigued, and I began to think about ways that I might in some way become involved in the management of Khazanah. I even fantasized about what prospect I might have of ultimately gaining control of this Malaysian wealth fund, just the way Mubarak controlled the Mubadala fund for Abu Dhabi. But how was I going to get there?

Well, the first thing I knew I had to do was to get as close as I

THE ART OF GREED

could to some of the most powerful people in the Malaysian government. Fortunately, I already had an excellent connection. During my days in London, while I was attending the Harrow school, I had made friends with Riza Aziz, the stepson of Najib Razak, then the Malaysian defense minister, as well as the son of a former prime minister and nephew of another. Najib's own political career trajectory made him an odds-on favorite to be elected prime minister himself one day. Riza was a few years older than me and attending college at the London School of Economics when I first ventured to meet him.

It only took a little reconnaissance to discover that Riza loved American basketball, and he often practiced or played in pick-up games between classes at a gym near campus. So I donned gym shorts and sneakers and went there to challenge him to a little game of one-on-one. Needless to say, Riza laughed. I must have looked ridiculous.

"*You're* challenging *me*?" he exclaimed, pointing to his own chest, his eyebrows seeming to jump up under the red and white checkered headband he wore to keep the sweat out of his eyes.

"Yes," I said calmly. "I'll even give you first outs."

Now Riza is only about five nine—really, only two inches taller than me! And so he was categorically not destined for the NBA, but he was physically fit and extremely agile, and he could run circles around me on the court, which he did every time. He beat the pants off me, as the expression goes. But I just took it all in stride, and a friendship was acquired, and even as I eventually left for the United States to attend Wharton, I had made a point to stay in close touch with him, as well as with his distinguished family.

As my last semester at Wharton was coming to a close, I formed my first company, registering it in the British Virgin Islands and naming it Wynton Group—because my goal was to win tons of money. Okay, I guess I was pretty brash and arrogant after all.

Anyway, when I returned to my homeland of Malaysia—or perhaps I should call it the adoptive homeland of my Chinese family—I set up my office headquarters in Kuala Lumpur, on the seventieth floor of the famed Petronas Towers no less. At that time, the towers were the tallest buildings in the world, the premier business address in the capital city of Malaysia, and one of the most important addresses across the entire Southeast Asia region, outside of Singapore, of course. Only the best-known Malaysian firms had their offices there—could *afford* to have their offices there. The only proof one needed to support that claim was to know that the towers are the headquarters of Petronas itself, the state-run oil company whose profits were almost single-handedly fueling Malaysia's emerging economic transformation at the end of the twentieth century and into the beginning of the twenty-first.

Now something I'm not particularly proud of: I prevailed upon my father to give me some of the money that I used to secure the ridiculously expensive lease on the offices in the towers. He complained about it incessantly for months after I signed the papers.

"Why the Petronas Towers?" he whined. "There's plenty of office space in Kuala Lumpur you can get for a third of the rent they're going to stick you for—and in some really beautiful and upscale parts of town too."

He was so damned old school. He didn't have a clue how the world works in the twenty-first century. I argued with him. "You don't understand, Father," I lamented. "Business today is all about appearances; it's about glitz and glamour and the ultra-modern sophistication that draws wealthy clients to you like moths to a flame. If you make a fantastic show of success, success will naturally come to you."

Then I added for good measure, "That isn't going to happen if your office is some back-bay storefront that looks like a Chinese laundry or a flower shop."

"Nonsense!" was all he said in response. But he gave me the money, albeit begrudgingly. However, it was not nearly enough, the old fool.

Undeterred, I was determined to do it up right, so I went out and secured several rather heavy business loans from local banks that, quite conveniently, my father had done business with over many decades. In some cases, my father introduced me to the bank's principals, however reluctantly. In other instances, he refused, but I went there anyway and just used his name whether he approved it or not. The plain fact was that I absolutely needed those loans so that I could afford the high-ticket rent of office space in the towers, but I also spent wildly on the most lavish appointments I could think of. Even now, it amuses me to remember the huge island boardroom in the very center of the space, surrounded by inch-thick floor-to-ceiling glass that, when privacy was required, could be frosted over with the touch of a button. The toilet seats in the restrooms that automatically adjusted to the height of the occupant! I spared no expense, and that office was described by the local press as the most luxurious in the entire country of Malaysia.

Most people would have ridiculed such opulence as nothing more or less than gross and unconscionable irresponsibility on my part. But I believed it was all quite necessary. It was imperative that I should massively impress the wealthy, powerful, elite individuals I was determined to do business with, whose universe I desperately wanted to inhabit.

At the same time, I continued my efforts to ingratiate myself with the family of Najib Razak, who, in 2004, had risen from minister of defense to the position of deputy prime minister. While I had not yet formally met Najib, a mutual friend had introduced me to one of his brothers, the one named Nizam. When I learned that Nizam was looking for office space, I offered him an ample suite of very attractive, already furnished rooms in Wynton's Petronas Towers headquarters, which Nizam happily accepted.

Here, I have to acknowledge that my earliest investment ventures were terrible failures. The first was a high-end condominium development only a few blocks from the Petronas Towers that fell through in the most miserable of ways. The most damaging part about the failure of that deal, however, was that I had convinced Nizam to go in as a coinvestor with Wynton. Meanwhile, I had gotten myself so much in debt to the banks that when the down payment came due, I was unable to raise the funds. Shortly thereafter, it took a very slick businessman fixer retained by the Najib family to bail both Nizam and me out of the horrible financial hole I'd gotten us into. It was worse than humiliating; the whole affair severely damaged my image and reputation in the eyes of the deputy prime minister and his family, especially his wife, Rosmah Mansor, who I would quickly learn was a powerful driving force in both Najib's personal *and* political life. One could never please Najib without first and foremost pleasing Rosmah. I could only pray that the damage that I had done was not irreparable.

From there, things got progressively worse. Because the next thing I did, I tried to broker a deal for the Kuwait Finance House—an Islamic bank that had also been involved in the condominium deal—to take over a much smaller Malaysian bank. That failed too, and when I subsequently became unable to pay the rent for several months—much less pay back the huge loans I had taken out just to set up shop there—I had to give up my ritzy office digs in the Petronas Towers. Those ghastly failures were extremely disappointing, I'll admit, but I'm not one to give up easily, and it was right about that time that I fortuitously learned about a new project in Malaysia called the Iskandar Development Region.

Iskandar was ambitiously conceived as a sprawling and spectacular state-of-the-art urban development project in Malaysia's southern state of Johor. It was designed specifically to become a financial hub and ultra-modern cosmopolitan city center to rival Singapore, complete with futuristic hotels, office buildings, and high-end shopping, and sitting just across the sparkling waters of the Johor Strait from Singapore itself. And to my extreme delight, I discovered that Malaysia's sovereign wealth fund, Khazanah, was looking for partners to finance this incredible construction project!

Here was my opportunity to leverage the invaluable connections I had fostered four years earlier during my fact-finding mission to the Middle East—and Abu Dhabi in particular—while still a student at Wharton. Yet far more important than even that, here also was my chance to get myself back into the good graces of the Najib family—and abundantly so, given both the financial and the political magnitude of the project. I also knew it could lead to a direct meeting for the first time with the deputy prime minister himself—my ultimate goal—and to meet Rosmah too.

There was no time to lose. There was an enormously lucrative deal to be brokered here, and I got right down to work. The first thing I did: In June 2007, I sent an email to Otaiba, in which I provided a description of the preliminary plans for the Iskandar development. In that email, I also strongly recommended to Otaiba that Mubadala should take advantage of this fantastic opportunity to invest and become a stakeholder in Malaysia's rapidly expanding economy.

And while Otaiba was my principal contact in Abu Dhabi, the exponential growth of the Mubadala wealth fund under the direction of its chief executive had only added to Al Mubarak's prestige and his power of influence as a highly successful fund manager. Skyrocketing oil prices over the preceding several years had enabled Mubadala to take significant minority stakes in some fancy, high-profile companies around the world—like Ferrari, one that I particularly liked and applauded. In effect, Mubarak had quietly gained control over a multibillion-dollar empire that was continuing to grow exponentially with each passing month.

From there on, I meticulously orchestrated everything that went down. I arranged the flights that whisked Khazanah executives to Abu Dhabi, where I set up the first meeting to introduce them to Otaiba and Mubarak, among others. Thereafter, I set up a series of meetings both in Abu Dhabi and in Putrajaya, just outside of Kuala Lumpur, a new city that had been built specifically to become the architecturally resplendent seat of the Malaysian government back in the 1990s. A colleague of mine, a well-traveled fellow by the name of Eric Tan and one of my first hires at Wynton Group, upon watching my plans unfold, exclaimed, "My god, Jho, you stage-managed those meetings exactly like the director of a Broadway musical in New York City."

I could only smile, because Eric was right. That is exactly what I had done, because I was determined that this deal would go exactly according to plan, and I wanted to leave absolutely nothing to chance.

In any case, one of those plans was, at last, my first private meeting with the deputy PM himself, in which I explained the details of the deal and graciously offered for Najib to take full credit for it. I would do all the legwork, I assured him.

Najib was skeptical to say the least. Who could blame him? He's standing there looking at this baby-faced upstart kid fresh out of school, with no other obvious credentials offering him the development deal of a lifetime.

"*You?*" he said, his eyes narrowing as he spoke. "You can deliver major investment capital from the Middle East? Is that what you're telling me?"

His skepticism only emboldened me.

"Think of it," I said. "On the day this project is approved, you will be standing in front of the Malaysian television cameras and news reporters with a golden shovel in your hands, breaking ground for this prestigious development project. And I don't need to tell you that Iskandar will directly challenge Singapore's preeminence right under their noses!"

The deputy PM pondered, stroking his chin with his right hand. He looked positively celestial.

Iskandar would almost certainly enhance Najib's persona and popularity among the Malaysian people, as well as his national and international stature as a political leader with the vision to lead Malaysia into the twenty-first century, and I was more than happy that he should take the credit for it. There was a catch, of course. As I was obliged to bet on only one powerful politician—or a single well-placed political family, as it were—it also would not hurt my personal interest in moving closer to the financial engines of wealth in Malaysia and beyond if the Iskandar deal helped Najib to significantly consolidate even greater power and prominence. The deputy PM and the Razak family collectively were a good bet; Najib's UMNO party had held power for the entire sixty years since Malaysia declared independence from Great Britain in 1957. The only thing that was important now, or so I thought, was that Najib should know and well remember that it was me who "gifted" him with this high-profile development deal.

So it was that I was there, in the magnificent grand ballroom of Najib and Rosmah's palatial official residence in Putrajaya, that night in August 2007, when all of the important principals and their elegant guests were gathered to celebrate the consummation of a breathtaking financial deal. Mubadala and the Kuwait Finance House had each agreed to take major stakes in the Johor development project that was, in the final design, even more lavish than originally conceived, to include five-star hotels, upscale residences, and a complete golf village along with the originally proposed financial center.

As with all of those critical business meetings, I had instrumentally organized this gala shindig as well, and I was there, hovering in the background, making sure everybody was having a good time—and that they were meeting the right people. I really didn't want any part of the spotlight that celebratory night, but I damn sure wanted the right people to know who the dealmaker behind it all was, who had made this gathering possible in the first place. That dealmaker was me.

And there was Rosmah Mansor, resplendent in the traditional brightly colored silks of Malaysia, smiling appreciatively as she greeted all the invitees as they arrived. You can imagine how I felt when, a short time later, she herself took the microphone in hand and addressed the throng of the very distinguished and influential people in that room, saying, among other things, "It is my great pleasure and privilege to thank Jho Low for bringing Middle Eastern investment to Malaysia." It was precisely what I wanted everyone in that room to hear and remember. And then I was ready to leave the party.

I was utterly shocked when Rosmah intercepted me at the door.

"Jho, dear Jho!" she cried effusively. "Are you leaving so soon?" In all of her finery, she came gliding toward me with her arms outstretched, embracing me and giving me a light peck on the cheek.

"Yes, Madame Rosmah," I demurred. "I'm afraid so."

"Oh, what a shame! I must thank you for this marvelous gathering," she said. But then she leaned in closely and confided, just above a whisper, "I want you to know that I forgive you for all that bad business with Nizam."

I was thunderstruck, fumbled for words. "Yes . . . no . . . I'm sorry. I mean, I have to admit I made some poor decisions there—"

Rosmah shook her head resolutely as she cut me off.

"No you didn't," she insisted. "My husband's brother is a loser. It's not the first time one of Nizam's crazy schemes has failed. Believe me," she said, her eyes rolling in her head. Then, putting her hands on my shoulders, she looked me directly in the eyes and said, "You have a good night, and thank you again for all of this," waving her right hand in a circle in the air. I realized and made note of the fact that Rosmah clearly reveled in celebratory lavishness such as this; the more decadent, the better. Good to know.

And that was that. Accordingly, on the morning after the party, Al Mubarak, on behalf of Mubadala, signed a contract to invest half a billion dollars in the Iskandar Development Region. I could not have been more delighted with the outcome.

My delight, however, was short-lived, to say the least. Khazanah Nasional categorically refused to pay me a broker fee for all the hard, diligent work I had done. The investment partners I had so tenaciously developed for Khazanah—the exceedingly wealthy partners, I might add—had not only made the Iskandar development a reality but, having now been introduced to an emerging Malaysia and formed a relationship with its rising political star of Najib Razak, were now poised to pursue future investment in our country. I could not fathom such ingratitude. The plain fact is, I was infuriated.

When I couldn't contain myself and confided my anger with Khazanah to Mubarak, he was unsympathetic, to say the least. He just shrugged and said, "What have you done, little man, other than introduce some powerful people to each other?"

"I did a lot more than that," I said. "I choreographed the whole thing."

"What, flying people around on planes to attend stuffy meetings?

Do you really expect the Khazanah board members to be impressed with that? Remember, they're the ones who control the money. Do you think they're going to just give it away?"

Mubarak's words only made me angrier, and I utterly detested being called "little man." But he was right.

At that moment, I decided that I needed, one way or another, to work my way into gaining control of a new and different kind of sovereign wealth fund, where I would have the power and authority to decide where the money would go. I wanted my name—or, I should say, the names of the financial entities *that I formed*—to be on those checks the way Al Mubarak directed the funds in Mubadala for Abu Dhabi. And I had a pretty clear notion about how to do just that.

Chapter 2

As angry and disgusted as I was with Khazanah's refusal to pay me a broker's fee, the Iskandar development project had done a world of good for my relationship with the Najib family. Over the course of working to bring Middle Eastern investment to Malaysia—and proving that I was the guy who could achieve that—I also seized the opportunity to help Najib and Rosmah with some personal matters—in particular, by forming an offshore company through which the couple could pay for their daughter's college education at Georgetown University in the United States.

To tell you the truth, I was shocked at how easy it was to set up this sort of offshore entity; you didn't need to be any sort of business or financial genius to get it done. For only a couple thousand dollars, there were plenty of financial services companies based in out-of-the-spotlight countries like Panama or the Seychelles that would happily set up an account or form a company. They would do all the paperwork and, most importantly, didn't ask a lot of questions.

In any case, you can imagine how pleased and excited I was when Najib and Rosmah proudly invited me to attend their daughter's high school graduation ceremony and after-party upon her completion of studies at the prestigious Sevenoaks School located in Kent, just a short hop southeast of London. I knew then I was making good progress in becoming more than a trusted advisor to the deputy prime minister, which was to say, I felt that I was becoming a friend of the family as well. This was crucial to my future plans.

At the same time, I kept looking hard at all aspects of the Iskandar deal to see if there was any room to leverage a bit more mileage out of the project for my own benefit after all the hard work I'd done to make it happen. After being shut out by Khazanah—and, frankly, to retaliate for that snub—I was determined to figure out a scheme to wrangle some major money out of the whole deal in spite of everything that had happened.

Financially speaking, virtually anyone could see that this massive Johor development was a hands-down winner and bound to become a resounding success if for no other reason than the incredible amounts of capital that were going to be poured into it. The financial newspapers across all of Southeast Asia, including Singapore, were abuzz with predictions of the economic boost the project would bring to the entire region, and they were simply giddy with delight over the huge investment of Middle Eastern money by Mubadala and the Kuwait Finance House. More locally, however, people in Malaysia were excited about the very practical aspect of the thousands of jobs the project would create.

And that's when it hit me. Starting essentially from scratch, the development plans for Iskandar involved building new roads and infrastructure, as well as the construction of new housing, office towers, and industrial complexes, not to mention shopping malls, hotels, and entertainment venues. In short, it would be, first and foremost and right out of the box, a financial and economic boom to the construction industry before it would be profitable to any other sector. Bottom line: There were big bucks to be made in construction at that moment.

So I did some digging, and I found two established construction companies that happened to be for sale. I thought that, if I could figure out a way to buy both of them, perhaps those firms could then win lucrative contracts on the Iskandar development. However, even if I were able to buy the companies on the cheap, we were still talking a pair of multimillion-dollar deals. And for me, there were some serious obstacles to raising the funds. On one hand, I was already in serious debt, in large part for all the money I'd borrowed and spent on the lavish Petronas Towers offices for the Wynton Group and its subsidiaries. That's not even to mention some other seriously in-debt ventures I'd gotten myself into.

On the other hand, to be brutally honest, I was still something of a nobody to the major banks in and around Malaysia and Singapore. After all, none of them knew anything about the pivotal role I had played in bringing the Iskandar deal into existence in the first place—especially in securing that Middle Eastern investment the papers were fawning over. That was partly my fault, because I'd deliberately stayed in the shadows during all of those complex negotiations.

Mind you, I have no regrets about that—staying out of the limelight had, in fact, very critically served many of my most key purposes in orchestrating the deal. Not the least of those purposes—as I stressed earlier—was my desire to bring myself much, much closer to the political leader who would ultimately become the Malaysian prime minister, specifically, by letting him take the credit for the deal. I envisioned that he would be much more valuable to me later on. But the truth was, I was learning, pretty much day by day that maintaining my anonymity, as a rule, would, in fact, almost always serve my purposes so well that it would remain one of my most valuable tools. What I had to do better, however, what the Iskandar deal taught me, was that I needed to devise ways to ensure that a share of the capital in such deals would flow more reliably to me—or to my control.

Yet the problem still loomed: In spite of everything I'd done up until now, I was going to need millions more dollars to buy those construction companies. So to begin with, I just figured that the easiest thing to do was to set up a couple of conveniently opaque offshore entities in the hope that I could use them to borrow more money. But that's when I got a sublimely simple but positively brilliant idea.

I had seen how the very scent on the wind of Middle East money had so easily opened doors among the already rich and powerful entities and individuals in Malaysia, from banks to politicians. When the visions of partnering with Mubadala to invest in the homegrown Iskandar Development Region danced in their heads, even the stodgy, stuffed-shirt, do-it-only-by-the-book board of executives at Khazanah had to sit up and take serious notice at this plum of an investment deal that I was orchestrating (even if they too failed to appreciate what I was doing to make that happen).

I began by forming an offshore entity in the British Virgin Islands, which I named rather officiously the Abu Dhabi Kuwait Malaysia Investment Corporation. I immediately sent free shares to Ambassador Otaiba of Abu Dhabi and to several minor officials connected to the Kuwait Finance House whom I'd met during the Iskandar negotiations. You see, I wanted this whole thing to look like there was a potent Middle Eastern component to this new investment organization—with deep pockets, of course—and also that there were some very prominent, high-powered, and highly respected individuals from that region who were behind the company. It was the only way I could think of to make the Malaysian banks take me seriously. And it worked like a charm.

In fact, it worked so well that it left me breathless. When we then sought to borrow money, the Malaysian banks that the ADKMIC targeted were practically falling all over themselves trying to lend us tens of millions of dollars and then tens of millions more on top of that! It was like they gave me a shovel and a wheelbarrow, pointed to the bank vault, and said, "Help yourself!"

Not only was I able to buy the two construction companies I was after, but I had enough cash left over to transfer a large chunk of the money to a Wynton Group subsidiary through which I subsequently turned around and took out a minority stake in the Iskandar land project itself. I was beside myself with glee at the supremely gratifying irony of that. Here, Khazanah had refused me a broker fee, so instead, I one-upped them, if you will, by becoming a coinvestor in the lucrative project right alongside Mubadala and the Kuwait Finance House! But I absolutely wasn't finished yet—not by a long shot.

Because next, I formed two more offshore shell companies, this time incorporating them in the Seychelles, where I learned such accounts or companies are shielded by even more secrecy than entities incorporated in the BVI. The names I registered for the two Seychelles entities were important and crucially pinpointed: One was called ADIA Investment Corporation, and the other was called the KIA Investment Corporation. To understand why this was so important, you have to understand that two of the most famous, multibillion-dollar sovereign wealth funds in the world at that time were the Abu Dhabi Investment Authority and the Kuwait Investment Authority.

Or: the ADIA and the KIA for short, and as they were commonly known in international investment circles.

Do you see what I did there?

If a banker or an investment entrepreneur didn't look too close, they might think they were dealing with one or the other of the richest and most prestigious wealth funds in existence. And I was already beginning to observe that many bankers and entrepreneurs, faced with the prospect of a potential windfall deal, indeed tended not to look too close. It was that simple.

Anyway, as soon as these two Seychelles entities were formed, I had each of them take out minority stakes in the two construction companies I had bought through my Abu Dhabi Kuwait Malaysia Investment Corporation. So now, this whole complex and apparently sophisticated arrangement made it look for all the world like I was partnering in a significant portion of the Iskandar development plan with the very best elements you could want—royals from Kuwait and Ambassador Otaiba and other high-ranking officials from Abu Dhabi, with the backing of two major Middle Eastern sovereign wealth funds, all invested in the construction firms poised to land long-term lucrative contracts in the project.

At the same time, of course, all of this was just a means to an end. I didn't really want to be in the construction business, nor that of real estate development *per se*, so the next part of my plan was to find a wealthy buyer to whom I could quickly flip the whole conglomeration. And the buyer needed to be somebody who wouldn't look too deeply into what I was selling. As a used car dealer might have put it, I needed somebody who wouldn't "look under the hood."

Fortunately, while my direct and influential role in being the first person to bring huge piles of Middle Eastern capital to Malaysia had gone largely unnoticed and unappreciated by the country's myopic banking industry, several influential countrymen did know of my instrumental role in bringing together all the investment parties in the Iskandar project. In fact, many regional officials were suddenly interested in talking to me. Most of all, they were keenly interested in the further investment cash that I promised everyone would soon be coming to Malaysia from Mubadala and any number of other wealth funds in the future.

Not the least of these was Taib Mahmud, the chief minister of the Malaysian state of Sarawak. Sarawak is located on the Island of Borneo, about a two-hour flight from Kuala Lumpur, eastward across the South China Sea, or an eternity by passenger ship, though that's partly because the boat stops all the way down in Jakarta en route. Sarawak is like one giant remote jungle; think Conrad's *Heart of Darkness*, only instead of African Congo, you have nothing but incredibly dense Indonesian rainforest that you need a team of natives with machetes just to hack your way through.

As the long-standing chief minister of the state, for over twenty-five years, Taib had been trying to drag backwater Sarawak and its scattered assortment of tribal peoples into the twentieth century, largely through wholesale logging of the state's rich timber reserves and more recently through intense development of dozens of sprawling palm oil plantations and refineries across the lands that were deforested by all that logging. I would add that he had gotten himself pretty damn wealthy in the process.

And while Taib was elderly—he was past seventy years old when I first met him—he was still mentally quite sharp and an astute politician. Thanks to his long and deeply entrenched tenure, he still retained an iron-fisted grasp on the reins of near-absolute power over his jungle state, and he was still a force to be reckoned with in the halls of government back in Kuala Lumpur. Intriguingly, however, he was not a particularly savvy negotiator, or even a remotely sophisticated financier. In the end, I found Taib to be, shall I say, malleable.

He was exactly what I was looking for.

Like many of the other state leaders, Taib was extremely interested in the prospect of obtaining substantial foreign investment to further promote his efforts to modernize Sarawak through industrial development. But his ideas were archaic, focused on local manufacturing, such as clothing for export, and increasing the export of minerals and forest products. I surmised these concepts were outdated artifacts from Taib's misty remembrances of British colonialism—and despotically exploitive British colonialism at that. Fortunately, when I raised my concerns about their viability, the chief minister was open to hearing both my critical concerns about Sarawak's current economic course and my recommendations for a more effective strategy going forward.

"You do not feel that more industry and export are the way to go?" he asked.

"Industrial development is fine," I said, "but why wait for foreign investment to make its way here?" Then, urging him to look proactively beyond the borders of Sarawak, I continued, "Here is an opportunity for your state of Sarawak to proactively invest in its own future, and your return on investment will be much quicker than through industrial development, which takes a long time to kick in. Not only that, but the Iskandar development project will benefit the whole national economy of Malaysia, so it will be a double win for Sarawak." And of course, the next thing I did, I told him about a couple of construction companies I had for sale.

I had an ace in the hole. I knew that Taib's vision for the future of Sarawak included at least one very forward-thinking idea—perhaps his only one—and that was ecotourism, a phenomenon that was just beginning at that time to burst on the international travel scene. Even then, the state of Sarawak was already internationally famous for its national wilderness parks, like Niah and Bako near the coast or the enormous interior mountainous rainforest of Gunung Mulu on the border with Brunei.

THE ART OF GREED

The way I pitched it, I told Taib to "forget the twentieth century; that's all in the past!" I told him that here was an opportunity to invest in a bona fide *twenty-first-century project.*

"You will be investing in an ultra-modern city that's going to become the envy of all of Southeast Asia, and you won't have to cut down a single tree in this beautiful pristine state you love so much." Needless to say, our conversation went swimmingly from there.

He liked it. In fact, he was starry-eyed with the whole idea of it. "You know," Taib confided, "as chief minister of this state for so many years, I have been obliged to recognize and accept the fact, I'm afraid, that logging and mineral export have been, dare I say it, necessary evils for the economy of Sarawak. For a long time, those industries have been the best—or rather, in reality, the only—economic enterprises that we could effectively undertake to improve the welfare of the people who have populated these jungles for many generations. Yet it's always caused me great anguish to see our great forests being clear-cut to the ground and the great lifeless pits of mud and stone left after the strip miners have done their work, both these activities rendering Sarawak's natural beauty into hideous wasteland, perhaps forever."

"Here is your chance to change all that," I said solemnly.

And so it wasn't long after our meeting that Chief Minister Taib bought the two construction companies lock, stock, and barrel from the ADKMIC. He then bought outright Wynton's minority stake in the Iskandar land project, which he acquired through a private holding company that he personally controlled, known simply as UGB. In this way, Taib quietly paid for his stake in Iskandar with a combination of cash—a prodigious mountain of cash—and shares in his holding company—so many shares, in fact, that I instantly became the largest shareholder in UGB!

It was a fantastic deal for me. So enormous was Wynton's markup on the sale that I netted $110 million in profit, and that was even after paying off Ambassador Otaiba (to the tune of some ten million dollars) and all the others, whose tacit involvement—just the presence of their names on the shareholder rolls—had helped the whole deal to work so smoothly and, from my point of view, so effortlessly, like clockwork.

It wasn't such a great deal for Chief Minister Taib. True, he now owned two major construction companies that could be expected to win lucrative building contracts that would yield substantial profits for him. However, it remained to be seen if his companies would, in fact, win those lucrative contracts; there were certainly no guarantees, and the competition would be fierce. Also true, Taib now owned a decent-sized financial stake in a development project that, as I've said repeatedly, was bound to be a huge success, meaning that his minority stake would increase in value exponentially. Here again, there were no guarantees. Still, in point of fact, there was considerable tangible value in the entities he had acquired, initially at the time of purchase but especially over time. And that, of course, was the rub, that it could take upward of two decades or longer for Taib's investments to start paying dividends. My return by contrast, was immediate.

Still, I had to imagine the chief minister to be happy with the deal. Because he had paid for the construction companies and the stake in the project through means or entities that he controlled and through which he would personally profit—and enormously so. As for Sarawak, well, it's really just a vast jungle after all.

The way I saw things, this was all strictly business. Besides, I was already looking past Iskandar to much bigger deals. Through all of this time, I had to admire the power and prestige that Khaldoon Al Mubarak commanded at the helm of Mubadala. If I had been impressed when I first met him during my college-age visit to Abu Dhabi, my admiration only increased as I observed the way he skillfully structured the fund's investment in Iskandar. Here was a guy who controlled billions of investment dollars, not mere trifling millions. As audacious as it might sound, I saw no reason why I couldn't create a sovereign wealth fund of my own, one based in Malaysia—with the help of some well-connected people, of course—but whose funds I would control. The issue was, where could I find the initial funds to get started? And who in Malaysia should I approach?

In Abu Dhabi, I had also learned from Ambassador Otaiba how most sovereign wealth funds had gotten their starts by investing oil profits, so after a bit of research, I decided to focus on the Malaysian state of Terengganu because of its rich offshore oil and natural gas reserves. Might as well stick to the basic model, I reasoned. But then, I discovered a number of happy coincidences, which I moved very quickly to exploit.

First, one needs to understand that Malaysia is technically a constitutional monarchy, not unlike Great Britain, except that, in my country, there are nine historic, hereditary Malay ruling families, all coming from different states, that share in presumably equal capacity the responsibilities and duties of the nation's monarchy, such as those are. In fact, the position of king is rotated on a regular basis among a chosen individual sultan from each of the nine royal families in succession. And it so happened that, right at the time I began to vigorously pursue the creation of a sovereign wealth fund for Malaysia, the sultan of Terengganu, Mizan Zainal Abidin, was, on behalf of his esteemed family, serving his tenure as the king, so he was indeed the perfect leader to approach about my plan. But there was more.

Again, much like Great Britain, the ruling class of the nine royal families are largely a figurehead times nine, with the role of the king primarily ceremonial. Malaysia does have a democratically elected government, not surprisingly modeled on the English parliamentary system, a legacy of many decades of British rule. Whether because of their symbolic status or simply because they are members of a very privileged class, among the Malaysian people, the Sultans are often viewed as lazy and self-entitled—a kind of leisure class among an otherwise hardworking citizenry. I choose to venture no opinion whether that perception is true or not. What I did know and what I was banking on is that, even amid their figurehead status on the national level, these ruling sultans maintained wide-ranging political power within Malaysia's individual states. That meant they often had control over local state revenues, which, of course, was of primary interest to me.

But I can say that the popular perception of the royals as lazy and indifferent was not true of Mizan. He was very smart and energetic, and I perceived him to be a doer. Or so I thought when I first met him.

Born of a conservative Islamic family and educated at some of the top schools in the UK, Mizan was clearly interested in doing productive work to foster business and industry that would advance the economic prowess of his beloved state of Terengganu. I had gotten to know him at a distance through his sister, who—through another wonderful coincidence—happened to be sitting on the boards of the two construction companies when I had acquired them. I had been quick to take full advantage of that connection: Mizan was one of the important Malaysian officials I had sent free shares of the ADKM Investment Corporation through which I had bought those companies, and then sold at such an enormous profit. So Mizan, just like Otaiba, had already profited handsomely from my savvy investment entrepreneurship.

In any case, the short version of the story of my brief dealings with Mizan is that I convinced the sultan king to create a sovereign wealth fund modeled on Abu Dhabi's Mubadala fund, with the full power to borrow money globally against the state of Terengganu's ever-accruing oil wealth. I even brought to the table some powerful elements from the prestigious investment firm of Goldman Sachs, led by the head of the firm's Asian operations—a kind of renegade, free-thinking, Wild West financial gunslinger by the name of Tim Leissner, whom I really admired for his sheer financial bravado. I'll be telling you a lot more about Leissner later on, but for now, the idea was that he and his team at Goldman would advise Sultan Mizan on matters related to the management of the fund, as well as procuring qualified global investors to generate rapid growth of the fund. With Goldman's support, I tried every way I could to convince the sultan that this would be a terrific economic engine to empower modern commercial and infrastructure development in his native state of Terengganu.

Then, in the spring of 2009 and just when we were ready to issue $1.4 billion in bonds to launch the fund, backed by the state's anticipated future oil receipts, Sultan Mizan got scared—way too scared to go through with it. He would later tell everyone that he was determined to protect the state's treasure, embodied as it was in their oil resources, and that he was simply doing what he believed was the right and upstanding thing by refusing to gamble with that vital treasure. I think that was political bullshit. I think he just got scared off by the numbers and by words like *billions*.

When Mizan abruptly shut the whole venture down, I thought I was screwed once again, with all my hard work down the drain. Here I was, on the cusp of reaching my dream of assuming control of a reasonably respectable sovereign wealth fund in terms of assets—which is to say, I thought that a billion or so dollars was a good start, even if I had much bigger plans in mind. I had already hired a crack staff of people I knew and trusted and whom I knew would follow my instructions in running the fund, only now to be thwarted by a so-called sultan and a powerless figurehead king who turned out, in the end, to be far more weak-willed than I had initially taken him to be and from what I could only now discern was just another weak-minded royal family to boot. Perhaps those gossipy allegations about the laziness of Malaysia's merry-go-round of part-time ruler-sultans were accurate after all. For me, there was never a time in my life up to that moment that I was more eager to make this thing happen. I really just had no time for any of this nonsense from the good sultan from the state of Terengganu.

But then, suddenly, fate smiled on me in a bigger way than it had ever done before. In April of that same year, Najib Razak was elected prime minister of Malaysia. I could not stop smiling at the thought of seeing my friends Najib and Rosmah once again—and soon.

Chapter 3

While the newly elected prime minister was obviously the most critical key to my plans for the creation of a sovereign wealth fund, I believed, rather intuitively, that he would actually be the easiest party to bring on board with the whole idea. There were a number of reasons for this, and it helps to know a little bit about Malaysia's political climate in the day to understand those reasons.

About half the population of Malaysia are considered to be ethnic Malays. Another thirty percent are Chinese and Indian Malaysians who, despite their numbers—and their presumed or potential political power, if viewed as a voting bloc—are mostly treated as second-class citizens, especially in the heart of the more modern-day, developed region of West Malaysia, also called Peninsular Malaysia. That is a fact of life that I can personally attest to. The remainder of the population are indigenous, tribal peoples scattered most notably across the remote jungle regions of the two states of Sarawak and Sabah in East Malaysia on the island of Borneo. These unfortunate tribal peoples were largely clueless to the complex, sophisticated, and often devious political and financial machinations that routinely operated in Peninsular Malaysia. Yet given that they duly exercised their constitutional rights by voting en masse in national elections, they were—dare I say it—as easily bought as the Indians of American folklore who reputedly sold Manhattan Island to Dutch settlers for the tidy sum of twenty-four dollars' worth of trinkets and beads.

And while that might be an exaggeration of sorts, the notion of "serving the will" of these indigenous tribes was certainly of interest to any maliciously ambitious Malaysian politician willing to buy a few votes along the way—and that, of course, was all of them.

What ought to be clear from all of this is that, as is so often the case in countries with diverse ethnic populations, the most successful political party or organization is going to be the one that is most adept at bringing together and maintaining a broad-based coalition among as many of those groups and their members as possible. And throughout Malaysia's modern history, no party had done this better than Najib's own United Malays National Organisation, also known as the Alliance Party.

Despite free and ostensibly democratic regular elections, UMNO had dominated Malaysian politics, in no small part by racking up an unbroken series of wins in every election since the country became an independent nation in 1957. But as the 2008 election approached, the UMNO was in utter chaos. That might have been in part because of the rampant corruption of then-PM Abdullah Ahmad Badawi, and it most certainly was a direct consequence of the worldwide economic collapse of that same year, but the once solid and reliable coalition that was the very lifeblood of the Alliance Party was fracturing at its very foundation and was in danger of complete collapse. The reasons for all of this political upheaval weren't of any specific interest to me; however, the financial opportunities they created absolutely were.

Amid all this chaos, the UMNO turned to the nation's favorite son, whose own father, Abdul Razak, had served as prime minister from June of 1972 to the beginning of 1976 and who may have served much longer had he not died of leukemia while in office, two months before reaching his fifty-fourth birthday. Having served variously as minister of finance; of defense; of education; of culture, youth, and sports; and, of course, most recently as deputy prime minister—and thus having projected at least the illusion of having toiled as a servant of the people in dutifully rising through the ranks—Najib was the party's obvious choice. Yet even as he had campaigned vigorously on a platform of restoring economic prosperity to the country, discontented ethnic Chinese and Indian Malaysians expressed their mounting displeasure with UMNO by voting in droves for the opposition. Nevertheless, by the slimmest of margins, in April 2009, Najib Razak became Malaysia's sixth prime minister.

And none of this could have happened at a better time for me. For one thing, the roaring success of the Iskandar Development Region that I had orchestrated less than two years earlier was still fresh in Najib's mind. As celebrated as Iskandar was in the press and media—especially the media controlled by the UMNO—the news of the project apparently still remained fresh in the minds of the voters too over the weeks and months leading up to the election. One could make the argument that the Iskandar deal was the lynchpin that held the party's faltering coalition together enough to sweep Najib to victory.

However, even more front-of-mind for the newly elected PM than this victory had been the major investment of Middle Eastern money in the project—an infusion of major capital that Najib knew I, and I alone, had brought to the table. Where most people saw Iskandar as urban economic development, Najib saw dollar signs. Whenever I accompanied Najib and his wife on trips to the Middle East, he was clearly mesmerized with the opulence in the extreme of the gleaming cities and appeared to be downright bewildered by the sight of the furious construction of even newer high-rise towers that went on round the clock, twenty-four seven. Suffice it to say that Rosmah's reaction to this practically pornographic display of wealth in excess was nothing short of rapture. So anyway, throughout those negotiations, I made sure to keep assuring Najib. "If we succeed in pulling off this deal with Kuwaiti and Abu Dhabi backing," I told the prime minister, "there's a lot more money where that came from."

Najib just stood there, rubbing his hands together, as though he was warming himself in front of a New England fireplace on a cold and snowy Christmas morning.

From his family's long and storied political history to his own career odyssey, no one knew the ins and outs of the wretchedly corrupt labyrinth of Malaysian government better than Najib, and he, perhaps more than anyone else, recognized that the slim margin by which he was elected was a clear indication of the enormous task he faced in restoring and rebuilding the UMNO to its former tight-fisted, authoritarian glory. And that, Najib also knew, was going to take a shitload of money to pay the right people to, let's just say, "procure" the support of state governors and local officials across peninsular Malaysia, as well as the island states on Borneo. It was also going to take a long time, meaning that, if Najib was going to get the job done, he was going to need to stay in office for a long time. That, in turn, meant that the new PM was going to need a huge war chest of ready and available cash to keep the payoffs coming. The longer he wanted to stay in power, the more money he was going to need.

Whereas Good King Mizan, for his part, was dragging his feet and agonizing about pulling the trigger to start up the Terengganu Investment Authority, there was simply no doubt in my mind that PM Najib would be enthusiastically eager not only to take over the state-based version of the fund but also to expand it wholesale into a broad-based federal sovereign investment fund with international reach. That was especially true when I explained how he would be able to use the fund as a ready and available political financing resource in support of his tenure as the leader of Malaysia.

The underlying principle is this: Under the guise of what's commonly called *corporate social responsibility*, the charitable wing of a typical sovereign wealth fund often underwrites scores of good-will initiatives like education scholarships and job-training programs or like building public parks and recreation facilities. I pointed out to Najib that he might very effectively use the abundant profits flowing from an aggressively managed sovereign fund to build affordable housing or create high-paying job opportunities—and to do it, say, in places around the country where UMNO needed votes. Of course, how he used the money would be entirely up to him, and if he needed to pay off some important political supporters or certain blocs of voters in certain states or districts, well, in Malaysia, that was just business as usual, really. As prime minister, he would be fully in charge of the fund, even if I ran it for him from behind the scenes, so no one, I assured him, was going to ask any questions.

All the while, of course, I pointed out to Najib that he could go around the country being very devotedly prime ministerial, cutting the ribbon on a new school or plunging a golden shovel into the earth to break ground for construction of a low-income housing development or manufacturing facility—all of this in front of the TV cameras for everyone to see what a fantastic job he was doing for the people of Malaysia. I don't think I need to tell you how much Najib liked the whole idea.

Yet I knew that if I was going to persuade Najib to take over the Terengganu Investment fund and nationalize it, I was going to have to aggressively stoke the Middle Eastern connection to procure robust financial backing of the fund—in essence, to back the initial $1.4 billion in bonds that the Terengganu fund was to issue and more after that. I specifically wanted that connection to be with a prince or a sheikh who was a member of one royal family or another in order to convince Najib that he was dealing with the uppermost and wealthiest echelon of the royal ruling class of the region, whatever country that prince or sheikh might represent. And I found the perfect connection in His Royal Highness, Prince Turki bin Abdullah Al Saud of Saudi Arabia.

It's kind of funny how I first became acquainted with Prince Turki. It was through the owner of a private and very exclusive strip club in Philadelphia only a stone's throw from Wharton—a nifty and highly discrete entertainment enterprise catering specifically to millionaire Middle Eastern businessmen and luminaries who, in their travels to the West, sought to enjoy the delights of sultry and seductive female models and abundantly flowing top-shelf alcohol and a host of other lurid temptations of body and mind and spirit. You see, casino gambling is not the only wicked vice craved by those misfortunate individuals who come from countries governed under the harsh weight of strict Islamic law. Need I say more?

Prince Turki was exactly what I was looking for. Most people think that if you're a Saudi prince or a prince from any of a host of oil-rich Arab countries, you're filthy rich with a bottomless pit full of never-ending cash flowing out of it. Yet that's not really true, except for the most well-connected families at the very centers of the political power structures of those nations. Frankly, I don't know which came first, the money or the power, but I think I have a pretty good idea!

Anyway, the prince was in a pretty tough spot. He was one of twenty children sired by his dear old Dad, the ninety-year-old King Abdullah. Not only did the existence of nineteen siblings tend to dilute rather severely his share of their collective anticipated inheritance, but the death of the king would further remove Turki by another orbital valence or two from the seat of political power within the Saudi ruling family. He was essentially going in the wrong direction, spiraling away from the aristocratic mega-center of Saudi power and the wealth that supports it. I don't mean to be cruel about it, but you could say that, as Saudi princes go, Prince Turki was kind of a low-rent royal.

What that meant in real terms was that Turki actually had to work for a living, which is to say, he needed to try to engage in some semblance of boots-on-the-ground business, especially if he wished to continue leading a dichotomous lifestyle that ranged from lounging in cushy traditional Islamic silk robes drinking freshly squeezed fruit juices while at home to the exhilarating and decidedly more decadent nightlife he favored when he traveled to the West, where the libations were far more potent. Thus, if Sarawak's chief minister, Taib Mahmud had been "malleable" when I succeeded in convincing him to acquire Wynton's stake in the Iskandar project, as well as to purchase the two construction companies I owned, Prince Turki was both malleable *and* hungry: He was ravenously hungry for any sort of financial venture that would radically ramp up his future income and shore up his net worth. To this end, Prince Turki had formed an oil and gas exploration corporation called PetroSaudi International in partnership with another interesting guy by the name of Tarek Obaid.

Let me tell you a little bit about Tarek. While Prince Turki could at least claim to have a genetic membership card placing him somewhere in the vast hierarchy of the familial royal ruling class of Saudi Arabia, Obaid was born of what you might call *common stock*. Yet Obaid wore his own mask of deception. Raised from childhood in Geneva, Switzerland, where, for a time, he worked for a small Swiss private bank, Tarek relentlessly portrayed himself as a big-time financier and Saudi royal, going so far as to allow his banking colleagues to refer to him as *Sheikh*, even though that term is reserved for royals or religious clerics in his country of origin. And as far as I could tell, this had worked fairly brilliantly for him, and it reinforced, for me, the notion that if you portray greatness and command in your demeanor and your dealings, you become great and authoritative in the eyes of others.

After graduating from the International School in Geneva, Obaid attended Georgetown University, in the United States, where, somehow, despite the fact that the university is two and a half hours away by Amtrak Acela, he turned up at the same nightclub in Philadelphia frequented by Prince Turki, presumably seeking the same brand of entertainment, no doubt, and Obaid was particularly known for favoring the booze. In any case, the two Saudis became friends and, eventually, business partners in forming PetroSaudi, with Obaid taking the role of chief executive officer.

There was at least one other crucial player in the mix at PetroSaudi. His name is Patrick Mahony, a product of Goldman Sachs and, later, a British investment fund called Ashmore. Mahony and Obaid had first met all the way back in 1977, when they were both attending the international school in Geneva, and they had stayed good friends ever since. In 2009, Mahony was hired by Obaid as PetroSaudi's director of investments, charged with the responsibility of aggressively ramping up the company's business interests by accruing greater and more valuable oil assets, as well as securing foreign investment in the firm. Mahony was a very ambitious guy—ambitious to the point of being reckless—and he would play an important role in successfully cementing the joint venture partnership between 1MDB and PetroSaudi.

When I first looked at PetroSaudi as a corporate-industrial entity, there really wasn't much there of tangible substance. Basically, they had bought exploratory drilling rights in geographical regions that, remote as they were, certain oil industry experts believed might prove to be very rich new oil fields just waiting to be tapped. Except there were some formidable complications, owing to the fact that those rights were in some pretty shaky places. Like a vast offshore region of the Caspian Sea that overlaid disputed territory between Azerbaijan and Turkmenistan. As if oil exploration as a financial investment all by itself isn't complicated, extraordinarily expensive, and risky enough—and, in this case, *undersea* oil exploration that is even more difficult—with this venture you could also get yourself into personal danger by injecting your team into the middle of a bona fide potential border war with gunships at sea! The other place was in some godforsaken region of northern Patagonia, in Argentina, known as Vaca Muerta that I think you could only get to by riding a burro and where the nearest McDonald's was probably about five hundred miles away. If you think I'm exaggerating, just think about this: *vaca muerta* is Spanish for "dead cow"!

Beyond these largely hypothetical goldmine interests—hypothetical in the sense that there were no guarantees whatsoever that even the most scientifically and strategically pinpointed exploratory wells would find massive underground oil reserves worth millions or even billions of dollars—PetroSaudi really had little or no other ongoing business to speak of. I had to laugh when I realized this, because, here, I had two Saudi fakers in Prince Turki and Obaid in charge of a largely fake Saudi company, at least if you looked at it in terms of the firm's hard assets and future prospects for growth. It was perfect!

And it was all I needed. The bottom line that must be understood was that what Prince Turki had essentially done was to parlay his royal pedigree to form a shell corporation to attract foreign investment from entities that wanted to get close to Saudi Arabia. So, in a way, you could say we were made for each other, hand in glove, so to speak. Turki and Obaid were looking for investors to prop up the net worth of PetroSaudi and, ostensibly, fund its future oil exploration operations, without getting their hands too industrially dirty. As for me, just as I had no interest in being in the bigtime construction industry in Iskandar, I was equally disinterested in being in the oil business *per se*—that is, in the industrial nuts-and-bolts work of finding, drilling, and extracting crude oil to sell on the world market. Rather, I was looking for a convenient home for over a billion dollars in cash generated by the bond issue of the Terengganu Investment Authority that would soon be transformed into a full blown federal sovereign investment fund by PM Najib. And Najib was anxious to rapidly grow the pipeline of Middle East investment in Malaysia, not to mention the political "donations" that he hoped would flow directly to him.

I will say this about Najib: His decades of government service had made him into a consummate, very savvy, and confident yet very shrewd politician, with a certain—albeit limited—flair for diplomacy. He had developed a way of giving off a vibe of genuinely caring about and earnestly desiring to improve the lives of the people of Malaysia, as well as being determined to promote aggressive economic expansion aimed at making his country a significant and respected player on the world stage. All of that exhibited concern may, in fact, have been genuine, for all I knew. But I tend to doubt it, because I could easily see that the twinkle in his eyes was always at its brightest whenever the talk turned to the potential for substantial political donations to the UMNO and especially to Najib's private and well-secreted bank accounts—both in country and among numerous international offshore havens.

That being said, I knew that I absolutely had to get these people together in the same room. And in August 2009, I did even better than that: I got them together on the same ultra-luxurious superyacht. First, I arranged a sumptuously extravagant Mediterranean vacation for Najib and his family aboard the RM *Elegant*, a gleaming, futuristic-looking yacht with such dazzling appointments that Rosmah squealed with delight the moment she boarded the craft. The *Elegant* featured fifteen staterooms and an enormous formal dining room crafted entirely of hand-carved Malaysian teak wood.

At the same time, I instructed Prince Turki to arrange to do the same, and I must say I was truly impressed and awed by how he completely outdid himself. Turki and his entourage shortly made their arrival on those same crystal clear blue waters off the French Riviera aboard the mind-blowing, $190 million, 269-foot *Alpha Nero*, one of the world's largest superyachts, which featured a movie theater, a glitzy discotheque, and an enormous swimming pool with a retractable cover that, when in place, doubled as a helipad. And when I saw Prince Turki waving madly from the bow of the enormous boat, his sunglasses gleaming with reflected sunlight and a wide, beaming grin on his face, I could only smile in bemused amazement and approval. Further down the deck of the ship, Tarek Obaid reclined in a white lounge chair, a sparkling flute of champagne in his hand. Contrary to every appearance, Prince Turki had only, in fact, chartered the *Alpha Nero*, though it had cost him the staggering sum of $500,000 for the week. But of course—and exactly as I wanted—Najib would automatically assume that the vessel was Prince Turki's personal and privately owned plaything. So now I had my target parties on two big yachts cruising on the same tranquil Mediterranean waters, and all I needed to do was bring them together.

Chapter 4

To this day, when I think back on it, it is almost inconceivable even to me how quickly things transpired that summer. In July and only weeks after Najib's election as the new prime minister, I had the pleasure of escorting him and Rosmah on a tour of the Middle East, introducing him to officials and dignitaries that I had come to know during my own travels there, as well as a few I'd never met before at all, in which case I finessed the introductions without missing a beat. I just acted like I was the prime minister's official emissary and guide, and you know what? Nobody even questioned who I was or what my title might have been or what I was doing there—although some people somehow got the notion that I was Najib's minister of investment! How great was that?!

We even met King Abdullah of Saudi Arabia—Prince Turki's father—and Crown Prince Sheikh Mohammed bin Zayed Al Nahyan of Abu Dhabi, and toward the end of a sumptuous formal dinner in the spectacularly glittering ballroom of the Emirates Palace Hotel, the prime minister stood up to announce the formation of a new Malaysian sovereign wealth fund that would be called 1Malaysia Development Berhad or, as it would become more commonly referred to, simply the 1MDB. "Berhad" is a suffix used in Malaysia to identify a public limited company, and 1MDB was actually the Terengganu Investment Authority converted into the federal entity that I and others had urged Najib to create. The sovereign fund was formally chartered to invest in green technology and promote tourism—both cosmopolitan and ecotourism—in order to create high-quality jobs for all Malaysians equally, whether they were of Malay, Chinese, or Indian heritage. Intended to help uplift the quality of life for all citizens throughout the country, its rather direct and to-the-point slogan was "1 Malaysia."

At that same dinner and speaking on behalf of the several Arab nations represented at the affair, the crown prince repeated earlier assurances of additional Middle Eastern financial investment in Malaysia alongside 1MDB, as well as alluding in appropriately vague language to a general commitment to back Najib's newly formed administration through a flow of generous political donations going forward. While the precise form that all of this economic good will would actually take was largely unspecified, it had been more than enough to win over Najib; the prime minister was seeing dollar signs again.

Then, less than two months later, Najib and Rosmah joined Prince Turki, the Saudi son of King Abdullah, with Tarek Obaid in tow, aboard the *Alpha Nero* as it cruised within sight of the ruggedly magnificent cliffs of Monaco. And it was there on the superyacht that the prime minister and the prince first met to discuss the formation of a partnership between PetroSaudi and the new 1MDB sovereign wealth fund.

I was there too, of course, to make sure everything went exactly as I had planned it. In fact, I had procured a $12,000 South Sea cultured pearl necklace with an eighteen-karat white gold clasp from Blue Nile, which I slipped to Prince Turki prior to the couple's arrival shipboard, instructing him to present it as a gift to Rosmah, just to ensure that the deal, as they say, would be sealed. As I fully expected, Rosmah gushed with delight when he presented her with the pearls. But believe me when I tell you, this was a mere bauble compared to the jewelry pieces I would buy for the First Lady over the next couple of years to ensure her continued favor.

Within days of their meeting, on August 28, 2009, Prince Turki wrote a letter to Najib—on official Saudi government letterhead, no less—proposing what he called a "potential business combination." Along with the letter, the prince enclosed a formal proposal crafted by Tarek Obaid for a business venture to which PetroSaudi would commit its oil assets—in other words, the supposed assets of the exploration and development right in the Caspian Sea and the Vaca Muerta—the estimated potential value of which the document placed at a very respectable $2.5 billion. For its part, 1MDB would put in one billion dollars in cash—thus putting to work capital that was presently sitting unproductively in the Malaysian fund's bank account, looking for a purpose. It goes without saying that Prime Minister Najib was enthusiastically in favor of making the deal, so much so that he barely asked any questions about PetroSaudi or its corporate-industrial track record. That was perfectly fine by me.

Now, I have to forewarn you that, from this point on, the details of how I was able to get the PetroSaudi–1MDB deal done get very complicated, both because of all of the players that needed to be involved and because of all of the financial and legal shit we had to do to make it all happen. And yet by throwing away the usual playbook, I was able to consummate the deal in record time.

I had learned by now that the mere appearance of possessing or controlling vast amounts of wealth or even just the appearance of having connections to individuals possessing or controlling vast amounts of wealth can easily open doors among otherwise scrupulous and skeptical banking and investment and lawyerly types who ask nary a question about that presumed wealth—or its legitimate origins. This is a phenomenon of human nature that I found to be particularly true if, in some way on one deal or another, any of these professionals are getting a nice fat piece of the financial pie.

Let me say it more simply: Greed, wrapped in the disguise of the routine performance of a minimally complicated service, has a distinctly unique quality of getting even the most astute and responsible people—highly trained professionals with the most impeccable credentials and the most ethical of intentions, mind you—to look the other way, in return for a maximally obscene windfall. This was a simple fact that I found I could reliably trade on just about every time I needed to.

It is also why I was so easily able to engage all sorts of highly respected experts—from banking and investment moguls to high-level corporate attorneys to political operatives and elected government officials to fund managers and business entrepreneurs and even to auditors and valuation experts whose job it was to catch financial wrongdoing—all designed to betoken an air of fiscal responsibility, due diligence, and unquestionable legitimacy to the deal, without having any of these players ask too many pesky questions. Oftentimes, once any of these professionals learned that so-and-so fund manager or so-and-so investment bank or so-and-so royal family member or so-and-so government official were involved in a multimillion or multibillion-dollar deal with international complexities, they had neither the time or the inclination to investigate too deeply. Each of these operatives more or less shrugged their shoulders and assumed that everything must therefore be on the up and up.

Consequently, they each performed their discrete but pivotal roles in the deal like it was just another day at the office, and then, after they'd done exactly what I wanted, they blissfully took their nice fat checks in payment of their colossal fees and went home. I insist that I wasn't doing anything illegal *per se*; I was just doing things more efficiently my way—cutting a little red tape, if you will.

So here's a case in point, and it's also where Patrick Mahony comes into the picture. I needed Mahony to go out and obtain an independent valuation from a bona fide industry expert of PetroSaudi's Turkmenistan and Argentine oil assets, which, in turn, could be presented to the advisory board of directors of 1MDB for its approval before the board would commit the one billion dollars that had been agreed upon in the deal. Accordingly, Mahony reached out to a former U.S. State Department official and highly regarded energy analyst with Lehman Brothers by the name of Jordan Traynor, one of the world's foremost experts on the economics of global oil. Why Mahony chose Traynor, however, was based solely on the recommendation of none other than Tarek Obaid, and Obaid had done so because he knew Traynor well. Only a few years earlier, Traynor had collaborated with Tarek's older brother, Nawaf Obaid, on a book-length white paper assessing Saudi energy resources and global markets. A marvelously convenient connection, don't you think?

Anyway, Mahony said flatly to Traynor, "We're looking for a valuation in the neighborhood of two and a half billion dollars," which was the figure that Obaid had given to PM Najib in his August 28 proposal. Mahony coyly added, "And we're looking for it real quick, so we're pleased to offer a premium fee for rush service, if you can accommodate us."

"Sure thing!" Traynor told Mahony. "I'll get right on it."

You have to love this, but here, for all intents and purposes, was an instance where one could tell a respected valuation expert the number you were looking for, literally in billions of dollars, and if you threw enough money at him by way of a handsome fee, he was very likely to come back to you with all of that and more. Sure enough, it took Traynor only two days to compile a technical analysis report that projected a top-end valuation of PetroSaudi's oil assets at a whopping $3.6 billion—over a billion dollars higher than Mahony had asked for! And so Traynor had done his part just like we wanted him to, and in return, he walked away with $100,000 for his trouble.

Now, to be fair, Traynor's report plainly indicated that his findings specifically represented a purely economic valuation based strictly on the quantity of crude oil that was geologically estimated to be in the ground beneath the Caspian Sea and deep below the mountains of the Vaca Muerta—figures that were given to him, amusingly enough, by PetroSaudi's own geologists. But never mind that. Because practically speaking, it was impossible for his analysis to take into account the additional costs—not to mention the politically charged dangers to personnel and equipment—of operating undersea amid the simmering border dispute between Turkmenistan and Azerbaijan. Nor did his analysis attempt to address the high probability for incurring additional operational costs that might result from the degree of difficulty of drilling for oil in the incredibly rugged and nearly inaccessible mountains of western Patagonia. The logistical and technological costs were impossible, really, for anyone to gauge, but they could conceivably turn out to be substantial. And, indeed, all of these extraordinary potential cost factors could erode away some measure of the profitability of either venture and probably both of them. Basically, the oil in the ground might well be worth upward of $3.6 billion, but the anticipated cost of getting at it was another matter entirely.

But I knew that no one involved in this deal was going to care about any of that, particularly after they saw that valuation number! It certainly wasn't going to matter to Prince Turki or Obaid, because they were only interested in getting their hands on a billion dollars in Malaysian investment money from 1MDB. I was also quite confident that these, shall we say, technical difficulties, were also going to be of no serious concern to any of the principal members of the advisory board of 1MDB either. And that was because I had personally handpicked most of them. They were people that I had done business with previously, and I had chosen them with Najib's blessings.

When we sat down together to select qualified individuals to sit on the 1MDB advisory board, I knew from the outset that Najib wanted to be accorded the highest position of chairman of the board, which encompassed the power to appoint and remove members, as well as to approve or veto the board's decisions. It wasn't so much that Najib wanted to have complete control over the financial operations of the 1MDB fund itself; rather, what he *really* wanted was complete control over each and every individual board member in charge of the financial operations of the fund. As I alluded to earlier, the historical hallmark of Malaysian political governance had always been that if you wanted to be in charge, you'd better plan on being in charge of everything and everyone, which is to say, you need to make sure there is not a single person or institution that can legitimately challenge your autocratic authority, because that could lead to your downfall. You might even conclude that this was the mantra through which the UMNO had solely retained power over the course of the country's entire sixty-year history since gaining independence.

This, too, was exactly the way I had wanted things to play out. I knew that nothing else could confer on the newly formed 1MDB sovereign wealth fund a greater sense of national officialdom, or garner greater international prestige as well throughout the globalized banking and investment world, than to seat the prime minister of Malaysia himself as the fund's chairman and recognized figurehead. Putting Najib at the head of the 1MDB fund was what you might call a slam dunk.

From there, Najib wanted to select a guy named Shahrol Halmi as the fund's chief executive. Halmi was a former consultant at Accenture in Malaysia, and of all the members that we would ultimately put on the board, I'd have to say that he was the one individual I knew the least about going in. However, when I researched his background, I was pleased to discover that he was something of an industry lightweight. So I knew right off the bat that he was going to be way out of his league in trying to grapple with the 1MDB fund even as it presently stood at a little over a billion dollars, much less when it grew into the multibillion-dollar enterprise that I was determined to create. And because of this, I knew he'd quickly be desperate for my help, and I'd be able to get him to do whatever I instructed him to do.

Now, any advisory board for a major financial organization of this type must include the names of some high-profile individuals from the world of international business and industry, and we were able to recruit our share. Among them were Bernard Arnault, CEO of the huge French luxury products conglomerate that includes Moët Hennessy and Louis Vuitton; Chang Zhenming, the chairman of CITIC Group, one of China's largest financial conglomerates; and Sheikh Hamad bin Jassim bin Jassim bin Jabr Al Thani (now that's a mouthful for you!), who was both prime minister of Qatar since 2007 and its chief foreign minister since 1992, just to name a few. And then there was my friend Khaldoon Khalifa Al Mubarak, CEO and MD of Mubadala, the Abu Dhabi sovereign investment fund, who had been so instrumental in consummating the deal to create and fund the Iskandar Development Region.

These were all very responsible and highly respected individuals around the world, yet the purpose of naming them to one's advisory board is largely theatric, designed to affirm an abundance of credibility and a clean reputation while also suggesting strong financial connections of the sort that would attract investors, venture capitalists, and the like—people and organizations and governments with lots of cash. A lot of times, you don't even have to pay these guys much, outside of maybe a small annual stipend and perhaps graciously footing the bill for their travel expenses and hotel accommodations should they suddenly feel the urge to attend an annual advisory board meeting once in a while. Or if they want to take a vacation in Tahiti or something like that. And the fortunate thing for me and my team, this being back in the good old days, over a decade ago, when the expectations of oversight by advisory board members were really lax, was that these icons of international industry were nothing more than figureheads who paid little or no attention to the workings of the organizations whose boards they sat on. Some of them may have sat on a dozen or more of them, which only made them even more oblivious to the internal workings of these various entities. The visible persona of 1MDB, in the eyes of the broadly based global business and investment community, was set, headed by Malaysian Prime Minister Najib and descending among all of these distinguished economic and political leaders sitting on the sovereign fund's advisory board.

So much for appearances and corporate protocol; now it was time to get down to the real business by bringing in the true operatives who were going to do the hard work, and, of course, I made damn sure to get a number of my own associates represented on the board. Two key appointees were Casey Tang as executive director and Jasmine Loo as legal director. Tang had been the finance director for a major Malaysian retail chain, and Loo—well, Loo was simply the craftiest lawyer I ever met. As for me, I did not take a position on the board at all, yet that too was by design. On one hand, I had spent the better part of four years since returning to Malaysia from Wharton relentlessly honing my relationship with Najib, to the point of gaining such enormous, implicit trust from the now prime minister that he gave me free rein to run the fund exactly the way I wanted to. And on the other, not having an official seat on the board would enable me to operate independently without having to deal with financial compliance issues from bankers or lawyers or financial regulators or government entities and on and on and on.

Yet again, it wasn't that I was planning on doing anything illegal. I was simply interested in cutting away all the red tape is all. And while it's true that, after I began putting all the parties into direct communication to finalize the details of the deal, I instructed everyone to destroy their emails after reading them, that was only in part to protect me; it was also to protect the members of the 1MDB board and the principals of PetroSaudi from any needless, nosy scrutiny by bank regulators or compliance departments. Why give away my most creative investor trade secrets?

But let me get back to Patrick Mahony's work. Having procured the rather startling valuation of PetroSaudi's oil assets, Mahony next needed to set up a business account for the new entity that would be formed by the joint venture with 1MDB and that would be incorporated in the British Virgin Islands. This took a little bit of doing, because a couple of banks turned us down—despite the fact that we indicated that the first thing that was going to be transacted was the receipt into the account of one billion dollars from the Malaysian wealth fund, an opportunity that you'd think any ambitious banker would jump at the chance for. I maintain that they did so because of the way we were operating on the fly rather than following the usual plodding protocols that banks always seem so fond of. Anybody who has ever dealt with a banking or investment organization knows that they can be pretty stodgy and impossibly rigid in the way they handle their business dealings, and they sometimes tend to get a little too nervous whenever they are faced with anything out of the ordinary, at least in my view of things.

Regardless, Mahony was finally successful in setting up the needed account through his own private bank, J.P. Morgan Suisse, perhaps thanks to their long history of working with Mahony in the past. The important thing was that they didn't ask any annoying questions about why a sovereign wealth fund needed a separate account with a Swiss private bank and that sort of thing. Oh, and most important of all, they didn't raise any objections to the stipulation that I would be taking a cut of the money as a fee for my work in putting the deal together. That was nonnegotiable; I wasn't going to get screwed out of a broker fee on the whole blasted thing the way I had been shut out by Khazanah on my Iskandar deal!

Next, we needed a savvy, gunslinger lawyer to help us sell the joint venture to the 1MDB advisory board and to take care of all the legalities involved. Once again, Mahony came through big time, retaining Edgar Rongst, a New Zealander with the prestigious U.S. law firm of Helmsley & Cruikshank, working out of the firm's London office. A U.S. law firm based in New York City—the banking capital of the world—now how's that for respectability? Even before Rongst and his team started to develop the PetroSaudi prospectus, Helmsley & Cruikshank was quite happy to comply with a request from Patrick Mahony asking them to draw up a document to transfer five million dollars to a broker who was "instrumental" in putting the joint venture deal together—and the attorneys didn't even blink when Mahony indicated that the recipient "broker" would remain unnamed in the official document. These guys were my kind of lawyers!

On top of that, the slide presentation that our counsel put together was simply first rate. Beginning with the initial formative injection of PetroSaudi's $3.6 billion in oil assets comingled with 1MDB's minority stake investment of one billion dollars, the glossy full-color Helmsley & Cruikshank presentation displayed a series of elegant, professionally designed diagrams that clearly charted anticipated money flows and projected profitability expectations. There was, however, one little wrinkle that we put in the presentation. I'll admit that we prevailed upon our lawyers to kind of bury this in the fine print, in a manner of speaking, but there was an unobtrusive clause in there that stipulated that the joint venture, once legally formed, would make an immediate payment of $700 million back to PetroSaudi, in repayment of a loan that PetroSaudi had extended to the joint venture.

This was, if I may say so, a brilliantly conceived part of my plan for the 1MDB fund that, for now let's just say, was a totally innovative idea intended to really put the fund's money to work by freeing up a ton of capital that I could use for further creative investment—to get the "biggest bang for the buck," as the expression goes. However, I knew that this was an unorthodox facet of the proposed agreement that likely would only confuse some members of the 1MDB advisory board and, for a few of them, might even become a serious distraction from the real business of approving the joint venture once and for all. That is why, in making my presentation to the board at a specially convened meeting in Kuala Lumpur on September 26, 2009, I did not mention anything about the loan repayment at all. And it all worked out perfectly, because nobody else in the room questioned or even mentioned it, and the meeting concluded, exactly as I had hoped, with the 1MDB board voting unanimously to approve the transfer of one billion dollars to the J.P. Morgan bank account that I had set up, through Patrick Mahony, for the joint venture with PetroSaudi.

The deal was done, but now I had to really hustle my ass off to make absolutely sure all of the critical—and enormous!—money transfers that were about to transpire would successfully navigate through a myriad of channels without a hitch.

To anyone not familiar with the digital-age mechanisms of international banking, the lightning speed at which millions of monetary transactions take place around the world would probably be almost incomprehensibly mind-boggling, especially when you consider that the amounts of such transfers routinely range in the millions and billions of dollars, and there are literally thousands of these transactions all happening at any given moment. It can be a pretty heady atmosphere for one to be immersed in, almost addictively narcotic in a way. Suffice it to say, the transfer of the one billion dollars in 1MDB funds would happen very quickly. But there would be some logistical complications that only I knew about and that I anticipated might take some bank officers and intermediary managers by surprise.

It went something like this: On the morning of September 30, Casey Tang sent a letter via courier to Deutsche Bank of Malaysia instructing them to proceed with the execution of two separate transfers from the 1MDB fund to the joint venture. One of the transfers was for $300 million to be deposited in the joint venture's new account with J.P. Morgan, the account that had been set up by Mahony, and that one would go off without a hitch. It was the other transfer that caused some confusion at Deutsche Bank, because Tang's letter instructed the manager who was newly put in charge of the 1MDB account to transfer $700 million to an unnamed account with RBS Coutts, in Zurich.

Fortunately, Casey was able to reassure the account manager by telling her in a phone conversation that everything was in order and explaining that the Coutts account was wholly owned by PetroSaudi. When she further inquired as to why the money was going directly to PetroSaudi rather than to the joint venture entity, Tang smoothly referred the manager to the repayment clause stipulated in the original agreement. That seemed to do it, and about a quarter after three in the afternoon, Kuala Lumpur time, and about six minutes apart, Deutsche Bank finally sent out two wire transfers, one for $300 million to the joint venture's new account at J.P. Morgan Suisse and the other for $700 million to the Coutts account in Zurich. However, the complications attending the latter transaction were not yet over, because two days later, on October 2, some minor bank employee working in Coutts's regulatory risk department got alarmed and sent an urgent message via email to 1MDB asking for the full name of the beneficiary of the $700 million transfer.

This time, the fund's CEO, Shahrol Halmi, explained in an email reply that the account was owned by a company called Good Star Ltd. that was based in the Seychelles and, just as Casey Tang had told the Deutsche Bank manager, Halmi indicated that the account was one hundred percent owned by PetroSaudi. This time, however, Halmi's perfectly reasonable explanation was apparently not solid enough for the skeptical managers at Coutts. Within a matter of hours, Casey Tang and I were on a Malaysia Airlines direct flight to Zurich, where we would meet face to face with the worried, hand-wringing Coutts bankers to placate them and satisfy their overwrought concerns.

While I generally try to avoid them, there are at least two crucial advantages to engaging in in-person meetings when they become necessary. The first is purely psychological, in that, whether you are in the financial sector or any other kind of service business, it is enormously more difficult to say "no" to your clients when they are sitting right across the desk from you, staring you solemnly in the face. The second is purely practical in a twenty-first century world that has been overtaken by digitally keyboarded instantaneous communication; namely, a productive oral conversation or negotiation very conveniently leaves no paper trail of the discussion the way that online Internet correspondence almost always insidiously tends to do, even if that paper trail actually consists of electronic keystrokes floating forever in the ethereal twilight zone of the Internet.

Nevertheless, as I approached this meeting, I had to think of a clever way to finesse this massive $700 million transaction, and on the fly, I came up with a slightly different story from the one that Casey had told the 1MDB account manager at Deutsche Bank.

"Gentlemen," I said, "I owe you all an apology. There seems to be some confusion here, which I'd like to clear up right now. Good Star is a newly formed investment management company, and the 1MDB board has decided to put in $700 million of its capital. I suspect the fact that Good Star is newly formed is probably the source of the confusion, and hence the source of your entirely appropriate concern."

And it worked. The Coutts bankers sitting around the conference table all looked around at one another, one by one silently nodding their heads in agreement, until they were all silently nodding their heads in agreement, like so many monkeys at the zoo, until one of them said, "Makes sense," and then another one said, "Makes sense indeed," and then they were all nodding in agreement saying "Makes sense," and that was that. It was that simple.

Like I said, getting these things done required everyone to do their part without asking too many questions. Most of all, and part of the reason Tang and I raced to Zurich in the first place, I didn't need the folks at Coutts talking to the folks at Deutsche. And this is also what I meant when I explained earlier that I needed a freer, more creative hand to make these kinds of deals fly, unencumbered by the bureaucratic red tape that invariably clogs up the old-fashioned, conventional banking channels. The bottom line was I wanted to get things *done*.

Sitting in first class on the plane ride home that afternoon, as I sipped a deliciously aromatic glass of Johnny Walker Blue Label, I texted a message to my executive partners at Wynton Group, some members of my family, and a few select others, typing: "I think we've just hit a gold mine!" It was fast approaching midnight in Malaysia, and I smiled when a Facebook post only seconds later and clearly in response to my text flashed across my mobile screen. It was a selfie from Seet Li Lin.

I need to tell you a little more about Seet.

Seet Li Lin was a smart, innovative workaholic I had met at Wharton, and he was a natural financial strategist whom I knew, from the moment I met him, I wanted on my team. As I mentioned earlier, he was from Singapore, although his family was by no means wealthy. In fact, the only way he was able to attend Wharton at all was through the generous sponsorship of the Monetary Authority of Singapore, known mostly as MAS. While MAS is essentially the central bank of Singapore, more crucially, it is also the city-state's chief financial regulatory agency. A powerful agency indeed, when you consider Singapore's international preeminence amid the global financial markets. And this is where Seet's talent and training and hands-on experience would become almost incalculably useful to me.

That's because, as part of his sponsorship by MAS and, in essence, in return for the full-ride scholarship to Wharton that his benefactor had given him, Seet was obliged to go to work for the authority for at least two years after graduation. And it was there, working on the financial regulatory side of MAS in Singapore, that

Seet learned all of the ins and outs of international investment regulation and oversight protocols, including where all of the loopholes were. Not only that, from his brief tenure at MAS, Seet also gained a keen appreciation and understanding of the jurisdictional gaps that often existed—and mainly still do—between different regulatory authorities or agencies across the boundaries of different countries around the world, from Europe to the United States to the Middle East to Southeast Asia. Some of them, Seet once told me, "were wide enough to drive a truck through." I knew from the beginning that this definitive insider information would prove invaluable to my future plans for 1MDB, so as soon as Seet had fulfilled the term of his employment obligations to MAS, I immediately hired him to an executive position as one of my partners at Wynton Group. Bottom line: Seet knew how to work the system, and he was one of the best hires I ever made.

So, anyway, I'm back on the plane out of Zurich after the prodigiously successful meeting with the Coutts bankers, and in response to my "gold mine" tweet, I get this Facebook selfie from Seet. In it, he is flanked by a pair of sultry women in skimpy cocktail dresses holding magnums of Dom Pérignon and partying hard as ever into the wee hours of the morning at some exclusive nightclub in Kuala Lumpur. The caption reads, "I feel the Earth move!"

Chapter 5

By about now, I figure you're probably wondering about me—about what makes me tick, what drove me to do some of the pretty outrageous things I did in my life. Or maybe you are wondering what it was that I was truly looking for. I've wondered about that too, and it's not a trivial question, at least not the way I see it. It seems to me that people who see themselves as having a well-defined purpose are the ones who are most able to achieve contentedness in their lives, even a measure of sustained happiness, however brief, from time to time. I'm not so sure about a purpose, *per se*, but I know I had a plan.

When I reflect on the students I encountered at Wharton, and even as far back as Harrow in Great Britain, it has always seemed to me, they were rarely as intellectually bright as they were fabulously wealthy and even more fabulously well connected, never as industrious in their studies as they were versed in the fineries of social indulgence. I learned that, as a vehicle for career advancement in the international finance universe, hitting the books and learning all those tedious market theories and investment formulas would only take a person so far. To my way of thinking, my university studies were simply no match nor any substitute whatsoever for making very familiar and longstanding connections with all of these children of the gods of the twenty-first-century aristocracies, the most powerful family cartels that rule the modern world every bit like medieval kings of old only more secretively, with much greater finesse and sophistication, and—for the most part—somewhat less barbarically.

What I can tell you from personal experience is that it is remarkable how simply interjecting oneself into the visible universe of such people as this, to occupy a prominent orbit somewhere in their solar systems, was so infinitely more valuable than securing an A in macroeconomics or getting an article published in *Forbes*.

My own family, after all, was reasonably well to do. How else would I have been able to attend Harrow and then Wharton? How else was I actually able to pull off the Shampoo party, but for the regular wire transfers for thousands and thousands of dollars at a time that I received from my father, Low Hock Peng, whom everyone called Larry? My father had made and lost several fortunes before finally making it big in textiles or, more specifically, through a series of circumstances that left him with a huge stake in a Malaysian garment manufacturer, which he was smart enough—or lucky enough—to divest himself of at enormous profit just when the stock had gone through the roof. Regardless, the wealth my family possessed at that time was chump change compared to the wealth enjoyed by the families of many of my fellow students throughout my formal education. Despite my second-son status—or perhaps because of it—I desperately wanted to change that.

I was born in George Town, the once-British colonial capital of the province of Penang Island, and as a small boy, I hated it there. Many people—I suppose tourists mostly—like to talk about the period British architecture and the tight and narrow interconnected streets in the dense shopping district of the old town sector of George Town, but to me, Penang was a stinking backwater cesspool whose best days were behind it. The capital just teemed with the descendants of the Chinese and Muslim immigrants who came ashore in droves a century earlier, during that long-gone colonial era when Penang was a critical Strait of Malacca trading hub on the long route between Europe and the Middle East, to China and Japan. And while my family was very well off by Malaysian standards, our Chinese origins meant, inescapably, that we would always be treated as second-class citizens within our own country, no matter how successful any of our family members might have been in business and industry—or even in politics, for that matter.

Over the years, I have come to realize how difficult it is for Westerners to grasp the full, ignominious weight and power that hereditary or social class still holds so pervasively among so many different Asian societies. There are circumstances where such discriminations go even deeper than those sociocultural distinctions; for example, my own Chinese cultural heritage has the gall to bestow preeminently the highest value on the firstborn son, to the diminution of any siblings that might follow. Being the third of my parent's three children, I remember the sting of inferiority, my being a person of second class by virtue of both ethnic ancestry in my homeland country and, of all ridiculous things, my order of birth into my own family. Very early on in my childhood, I resolved that I would positively refuse to let any of that hold me back from making my mark in the world. I would show everyone, including my less-than-sympathetic father, how absurd and cruel and evil—and artificial—such distinctions formed by class or origin or fate truly are.

So I hated Penang and its backward ways and provincial mindset, and no one in my family was happier than I was when my father decided to settle in London and place me in the Harrow School. Yeah, I guess my father had done okay, but it was at Harrow that I got my first insight into the great paradigmatic chasm between possessing several millions of dollars languishing safely in modest interest-bearing Swiss and off-shore bank accounts to support our family's better-than-average lifestyle and the possession and political control of several billions of dollars sufficient to underwrite the truly fabulous, jet-setting, world-traveling, multiple-palace-dwelling lifestyles of my fellow students, who came from the richest sectors of an array of aristocratic societies. One might describe it this way: Owning a really humongous bank account is good, but owning the whole bank—along with that bank's power of investment—is much, much better. Or to state it differently, if you own a big bank account, you can buy a lot of stuff; if you own the bank, you can *do* a lot of stuff.

And I knew right from the start that those were the students I wanted to seek out, to get to know intimately, and to make friends with. They were the ones I wanted to be like—or so I thought at the time, though perhaps it wasn't that I wanted to be like them so much as I wanted to possess the same power and prestige they—or, more accurately, their families—seemed to hold. Because, as I've said all along, I was determined to be my own man and someone capable of moving investment mountains. And by the time I got to Wharton, I was already learning how the world of international banking and entrepreneurial investment worked, as well as coming to understand the critical positions of power and authority through which the wealthiest regions, institutions, prominent families, and individuals held sway in that milieu: the heady, intoxicating world of high finance that I longed to be a part of.

Theirs was the elite social circle that I absolutely wanted to be a part of. More imperatively, theirs was the financial circle in which I was determined to be player. As I looked around at my Wharton classmates, I theorized that one way to convince them that I was one of them was simply to act as though that was indeed true. I have no idea what a glance at the admissions demographic statistics at Wharton might reveal, but I can tell you that the most prominent families from across a broad collection of Middle Eastern and Asian nations were well represented among the student body, and it was on those kids that I concentrated my attention.

On campus, I played my role just like a Hollywood actor in a dramatic blockbuster movie, and I guess you could say that the over-the-top extravaganza I staged for my twentieth birthday party was just one outrageous act in the context of the larger drama. I drove around in a bright, candy-red Lexus SC 430 convertible. It was leased, but I let on that I'd paid cash on the barrelhead for it. When a rumor got started that I was some sort of royal prince in Malaysia, not only did I do nothing to quash it, but I cultivated that image by acting princely—or the way I imagined a prince is supposed to act. *Darn it all, I really was the Asian Great Gatsby!*

It's something of a curiosity, but I also knew that people from across the Arab world, aristocratic Middle Easterners in particular, often demonstrate an extreme fondness for casino gambling. It's really no mystery, once you realize that gambling is prohibited throughout most of the Islamic world. Such an irony! You have a huge stash of cash burning a hole in your pocket, and your religion forbids you to play with it? So when they come to America and the Caribbean, they flock to the glitziest and most decadent casinos like moths to a flame, presumably to feed their wicked pleasure somewhere out of the sight of Allah.

I have to admit that I too occasionally get a rush from the thrill of high-stakes gambling; I regularly rented stretch limousines and invited my new wealthy friends on junkets to Atlantic City, where we'd be at the gambling tables until the sun came up.

Here's a funny story about that. One of our favorite gambling haunts was the Trump Plaza Hotel and Casino. When I learned that Ivanka Trump had transferred from Georgetown University to Wharton in 2002, I immediately wrote an invitation to her to join us on our next AC gambling junket. Know what she said in reply? She said—no lie—she said that she *wouldn't set foot in one of her father's sleazy casinos*! What a riot! Of course, at the time, no one in the world—including Ivanka—could have any idea of what her famous father would outlandishly accomplish in American politics and on the world stage of foreign affairs some fourteen years later.

And to be clear about it, my inviting Ivanka to party with me in Atlantic City really had nothing to do with Mr. Trump; that's the gods' honest truth. Dare I admit it? No, it was that Ivanka was just drop-dead gorgeous to me—a statuesque, hot, 5'11" American blonde that I full well knew I didn't have a snowball's chance in hell with. Nevertheless, she was absolutely the kind of girl I liked to have around me—and my friends—whenever I partied. Her rejection of my invite actually turned into a unique opportunity later on, one that few people can say they've ever experienced. But I'm going to tell you all about that in context later on. It's an interesting story, so you might want to stick around for that.

Moving on, that same year, one evening in 2002, I was having scary, almost supernatural luck at the tables, and at one point, I was up over $200,000! That was until I lost every cent of my winnings during a single, withering, champagne-fueled, two a.m. session at the roulette table—alcohol being, of course, another strict Islamic taboo quite popular among my Arabic classmates. You should have seen the look of horror on my friends' faces that night; they all turned white as sheets when the beautifully cleavaged croupier slid the last of my chips across the green felt to her side of the table. I just smiled at them and ordered another magnum of Cristal for the limo ride home. It all just added to the aura I wanted to create, so, as far as I was concerned, it was a good night.

Maybe you find all of this distasteful, all these things that I did to ingratiate myself with the wealthiest and most well-connected people I could find at Wharton, the apparent superficiality of it all, like it was all one big lie. There's a famous quote or saying attributed to Gandhi, something about becoming the change you want to see in the world, or words to that effect. The way I looked at it, I was working fervently to change who I was, to become the kind of person I wanted to be. That happened to be, in my mind, someone who was respected in the global financial investment space—a guy who could get things done. You can only get so far by fitting yourself to the world, I reasoned, yet in order to change the world, I needed to change myself. That notion seemed like a natural and logical corollary to Gandhi's words, at least the way I saw things, and the bottom line was that I had real aspirations to do great things; what, in the end, is truly wrong with that?

It's a difficult thing, you see, to try to come to terms with some of those vile indoctrinating beliefs we are fed when we are growing up, about our limitations, those stereotypical societal beliefs about what we can and cannot accomplish with our lives. Beliefs that choke our human ambitions, that tell us not to try because we will never succeed. Well, I was trying to overcome all of that dispiriting baggage, and it was all I could do to play my Hollywood role to bury my intense and deeply rooted feeling of inferiority and to act like—and thus become—the person I desired so much to be. At least, that is what I would have told my shrink if I had one.

Even if it was true that I had misrepresented myself to my wealthy Middle Eastern friends, I want to point out that it was only through them, after all, that I was able to arrange my tour of the Middle East, where not only would I learn for the first time about sovereign wealth funds and how I could make one work for me, but I would also establish the important connections that would enable me to acquire control of such a fund.

So what's wrong with a few fibs?

Chapter 6

As soon as I returned from Zurich, I immediately began disbursing money from the Good Star account to the people who had been instrumental in getting the deal done. In particular, over the course of about three months, I sent over $150 million to Tarek Obaid's J.P. Morgan account in Switzerland, which he, in turn, filtered out to PetroSaudi executives and other important principals, including, for example, some thirty-three million dollars to Patrick Mahony and another seventy-seven million dollars in total to Prince Turki, spread out over the course of 2010. Five million dollars went to Casey Tang for his vital role in convincing Coutts to grant its approval of the asset management agreement with Gold Star, to which Tang was a signatory on behalf of 1MDB as the fund's executive director. As for attorney Edgar Rongst, he shortly left Helmsley & Cruikshank to become chief counsel for PetroSaudi UK at an obscenely generous salary worthy of his legal talents—and his dedication to discretion in all matters relating to his new firm.

I also handsomely rewarded my inner circle for all the work they had done, starting in particular with the executive team at Wynton Group and reaching beyond to the firm's invaluable outside advisors, who had so ably assisted us in a myriad of ways. In particular, Eric Tan received an initial payment of eleven million dollars at the beginning of 2010 and another thirty million by the end of that same year. Eric, whom everyone called "Fat Eric"—affectionately so—was not a member of the Wynton Group. I guess you could think of him as a kind of unaffiliated freelance businessman and a facilitator. Accordingly, Fat Eric was not aligned with any particular banks, financial organizations, or corporate entities, such that he was free to fulfill any number of roles to support my extreme deal-making vision. He was like a utility player on an American major league baseball team, able to play many positions on the field, and as such, Fat Eric would become indispensably valuable to me, as he operated, let's just say, at the evolving frontiers of innovative international investment of a kind that had never been tried before and that I alone had conceived and would put into action. When I needed a "guy"—a jack-of-all-trades—to act as the representative for one of the many companies or accounts I would set up going forward, Fat Eric was that guy. And it worked out really well too.

I'm not going to tell you how much I paid Seet, who was really my right-hand man at this stage of the game and was also a signatory to the asset management agreement on behalf of Good Star. Suffice it to say that he was abundantly compensated.

I will reveal that I sent three million dollars to my sister, Low May Lin. May Lin is an exceedingly sharp corporate attorney, who, at the time, specialized in offshore and trust management, and she had provided all of the expertise I had needed in setting up Good Star, as well as a host of other offshore entities I would need to move and position 1MDB money to where I needed it.

Now here's where it gets really interesting, and, I think, you'll get an idea of the big plans I had for investment in prime U.S. real estate—professional, commercial, and residential properties. I opened a private account, known as an IOLTA, with one of New York City's top white-shoe law firms, McCarter & Maxwell. If you're not familiar, *white-shoe firm* refers to a long-established, highly respected law firm known for its prestigious professional services to the upper of upper-class elite and staffed exclusively with Ivy League law school graduates. McCarter & Maxwell, a prominent New York and U.S. firm since their founding all the way back in the mid-1800s, truly fit the bill. Furthermore, you might also not know that IOLTA stands for *interest on lawyer trust account*. Suffice it to say, you might think of an IOLTA as a kind of slush fund through which one can make transactions, under the secretive cover of attorney–client privilege. Although, the lawyers at McCarter & Maxwell would probably scream bloody murder if they heard me call an IOLTA a "slush fund." In fact, they'd probably try to sue me!

Anyway, I began pouring what would eventually amount to a total of over $368 million into my IOLTA with the firm. This was the money I would use to buy U.S. properties—and discretely, through the channels of the law firm. Of course, the partners at McCarter & Maxwell would reap a tidy profit in legal fees from handling the real estate transactions, as well as from short-term interest on the client money they were holding in the IOLTA.

But here's the really interesting part. The Good Star and other funds were technically in Swiss or offshore accounts, and I needed a way to get them into the United States for the purpose of building the real estate empire I had in mind. So two things to know: First, unlike bankers, lawyers are not required by law to investigate or conduct due diligence on their clients. So I knew they would not be nosing around trying to figure out where the IOLTA funds were coming from. Heck, they were going to make a ton of money in the arrangement as well, so what the hell did they care? And second, our collaboration was protected—*legally* protected, that is—by attorney–client privilege. So, for privacy's sake, as well as the ability to move money without a lot of red tape, the arrangement with McCarter was ideal for everyone.

Finally and not the least crucially, I invested about six million dollars with a couple of upscale jewelers based in Singapore for gift items I instructed to be sent to Rosmah Mansor, things like a couple of diamond rings and some emerald earrings and a ruby necklace, baubles that I knew would truly please her—and, in turn, would please Prime Minister Najib as well.

Look. The only other thing I'm going to say about Good Star is that, while it had the appearance, to Coutts and a few other parties perhaps, of being an asset management vehicle, it was not really that, but it was, in reality, the only entity over which I wielded one hundred percent, total control. Because I believed that only I knew what I wanted to do to build a financial empire that would ultimately benefit everyone—including the 1MDB sovereign fund and its mission to develop Malaysia, our financial backers in the Middle East (and soon other nations around the world, I hoped), and, of course, me and my associates.

When all of this blew up in my face a few years later, if you had read the newspapers back then—and even still today—everywhere from the outrageously salacious headlines to the more objective, conservative financial pages, they all said that, immediately after the PetroSaudi–1MDB joint venture was formed, I went on some sort of wildly, extravagantly out-of-control spending spree even before the ink was dry on the written contract.

When they got wind of my real estate purchases, the tabloids were downright, despicably gleeful in reporting the details of how I acquired a luxury condominium for thirty-six million dollars in New York City's Park Laurel building on Central Park West—the first acquisition I made using the McCarter & Maxwell IOLTA funds, by the way. How they went on and on about the duplex's 7,700 square feet on multiple floors with floor-to-ceiling windows looking down spectacularly on the park and the Hudson River! Or when I plunked down thirty-five million pounds sterling for the Stratton Penthouse in London, opposite the Ritz Hotel in the "upmarket" (as one newspaper put it) Mayfair district. That place had this amazing rooftop terrace with breathtaking views across the lush manicured gardens of Green Park to Buckingham Palace. And, of course, there was the exclusive Hillcrest property in Beverly Hills, California, known as the Pyramid House; that home cost only twenty million dollars, although, of course, that was before we tore down a substantial portion of the original twenty-room mansion and invested another thirty million dollars to rebuild a much grander edifice in its place, with both indoor and outdoor swimming pools and a bowling alley (yep, IOLTA funds here too!).

What these scurrilous news stories failed to report, however, was that all of these properties were not strictly for me personally, but rather, they would be used as convenient, safe-haven residences abroad, where the prime minister and Rosmah often stayed when they visited the U.S. or the UK. So, in an important sense, the properties were there for the benefit of all of Malaysia when Najib traveled on diplomatic missions overseas, as he conducted the people's business as it pertained to international affairs. The many residences would also be used by Riza Aziz, the prime minister's stepson, as he traveled about the world on business. So in effect, they all *belonged*, directly or indirectly, to Malaysia. As for me, well, I was jetting around the world so continuously that, on those occasions when I may have stayed in any of these homes, it would typically have been for no more than a day or two between business trips, so hectic was my travel schedule.

Yet the media—particularly the Malaysian press—also got it very wrong when they criticized and sensationalized the bona fide real estate investments I made strictly on behalf of 1MDB, such as when I successfully acquired the world-renowned L'Ermitage hotel, just off the Sunset Strip, in Beverly Hills, with an all-cash bid of just under forty-five million dollars. L'Ermitage is a $1,000-a-night, world-class hotel and one of only a handful of the most exclusive destinations of choice among the most sophisticated world travelers, whether for business or pleasure. My plan was for this Beverly Hills gem to be just the first foray of 1MDB, not just into the acquisition of exclusive, high-value (yet somewhat passive) real estate holdings, but also as an aggressive investment into what I saw as a looming opportunity in the potentially highly lucrative hospitality and travel industry. At that moment, I saw this industry as a sleeping giant, and in this, I think I can say that I was ahead of the curve.

I astutely acquired the hotel in early 2010, just as the whole world was beginning to try to dig out from under the economic crash of 2008, and over the ensuing years, the hospitality and travel market took off like a rocket. It continued to explode exponentially with no ceiling in sight right up until the day—only a scant couple of years ago—when it was completely shut down by the COVID-19 pandemic. The fact was, my plan was that 1MDB would acquire a whole assortment of such top-end, monumentally desirable hotel destinations in the most glamorous cities around the world.

Imagine: a Malaysian sovereign entity becoming famous among the world's most elite travelers, the movers and shakers of international business, finance, and investment! If you have any difficulty grasping how powerful that kind of upscale notoriety might be for 1MDB, think about the fact that one of the major factors—and possibly the single most influential factor—that enabled Donald Trump to become the American president was undeniably the recognition factor that derived from having his name plastered over office buildings, beach clubs, casinos, and golf resorts all around the world.

It was no coincidence, by the way, that one of the most important and influential real estate developers that my New York attorneys talked to extensively—at my urging—was Donald J. Trump. I had learned about Mr. Trump as early as my high school days at Harrow, and I became fascinated by him, and more particularly intrigued by the kind of mythic universe that he seemed always to move within.

When I got to Wharton, however, I was surprised to find that, among some circles at his alma mater, the Trump name was something of a joke. Some of the students and even the professors ridiculed the man, disparaging both his arrogance and what they insinuated was his overblown reputation. Long story short, while nobody disputed the fact that Trump had made millions upon millions of dollars—and, no doubt, lost millions upon millions as well—even then, at the beginning of the millennium, the value of his corporate enterprises, as well as his total private net worth, were subject to serious debate. Trump was both loved and hated by Wall Street and the big banks as well, probably in nearly equal measure, and when the New York press dubbed him "The Donald," beneath a thin veneer of recognition and respect, the moniker also carried with it an implied but palpable subtext of mockery and disdain, for both the man and his methods.

Yet I looked at Donald Trump's brash, enterprising brand and his radical entrepreneurship and thought to myself, *What the heck is wrong with all of that?* If, indeed, a large measure of his wealth was on paper—even if much of that wealth was predicated on debt that he had acquired—my take on it was that it was really way much more than that. I always saw debt as "money in transit," if you will—that is, money traveling between one big deal going to yet another even bigger deal. Seemed like perfectly sound business investment practice to me. I mean, what's the use of having millions of dollars if you don't parlay that capital into a deal worth *billions* of dollars? That was my way of thinking, and I was intrigued by the way that Trump had made a name for himself, essentially by being unorthodox—and fearless—in his approach to business, by making up his own rules, by finding a way to make the deal, by going into the negotiations bigger than anybody else. No matter what the people in New York said about him, he had become, through his own determination, a force to be reckoned with. I had to admire this.

So, whatever the actual circumstances might have been with respect to his financial status, I honestly believed he might be able to help me find, or perhaps build anew on behalf of 1MDB, a really terrific hotel in a prime location in New York City, which I planned to make into something that might compare with the internationally known reputation of The Plaza or the Four Seasons or the like or an East Coast sister hotel to L'Ermitage.

I told you earlier about how I had invited Trump's daughter Ivanka to come gambling with me and my friends down to her dad's casino in Atlantic City and how she turned me down and how that rejection had led to something even more significant later on. Well, here it is.

By any standard of feminine beauty, Ivanka was a stunningly glamorous young woman in her college days—still is today—such that any ambitious guy certainly would have been delighted to be in her company in any capacity. So, no question about it, I found her beautiful and alluring, but in a strange way, I think I was even more vicariously attracted to her sheer celebrity, her public persona almost as an entity in itself. Whether one likes the Trump family or not, even at this early stage of her life, Ivanka had already begun to build a multifaceted brand of pop-culture celebrity that seemed to have numerous crossovers, from business entrepreneurship to fashion design to politics and even to entertainment and social media. When I received her note politely declining my invitation, and somewhat on a whim, I wrote back that I was sure she was joking about her father's "sleazy" casino, that I'd gotten a good "chuckle" out of it, but also telling her how much I admired her father and his work, and expressing my hope that I'd get to meet him in person someday.

Well, I don't know if it was intended as a kind of consolation prize, but a couple of months later, I got an email from Ivanka. It read, "My father is coming down from New York to visit me this weekend. Would you like me to introduce you?"

"Absolutely," was my one-word reply, and she arranged for us to have breakfast together that Saturday morning at the famed Walnut Street Café, right in the heart of the metropolitan UPenn campus.

Bright and early, at the appointed time, I picked up Ivanka from her campus residence, and we took a cab to the café. When we walked in together, Mr. Trump was already seated at the table that had been reserved in advance. It was one of the rare times in my life that I actually felt nervous—in fact, extremely so, as if this was that fateful date when your girl introduces you to one or both of her parents, even though, of course, it was nothing of the sort. And I realized it was Mr. Trump I was nervous about impressing, not his daughter.

He did not stand when we approached the table, and as Ivanka made the perfunctory introductions, Donald Trump regarded me with a kind of blank, puckered face, as if he had just sucked a lemon or something. He looked from me to Ivanka and back again, like a mathematician doing a complex calculation in his head, only something wasn't computing. When, at last, we sat down, he seemed to take deliberate notice of the space between us, as if trying to gain some empirical data points of meaning from whatever distance apart from each other we settled in our chairs.

The truth was, I had amply prepared myself for the steely reception I fully expected to receive from Ivanka's father. There was no possible way to overlook how incongruous we were going to look standing there together, Ivanka a statuesque blonde just under six feet tall, taller still in moderate heels, and me, a pudgy Asian guy barely 5'7" with my thickest-heeled shoes on, squinting through wire-rimmed glasses. Even if Trump was well aware that this meeting was strictly about business, that it certainly wasn't a "Daddy meet my boyfriend" moment, I had to presume that Donald Trump would expect that *any guy* that Ivanka would take the trouble to introduce to him—for any reason at all—would have to be some dude with the imposing drop-dead Aryan good looks and chiseled physique of, I don't know, say, Dolph Lundgren or somebody. But I didn't really care about any of that, and I wasn't going to let whatever deep-seated prejudices that might be lurking in his subconscious deter me from my mission—to see what I might be able to learn from him of substance.

In the end, Donald was very cordial, and our meeting went very well. The very first thing, he made sure I knew that Wharton was his alma mater.

"I went to Wharton, you know," he said, looking at me inquisitively, apparently for confirmation that I did indeed know this and that I was duly impressed.

"Of course," I smiled as I replied.

"Graduated in the top three of my class," Mr. Trump interjected, practically before I could get those two little words out.

He then asked me what I wanted to do once I graduated. I told him that I was not entirely sure but that I wanted to be involved with international financial investment or trade and that I wanted to do so on a grand scale.

"I want to play a major role in the burgeoning globalization of business and industry in this new century," I said, adding, "I think the growth of international investment opportunities is going to be astronomical over the next several years."

Trump nodded approvingly, stirring his coffee.

"That's good," he replied. "And you're absolutely right."

It's funny, but, for some reason, I vividly remember he took his coffee black but only after stirring a shocking number of spoonsful of sugar into it.

"You should read my book," he said. He was referring to *The Art of the Deal*, which he originally published in 1987. "I'm always telling people," Trump continued, "if you're going to do something, you should try to do it big—as big as you possibly can. Like, if you're going to be thinking anyway, you might as well think big."

Mr. Trump paused, looked at me pensively, as if he was trying to size me up and to determine whether I would fully appreciate the next bit of advice he was about to give. "Sometimes," he said, a wry smile crossing his face, "sometimes all you have to do is make the deal look a lot bigger than it really is. When you make the deal look really big, it becomes really big, because a lot of the major investors just can't resist the opportunity to be involved in it. They're afraid as hell of being left out. And before you know it, it's a megadeal."

While today there is little else that I remember from my first meeting with Donald Trump, I never forgot this rather simple advice he gave me. It was already exactly the way I felt about such things.

For what it's worth, nothing substantive ever came of my lawyers' initial overtures to Donald Trump, but even then, I believed our paths would cross again one day, as I hoped they would. Of course, everybody in the world knows what "The Donald" accomplished just a little over six years later. Nobody back then would have given him a snowball's chance in hell, but even before Donald Trump became president of the United States, I surmised that he would be an important and influential individual to know and with whom to develop some business ties.

But I seem to have digressed, so please forgive me. Let me get back once again to my plans for 1MDB.

There was much more to my plan than simply acquiring and owning a group of the world's most prestigious hotels, even if that might be great fun in its own right. But I had also learned from

Ambassador Otaiba that Abu Dhabi's Mubadala wealth fund had recently acquired the hotel management company known as the Viceroy Hotel Group. In fact, the ambassador had willingly offered his official influence with the seller of L'Ermitage, who happened to be U.S. real estate billionaire Tom Barrack Jr. and who had some three decades earlier worked with Otaiba's father when Barrack was a young lawyer.

Anyway, Otaiba's influence may well have swayed the deal in my favor, and, in return for his help. I promised Otaiba that I would rebrand L'Ermitage as a Viceroy Hotel. Why I did this should be self-evident by now: I was working to further cement the connection between Middle Eastern money and Malaysia, more specifically to investment in the emerging development of the Malaysian economy by wealthy Middle Eastern nations. So you see, I was trying to transform 1MDB, right from its inception, into an international entity comparable to Mubadala and other storied sovereign wealth funds in countries around the world that had themselves taken decades of internal and foreign investment to achieve such lofty reputations. To turn a phrase, I wanted 1MDB to be playing with the big boys on the international stage right from the start. And today, by the way, L'Ermitage is a renowned premier member of the Viceroy Group.

By contrast, it is worth reviewing what all the fund managers back in the Kuala Lumpur offices of 1MDB were accomplishing—or, more accurately, not accomplishing. Like all major investment sovereign funds, 1MDB had hired a team of blueblood fund managers—starry-eyed recent Ivy League graduates whose only thought was that there was nothing more noble than working for "the good of the nation on behalf of its people" through their employment with a dedicated sovereign fund. Despite their array of university pedigrees from Harvard Business School and the like, the best these guys could muster was a misguided plan to turn a section of Kuala Lumpur into a financial hub to rival Singapore and Hong Kong.

The team nicknamed their flagship initiative Project Wall Street, but in terms of both scope and scale, it paled in comparison to the Iskandar Development Region. Nevertheless, I tried to help the fund managers get the project off to a flying start. First, I interceded with Prime Minister Najib to grant the 1MDB fund parcels of vacant land in the center of the city—at bargain-basement prices—to be dedicated to the development. The plan called for Abu Dhabi's Mubadala fund to invest billions into the financial center, and after the fund managers spent some two million dollars to arrange a launch party to celebrate the initiative, I used my connections to invite the crown prince himself to attend the gala. However, at the very last minute, circumstances at home prevented the crown prince from appearing at the party. And as far as I know, the launch was never rescheduled, and most of that two million dollars' worth of preparations was simply lost. Worst of all, however, Project Wall Street simply floundered from that point; it never came to fruition, and the whole affair became a total loss.

So these Ivy Leaguers couldn't manage to pull off a modest development in their own back yard, and the truth was that many of them quit their jobs after less than a year, all of this while I was almost single handedly leading the effort to turn 1MDB into a world-beating economic empire and financial powerhouse. It's like I said earlier, about the difference between what the classroom lessons at Wharton offered and the far more invaluable connections one could make on that campus that would later afford the opportunity to do business on a much larger scale.

Moving on then: My direct involvement in handling these business dealings, particularly with respect to the real estate acquisitions, enabled Najib to stay at arm's length from the day-to-day operations of 1MDB and, let's just say, its "subsidiaries." To my way of thinking, the prime minister didn't need to know where the funds I used to buy all these luxurious homes had come from, and for his part, Najib never asked.

Meanwhile, even as he and Rosmah enjoyed the use of these fabulously appointed residences—Rosmah particularly loved the Pyramid House on Hillcrest in Beverly Hills because it was less than ten minutes away from one of her favorite shopping haunts, that being Rodeo Drive—I made sure that the prime minister began receiving a regular stream of millions of dollars in political funding, much of that going into his private offshore accounts. That was all Najib needed to permit me to run the fund pretty much independently of the board of advisors.

Keeping everyone in the Razak family happy and comfortable quickly paid enormous dividends for me, because, honestly, when the advisory board finally got wind of the $700 million Good Star transaction, I got way more pushback from some of the members than I ever expected. In fact, when a group of them objected to the transfer and began loudly demanding that PetroSaudi return the money so that it could be invested in the joint venture as originally agreed, I urgently needed enormous help from Najib to quell a potentially serious uprising. And I got it in droves.

While I had been able to exert enough influence over Najib to induce him to seat a number of trustworthy decision-makers on the 1MDB board, naturally, I was not able to handpick the entire slate of advisor-directors—much as I would have liked to. I'm talking now not about the innocuous figureheads, many of them foreign nationals, from the realm of the international rich and famous who were there just to pretty up the board but, rather, about those board members who tried to be serious about their hands-on roles in directing the day-to-day operations of the sovereign fund. Those reputable individuals, bless their little hearts, thought I'd actually let them be in charge of directing the investment operations of the 1MDB fund all by themselves.

One of the most prominent among the objectors was Mohammed Bakke Salleh, a dyed-in-the-wool chartered account and a hardline, by-the-book product of the London School of Economics, whom Najib had appointed chairman of the 1MDB board. It was not one of Najib's finest appointments, but I was obliged to respect his wishes. I became very alarmed when Bakke suddenly started pressing his demand that an independent audit be conducted of PetroSaudi's oil assets, assets that were supposed to be going into the joint venture, he argued. I could not afford to jeopardize the generous valuation appraisal that Patrick Mahoney had obtained from world oil market expert Jordan Traynor, and all I can say is thank god I managed to persuade Najib, as the head of the whole shooting match, to rule that there would be no such thing. Upon being rebuffed in this public way, Bakke was deeply incensed, but he chose to simply resign quietly from the board without making a big stink about his dissatisfaction, to my great relief. I knew that his departure would create murmurs that would reverberate through the financial world, but I believed I would be able to weather that storm one way or another.

However, when Bakke's resignation was followed less than a month later by that of another prominent board member, I realized I had to do something to quell any further dissension, or this whole thing was liable to fall apart. I also needed to strenuously bolster the prime minister's trust in me, so, in January 2010, I quickly organized another state visit to Abu Dhabi. As I always did, and even as urgent as the present crisis situation was, I stage-managed this junket down to the minutest detail. Up until this point, most of my contact with Tarek Obaid was via email. But, given the gravity of the situation, this time, I called him. After the exchange of some cordial pleasantries, I got down to business.

"This is a delicate matter, Tarek," I explained, "but I'd be very grateful if you might possibly intercede with the Saudi royals, to encourage them to be very reassuring in their private conversations with the prime minister and First Lady—especially the First Lady."

"What do you have in mind?" Obaid asked.

"What I'm thinking of is if you could see your way to asking the royals to use words and phrases like 'mutual trust' and 'common bonds,' or 'friendship' and 'personal connection,' that sort of thing—anything to reassure the prime minister and his wife of the reliable and ongoing nature of the connection between our two nations."

Basically, this was to leave unsaid that I wanted Najib to be reassured that the political contributions to him and to the UMNO would continue to flow from Middle East royals like water from the mountain.

"I understand your concern," Tarek replied. "It's clearly in everybody's interest that Saudi Arabia and Malaysia continue to cooperate to advance their friendly political ties and mutual economic prosperity," he monotoned like a press release from the Department of State, but I knew Tarek got the message.

I thanked him profusely, but then I couldn't help but add, "And if it isn't too much, Tarek," I said, "if the king would express his close personal friendship with Najib—and Rosmah—I think it would go a long way toward fostering that cooperation, and I know that Najib would really take it to heart."

"Of course," Tarek closed. And then he gave a slight laugh. "Isn't it amusing," he added, "how our great and powerful leaders so often seem so pathetically insecure as to need such petty reassurances? They can be like little children seeking favor from their mommies and daddies." And then he hung up.

To my delight, not only did the Saudis get my message, but they exceeded anything I could have imagined when they honored Najib by presenting him with the kingdom's highest civilian award with all the fanfare of an official ceremony at a state dinner. It was the kind of massively ego-boosting pomp that fed Najib's addiction for praise and recognition, though, of course, the award itself was about as meaningless as all the medals and ribbons you always see on the chest of the average military dictator's parade-dress uniform. Nevertheless, the well-publicized ceremony made for great front-page press back home for the prime minister, providing very positive media coverage that only served to strengthen his advancing hold on political power over the Malaysian people. Najib knew or, at least, believed that I was the guy behind all of this, and that fact, coupled with the departure of Bakke and some of his fellow stuffed shirts from the 1MDB board, created an exquisite and breathtakingly timely opportunity for me.

But I had to work fast. I immediately but very quietly began meeting with various members of the board, one-on-one over coffee or lunch, to make it clear to them, however obliquely, that I was the prime minister's direct representative with respect to all matters concerning 1MDB. It's funny how easy it was to convince them of this, especially when you consider that I had no official seat on the board or any sort of official government title to speak of. But, after all, who were they going to ask, in any event? It was abundantly clear that none of them would have had the balls to confront the prime minister directly about me or my role—especially now, with his power only increasing exponentially, seemingly by the hour. They all feared him, and that played to my advantage. Even further, I remember warning one particularly cranky board member that, if he persisted in belligerently asking too many probing questions about the PetroSaudi joint venture, he seriously risked insulting the Saudis, who, I pointed out ominously, "just gave the PM the equivalent of a twenty-one-gun salute. Do you want to be the one guy responsible for blowing up Malaysia's—and Najib's—amazing new diplomatic ties with the Middle East? Do you want to be the one that causes an international incident?" Naturally, the board member backed off after that.

Plus, now we had crucial vacancies to fill on the board, and I happily made the most of that opportunity too, by steering Najib to appoint people I knew I could count on to work with me—or, at the least, not get in my way. I wanted no further scrutiny or resistance from old-school fossils lacking any semblance of future-thinking vision.

To fill one of the at-large seats, I persuaded Najib to appoint a Malaysian Chinese from my hometown of Penang who just happened to be one of my father's former business partners and, honestly, somewhat past his administrative prime at this point. No matter.

To fill the chairmanship vacated by Bakke, we designated a fellow by the name of Lodin Wok Kamaruddin. We chose Kamaruddin primarily because he was a lockstep UMNO loyalist who would set his hair on fire for the party or even fall on his sword in expression of his loyalty to Najib. Mostly, he absolutely wouldn't question anything the prime minister wanted to do, so he was a perfect candidate for the 1MDB board. Beyond that, Lodin was pretty much a nondescript itinerant business executive with an unremarkable track record and an MBA from the University of Toledo. The one in Ohio. In the United States. In case you were wondering.

So in the end, I was able to turn this early and potentially disastrous shake-up among the executive team of 1MDB into a really good thing, because I used it to solidify my control over the board—with Prime Minister Najib's blessings, of course—and to eliminate any further objections to my directives from meddlesome members. Directives that they believed were coming straight from the prime minister, that is. In effect, I had cleansed the board of any naysayers while making it abundantly clear to the remaining members who was really in charge of the fund. Once all that was straightened out, I could better focus my energies and attention on the investments—and the investors—I wanted to pursue, in the manner in which I wanted to pursue them.

I was convinced that the best way to attract the right people was to entertain them and to do it in a way they had never experienced before or even imagined. In a word, I partied and invited all kinds of characters to my parties—rather publicly, in fact. The press had a field day following and reporting my exploits and trying to identify as many of my guests as they could. Only now it wasn't just the Asian and British tabloids; well-respected Western newspapers such as the *Wall Street Journal* and the *New York Times* struggled to figure out who I was and where I came from, describing me as some new Asian "billionaire whiz kid of Wall Street." Fortunately, they could never quite pin down my origins, and thanks to the great care I had taken to remain unofficial and strictly behind the scenes with respect to 1MDB, there was no easy way for anyone to connect me to the sovereign fund. But oh how they loved printing the stories about my lavish spending—"decadent and obscene," as one newspaper described it—in the most exclusive clubs in New York City, Vegas, and LA!

Well, to be perfectly honest about all of that, let me concede right here and now that I did indeed spend millions of dollars on entertainment and parties—lots of mind-blowing, outrageous, over-the-top crazy parties, whether they were staged affairs or just impromptu gatherings that came together after signing a deal. And let me remind you, those parties were all about the deal.

Let's see. Over the span of about eight months, from that October in 2009, when the PetroSaudi joint venture was officially completed and the money was transferred, to about June of the following year, I spent about twenty-five or thirty million dollars between Caesar's Palace and the Sands Hotel in Las Vegas. (I may have run up some bills at a couple of other casinos outside of Vegas as well; America is just full of casinos nowadays!) That was for entertainment, mostly fantastic parties that lasted for two or three days and included a star-studded list of celebrities, many of them from the movie and music industries. I also hired scores of gorgeous models, sometimes Playboy Playmates, just to mingle with crowd wearing skimpy cocktail dresses or to lounge around the pool in the scantiest of bikinis.

For travel, I think I paid out about four or five million dollars to a company called Jet Logic, for leasing jet airliners and for chartered flights. Hey, how else was I supposed to get all my distinguished guests to and from those great parties? Another three million dollars or so went to Yachtzoo for the rental of those lovely superyachts. I will confess that I lost track of how many millions of bucks I dropped in the ultra-exclusive nightclubs and the ritziest bars in Manhattan and Brooklyn, in New York City, entertaining the rich and famous celebrities from Fifth Avenue or Broadway and beyond, to Hollywood and Silicon Valley; West-Coaster elites are always visiting New York, you know, not to mention that there are plenty of movie and pop music stars that make their homes right there in the Big Apple. I wanted to get to know as many of them as I could.

And that was why I also rented a suite of rooms, for about $100,000 a month, at the Park Imperial on West 56th Street, with panoramic views of both Central Park and the Hudson River. I made the Park Imperial my base of operations in New York because the hotel was something of a magnet for celebrities in the entertainment industries. Some stars actually lived there on a regular basis at different times of the year, like rapper Sean "Diddy" Combs, while many others from around the world stayed at the Park Imperial when they were performing in New York or making appearances on local television shows. In fact, when I first arrived, the British actor Daniel Craig of James Bond fame was staying at the Park Imperial while he was performing on Broadway.

So you see, even to this day, I do have a general handle on what I was spending way back then, at least for the most part. And it's true: I did embark on what would have appeared to most people as an outrageously wild and extravagant lifestyle.

Notice I said that's the way it "would have appeared" to people. I think the media must have knocked themselves out looking for adjectives to describe how "reckless" and "chaotic" and "out of control" my partying was. But I can assure you it was not that way at all. Look, I'm not a big drinker, and I've never done drugs, and as far as women and sexual exploits, well, let me just say I'm no Hugh Hefner and leave it at that. Yet all of these evil little diversions, these "vices" if you want to call them that, go hand-in-hand with the image and excesses of celebrity life, whether perceived or real. For the rest of us, it's part of the aura, the lure to be in the company of the rich, the famous, the really glamorous people. Hey, if you want certain people—like the powerbrokers and the dealmakers and the financial heavyweights of the world, for example—to come to your parties, you've got to give them what they want.

So all of this crazy party madness, you see, was far more calculated for effect than you could ever imagine—easily as well calculated as my real estate investments were for keeping the Razaks happy while, at the same time, throwing a bone to the board at 1MDB. And if my lavish entertainments, as regularly chronicled in the pages of the *Times* and the *Journal*, attracted the wolves of Wall Street and the investment gunslingers at Goldman and J.P. Morgan and Deutsche Bank and all the rest of the one-percenters at the top of the personal and professional wealth pyramid, so much to the good for me. The bottom line is you don't get the opportunity to invite these kinds of high rollers into your international business and investment circle by buying them breakfast off the Dollar Menu at your local McDonald's.

As for what the advisory board at 1MDB back home might have thought about it, well, all of this was just the cost of doing business, the way I saw it. I knew that I needed to make a big splash in order to gain the attention of the glitterati of the world, as well as to gain entry to that powerful, exciting, and influential world myself.

Although, there was one "perk" I will admit I bought, mostly for myself. With all of the business dealings I was involved in, I was constantly flying around the world, traveling from Kuala Lumpur or Singapore or Hong Kong to Zurich, Paris, or London or to New York, LA, or Vegas in the States and then flying back home only to do this arduous circuit all over again. I think I was spending more time on airplanes than I was on the terra firma of planet Earth.

Don't get me wrong; I loved being in constant motion. I thrived on it, as if travel itself was what kept the blood pumping in my heart. Whenever I was in flight, high above the chaos of the land or the unseen depths of the ocean below, crossing from one continent to another, I felt exhilarated and alive, empowered to live by my own rules rather than those of any restrictive government down there on the surface. One time, Seet and I were flying to America; I think it was the first or second time we were flying together to New York. We were just finishing up some business as the plane was making its approach to Newark Liberty International Airport, in New Jersey. As I gazed out the window at the New York City skyline to the east, I mused to Seet, "You know, sometimes I genuinely feel like a citizen of the world more than a citizen of any individual country."

Seet was curious. "Why do you think that?" he asked. But before I could answer, he continued, "Do you think it's because we're up here, highfliers doing international deals among different nations and trying to benefit the interests of all of those nations at the same time?"

I pondered that statement for a moment, smirked to think how Seet's summarization could have been concocted by some crafty advertising executive just across the Hudson River there, over on Madison Avenue.

"I suppose that's it," I sighed inconclusively. But, quietly, in that moment, I couldn't help but think of my father, and of my Chinese-Malaysian heritage, so restrictive and so thoroughly outdated in the modern world, where the World Wide Web and economic globalization provides open access to everything for everybody.

Still, air travel is and always was a very hectic, energy-draining way to carry on my affairs, and after a while, I got tired of the tedious rigmarole of constantly leasing jets, and I had absolutely no patience for the bureaucratic ordeal of flying with the commercial airlines, with their convoluted, nightmarish security protocols and their incessant, aggravating flight delays without explanation. So I bought my own private jet, a Canadian-made Bombardier Global 5000, for a little over thirty-five million dollars. This thing was really cool; I had it outfitted with a private sleeping quarters and an office complete with Wi-Fi and a fax machine. And on board my own aircraft, following the self-directed flight plan of my own life, there was no daytime or nighttime *per se*; there was just a kind of virtually streaming business time for getting deals done. I could conduct business from any map coordinates around the globe at any moment in Greenwich Mean Time—or any other arbitrary time in the world. Inevitably, there was time to get some sleep at will, whenever that might be necessary, those little slices of death that even the best of us must endure.

I could argue that my buying the Bombardier was, in the long run, really a benefit to 1MDB, because it made me about as nimble and flexible as any enthusiastic entrepreneur could possibly be. I could be in any city in the world in only the time it took to jump on board and fly there, whether it was New York or LA to sign an investment deal or Zurich or London to give the nervous bankers there some reassuring hand-holding (they were always worrying themselves silly!) or Las Vegas to orchestrate another outrageous celebrity party. But I'll tell you a little secret: That jet became my private haven.

It wasn't long after I bought the aircraft that, for all practical intents and purposes and despite all the beautiful homes I was also acquiring for myself in Asia, Europe, and America, I found myself virtually living my life within its Spartan yet comfortably adequate confines. What I discovered was that, as much as living in a resplendent mansion located in some dynamic and desirable city anyplace in the world might be a wonderful thing, to me, there was nothing quite like living in a well-appointed place that was actually capable of traveling under its own power to any of a thousand other luxuriously desirable places anywhere around the world—a mobile sanctuary if you will. I believed I deserved such a sanctuary. Still, it was kind of tight inside that cabin.

And that's also when I determined that, some day, I was going to get myself a superyacht like the RM *Elegant*—or even the stunningly magnificent *Alfa Nero*. That way, I could have the resplendent mansion, the sanctuary, and the worldwide mobility all in one place.

Eventually, however, I realized there was a problem. I was running out of cash! Can you imagine? I was a little surprised by it myself, how easily I had invested $700 million, just like that. Of course, there was only one thing to do. I simply had to go back to 1MDB for more money.

Isn't that obvious?

Chapter 7

There is something about partying in New York City that is unlike partying in any other city on the planet. When I reflect on my most itinerant days back then, I am honestly grateful for having had the opportunity to visit so many of the world's most cherished, most beautiful, and most romanticized cities. Whether those steeped in history, like London and Paris and Rome, or the startlingly modernist, almost avant garde cities like Dubai and Singapore and Shanghai, I loved them all, and you could have a simply fabulous time in any one of them. And yet when it came to celebrations or happenings meant to mark special occasions or achievement, or just to have a good time for the hell of it—I'm talking about over-the-top extravagant partying here—I think all of those great cities are just trying their damnedest to be New York City.

Because in New York, you can be sitting at a table in a tiny nightclub anywhere from the Upper West Side or midtown to Greenwich Village or SoHo or even in one of a dozen restaurants along Arthur Avenue in Brooklyn—where they're serving you the best Italian food you've ever had in your life—when some famous celebrity walks past you like it's nothing. It could be actor-director Robert De Niro or actress Meryl Streep, comedian Billy Crystal or country singer Keith Urban; you might even catch a glimpse of megastars like Beyoncé and Jay Z or Cher. Back in the day, before his tragic murder, one could have seen John Lennon and Yoko Ono strolling through Central Park on a sunny afternoon. And this is not just about the folks who happen to live in the city like the ones I mention here; on any given day or evening, you might encounter any one of a thousand celebrities simply passing through from anywhere in the world, who feel comfortable moving through New York as if it was just a familiar part of their own neighborhood.

In some ways, this is just astonishing, and in no other city in the world does this sort of thing happen so routinely, so nonchalantly, so "ho-hum" matter-of-factly, at least as far as I could ever discern. The only way I can find to explain it is that the level of sophistication there is just unparalleled. Oh, there might be a few photographers about, snapping some pictures for the gossip pages or the entertainment section of the newspapers, but, mostly, there are no rabid paparazzi sticking their cameras in peoples' faces and trampling over everybody to get their "money shot" of the latest celebrity making news. For the most part, everybody in New York seems to just go about their own business; yet if there might be an opportunity to join into a celebrity celebration, well . . . .

If I was a little dumbfounded when I first observed this phenomenon, I was also determined to leverage it to gain the kind of visibility among the rich and famous that I was seeking. Here, at this point, it's also important to point out that all of those desirable New York clubs were not just populated with Hollywood A-listers; they were also filled with Wall Street powerbrokers and dealmakers, whose attention I also wanted to encourage. According to the *New York Post*, which, practically from the moment I moved into the Park Imperial, began to keep regular tabs on my nightclubbing activities, I set records for running up bar bills at several of the hottest and most exclusive clubs, including $160,000 in a single night at Avenue, a then-very-new club in Chelsea, in lower Manhattan. That was in 2009, during Fashion Week. I seized every opportunity to make an impression—like the time I spied actress Lindsey Lohan in a club in Tribeca and immediately sent twenty-three bottles of Cristal champagne to her table—at roughly $900 per bottle. In fact, night after night, in club after club, I splashed Cristal around like it was water.

Sometimes I ordered Patron tequila for everyone in the place, and I'd have to say that dropping $30,000 on a weeknight, for no special occasion or reason, became pretty routine for me when I went out to show my associates a good time.

You'll laugh, but I can tell you one group of people all this freewheeling spending made me exceedingly popular with was the owner-proprietors of all these clubs! Believe it or not, the guys who run these high-end venues are by no means just simple bar owners sitting behind a line-up of beer taps. More often than not, they are ambitious, enterprising, entrepreneurial people who form consortiums to operate a phalanx of exclusive nightclubs for the Hollywood-worthy glamour set in all the great cities. In the U.S., for example, they might operate clubs in New York and Miami and Vegas and Chicago and LA. Yet, in order to be successful, one needed to get the biggest stars to actually come to those clubs, to draw in the monied high rollers who go to such places hoping to get a glimpse of one or more of these stars. That's right: These nightclub owners needed to coax celebrities of all types essentially to make appearances in their establishments—*paid* appearances. It's one of Hollywood's closely held little secrets that even the biggest box office movie stars accept payment to attend events or make candid appearances in particular venues. And in order to get those celebrity bodies into their clubs, the owners either hire entertainment promoters or, in essence, become celebrity promoters themselves.

It's kind of a long story, so I'll try to just give you the highlights here. One of the celebrities that I was thrilled to invite to my events on a regular basis was Paris Hilton, the actress and heir to the Hilton Hotels fortune. Truth be told, I admit I had fanaticized about her from back in my first years in America, during my college days. In fact, I took a lot of ribbing from my friends and classmates at Wharton because—I admit it—I incessantly watched, over and over again, Paris's debut full-length movie, *House of Wax*. What a godawful film!

Well, regardless, now I was knock-kneed with delight just to have her with me. One such junket was a ski trip I arranged in

November 2009 to the Canadian ski resort of Whistler, high up in the spectacular mountains of British Columbia, about two hours northeast of Vancouver. I had hoped to make this into an annual weekend-long event.

At first, she declined my invitation—repeatedly. But I persisted until, at some point, Paris seemed to relent, asking timidly if she could bring a friend—not a romantic friend, she confided, to my great relief—more of an associate in the talent-booking business. Naturally, I said, "By all means." I imagined, of course, that her purpose in bringing a friend along was so that she would feel safe and more comfortable, and I thought, *So be it*; I certainly always wanted the guests at all my events to be comfortable and to have a good time.

His name was Joey McFarland, and when I first met him, I kind of dismissed him as a wannabe celebrity promoter and dealmaker who longed to be something much bigger in the glare of the Hollywood lights, like a filmmaker or big-time movie producer—or even a director. Having, by this time, hung out with some of Hollywood's biggest stars and elite personalities, I thought—perhaps somewhat arrogantly, I'm forced to admit—that I could tell the winners from the losers. Don't get me wrong; he seemed like a nice enough guy, and I was seriously in debt to Joey for being the ticket that brought Paris Hilton to Whistler that very first time, and consequently, I would happily suffer his company when it meant that I would also have the pleasure of hers. But then he and I got to talking.

"Acting's not my thing," Joey told me. "Sure, I get to meet a lot of famous people as a promoter, but it's really a lot like being somebody's errand boy, chauffer, nursemaid, house servant—all of that and worse. Half the time, you feel like all you do is clean up messes for spoiled, privileged children and get them to school on time."

"Sounds pretty terrible," I consoled. "Not exactly the image I have of Hollywood."

Joey shrugged. "Eh, people are people. You treat them like stars, they begin to act like stars. It's still the most exciting place to work that I can think of, and I wouldn't have it any other way."

"But I assume from what you're telling me, that you want to move on from event promotion to something bigger," I suggested.

"You want to know what I really want to do?" he asked, looking me deadpan in the eyes. "I am determined to create a completely new, full-fledged, first-class movie production company—a company solely focused on making blockbuster films." He said it with such conviction that I was immediately certain that he would succeed. I also realized that I had grossly misjudged him upon first meeting. Suddenly, I wanted to be Joey's best friend. Paris could wait.

What was most ringingly clear from our conversation was that Joey was just an out-and-out, unabashed movie buff. Such enthusiasm for the pure art of the cinema was refreshing, and, more critically, I happened to know somebody else who shared McFarland's passion in equal measure. Somebody aside from me, that is. His name was Riza Aziz, and by the luckiest of coincidences, Riza had also come along on this ski trip to Whistler. Not only that, but Riza was now living pretty much full time in the Pyramid House, in LA, on one hand helping me to invest the money from the 1MDB fund while on the other looking for some enterprise that would fulfill his own vicarious desire to play a role in the Hollywood entertainment industry at the executive level.

It goes without saying that, before that ski trip was over, I got Joey and Riza together in a private meeting, and it was, as Bogart says in the classic film *Casablanca*, the beginning of a beautiful friendship.

Only ten months later, in September 2010, we formed Red Granite Pictures, with Riza and Joey serving as chairman and vice chairman, respectively. The company initially set up offices, quite conveniently, in a suite of rooms at L'Ermitage Beverly Hills very shortly after I had acquired the hotel, though this arrangement would only be temporary until we could find a suitable permanent location. As per my usual preference for staying behind the scenes with these kinds of ventures, I once again took no official position within the company, although I would provide millions of dollars to get Red Granite off the ground. And while the papers were signed that September, we deliberately kept relatively quiet about our new entity until we could make a sensational splash with an official announcement at the Cannes Film Festival in May 2011, a high profile announcement that would grab the headlines of *Variety* and the *Hollywood Reporter* and all the other entertainment industry news outlets.

I have to tell you something quite personal now, in connection with all of this, because, for me, the very notion of becoming intimately involved in the motion picture industry was a colossal fantasy that was nothing short of narcotic in its appeal. All my life, I had always been fascinated by the movies, and when you get down to the best of the best, for me at least, that always meant the alluring glamour and phantasmagorical grandeur of American movies created on a scale that only Hollywood can produce. When I was growing up in Penang and, I'd say, right up until the years that I lived in London while I attended Harrow, there was nothing more seductive and desirable about the West than American feature films and the fantasy lives and worlds those movies seemed to portray so seamlessly as living, thriving separate realities.

I suspect that same fascination may have held true for Asian kids born all across the subcontinent from India to Malaysia and even beyond to Indonesia and the Philippines. Among those cultures, there was really nothing to compare with American feature films. And while that may have changed somewhat over the past twenty-five years or so with the rise of the movie industry in places like India and Australia, it's worth noting that, despite the fact that the film industry in India can be traced all the way back to the 1890s, modern filmmaking in India still closely mirrors the time-honored methods and models of filmmaking created by the masters of America's Hollywood. They don't call it Bollywood for nothing.

To his credit, and to my delighted surprise, Joey McFarland had already established some respectable Hollywood connections, and Red Granite got off to a reasonably promising start with its debut film, the romantic comedy *Friends with Kids*, with notable stars John Hamm and Megan Fox leading the cast. Immediately following that film, Red Granite executive-produced the dramatic thriller *Out of the Furnace*, which impressively featured a full slate of even bigger stars in Christian Bale, Forest Whitaker, Zoë Saldaña, Woody Harrelson, Willem Dafoe, Sam Sheppard, and Casey Affleck. But I really wasn't satisfied with that; I wanted something much bigger.

One evening, in a luxury suite at the Palazzo, in Vegas, long about three a.m., as one of my parties was winding down (it would restart at dawn the next morning with a sumptuous smorgasbord champagne breakfast out by the pool), I was lounging on an oversized leather couch with the actor Leonardo DiCaprio. Leo held a crystal snifter of Rémy Martin Louis XIII cognac, in his hand, and, apparently, he was so enjoying the heady aroma that wafted from the glass that he barely took a sip. I was content with a cold bottle of Corona Extra, and we were both smoking Arturo Fuente cigars, the curls of smoke dancing seductively in the soft lighting of the room as it rose pleasantly toward the ceiling. I listened intently as the actor was explaining all of the difficulties that he and famed director Martin Scorsese were having in trying to launch the production of his newest film—that is, if they could work out a solution to all the obstacles they were encountering.

The movie was called *The Wolf of Wall Street*, and it was based on the memoir of the same title written by Jordan Belfort, a Wall Streeter whose investment firm, Stratton Oakmont, had sold worthless penny stocks to mom and pop investors and institutions and defrauded them of tens of millions of dollars in the process. As despicable as his actions had been, and despite all the lives he had probably ruined, Belfort had spent only twenty-two months of a four-year sentence in prison after being convicted of securities fraud, writing his memoir shortly after his release. DiCaprio was so intrigued by Jordan that he had fought—and won—a bidding war with none other than Brad Pitt for the movie rights to the book. In his career, DiCaprio had played similar characters before, like the master impersonator Frank Abagnale Jr. in the movie *Catch Me If You Can*, and he was on the cusp of signing to play Jay Gatsby in yet another movie remake of *The Great Gatsby*, this version to be directed by Baz Luhrmann. With the screen rights in hand, now

DiCaprio was struggling to get the film version of Belfort's story into production against some pretty formidable odds.

I knew very little about how things worked in the Hollywood moviemaking scene, but the main difficulty that Leo and Scorsese were having was a predictable one. In simple terms, you might describe it as a pitched battle between artistic integrity and directorial control and the not-insubstantial costs of financing the film. In Hollywood, it seems a curious but inherently unavoidable equation that, as the need for artistic integrity increases, so too, does the cost of making the film, often significantly so, depending on the force of the director's predilections.

"So it's a matter of money?" I asked, thinking I might just be the guy holding the solution to that particular problem.

"Well, actually, it's more complicated than that," Leo explained. "It's the script. You see, we hired Terence Winter to create the screenplay from Belfort's memoir. Terry, if you don't know, was one of the writers behind *The Sopranos*, and he did a slam-dunk job with *Wolf of Wall Street*, just as we knew he would."

Leo paused, took a long drag on his Arturo Fuente, and then, forming an O with his lips, he exhaled a long plume of bluish grey smoke out toward the ceiling. I was pleased that he appeared to be very relaxed and enjoying himself, but I was fascinated and anxious for him to continue.

"The problem is that the script is full of all of the fucking outrageous shit that Jordan Belfort and his colleagues really did—the sex, the drugs, the booze, the nudity—all of that you-can't-make-this-stuff-up shit, you know what I mean? Cuz I gotta tell ya, you can't fucking believe all the crazy shit these guys did!"

"So you're worried about the censors?"

"Censors? Pffftt! Hell no!" DiCaprio scoffed. "There are no censors here. We're fighting with the studios. A while back, we had a development deal with Warner Brothers until some of the empty-suit execs over there got cold feet and pulled out."

"Why?" I asked.

"You have to understand," Leo said. "If we do the film the way

Scorsese wants, it's gonna be an R rating, and I mean an R flirting right on the border with being an X rating. Even the studios try to hide that rating with what they call NC-17 these days. And most of the time, you just have to scale back to avoid an NC-17 at all costs. Either way, it's going to cost around a hundred million dollars to make the picture. The studios are all worried that not enough people will go to see an R-rated film to make back the hundred million, much less make a decent profit at the box office."

This was utterly amazing to me. Here were two of Hollywood's elite and most popular personalities—the legendary director Scorsese at the top of his field, fresh off winning the best director Oscar for his film *The Departed*, and arguably the film industry's most bankable star in Leo DiCaprio (who coincidently had led the all-star cast of *The Departed*)—and even they, with all their presumed power and high-profile influence, had to fight for artistic control of the creative content that would go into the movie that they had conceived and were trying to make into a reality.

Leo sipped his cognac and said, "Marty has been struggling to adjust Winter's screenplay for, like, almost the past six months, and I think he's getting frustrated with the whole damn thing. I'm worried he's going to just throw in the towel and give up on this one."

There followed a contemplative pause in our conversation, a silence broken only by thick, breathy pulls on the cigars, the tips glowing red.

Finally, I said, "So you need a hundred million?"

"That's what Scorsese thinks."

"What if I was to tell you that I think I can provide all the financial backing that you and Scorsese need to make your film, and what if I was to also tell you that I know a couple of producers forming a new production company who I'm quite confident will allow you complete artistic control over the content of the final film—guys that will let you do whatever you want with your screenplay?"

As you can probably guess, it wasn't long after my conversation with Leo that Red Granite Pictures bought the film rights to *The Wolf of Wall Street* for one million dollars and also signed an agreement to coproduce the film in collaboration with DiCaprio's own production company, called Appian Way. Pretty soon, Red Granite moved into its brand new offices on the Sunset Strip, into the same building where Appian Way was headquartered, and that, of course, was no coincidence.

The Wolf of Wall Street would be released in December 2013 and feature, in addition to Leo, a star-studded cast that included Margot Robbie, Jonah Hill, Matthew McConaughey, and Rob Reiner, among others. DiCaprio won a Golden Globe Award for Best Actor in a Motion Picture—Comedy, and the film received five Academy Award nominations for Best Picture, Best Director, Best Actor (for Leo), Best Supporting Actor (for Jonah Hill), and Best Adapted Screenplay (for Terence Winter). The movie opened to critical acclaim and became a box office smash hit, despite that nasty little R rating. So much for the timid little empty suits at the vaunted major studios, so afraid of a little cinematic controversy. In the end, *The Wolf of Wall Street* would put Red Granite Pictures on the Hollywood map, and I had been the one to kick-start that.

Chapter 8

People said that I had massively diverted funds from the 1MDB–PetroSaudi joint venture. What was actually the truth was that I had a much broader and mightier vision—as I've stressed from the start of my telling you all of this—for what a strong and robustly aggressive sovereign wealth fund could accomplish for Malaysia, which is to say, I never saw the $1.2 billion that 1MDB put in as intended solely to back the risky fortunes of a single oil exploration company. Don't you think that would be foolish? Especially, as I've already explained, when you consider that, while yes, if PetroSaudi struck pay dirt by successfully discovering enormous reserves of oil either under the Caspian Sea or in South America—or even both!—the venture would have been worth untold billions, thus dwarfing 1MDB's initial contribution. In that case, nobody would have been worrying about a trifling $700 million. Instead, we'd be talking more like seven hundred billion, with a B. But on the other hand, the venture could also easily go bust; that's the nature of the high-risk speculation that comes with the territory of oil exploration, if you'll pardon the pun. There simply aren't any guarantees.

Even if the venture was to prove successful, it might take a year or longer for PetroSaudi's exploratory work to find the theorized oil reserves and another year or two after that for extraction to begin and even longer for profits to begin to flow. To my way of thinking, I wasn't exactly diverting the funds that 1MDB had contributed; I was *diversifying* them. And in doing so, I was protecting 1MDB's investment interests. I wanted to show results sooner rather than later; I didn't have time to wait for PetroSaudi to strike that proverbial oil well gusher. But that doesn't mean I was happy with the way things were going, either at PetroSaudi or at 1MDB. Then again, what did I know about oil wells?

Patrick Mahony, Tarek Obaid, and Prince Turki had each received substantial cuts from the Good Star account, yet there did not appear to be much progress happening with respect to the anticipated oil exploration. I admit I was getting impatient. I didn't need PetroSaudi to strike it mega-rich, but I needed for it to at least look promising enough on the books that no one would think twice or get nervous about the company's viability. I had other deals to make, and I wanted to be able to point to PetroSaudi as a going concern on the cusp of monumental success. But at one point, shortly after PetroSaudi purchased two oil-drill ships, I had an enlightening phone conversation with Patrick Mahony. An enlightening, confusing, and well, a very wryly, darkly, just about almost humorous conversation.

"I see you purchased a couple of drill ships," I said. "Is that going to help you get started with making some progress with your oil exploration plans?"

"Well, not exactly," Mahony replied.

I was perplexed. "Why not?"

"Well, you see, we leased both of those ships to Venezuela—to their state-run oil company."

Now I was even more perplexed—incredulous, in fact.

"Why would you do that?" I practically stammered.

Mahony shrugged his shoulders, his face turning into a question mark. "We got a good deal," he offered meekly, half telling, half asking.

I had absolutely no words to respond with. I simply could not process this. I said to Mahony, "Please find some oil, will ya?" and I hung up the phone.

Thus gaining little traction in the hard work of oil exploration, the Three Stooges of the petroleum industry next started looking around for other opportunities. Patrick Mahony had an idea about investing in a U.S. oil refinery, but doing that would require another substantial infusion of capital into the joint venture. In fact, all of the ideas they looked at—that is, those that offered the magnitude of financial scale that I was looking for—were going to require getting more cash into the venture. Consequently, there was some discussion about bringing a prestigious California-based private equity firm into the deal as a means of raising the necessary extra capital. As it turned out, neither the refinery acquisition nor the equity firm participation would ever come to pass.

There was only one thing left to do. If I was going to get this thing really moving, it was clear that I would need to go back to Prime Minister Najib to persuade him to invest more 1MDB money into the joint venture.

And here is where all of my work in selectively configuring the 1MDB board of advisors really paid dividends. It's also where Tim Leissner (remember him, the head of Goldman Sachs' Asia operations?) comes back into the picture. Last but certainly not least, it was but one of many instances where everything I had done to take care of the Razak family was, in a sense, reciprocated in kind.

Oh my god, where do I begin with explaining all of this? Let's start with talking about what Tim Leissner had been up to all this time, and then we can look at what the advisory board was doing, which played into Najib's willingness to take my advice to put more 1MDB capital into the joint venture.

It's no secret that Tim Leissner really didn't know whether to take me seriously or not at the time he and I first worked together in trying to set up the Terengganu Investment Authority, both of us struggling to get Sultan Mizan to go forward with issuing the $1.4 billion in bonds. I was, after all, pretty fresh out of school, and, as you're probably sick of hearing me complain, I had gotten no tangible credit within the financial world for bringing together the Iskandar development project. So no one at Goldman or any other of the big banks really knew me very well. But after what Leissner had seen me accomplish in persuading Najib to take over the TIA, imperiled as it was by Mizan's lack of resolve, and transforming it into the national 1MDB fund, well, he started to pay attention to what I was doing. After all, that transformation effectively removed him as the investment advisor to Mizan, at least as far as the TIA was concerned. Like any good emerging markets guy, Tim kept a close eye on 1MDB, looking for ways he could earn fees for Goldman while helping the new fund raise money through international investment or asset acquisitions—and make a few bucks for himself as well. That meant he stayed in touch with me fairly regularly. In fact, it was Tim who first floated the idea of bringing in the California-based private equity firm to raise more capital for the PetroSaudi venture.

For many months prior to all of this, Leissner had been steadily laboring to further convince his bosses back in the United States that there was significant money to be made by investing in emerging nations in Southeast Asia—and in Malaysia, in particular. One place he saw riches was in the jungles of the state of Sarawak, with its abundant timber resources and the perfect geographical and climatological conditions for producing millions of gallons of palm oil annually on sprawling plantations that could be built as soon as those teeming jungles were clear-cut of their valuable timber.

I acknowledged earlier that I admired Tim's creative, shoot-from-the-hip and rules-be-damned approach to international investment ventures. In this, we thought alike. I cannot say, however, that I always agreed with his methods.

For example, in trying to curry favor with Taib Mahmud, the chief minister of Sarawak, Leissner had cozied up to the minister's niece, going so far as to take the Muslim name of Salahuddin as part of his conversion to Islam prior to marrying the girl. The marriage never happened, not surprisingly, and I strongly suspect that Leissner never had any serious intention whatsoever to marry her in the first place, but the ruse certainly had played well in the eyes of Taib, even after the marriage was broken off, ostensibly by mutual agreement. That "courtship," if one may call it that, ended sometime toward the end of 2009, coincidentally about the time that 1MDB came into being.

Subsequently, over the summer of 2010, Leissner conveniently set up an internship at Goldman's Singapore office for the daughter of the Malaysian ambassador to the United States—a close ally and staunch supporter of PM Najib. The internship was risky enough on its own merits, because it came perilously close to a violation of the U.S. Foreign Corrupt Practices Act of 1977, which essentially bans bribes to overseas officials as a means to win business and widely interprets bribes to include just this sort of potentially conflictive arrangement.

But then Leissner took things an intensely riskier step further when, fresh off his "breakup" with Taib's niece, he began a brief love affair with the ambassador's daughter. What can one say? I'm no expert, but I suppose it's true that Tim was a reasonably good-looking guy and charming in ways that made him naturally, almost inherently attractive to women. His string of affairs was already legendary among his colleagues throughout Goldman and even beyond. Rival bankers had complained that his amorous relationship du jour—this one with the CFO of Malaysia's largest satellite television services provider—gave him an unfair advantage in the intense, ongoing negotiations over which bank would land the contract to handle the company's IPO, a battle Leissner eventually won for Goldman.

But here's the funny thing about Leissner's liaison with the ambassador's daughter: little more than a week after she finished up her Singapore internship under Leissner's "tutelage," 1MDB signed a one-million-dollar contract to retain Goldman Sachs as advisor on the Malaysian authority's plans to build a massive hydroelectric dam in Sarawak. Interesting coincidence, don't you think? Now to be fair, to a megabank like Goldman, the one million was chickenfeed, and, for a variety of reasons, the proposed dam project never got off the ground. But Leissner knew how to follow the money, and his blossoming connections within Malaysia led to another, much sweeter deal with the state government of Sarawak—that is, for all intents and purposes, with the same Chief Minister Taib whom I'd convinced to invest heavily in the Iskandar development project.

Specifically, the Sarawak state government wanted to raise a substantial amount of cash, ostensibly to develop renewable energy resources and also to fund the incessant building of palm oil plantation and production facilities. And they wanted to do it fast. The plan was for the government to sell $800 million in bonds with the administrative help and expertise of Goldman. Normally, the way such agreements work, the bank, be it Goldman or one of the other established investment firms, would partner with the state government to line up major institutional investors, such as mutual funds or corporate pension funds. Because the work of selling bonds for governments in this region was relatively easy and routine and considered to be largely risk free (governments are less likely to default than corporations), the standard fee that most Asian, European, and even U.S. banks charged for bond issues like this one runs about one million dollars.

However, Leissner helped work out a deal through which Goldman bought the entire $800 million bond issue, lock, stock, and barrel. That allowed the government to get the cash it sought immediately and without having to go through the usual and prolonged dog and pony show to attract a sufficient complement of institutional investors to buy all the issued bonds. No muss, no fuss. But, for its part in this rapid-fire deal, Goldman got the bonds for dirt cheap, and by the time they had sold off the entire issue to various institutional investors—to the aforementioned mutual funds and pension funds mostly—the bank had reaped a profit of over fifty million dollars on the deal. Just to be clear, that's fifty times what the customary fee would have been for administering the sale of the bond issue. Now, Leissner was indeed generating serious money for Goldman—and in record time too.

That aspect of the deal didn't go unnoticed. Because Global Witness, an international financial watchdog NGO charged publicly that many of the very lucrative local contracts that were underwritten by the money that Sarawak had received for the bonds went to a conga line of companies owned by Chief Minister Taib's relatives. You see, that's the way things generally work in Malaysia, and, to the best of my recollection, nothing ever came of the accusations put forth by Global Witness in terms of any inquiries or legal action.

Nevertheless, Leissner's interest in investment in Malaysia—and in Sarawak in particular—had dovetailed nicely and quite serendipitously with Najib's rise to the pinnacle of power as prime minister and right at the time that he was seeking to win back support for the UMNO party, not to mention, of course, even greater power and influence for himself. It also dovetailed equally well with the formation of 1MDB; here, you have to remember that the sovereign fund was formally chartered to invest in green technology and promote high-quality jobs through ecotourism, putting Malaysia and its people "first" under the fund's nifty slogan "1 Malaysia." And for all its untamed wilderness, there was perhaps no place on Earth better suited for ecotourism than Sarawak.

On March 1 of that same year, 2010, the newly reconstituted advisory board of 1MDB met for the first time since the departure of Bakke and others, and it was also the first time they met in their new, permanent offices on the eighth floor of Menara IMC, a shimmering glass skyscraper near the Petronas Towers in Kuala Lumpur. Thanks to the more loyal replacements that Najib and I had installed in the place of the narrow-minded naysayers, the board was much more in tune with the prime minister's wishes for the fund, as well as his desires with respect to socially responsible political initiatives it should undertake, initiatives that would naturally help support and strengthen Najib's premiership. Accordingly, Chief Executive Shahrol announced the formation of a charity arm of the sovereign fund that, as its first order of business, would immediately begin funneling millions of dollars into Sarawak, and a proposal was raised to provide over a half million dollars for housing for the poor and school scholarships in Sarawak. The measure was passed by the board without debate—or dissension.

A PR-style visit to the jungle state by Najib was in order and was quickly planned and executed. I can still vividly picture in my mind the television news video footage of Najib addressing the assembled crowds when he visited Sarawak a few months later. It was almost comical, Najib standing at the podium, sweating profusely in the searing sun, undoubtedly very uncomfortable with the eye-watering sights and grossly unpleasant smells, and vastly out of his element of limos and yachts and planes and mansions and statehouses.

More seriously, it would be hard for me to exaggerate the grinding poverty and—there's no kind way to say this—the deplorable ignorance of the mostly tribal people there, many of whom literally live in longhouses in the jungle with no electricity or running water, and who subsist largely on hunting and fishing, and perhaps growing some meager crops. And yet, the way things were constituted, this godforsaken state was a crucial key to the UMNO party's ability to retain a stranglehold on national political power. In point of fact, the only reason Najib's visited Sarawak at all was to stump for party candidates ahead of local elections there, and in speaking to the unwashed masses, he had the unmitigated nerve to flat out tell them that he would provide further federal funding for local development projects and education initiatives *only* if the ruling UMNO candidates won! "You help me, and I'll help you." He actually said that, despite the presence of the cameras of numerous Malaysian television networks.

All of this made my task of approaching the prime minister to persuade him to plunge more money into the PetroSaudi joint venture that much easier. Najib knew very well that the money being used to consolidate his increasingly unilateral political power was coming, through one convoluted, well-protected channel or another, from the 1MDB fund. He was content, apparently, to rationalize that the millions of dollars flowing into his personal accounts—and especially into his private political war chest—somehow equated to the fund's social responsibility project outreach through which he doled out some of that money to his political supporters and operatives. That money, at least some of it, and if only for the sake of appearances, was supposed to be going toward doing good for the people of Malaysia—building schools and decent housing and infrastructure, for instance. And that was the way Najib chose to regard it, though he fiercely avoided looking too deeply into that aspect, lest he discover that his friends and associates and political cronies were keeping the lion's share for themselves. He undoubtedly knew this, regardless.

Nor did Najib want to be too knowledgeable about the specific business or investment dealings—or, for that matter, the overall financial health of the sovereign fund. He preferred to allow me to run things while he stayed out of it—at arm's length, if you will. This too was very much to my advantage, because I wouldn't have to provide any of the gory details regarding the ongoing business, or to explain why, frankly, I was disappointed in the performance of some of my investments, like the L'Ermitage hotel and other real estate acquisitions, which hadn't taken off like I expected. Just like oil exploration and resource development, sometimes these ventures take time to gather steam, and I wasn't sure Najib would understand, or would have the steely patience to stay the course. I was even more loathe to the prospect of possibly having to reveal my displeasure with the dismal performance of the Ivy League, kid-crew 1MDB project managers whose only promising initiative, the so-called Project Wall Street, had been a complete flop.

Nevertheless, I wasn't going to take anything for granted, so in my proposal to the prime minister to put more money into the joint venture, I couched my appeal largely in terms of keeping Prince Turki happy and, more broadly, as a crucial means of ensuring and expanding friendly ties with Saudi Arabia. We absolutely did not want to jeopardize that, I told Najib. In documents subsequently provided to the advisory board in connection with the new lending, PM Najib argued that it was justified "in consideration of the government relationship between the Kingdom of Saudi Arabia and Malaysia." As one might have anticipated, the documents focused primarily on the Middle Eastern political imperatives to further support the provision of the additional funding, and said almost nothing about the fundamental practical soundness or the financial investment advisability of the move.

So it went. On September 14, 2010, and just under a year from the date that the original PetroSaudi joint venture agreement was

THE ART OF GREED

signed, the 1MDB board sent over another $800 million at the authoritative behest and with the full approval of Prime Minister Najib. Just like that. But there was something of a catch.

While I now had more capital to work with, an ever-increasing amount of money was going, directly or indirectly, to the one (and only) man who could keep the money flowing from the 1MDB spigot. I'll tell it like it was: Najib began to put greater and greater pressure on 1MDB to provide him with millions upon millions of dollars to support his political aspirations, and that's just a fact. Taking care of his family was also getting increasingly expensive, what with the investment of millions of dollars in the effort to launch Red Granite Pictures for Riza Aziz, as well as to pay for the first couple's luxurious lifestyle, including expensive travel junkets to so many of the world's most exotic places.

There were other drains on this new infusion of capital as well; principal among them was Chief Minister Taib, for just one example. On one hand, Taib felt that I had cheated him, or taken advantage of him, in the deals we had consummated in connection with the Iskandar development project. Regarding this, I felt I had done no such thing. I was just a better businessman than he was; that's all that happened there. If Iskandar hadn't done quite as well for his pocketbook as Taib had expected, well, those are the risks of real estate and infrastructure investment.

On the other hand, and despite getting the short end of the stick in Iskandar, Taib was no dummy; he could see exactly what Najib was doing to buy votes in regions where the UMNO had lost support and to lock up political backing for himself across Sarawak. He had surmised how Najib was paying for it. So now Taib was demanding payback. In order to placate the chief minister, I persuaded Petro-Saudi to use some of the newly invested 1MDB cash to purchase one of Taib's companies—at an excessively rich price, I might add. I just needed to keep him happy, and, at least in this case, the acquired company would show up as an asset on PetroSaudi's books.

In the end, none of this solved the looming and significant problem of figuring out a way for 1MDB to show a respectable profit on the books. I needed some kind of stopgap measure that would buy time until my strategic investments would take off, as I was downright certain they would.

What we came up with was some really creative accounting.

What we all agreed to do—and by "we," I mean Patrick Mahony and Tarek Obaid at PetroSaudi, along with Shahrol Halmi on behalf of the advisory board—was to turn 1MDB's initial investment of one billion dollars into an Islamic loan of $1.2 billion due in ten years. This would accomplish two things. First, 1MDB could book the difference of $200 million as profit through 2010. Second, PetroSaudi would have until the year 2020 to repay the loan. While that part of this maneuver may have amounted to kicking the can down the road a bit, I was nonetheless absolutely confident that ten years was way more time than we would actually need to pay the loan back.

As you might imagine, however, 1MDB's accounting firm, Ernst & Young, didn't like this innovative idea—not one bit. So, with the help of the prime minister, we simply fired Ernst & Young and hired KPMG and the fund's new auditor. In their proposal, KPMG stipulated that they would take on the account only if 1MDB certified that the business with PetroSaudi was sanctioned by the countries of Malaysia and Saudi Arabia. Malaysia was easy; I instructed Najib to write a direct order to the advisory board to fire Ernst & Young and to hire KPMG, and the word of the prime minister was clearly good enough for the principals at KPMG. Saudi Arabia would be trickier, what with Prince Turki being something of a lesser prince subsisting at the outer fringes of the royal family, like an idiot cousin that no one in the family talks about, and one whose role in government was negligible at best.

Yet here is an object lesson in the sheer, blind, brutal power of wealth. Consider this: Somewhere in the minutes of the meeting of the 1MDB advisory board convened in September 2010, there's a notation written by the recording secretary that reads, "At the very least, KPMG requires a document to confirm that PSI is related to the royal family." So, it was easy enough for Mahony and Obaid to trump up the crucial corporate role that Turki played in PetroSaudi International's operations. The claims were baseless, of course. By this time, Prince Turki was spending most of his time sampling the earthly delights of the nightlife in Philadelphia and New York—that is, when he wasn't lounging on leased yachts in the warm waters off the French Mediterranean coast and sampling the earthly delights of the nightlife in Monte Carlo or San Tropez. Besides, no matter what Turki's marginal role in the company might have been, it hardly amounted to any sort of certification whatsoever that PSI was sanctioned by the Saudi government, and yet this simple written assurance from Mahony and Obaid was enough for KPMG! Ultimately, KPMG was hired, they signed off on the accounts for 2010, and they allowed 1MDB to book the value of the PetroSaudi loan just as the advisory board pleased.

Unfortunately and much to my own frustration, this would not be the last time that the advisory board would have to engage in some circus-ring financial acrobatics as a last-resort means of keeping the 1MDB fund in the black.

Yet there was something else that was even more troublesome to me, and that was the way the principals at PetroSaudi had conducted themselves through this whole ordeal. At one point, Patrick Mahony actually tried to blame PetroSaudi's financial failures on my lifestyle! He had even suggested to Obaid—behind my back—that Tarek should tell the prime minister that PetroSaudi had lost a number of good deals to rival competitors because of my partying! These guys were ready to throw me under the bus! You can imagine how furious I was, not just at the lies but also at the very idea that Obaid might go over my head to the prime minister.

Fortunately, I shut that down immediately, in a conference call with the two of them.

"Nobody interferes with my end of these dealings," I shouted into the phone. "I've worked too damn hard to gain the prime minister's trust, and I won't have you two guys fucking it up."

There was silence on the line, so I took full advantage.

"You call yourself oil men? You buy a couple of oil drill ships, and instead of using them for actual exploration—no, you don't do that. You lease them to an OPEC nation that already has billions of barrels of untapped oil? What are you going to do to find our own oil? Shall I give each of you a shovel so you can go out in the field and dig for it?"

"Look, Jho," Mahony whimpered. "Please calm down. We're doing the best we can—"

"You're doing nothing," I roared. "What do you suppose Najib would think if I told him what you did with those oil ships? I can tell you this: I hope you made good friends in Venezuela, because if PetroSaudi blows up, that's where you're going to be hiding!"

And that, pretty much, was the conclusion of that conversation. It wasn't long after that Mahony acquiesced on behalf of Obaid and himself, sending me a text in which he promised, "We will never go around you." And while that might have been the end of it, I became resolutely determined to look beyond languishing PetroSaudi for other, more promising deals to enhance significantly the capital growth of 1MDB. Little did I know at the time, but there would be more trouble coming out of PetroSaudi very soon, and it would be far more serious; in fact, it would be deadly.

But, as luck would have it, right about this time, I got wind of an intense real estate battle that was brewing over a group of four- and five-star hotels, the flagship of which was London's famed Claridge's Hotel, in the Mayfair district. One of the most iconic hotels in all the world, Claridge's was founded back in 1856 and operated continuously through both world wars. The ongoing real estate battle was for control of Coroin Limited, a privately held asset management company based in England that owned Claridge's Hotel, along with several others.

One of the players in this bidding war was Robert Tchenguiz, a widely known real estate entrepreneur famous for his own flashy lifestyle. Tchenguiz's own story was pretty amazing; the descendant of an Iraqi-Jewish family that had moved to Iran only to be forced to flee during the Islamic Revolution in the late 1970s, finally settling in London. But it wasn't Tchenguiz I was most interested in getting to know; it was his principal financial backer, which happened to be the Middle Eastern fund known as Aabar Investments PJS, and was headed by its chief executive, Mohamed Badawy Al Husseiny, an American with Kenyan roots, and there was even more gold here. Because Aabar was wholly owned by IPIC, the International Petroleum Investment Company, a seventy-billion-dollar sovereign wealth fund owned by—you guessed it—the government of Abu Dhabi. IPIC's managing director was a wealthy Arab businessman by the name of Khadem Al Qubaisi. Both Husseiny and Qubaisi would ultimately be critical to my greatest successes going forward.

That said, I was indeed genuinely interested in getting a share of the Coroin Limited acquisition for its own merits. Let me add, by the way, for all those rancorous skeptics back then who deemed so foolish my efforts to acquire, on behalf of 1MDB, numerous prestigious hotel properties like L'Ermitage in LA and across America, as well as in London and around the world, what do you think of that idea now? Here was no less the highly respected and enormously wealthy Abu Dhabi sovereign wealth fund of Aabar Investments PJS, under the controlling authority of IPIC, going after precisely the same kind of luxury travel and entertainment assets that I had so vigorously pursued years before. What do you think of that? Perhaps I hadn't been so foolish after all, no?

Much the way Tim Leissner had reacted when I first met him, I don't think that real estate investor Robert Tchenguiz took me very seriously either, when I first gained an introduction to him through a wealth management advisor that we both happened to know. But that attitude changed very quickly in one of our subsequent meetings in his London office, sitting in his very comfortable oak-paneled conference room, when I deftly slid a single sheet of crisp stationery across the highly polished mahogany conference table to him. It was a letter from Shahrol and the 1MDB board pledging one billion pounds toward the acquisition of Coroin Limited, and Tchenguiz just looked at me blankly after he read it. But then I really blew his mind when I wrote out a check from Wynton Group, right then and there on the spot, for fifty million pounds. Sliding the check across the table to him, I said nonchalantly, "You can start with this." He was dumbfounded.

Anyway, the long and the short of that potential deal was that our bid failed; the shareholders of Coroin turned down our offer. And while it was a shame we didn't win that one, it was, after all, the exercise through which I became friends with Al Husseiny; he and I really hit it off right from the start. Husseiny was stars-in-the-eyes awestruck whenever I talked about my Hollywood and New York friends, like DiCaprio and Scorsese and Paris Hilton, or music industry folks like Jay-Z and Swizz Beatz and several others whom, by this time, I'd also met and become friends with, all thanks to those fantastic parties and events I had been throwing since the successful founding of 1MDB.

Which, I remind you, I was also roundly ridiculed for in the tabloids and in financial investment circles—my so-called decadently outrageous, allegedly self-destructive party antics. But, you see, my strategy was working. Case in point, Al Husseiny became one of the most enthusiastic and regular revelers at every one of my gatherings; this guy who sat on top of billions upon billions of dollars as the chief of Aabar Investments PJS would not miss a chance to party with me! And he was not the only guy with tons and tons of money under his control who became a regular—not by a longshot!

As garish and as vulgar and as sinfully hedonistic as it may have appeared to some very straight-laced people—indeed, some very psychologically repressed people, in my humble opinion—*my strategy was working*!

Chapter 9

Even as I sit here writing this, I cannot tell you where I am writing it from, because doing so would put me in serious peril from the people who are seeking me, whether it is those who do so under the guise of the legal authority of one government or another, or from the scarier ones who just want to see my head on a pike. In fact, any inadvertently illuminating clue I might unwittingly disclose in telling you my story could be detrimental to my continued freedom, let alone my life. So you see, I remain true to form, being the risk-taker I've always been my entire life by relating all of this to you so openly and in such detail.

Here's what I can tell you about my present situation.

I am relatively safe, thanks to the help of several agents of a certain government—actually, agents of a couple of governments or, at least, certain factions of those governments—as well as some very interesting, rather free-thinking people who would profess allegiance to no governmental authority at all, who, in fact, would scoff at the very idea. As to how safe I am, or how long I might reasonably expect to remain so, well, that probably depends on a number of variables, some of them rather unpredictable, unfortunately. After all, government regimes are subject to change; sometimes such change may be anticipated, but, oftentimes, regime change is totally unforeseen and even shocking in how quickly it can occur. You look at what's happened in recent years with the bloody coup in Myanmar, or what China has been systematically doing to exert greater and greater political and economic control over the once-but-no-longer-democratic city-state of Hong Kong. Even as the presumed rock solid premier democracy of the world, the United States saw a violent insurrectionist attack on its Capitol Building, when Mr. Trump was deposed through a questionable, possibly rigged election!

The point is, I'd be a fool not to acknowledge that my protectors could turn against me in a heartbeat, should the government they loyally serve become, in effect, a whole different government that they would then nonetheless be obliged to serve with equal vigor and fidelity. The key to survival in party politics, after all, is to always be with the party that happens to be in control.

As for those who are helping me who would serve no country at all, well, you can just imagine how difficult—impossible, really—it is to calibrate the depth and strength of their loyalty or to predict what sort of changes in the political winds—or, more likely, the financial ones—might impact their attitude toward me.

Suffice it to say, it is rather important that I take very good care of my people, and, like in all things, that usually means with cash. In fact, if you were to ask me how long I expect to remain safe, holed up where I am, you might as well ask me how long I expect my money to hold out. It's really a pretty direct correlation at work here: The more money I have to spread around, the safer I am. It's that simple.

Nevertheless, the day may come—and very soon, I fear—when the rising "price on my head," figuratively speaking, exceeds my ability to outbid the going security premium, when, for example, the U.S. Department of Justice or the Malaysian government or some Middle Eastern government for that matter, wants me taken into custody more earnestly than I am able to pay my protectors to thwart their efforts to grab me. I don't mean to obfuscate the hard facts, so let me state it more plainly: If I've learned anything from my experiences at the apex of international financial deal-making, it's that everything is for sale, and it's just a matter of the price. And that includes me.

Or a radically different day may come, when some former financial associate or competitor suffers from some bizarre and misguided notion that I cheated him so badly that he wants blood over gold, no matter the price. On that day, I'll wake up, and the next thing I'll see when I open the front door is this former associate or competitor—or his henchman—pointing a Glock 19 at my forehead, and it'll be the last thing I see. That's why, by the way, I don't open the front door. I have people who take care of that sort of thing. Still, something like that little scenario could happen, you understand. But let's not talk about such unpleasantness any further, at least for now.

Because right now, I live fabulously well; a "mansion in the jungle" you might call this place, and it has all of the amenities you would expect—the swimming pools, the spa and sauna, the fully stocked bar and wine cellar (there's actually a couple of those), the home theater, the elegant outdoor decks with spectacular mountain views—all of that good shit. The compound itself encompasses over 550 acres, including several golf courses and clubhouses, and, of course, no exclusive retreat would be complete without a helipad. This one also happens to have a protected airstrip as well, capable of handling jets up to the super midsize class.

Though now quite limited, there are still a few outside places I am able to travel with relative freedom, as long as I do so quietly and without fanfare, accompanied by a couple of armed associates, and, for the most part, as long as I stay within the regions controlled by those friendly governments I alluded to earlier. And even with that, there are occasional, carefully orchestrated exceptions when I travel beyond my protective sphere to the outside world, mostly to do business in a handful of important cities across Asia and along the Pacific Rim. All things considered, it is generally more prudent to bring the outside world to me, to the extent that it's possible to do so. Matter of fact, during the pandemic, a nurse practitioner was brought here on separate occasions to administer my two COVID-19 shots. She was quite attractive too, I must say. So you see, all the comforts of home but none of the chores.

Except, please do not think ill of me when I tell you that, in so many ways, it is killing me to be mostly forced to stay right here, within this compound. It is like living an excruciating, self-imposed exile from the entire world. I might as well be wearing one of those location-tracking anklets so popular with modern law enforcement these days. A while back, I told you about how I flourished even as I spent so many of my hours in the confined quarters of the cabin in my private Bombardier jet. But at least that aircraft could take me at a moment's notice wherever in the world I wanted to go. I was as free as the proverbial bird, and I think I can say I made the most of it. I breathed deeply the whole wide world, in and out, like a precious, life-giving ether, and I thrived on it.

I miss that freedom so severely, like someone has ripped out my soul. It violates my nature to be relegated to any such realm of prolonged sequestration as the one I am in now.

At any rate, if I can't travel the world as freely as I did before, let me assure you I nevertheless have abundant access to it. As geographically isolated as we are, this remarkable little palace nevertheless has impeccably reliable Internet access, Wi-Fi, cable television—the works. In short, all manner of the most sophisticated communications capabilities in use today. In fact, there is an ultra-secure safe room within the mansion complex, a kind of control center that looks like it might be a secret Interpol operations lab, from which a couple of technicians monitor everything from the physical security of the grounds to cyber-security, including the integrity and encryption security of the information that flows in and out of this sanctuary, to and from the Internet itself. And in case you are wondering, yes, I am able to cloak my identity online. In fact, this whole place is like something out of a James Bond movie.

So make no mistake about it: I still have eyes and ears on the world, I know what is going on just about everywhere, and I know it in real time pretty much as it is happening and almost always before it gets reported on the evening news. You might be surprised when I tell you that two publications I follow very closely are Malaysia's own venerable English-language business weekly, the *Edge*, and the London-based—and somewhat radical, in my view—*Sarawak Report*.

I say it may surprise you because I'm sure you are well aware that the reporters and writers at those two distinguished news organizations aren't exactly my biggest fans, and the op-eds that the two papers regularly publish appear to scream more loudly than anyone else for my immediate capture, prosecution, conviction, and imprisonment. That does bother me a bit. Don't they want to hear my side of the story? Aren't newspapers supposed to be dedicated to publishing the truth? The hard facts? Yet I have always found it extremely useful to know precisely what your adversaries are saying and thinking. So, indeed, I read the *Edge* and the *Sarawak Report* right along with the *LA Times*, the *London Times*, and the *Wall Street Journal*.

Suffice it to say, therefore, I see the legal proceedings and court cases going on from Malaysia to the U.S., I see the allegations and indictments that are being brought by prosecutors and contested (or not) by the defendants, I see the settlements that, one by one, seem to be coming down from the financial investment behemoths like Goldman Sachs and Deloitte and J.P. Morgan and all the others—you know, the enormous, eye-popping settlements that are invariably attached to the disclaimer that "the firm admits no wrongdoing" or some such other line of total bullshit.

And I see the several actors, the individuals who played prominent roles in the 1MDB "scandal," as the press and everyone else now seems to refer to it, who, one by one, have been carted off to separate federal prisons following their convictions on a variety of criminal charges from bank fraud to conspiracy and more. Not the least of which being former Prime Minister Najib, who, of course, sits at the top of this whole mess. I keep myself informed of developments in the no-holds-barred legal battle he is waging to appeal his convictions and get himself out of what presently stands as a twelve-year jail sentence. And yeah, I know all the terrible things that are being said about me in the press and in the financial world.

Now if I were to say to you, here in this writing, that all of this prosecutorial backlash against the operations of the 1MDB fund is nothing but trumped-up lies and deceptions and falsehoods, that the indictments of people and institutions are all part of a colossal witch hunt by legal and regulatory government authorities—representing several governments—trying to pin the blame for this whole fiasco on someone else, you'd probably laugh in my face. Your reaction would probably be "Well of course you'd say that, seeing how you're wanted by authorities in several countries where you face trial on criminal charges that could put you away for life." You might think me no better than the mega-firms that have paid billions of dollars in fines and restitution, yet have "admitted no wrongdoing." You might also accuse that, like Najib and his attorneys have been doing in court, I would say or do anything to save my own skin. And I can understand why you might feel that way.

But that doesn't change the fact, like it or not, that there is plenty of deception and falsehood at work here, as everyone tries to cover their own asses for their part in what went wrong. That's just an undeniable fact, and this is always the case in the financial world when massive international deals with so many moving parts implode thanks to weak links in the chain. Yet hopefully, you'll take me more seriously if I openly acknowledge that there was also plenty of wrongdoing involved. And yes, looking back on it all, I made some mistakes myself.

On the positive side, I had mastered the brave new world of the twenty-first century's globalizing economy, where sovereign countries no longer sought to invest their wealth solely within their own borders on things like infrastructure or education but also to invest for profit in other nations and in the promising but often riskier fortunes of multinational corporations or business ventures. I learned how to work seamlessly with the most prestigious sovereign wealth funds in the world while, at the same time, developing a knack for leveraging some very nimble offshore banking resources that, shall we say, were somewhat less myopically constricted in their approach to international financial dealings. Firms that didn't play strictly by the book, that were more open to innovation and to the novel idea that hadn't been tried before.

At the same time, I also think I did a pretty good job of attracting to my inner circle the kinds of people who possessed the access to wealth and resources—and the power and perhaps more importantly the will to use them—characteristics that are a foundational requirement for participation in that brave new global economic world, where everything is on the table. All that's needed to prove that point is a quick look at the guest list of so many of the events I hosted around the world. In spite of the criticism those galas inspired, I believe I was adept at attracting people who out-and-out *wanted to do business*. Plain and simple. If they just wanted to get *more rich*, well, what the hell was wrong with that? The point is, I possessed the unique ability to identify the individual who had the determined mindset and the steely nerve to be a speculative dealmaker on a grand scale. It takes a special kind of person to do that. Call them the burning desire people.

What I could not do, at least not completely, was judge the true character of that individual with any measure of certainty or know how that actor would respond to the wealth and power I would put in their hands.

And that included Malaysia's once-upon-a-time favorite son, Najib Razak. When I first got involved with Najib, during the days shortly before his ascension from deputy prime minister to prime minister in 2009, I thought I had gotten to know the man very well. I thought he was someone who truly wanted to be a man of the people for Malaysia in-country while also being, internationally, a statesman and diplomat representing the best interests of Malaysia to the other nations of the world. As I would learn ten years later, I had been quite wrong in my assessment.

This tale begins with a murder in October of the year 2006 and a horrendously gruesome one at that. The victim was Altantuya Shaariibuu, a statuesque, world-class Mongolian model and rising international social media celebrity. But don't be mistaken, Altantuya was not just another pretty face and another thinly curvaceous body strutting the fashion runways from Paris to New York to Milan. Oh no, Altantuya was whip-smart, well-educated, culturally sophisticated, and intensely ambitious. She may also have been a little too headstrong for her own good.

She spoke several languages and was especially fluent in Russian and French, working as a translator in those languages in addition to her stratospheric modeling career. Which is how she happened to become entangled in the complicated negotiations between the Malaysian Defense Ministry and a French defense contractor conglomerate known as Direction des Constructions Navales, or DCNS, over a deal to purchase a fleet of French-made nuclear submarines for use by the Malaysian Navy. DCNS, you might be interested to know, is steeped in French history, legitimately tracing its roots back nearly 400 years to its founding in 1631 by none other than Armand Jean du Plessis de Richelieu, a.k.a. *Cardinal Richelieu*!

Can you imagine that?

Anyway, Altantuya was hired as an interpreter by one Abdul Baginda, the high-ranking Defense Ministry official at the head of the negotiations and a very close friend of then–Deputy PM Najib. She also became Abdul Baginda's mistress, though it's not clear which position came first. Regardless, after the submarine deal was concluded in early 2006, Altantuya demanded her commission of $500,000 for her "integral" role in the negotiations—the amount she claimed Baginda had promised her. Baginda flatly refused her demands, profusely denying that he had promised her anything of the sort.

Altantuya was not a woman to take "no" for an answer, so in response, she made at least two trips from Mongolia to Kuala Lumpur, one in July and the second in October, bringing along two of her close friends, and together, the three women virtually terrorized Abdul Baginda on a daily basis. They went to his downtown office numerous times during the day to demand payment very loudly and very publicly, making quite a scene, as I'm sure you can imagine. And in the evenings, they even went to his palatial mansion in the exclusive Damansara Heights to harass him there as well. The women caused Baginda such distress—not that he didn't deserve it, mind you, for breaking his promise—that he hired a private investigator and bodyguard who went by the one-word name of Bala to shield him from his former—now scorned—lover. Even more critically,

Bala's most essential task was to keep Altantuya as far away as possible from Abdul's unknowing wife and daughter.

And it didn't help matters that the defense minister was facing accusations in the daily press of accepting more than $100 million in bribes from DCNS, something that the Mongolian model could almost certainly shed some light on as a witness under oath, should the matter ever come before a Malaysian court of law. One imagines she would have been more than happy to testify too—that is, until she got her cut.

You can guess the outcome of all this. Late on the night of October 19, 2006, Altantuya and her friends are out on the street, shouting epithets and expletives through the steel security gates of Abdul Baginda's sumptuous home. An unmarked car pulls up swiftly, two policemen get out—in uniform, according to Bala, who witnessed the whole chaotic scene from the grounds of the defense minister's home. They grab Altantuya and forcibly push her into the back of the car, and just as swiftly as they arrived, they speed off, the tires screeching on the pavement. They take her to the police station, but they do not stay there very long before they drive her to a remote forest just outside of a place called Shah Alam. There, on orders from the ranking officer, Inspector Azilah bin Hadri, the other officer, Corporal Sirul Azhar Umar, shoots Altantuya twice in the head, "execution style," as they love to say in so many American gangster movies. But then, in a bizarre effort to destroy any trace of her DNA that might be absurdly comical if it weren't so horrific, the two officers remove all of the dead woman's jewelry and clothing, they place high-powered C4 explosives under her corpse—a type of explosive available only to the military—and they detonate the C4, blowing her body to bits. Of course, all that accomplishes is to spray the unfortunate girl's DNA all over the woods while at the same time making identification just a bit more challenging—and a lot gorier—for the criminology forensics experts.

When Altantuya fails to return to the hotel that night, her worried friends file a missing person's report the following morning. The investigation leads very quickly to Officers Azilah and Sirul—Bala, the private investigator, was able to identify them both by name—each of whom, under interrogation, separately lead police detectives to the spot where Altantuya was murdered. And inevitably, some samples of her DNA are successfully taken from the site, I imagine ingloriously scraped off a tree or a rock or something by a forensics expert with a really, really strong stomach. Yuck. The two officers were immediately arrested.

Now, one thing that it's important to know about all this is that Officers Azilah and Sirul were not your ordinary precinct cops on the beat writing traffic tickets to hapless confused tourists run amok in their rent-a-cars amid Kuala Lumpur's labyrinthine maze of streets and alleys and byways. Far from it. Instead, they were members of a special actions elite tactical unit of the Royal Malaysian Police, known as the Unit Tindakhas, or UTK. However, in reality, the UTK—surprise, surprise—was Najib's personal security detail, a kind of royal guard or secret police, if you will, that reported directly and solely to the deputy prime minister. Except that these guys were no secret to a lot of people in Malaysia. Basically, the UTK were Najib's henchmen. So the optics of this spectacularly monstrous killing were not very good at all for the deputy PM or for his designs to one day become the PM. Despite that connection, Najib, of course, denied any knowledge in the matter of Altantuya's untimely death, and he condemned it accordingly, as any good national political leader would.

The trial commenced in 2007, shortly after I had returned home to Malaysia from Wharton, in the U.S., and at a time when, as you already know, I was deeply immersed in aggressively trying to launch myself into international business. Of course, I was well aware of everything that was going on with the court proceedings; everyone in Malaysia was. After all, the proceedings took over 180 days, spilling into the spring and summer of 2008, with the lurid details splashed all over the morning papers and broadcast ad nauseam over the television news and the Internet. Flip on the radio, turn on a TV, every news program, every talk show—they'd be talking about the trial. You couldn't escape it. You might say the case was Malaysia's version of the sensational O. J. Simpson murder trial in the United States, which had captivated the whole world back in the 1990s, or so it seemed back then. It was all a pretty ugly affair in my country's history, particularly as it involved at least one high-ranking government official in Abdul Baginda. That seemed to magnify the national impact.

Still, if you tried really hard, you could imagine that the link to elected leaders in the Malaysian government ended with the defense minister. If you tried really hard, you could imagine that Najib was telling the truth, that he knew nothing about the killing, despite the fact that it had been carried out by two members of his personal UTK security force. You could even rationalize that it was just unfortunate to have happened, so to speak, on his watch as deputy PM. And I tried really hard to believe these things.

Certainly, I wasn't alone in this, because the citizens of Malaysia seemed to believe them as well, because they subsequently elected Najib as prime minister in 2009, a year after the first trial ended. But you see, I had an ulterior motive. I had a burning desire to be the financial and personal advisor to a prime minister in charge of an enormous sovereign wealth fund, and, simply put, I had my best shot with Najib. Rationalization is a powerful thing, don't you know. And rationalization aside, the trial ended without finding any direct connection between Altantuya's grisly murder and Najib Razak. And that was good enough for me.

Three people were indicted for Altantuya's murder, the two police officers and the defense minister, Abdul Baginda himself. The trial itself was a media circus, much like the O. J. trial had been. Even before the proceedings got started, there seemed to be a whole hot mess of shenanigans going on. The presiding judge was replaced, then the prosecutors assigned to the case were also replaced, then there was a highly publicized shake-up among the defense counsel, and the next thing you knew, they were also replaced! It was like a game of musical chairs.

Private investigator Bala had been the prosecution's star witness, yet as the trial was drawing to a close in July 2008, the man in the know who had been Abdul Baginda's protector abruptly issued a detailed statement, sworn and signed by him, in legal circles known as a *statutory declaration* (SD1), in which he severely criticized the way the prosecution had pursued the case, also claiming that important evidence was being suppressed and—worst of all for Najib—providing damaging information that strongly implied that the deputy PM was indeed involved in Altantuya's murder and possibly deeply so. But then Bala took things another step further when he held a press conference on July 3, at which he released his sworn document to the media. SD1 went viral on social media overnight. Bizarrely, the very next day, July 4, Bala immediately and hastily convened a second press conference in which he released a second statutory declaration, SD2, in which he retracted, revoked, and downright contradicted substantial portions of SD1. So now what, you say?

Long story short, the prosecution pressed on, despite Bala's conflicting documents, and when the trial was concluded, Officers Azilah and Sirul were convicted. Actually, they were convicted in the lower district court of Shah Alam; then their convictions were overturned by the court of appeals when the attorneys for the defense successfully (and correctly, one has to admit) argued that the prosecution had failed to establish any motive on the part of Azilah and Sirul to commit such a heinous act; then the two UTK police operatives' convictions were reinstated—or *upheld* I think is the right word—by the High Court of Malaysia, sort of akin to the U.S. Supreme Court. Offhand, I'm not sure the exact reason the High Court gave for this reversal; I guess the judges just figured, motive or not, Azilah and Sirul had clearly done the deed, so they were clearly guilty of killing a human being, whether they had an actual reason for committing murder or not.

The defense minister, on the other hand, went off scot-free. In fact, Abdul Baginda was swiftly and summarily acquitted of all charges—shockingly, without even having his defense counsel called before the court! Then again, a sober and fiercely objective observer might simply shrug his shoulders and repeat, "Well, that's the Malaysian justice system for you." If however, you were rooting for Najib, as, of course, I was, you could once again try to imagine that Baginda's acquittal validated the contention that the then-sitting Malaysian government officials indeed had nothing to do with Altantuya's murder, that deputy PM Najib and his cronies were blameless in this despicable business, that it was the inexplicable work of two renegade UTK thugs who simply went off the reservation, even if their reasons for doing it might forever remain a mystery.

As I said earlier, you had to try really, really hard to imagine—and swallow—the plausibility of these sorts of explanations; call it a kind of leap of faith, if you will, albeit a breathtaking one at that. But it was vaguely possible to accept them if you were an eternal optimist, like me. I mean, think about it. What else could I do? I really didn't have any alternative; Najib's UMNO party had held an unbroken string of sixty consecutive years in power. Just as a reminder, that sixty years also happened to represent the entire length of time Malaysia had been in existence as an independent sovereign nation. So, like, they had a perfect record. How can you fight that sort of thing? When all the chips are on the table, you have to go with the winner.

Bottom line: There simply was nobody else to bet on, and I was willing to give Najib the benefit of the doubt. Besides, if I didn't trust in Najib now, all of the meticulous hard work I'd put into currying favor with his stepson, Riza Aziz, while I lived in London attending Harrow would have been a complete waste of my valuable time!

Was I compartmentalizing the whole nasty affair? Probably.

But here is what came crashing to light many years later: After the sensational uproar he had caused with his dueling statutory declarations, Bala had been forced to hastily flee the country, first to Bangkok and ultimately to Chennai, India, taking his entire family with him. They left that very evening of July 4, as a matter of fact, mere hours after Bala released SD2 at his second press conference. Circumstances would oblige him to reside in Chennai for the next five years.

When he finally returned to Malaysia, in February 2013—whereupon he boldly began to campaign for the opposition party against

Najib in the 2013 election cycle—Bala revealed that his largely contradictory statements embodied in SD2 had been coerced. He also reiterated claims he had made much earlier during his banishment from Malaysia: that it had been Najib and his wife Rosmah who, in 2008, had directly ordered him to leave the country, further instructing him to take up residence in India until Najib became prime minister. Bala also claimed that he had been verbally threatened by Nazim Razak, Najib's younger brother—the same guy I had gifted with free office space within Wynton Group's headquarters in the Petronas Towers some years earlier. Nazim confronted Bala, pointing a finger at his chest, "precisely in the manner of a pistol," Bala is reported to have said, ominously telling the private investigator to get his family out of Malaysia, "if you love them and are concerned about their safety." Yet, curiously, even as he left under such threatening circumstances, all of Bala's living and travel expenses for his family's entire five years in Chennai had been fully covered by Najib, delivered to him by a go-between who shuttled regularly between the two countries—handing Bala a fat bundle of cash with each trip.

But when he finally returned to Malaysia, Bala would no longer be silenced. The problem was, he made so many wild accusations that it was difficult to pinpoint which of them were true. Or how many of them were. Or if all of them were true. As he had sworn in SD1, Bala again directly implicated Najib in the murder of Altantuya, insisting that the deputy PM had direct knowledge of the hit and very likely had been the one who ordered it. But Bala further alleged that, in some weird tandem with Abdul Baginda, Najib too had been regularly sleeping with the Mongolian model, and Bala went so far as to suggest the mind-blowing possibility that, when Rosmah inevitably discovered her husband's indiscretion, it was she who had demanded the killing of Altantuya in retaliation—to punish both Altantuya and her husband, one assumes.

It sort of made sense. If it was true that he was also having an affair with Altantuya, Najib could easily have imagined that, once the scandal leaked out, his chances of becoming prime minister would be nil, his rising political career utterly destroyed. Najib, as we know, would do absolutely anything in his power to prevent that from happening. And for her part, Rosmah knew full well that, once Najib's career was over, so too would be her extravagant gravy train lifestyle of obscene wealth and gaudy palaces and jet-setter world travel and untethered shopping and jewelry, jewelry, jewelry. It was stark, eye-blinking kismet for both of them. Altantuya had to die, apparently, and that was that. It was the only solution to both of their problems.

Could Bala have really known about any of this? Think about the fact that he was, by trade, a private investigator, presumably an expert highly trained and handsomely paid to dig up people's ugly secrets and hidden dirty deeds. However, in one of the biggest ironies of all time, in the case of the dalliance of the highly placed deputy PM and the exotic foreign model, we'll never know for certain, because, less than a month after he returned to Malaysia, Bala dropped dead of a massive heart attack on Friday, February 15, 2013, taking his secrets to the grave with him. You can't make this stuff up.

But the trail doesn't exactly end there, either. Some six years after Bala's untimely death, and ten years after his original conviction for the grisly murder of Altantuya, in December 2019, Inspector Azilah sent word through his attorneys to federal prosecutors stating that he wanted to come clean by fully revealing the circumstances surrounding the whole terrible episode. Naturally, the lawyers in the attorney general's office were very interested in what Azilah might have to say, and later that month, the former police inspector swore out a damning statutory declaration of his own. In it, Azilah revealed shocking evidence that the orders to "eliminate" Altantuya had come directly from deputy PM Najib Razak, face to face. Only thing was, Najib also "secretly" told Azilah that Altantuya was actually a foreign spy and a serious threat to national security!

For the attorneys, this was not hearsay, which would have been inadmissible in court; this was direct, legally actionable evidence. Azilah stated that he was personally instructed—that is to say, directly ordered by Najib himself—to eliminate Altantuya and was further assured by the deputy PM that, because she was a foreign agent engaged in malicious spying activities against the Malaysian government, this extreme action was critical to the national interest. Unbelievable, right?

Concurrent with serving this bombshell statutory declaration to the prosecutors, Azilah's defense attorneys also petitioned the federal court, seeking to have their client's conviction and sentence set aside due to the fact he was following the explicit orders of his superiors "to kill a foreign spy" and, therefore, should not be forced to suffer such extreme and unfair consequences for doing his sworn duty.

So there you go.

Why, you might ask, had the former police inspector waited so long, and why was he suddenly willing to speak now?

Simply put, Azilah had played the good foot soldier for ten years, the devoted, loyal, and belligerently tight-lipped "name, rank, and serial number" subordinate, clinging for over a decade to the false hope that one day—once he advanced to prime minister—Najib would pardon him, perhaps even exonerate him somehow. Hell, make him a national hero even. After all, he believed he had done a great service for the state; he and Corporal Sirul had gotten rid of a dangerous foreign spy. Maybe Najib would do all that and more once all the dust had settled from the sensational trial and once the people of Malaysia had forgotten about it or perhaps moved on to other salacious, newsworthy scandals. There's always plenty of new ones to choose from!

Regardless of the manner, Azilah had hoped to be released from bondage and returned to freedom, even if, on the other hand, it had to be done quietly. Not to mention he also expected to be vastly rewarded by Najib for his undying loyalty and devotion; a nice big house in the country, a couple of cars perhaps, but certainly a bountiful income for the rest of his life would all do nicely. That wouldn't be asking for too much.

However, by the time of Azilah's statutory declaration, not only had Najib fallen dramatically out of power, having lost miserably in the 2018 election—thereby almost singlehandedly ending that sixty-year winning streak of the UMNO party—but the former PM was also in very hot water, facing serious charges of his own for abuse of power, money laundering, and multiple counts of breach of trust and on and on.

Azilah's star, you might say, had fallen like a rock. Faced ultimately with the death penalty once all of his appeals were exhausted, Azilah began to sing like a canary, as the mobsters in American Mafia movies call the guys that finally crack under pressure and turn state's evidence.

So the saga of Altantuya's murder continues. The fate of the two former police officers also continues to wend its way endlessly through the Malaysian court system as I write, and where things end up remains to be seen. God knows it could go on forever, like a daytime soap opera or something.

But, once again, I have to apologize for getting ahead of myself.

Matter of fact, I just noticed the sun is up, and I happened to glance at my Patek Philippe Nautilus. Right now is about the usual time I stop by and wake up the boys in the COM security room to confirm that nothing unusual is showing up on the radar, if you'll excuse a rather amusingly outdated expression, technologically speaking. No prowlers peering at us from the woods, no hackers trying to poke through the ether of the Internet. It already looks like it's going to be another boring ho-hum day here at the compound.

Chapter 10

Even though Al Husseiny, Aabar's chief executive, and I seemed to hit it off very quickly and quite fluidly, it's fair to say my relationship with Al Qubaisi had gotten off to a comparatively rockier start. Qubaisi, you'll remember, was the managing director of the Aabar fund's parent company, Abu Dhabi's massive sovereign wealth fund known as the International Petroleum Investment Company, or IPIC. Suffice it to say that Husseiny and I experienced a couple of unfortunate misfires in our initial efforts to find ways to team up Aabar and 1MDB in new, collaborative investment opportunities and money-making ventures.

The first had been the failed bid on Claridge's Hotel and the others in the Coroin group. That, of course, was nobody's fault; our bid had been legitimate, even generous, certainly worthy of consideration. The sellers had simply declined to pick it up, which was certainly their prerogative; you can't make a client do something that would have been really good for them if they fail to see it that way! Yet that experience only made Husseiny and me more eager to find ways to work together, which is to say, for the investment funds we controlled in Aabar and 1MDB to work together, and, by the middle of 2011, I brokered a deal for Aabar to acquire a substantial stake in RHB Bank of Malaysia for $2.7 billion. Unfortunately, RHB's stock prices plummeted sharply within months of the acquisition, and Aabar sustained paper losses of hundreds of millions of dollars.

THE ART OF GREED

Still determined, Husseiny and I next collaborated to put together a joint venture between Aabar and 1MDB in the form of a separate fund to invest specifically in commodity markets. The joint fund's first acquisition was a large stake in a massive Mongolian coal mine. And, wouldn't you know, right after that, China's economy went into a nosedive, coal prices crashed as factories were idled, and our Mongolian mine investment tanked! I'll admit that, regardless, Husseiny and I both profited quite nicely on the deal, because we had been prescient enough to extract a multimillion-dollar fee payable from the seller for the work we had done to bring in Aabar and 1MDB as the partnering buyers.

But when Al Qubaisi was advised of these early investment hiccups, he was pretty damned angry about what he rather saw as financial failures. And while I couldn't really blame him, in point of fact, you really couldn't predict the sort of things that happened to RHB Bank, or what the Chinese economy was going to do tomorrow. To me, these snafus represented new and bigger opportunities. Somehow or other, I would make up for these losses ten times over by involving Aabar and IPIC—in conjunction with 1MDB, of course—in an even bigger deal. The thing I surmised about Qubaisi, almost from the moment I first met him, was simply that, in his mind, the bigger the deal, the better. It appeared that the best way to make it up to him for a couple of little deals that didn't perform as expected was to propose a much more enormous deal with even bigger stakes and profit potential—and risks too. Like all of this was some sort of high-stakes casino game to him. But you better win in the end.

There was just one other thing you needed to know about Qubaisi, but it was an extremely important thing. For the privilege of doing business with him, he generally demanded a substantial kickback. That's just the way it was, yet I refused to be daunted.

The plan I had in mind would make 1MDB's joint venture with PetroSaudi look like pocket change, but it would also require the cooperation of a wider collection of powerfully positioned people and the organizations they represented to make it happen. It would also solve, at least temporarily, the cash flow problems I was having with 1MDB—you know, to paper over some of the holes left by the cash that I had diverted to Good Star to fund my other investment plans for the fund, as I've stressed before. But we'll get to that part a little later on.

This next deal started with Goldman Sachs, where Tim Leissner was hard at work preparing to sell an issue of $3.5 billion in bonds for 1MDB. The Malaysian fund planned to use the funds to purchase a group of coal-fired power plants across several countries, from Malaysia to Egypt, Pakistan, Bangladesh, the UAE, and elsewhere. It would then consolidate these vital electricity-producing plants into a single megacorporation and launch an initial public offering (or IPO) for the new company on the Malaysian stock exchange. Thus consolidated under a single entity, the theory went, the power plants would be worth a lot more than when they were individually owned, and 1MDB expected to earn in excess of five billion dollars through the IPO.

However, there was one difficulty. Since the relatively nascent 1MDB fund had not yet offered a U.S. dollar bond issue to international investors, it consequently had not yet earned a credit rating. That's where I wanted IPIC to come into the deal—as a highly respected sovereign fund with, like, probably the strongest credit rating in the whole fucking world—to guarantee the issue and allay any possible fears or reservations among potential investors. In return for guaranteeing the 1MDB bond issue, IPIC got first crack at buying a huge stake—at a bargain price—in the newly formed power company conglomerate.

This was getting into some pretty big stuff for 1MDB, although it was the kind of deal that Qubaisi might routinely—and unilaterally, I might add—sign off on before his first coffee break in the morning, with the full weight and power of IPIC behind his signature. This situation, however, was a little different, again owing to the fact that 1MDB being essentially the new kid on the block, and it turned out that, this time, Al Qubaisi's boss wanted to have final say before signing off on the deal. And Al Qubaisi's boss was Sheikh Mansour bin Zayed, one of nineteen children of the original founder of the United Arab Emirates, whose net worth of forty billion dollars made him one of the richest people in the world. Sheikh Mansour had also recently become famous for buying, in 2008, the Manchester City Football Club for £210 million and promptly building a new state-of-the-art stadium for the soccer team, spending another £150 million. But even more importantly, Sheikh Mansour's exclusive and exalted position as chairman of the seventy-billion-dollar IPIC made him also one of the most powerful people in the world, financially speaking.

Qubaisi was Mansour's supremely trusted right-hand man, so much so that, in certain very inner circles, the sheikh was known to blithely apply his signature of approval to anything Qubaisi set before him without even bothering to read any of the accompanying paperwork. So, with Qubaisi's help, I arranged a meeting between Tim Leissner and the sheikh, at which I would also be present, to discuss the proposed collaboration and the 1MDB bond issue. Such a meeting was exceedingly rare, and when Tim and I flew to Abu Dhabi for that conference, he and I became a couple of only a handful of foreigners from across the entire world ever permitted to meet face to face with the reclusive Sheikh Mansour. Needless to say, the meeting went very well, because when our presentation was over, Mansour happily signed off on the deal. And that was all we needed. Oh, and I also noticed in passing that the sheikh barely even looked at the documents that Al Qubaisi had laid out on the desk in front of him. As I reflected on that, settling back in my plane with a cold bottle of Pilsner Urquell lager as we lifted off the tarmac at Abu Dhabi International Airport headed for home, I could only smile at the thought.

Sometimes, for all of the uber-confidence I strived to outwardly project, I would be lying if I didn't acknowledge the nagging inner insecurity that plagued me incessantly and yet for no reason that I could rationally identify or define. It often came to me in a recurring dream in which my evolving deal of the moment appeared as a game of Jenga, the blocks being the components of the deal, or the principal characters, where the loss or failure of just one block could bring the whole edifice crashing down. And that dream often felt more frighteningly vivid the more spectacular the deal, and another reason, I suspect, that I did not like to sleep. *The dream is stupid*, I kept telling myself, because I could always find a way to complete the deal no matter how complicated.

Case in point: The arrangement between IPIC and 1MDB was unorthodox, to say the least—even groundbreaking. I don't know of any other instance, before or since, where the sovereign wealth fund of one exceedingly wealthy country would guarantee a bond issue or similar investment offering of another emerging one, which, in turn, would help raise billions of dollars for the latter. I asked Leissner about it.

"Well, Jho," he confided, "the fact is, a number of the investment executives in our Singapore office had serious reservations about the plan. In fact, David Ryan, the president of Goldman's Asia division, was so concerned he actually possessed himself to personally visit 1MDB's offices in Kuala Lumpur."

I was shocked. "You're kidding!" I exclaimed. "So Ryan actually confronted some of the executive staff right in their own offices?" This was a sobering thought; the whole deal could have blown up right there.

"I believe he did," Leissner replied, "and from what I know of their meeting, I can tell you I don't think he was impressed."

But Tim had an ace up his sleeve. His previous successes in Southeast Asia, like the fifty-million-dollar profit that Goldman had made on the aforementioned Sarawak bond issue, had put him in excellent stead with the top brass at the bank's global New York headquarters on Wall Street, and in particular, with company president Gary Cohn. Not only was Cohn extremely bullish on Asia investment, but he also seemed to see the "water coming from the mountain," as Leissner put it, when it came to making tons of money from working with government-backed sovereign wealth funds, which he also presumably saw as being about as minimum risk as you could get. In fact, Cohn had created a cross-divisional unit within Goldman specifically designed to work hand in glove with such sovereign funds, whether through coinvestment or by devising hedge-fund strategies for them at a fee, or basically to create or enable whatever mechanisms the funds needed to construct to raise capital—enormous sums of capital, to be specific. Cohn even came up with a term for working with sovereign funds. He called it, "monetizing the state."

I loved that!

"So you see," Tim continued, "it was pretty easy to convince Cohn to override the naysayers and give his blessing to our little IPIC–1MDB bond issue collaboration. On one hand, we had the approval of Sheikh Mansour himself, backed by the government of Abu Dhabi, and on the other, even if 1MDB is still a little fish in a big pond, we also had Prime Minister Najib's endorsement of the deal, carrying along with it the backing of the Malaysian government as well. You could say that all of this really greased the rails to make this deal happen very quickly."

Leissner paused, seemed to gaze off into the distance, and then added, "But, of course, we were preaching to the choir anyway. Because Gary Cohn is hopelessly in love with Asia and 'its vast, untapped wealth.'" He said that last part with both hands raised, making air quotes with his fingers.

I want to further explain that, for my part, I was simply trying to catapult 1MDB into the big leagues of global investment, as well as to raise Malaysia's stature in the eyes of the other nations of the world. And I wanted to do it quickly, efficiently, without wasting a lot of time wending through the traditional, endless conventional bureaucracy. Much as it might have pained me, I couldn't really dispute Tim's characterization of 1MDB as a "little fish." Certainly, this was, in my mind at least, an ignominious fact comparative to all of those breathtaking sovereign funds of so many of the Middle Eastern nations. I was in a hurry to change that, and I was determined to do it my way. I wanted very much to banish that damn Jenga dream permanently from my mind.

If I may use a metaphorical analogy, if IPIC's formal guarantee of 1MDB's first-ever major bond issue was unusual—and it certainly was—what I wanted was to put the 1MDB fund on the express tracks to the big time. And if that meant bypassing some of the local station stops along the way—the ones that some less innovative and less daring and less visionary financial investors believed were obligatory stops (like tediously building a credit rating, god help us)—well, so be it. Yet there was a substantial price that had to be paid for all of this fast-track efficiency.

In a word, it seemed that everybody wanted their cut.

Perhaps I should have realized it sooner, but, now, in hindsight, I see how there was a growing problem with these huge deals, and it was a problem that only got bigger and bigger as the deals themselves got more and more enormous and increasingly potentially even more lucrative. Mainly, the problem revolved around the rapidly expanding cast of characters that I needed to involve in each successive deal, each of them demanding larger and larger payoffs for their individual roles in bringing about the consummation of the deal. This was despite the fact that, more often than not, these players or operatives or partners—call them what you will—were already pretty fabulously wealthy to begin with, to my way of thinking. Maybe it was simply a matter of scale; when you're worth billions, a couple hundred million doesn't amount to much, relatively speaking, so why would someone with that kind of means even bother to extend the effort needed to get involved, much less take on the perceivable risk that went with it? Or was it all simply unabashed, insatiable all-consuming greed? I don't know, but the increasingly steep demands for compensation were leeching more and more cash away from the future investments I wanted to make with all that capital, as well as doing a disservice to the 1MDB fund. I'm talking about mega-investments that would have yielded even greater returns for all of us, not just a few people, while, at the same time, also benefiting the people of Malaysia. Didn't these people understand that?

But let me continue.

So needless to say, the deal went through, and Tim Leissner followed pretty much the same game plan as he had when he sold $800 million in bonds for Chief Minister Taib on behalf of the state of Sarawak some years earlier. Which is to say, Goldman Sachs bought the entire bond issue from 1MDB through the arrangement of two separate but equal $1.75-billion bond issues, the first in May 2012 and the second in October of the same year. Internally and for whatever reason, the Goldman bankers named the two transactions Project Magnolia and Project Maximus, respectively. I have no idea why the bond issues required names, but that's what they called them.

To state it more plainly, Goldman directly paid out in cash to 1MDB the full amount of $3.5 billion even before ensuring that the bank had the needed investors lined up to buy the bonds. And once again, just like Chief Minister Taib had done with the Sarawak bonds, this was a great way for 1MDB to raise the funds very quickly without having to obtain credit ratings from the big agencies like Standard & Poor's or Moody's.

But, speaking to my earlier point about the premium to be paid for all of this fast-track, cut-the-red-tape efficiency, Goldman demanded a fee of $190 million to underwrite each issue; that would be a total of $380 million for the entire $3.5 billion bond issue or a whopping eleven percent of the bonds' value! Strictly on a percentage basis, this outrageous amount even far exceeded the fifty million dollars Goldman had charged for buying up the full complement of the Sarawak bonds, which, by comparison, amounted to just over six percent of the bonds' total value. Even that was monumentally excessive; as I told you previously, the going rate for any bank orchestrating these kinds of bond issues in Southeast Asia was a paltry one million. If this was to be the new standard, you can clearly see why Gary Cohn was so gleeful over the future prospects of investment in Asia, for sure. But as far as I could see, this wasn't "monetizing" the state; it was more like plundering the state.

And it certainly wasn't what I'd had in mind.

As you can imagine, the fee presented a major stumbling block when Leissner gave his presentation of the deal before the advisory board of 1MDB. Attorney Jasmine Loo, one of my most trusted contacts on the board, filled me in on the details of how the meeting went. She told me that Tim kept trying to emphasize the very real expectation that the fund would make a killing when it ultimately IPOed the giant power-asset conglomerate that was to be formed.

"It was like some of the board members didn't want to wait that long for the payoff," Jasmine lamented. "And when that wasn't compelling enough, Tim got pretty angry. He kind of scolded the board by reminding them that 1MDB was not putting a single penny of its own money into the acquisition of all of these essential power assets."

That much was true: All of the $3.5 billion was coming directly from Goldman. And as Tim insisted repeatedly in the course of the meeting, it was Goldman that was taking on all of the financial risk, because 1MDB would get its money immediately, without the "rigorous ordeal," as Tim put it, of actually having to find qualified buyers for the bonds.

But here was the kicker: By that last very terpsichorean bit of twilight logic, apparently, the 1MDB board was supposed to have $380 million worth of ecstatic gratitude for Goldman's beneficent stewardship—and outright purchase—of the dual $1.75 billion bond issues. What likely never came up through this whole discussion, I suspect, was the fact that, once again, as it had with the Sarawak bonds, Goldman would have the privilege of purchasing the entire 1MDB bond issue at a deep discount, and the bank was sure to make a major killing of its own when it turned around and sold them to investors at a much higher premium than it had paid.

All I could say about this was *wow*. Even measured by the biggest, most excessively opulent Wall Street standards, this was going to be a huge windfall payday for Goldman. Calling it a *payday* didn't even seem sufficient to cover the sheer magnitude of it! Oh, and make no mistake, Tim Leissner personally stood to do very well for himself by the deal; in 2012, Goldman paid him more than ten million dollars in salary and bonuses in reward for bringing in the new business, making him one of the highest paid executives at the bank for that year.

Goldman's greed over the fee (and let's be plain; it was Leissner's greed as well—particularly as it was revealed to his highly jealous peers across the organization) damn near caused a revolt among the board that could have blown the whole thing up—that is, if I hadn't taken preemptive steps to make sure Najib would give his authoritative blessings to the deal and effectively override any objections from any of the board members, from Shahrol Halmi on down.

By this time, gaining Najib's backing had actually become quite easy. All that was needed to lock in Najib's unequivocal—and quite enthusiastic—approval was to make sure that, one way or another, the deal resulted in more streams of money flowing into his personal and political slush fund accounts. Nor did it matter to the prime minister where the money came from, although the more unobtrusive the source—and the less Najib knew about it—so much the better. That meant trying to squeeze as many degrees of separation between the direct sources of cash flowing into Najib's war chest and the large and rapidly expanding pool of investment money moving into the coffers of the 1MDB fund. This too was a relatively easy thing to facilitate.

As soon as the $3.5 billion from Projects Magnolia and Maximus were transferred to 1MDB, the fund quickly made its first two major energy sector acquisitions, first buying a group of power plants scattered across several Asian countries from Tanjong Energy Holdings, a huge multinational corporation owned by Malaysian entrepreneur and billionaire, Ananda Krishnan. That acquisition alone cost 1MDB $2.7 billion, but, in short order, the fund made its second major multibillion-dollar acquisition, buying another cluster of power plant assets located throughout Southeast Asia and owned by the Genting Group, a large, Malaysia-based, primarily casinos and plantations conglomerate.

Now, in both of these cases, 1MDB overpaid for these acquisitions, and I would say they did so rather substantially. In return for these generous overpayments, however, millions of dollars in donations started flowing into various accounts in 1MDB's "charity arm," the same one formed by Chief Executive Shahrol in the days prior to funneling millions of dollars into the 2011 Sarawak state elections (in support of UMNO-friendly candidates) and also the same "goodwill" arm of 1MDB that was under the direct and essentially exclusive control of Prime Minister Najib himself—and, by extension, his wife, Rosmah, it should be noted. And the prime minister's formula for felicity in his marriage could be summed up in five words: *What Rosmah wants Rosmah gets.*

This influx of "charitable" contributions came, coincidently, from various companies or organizations owned by Ananda Krishnan—to the tune of over $170 million alone—as well as more millions originating from the Genting Group directly, ostensibly as part of Genting's desire to "give back" in support of its Malaysian homeland. And of course, Najib and Rosmah were free to use these millions of dollars of donated funds any way they pleased.

There's just one other revealing thing that I ought to mention about 1MDB's purchases of energy assets from Tanjong and Genting at higher values than they were actually worth. Would you like to guess who provided to the advisory board the financial valuation necessary to justify the purchase of those assets at the inflated prices? It was Goldman Sachs.

Neatly done, don't you think? In any case, at least Najib was happy, which perfectly suited my purposes. I also had to look out for my own interests and desires so that I could continue with my own unique and targeted program of joint ventures and major global investments on behalf of 1MDB. Look at it this way: If I didn't step in to gain a measure of control of some of the bond money, the incompetent investment managers at the sovereign fund might easily fritter away the lion's share of that money on hopelessly misguided and mismanaged boondoggles like the failed Project Wall Street in Kuala Lumpur that never even got off the ground. As I've said before, I had much bigger things in mind for 1MDB.

And then, of course, there was also the matter of appropriately remunerating Al Qubaisi and Al Husseiny, both of whom obviously wanted their cut for the integral roles they each played in making the deal happen. Certainly, they deserved something of real substance for putting the IPIC fund at moderate but not inconsequential risk in backing—and, in fact, guaranteeing—the bonds for 1MDB. It was the amount of the reward they demanded for their service that was initially shocking to me. I remember shaking my head and thinking, at the time, that maybe I just didn't fully understand how things actually worked at this level, that perhaps I had underestimated the stratospheric scale of the monies involved that was apparently quite typical when you worked with prestigious organizations like IPIC.

But the truth was, from the time I enrolled at Wharton and even before that, I was always determined never to think small. It was the same message I'd gotten from Donald Trump so many years earlier when I first met him at the Walnut Street Café, near the UPenn campus, sitting alongside his daughter Ivanka. So all of this, working in collaboration with major sovereign funds like IPIC and Aabar, it was all massively exciting to me, now operating as I was in the upper reaches of a financial atmosphere, where the thin, ethereal air itself was almost narcotic in its effects, and I was fast becoming addicted to it. And I simply didn't question anything that Qubaisi or Husseiny said or what they wanted; I was just grateful to finally be associated with them, to be making international deals with them, and I felt that there was much that I could learn from them.

In order to take care of the immediate needs of all three of us, Qubaisi and I devised a really clever plan. We established a new corporate entity based in the British Virgin Islands under the name of Aabar Investments Ltd. I'll admit this was a little bit dodgy, but Qubaisi and I believed it was necessary to the interests of everyone concerned. The name was intended to mirror Aabar Investments PJS, the IPIC subsidiary controlled by Al Husseiny that was involved in association with Robert Tchenguiz in our failed bid to buy the Coroin group of five-star hotels, including famed Claridge's in London. And that was because Qubaisi, Husseiny, and I wanted to be able to transfer funds into this new entity, Aabar Ltd., without having banks or auditors or compliance departments asking too many questions about the transfers. To them, hopefully, Aabar Ltd. would just look like another subsidiary of IPIC, even though we set up the Ltd. account with a completely different bank from the several others that handled the various accounts of the Aabar PJS subsidiary.

To smooth things even further, the corporate documents filed with the BVI listed Qubaisi and Husseiny as the directors of the company, just as they were listed as executives at Aabar PJS.

Suffice it to say, this worked exactly as it was intended. Such that, on May 21, 2012, Goldman deposited the $1.75 billion proceeds for Project Magnolia, the first bond issue, into the bank account the 1MDB energy subsidiary that had been set up. Barely twenty-four hours later, $576 million was moved into the account of Aabar Ltd. Five months later, around mid-October, Goldman launched Project Maximus when it deposited the $1.75 billion proceeds for the second bond issue into the 1MDB energy subsidiary account. And again, like clockwork, less than a day later, another $790.3 million was seamlessly transferred into Aabar Ltd.

Did I say that all this worked as it was intended? Perhaps that was an understatement. It all worked like a charm!

That may have been in part thanks to Al Qubaisi's ingenuity in creating yet another layer of security through which we were able to filter the transfer of the funds. It went like this: Shortly after the financial crisis of 2008, Qubaisi had very shrewdly acquired Switzerland-based Falcon Private Bank, buying it from AIG, the American insurance conglomerate. AIG had been hit really hard by the crisis, forcing it to sell the bank, as well as other major assets, to try to right itself. So Qubaisi buys the bank using funds from the original Aabar subsidiary of IPIC, but it essentially becomes *his* bank, which is to say Qubaisi owns and controls it, as well as handpicking everyone who works for it. He simplifies the name to Falcon Bank.

Why this is so important, you must understand, is that Qubaisi acquires Falcon Bank at a critical time in the aftermath of the worst financial crisis in many decades, and perhaps one of Wall Street's dirtiest, when you think of the complicit behavior of the banks in utterly bad-faith dealings like the subprime mortgage scandal that caused outrage in the U.S. And what generally happens after these periodic scandals is that international monetary authorities in the U.S., the UK, and Europe get their collective noses out of joint, and they react by exerting greater pressure on, let's just say, client-friendly banks in places like Switzerland, Singapore, and dozens of offshore banking hubs around the world to "clean up their acts." What that means in practical terms is that, virtually every major scandal that comes along is usually followed by a significant spike in regulatory and compliance scrutiny, both external and internal, forced on the banks by those outraged Western governments, usually led by the U.S. Department of Justice—never mind that the 2008 crash actually started in America, right there on Wall Street. This pressure usually subsides in about a year or two, when things more or less go back to normal. It's like a weird but standard part of the international banking cycle, the way it works.

So in any case, here was Al Qubaisi, at a moment of peak hypervigilance among international regulatory authorities and watchdogs, as well as increased pressure on internal bank compliance departments, sitting pretty on top of his own, personally controlled Swiss Bank. Naturally, of course, when the nearly $1.4 billion of 1MDB funds from the two bond issues transited through Falcon, none of the banking executives or the compliance experts working there was going to raise any red flags.

Uh-uh, no way.

Consequently, when the funds then flowed—rather routinely for all outward appearances—from Falcon Bank based in Switzerland to Aabar Ltd.'s bank account based in Singapore, nobody at Aabar Ltd.'s bank—a relatively small and innocuous bank called BSI that was, in fact, owned by the Italian insurance conglomerate Generali—had any reason to raise an eyebrow at what would have appeared to them to be nothing more than business as usual within the financially rarefied realm of massive sovereign wealth fund investment. You see? I told you I could learn a few things from Al Qubaisi.

Although in actuality, I had another ace in the hole at BSI: Our account manager there was a veteran Singaporean banking executive by the name of Yak Yew Chee. Yak was well known to me and to my family. Originally with Coutts, he had been my father's banker, helping my dad to manage and invest his modest fortune, and when

I came of age—or even a little before coming of age, when I was still in school—my father had instructed Yak to open up for me what, if I recall correctly, was my first-ever major bank account. Naturally, it was Yak whom I engaged to set up the account for Good Star that would eventually top one billion in assets. Now, normally that kind of capital would raise red flags with Coutts's compliance department, but consummate banker—and strong personality—that he was, Yak easily convinced the nervous compliance people at Coutts that, as the saying goes, "there's nothing to see here."

Bottom line: On one hand, Yak knew the enormity of what was at stake here, the magnitude of the deal at hand, and conversely, I knew I could trust Yak to perform his role according to my direction, so when Yak left Coutts to join BSI, my accounts, as well as those of the various people I advised, went with him. I needed forcefully persuasive guys like this on my team—as long as they could take direction from me, of course.

Naturally, we were all delighted when the full 1MDB bond issue was successfully completed, even those who really didn't exactly know all of the nuances of the deal as I have explained them to you here. When I think about it now, I guess that would have been just about everybody except Husseiny, Qubaisi, and me. Well, maybe Tim Leissner knew the circumstances too, but he didn't care; he had his ten million in salary and bonuses. For my part, I was particularly pleased by the factors that really distinguished the bond sale from my previous biggest accomplishment, which had been the execution of the PetroSaudi–1MDB joint venture.

I had to be honest with myself—in the PetroSaudi deal, I had been relegated to working with a marginally viable oil exploration company with a questionable future, headed, in part, by a third-rate, economy-brand Saudi prince, and I'd had to put on a pantomime act of sorts while I made up plausible stories for the bankers in Zurich and elsewhere about where the monies were coming from and where they were going to, and why they were transiting the way they were.

In stark contrast, with the issuance of 1MDB's first major public bond offering to the tune of $3.5 billion, I was working in collaboration with the international powerhouse financial professionals and the esteemed organizations whose world I had longed to be a part of since I was a kid at Harrow. Just think of the list that this included: Goldman Sachs and a string of executives leading directly to its president and CEO Gary Cohn, as well as Abu Dhabi's internationally renowned IPIC and Aabar sovereign wealth funds and their internationally recognized managing directors of Al Qubaisi and Al Husseiny. Politically, it included Prime Minister Najib and now Sheikh Mansour bin Zayed, a bona fide member of the UAE's governing elite and famously, as mentioned earlier, the secularly savvy owner of the Manchester City Football Club.

Suffice it to say, these were at last, for my sake and the sake of my career, people and organizations whom no one would question about the origins or the destinations of the (rather massive!) funds they controlled and routinely directed without fanfare from one place to another. In other words, transferring funds through and among these entities and players did not require any kind of dog-and-pony show performance from me—or anyone else. And I insist that my goal throughout all of this remained the same: to carve out a place of international collaboration and respect for 1MDB right alongside the major and most prestigious sovereign wealth funds of the world and, in so doing, to greatly benefit the people of my homeland of Malaysia.

What I'm trying to say here is that the bond issue deal achieved a level of interconnected professional sophistication, international prestige, and banking investment competence that made the Petro-Saudi–1MDB joint venture look like school children trading for American baseball cards and bubble gum in the schoolyard at recess.

At the same time, I have to admit that, when the deal was finally consummated, we all had a shitload of capital to play with—the kind of money that makes you downright giddy like a schoolboy! For starters, a total of about sixty-seven million dollars was moved from Aabar Ltd. into bank accounts owned by Al Husseiny at BHF Frankfurt, Germany, and Bank of America in the U.S.

To be perfectly honest, I really have no idea what Husseiny did with all of that money, and it remains a mystery to me to this day. But that was his business. Additionally, over a period of several months, a substantial stream of money totaling almost $400 million flowed from Aabar Ltd.'s BSI accounts into the bank account at Edmond de Rothschild Bank of Luxembourg owned by Al Qubaisi's private company, Vasco Investment Services. However, just like I had with PM Najib, I knew and fully understood that Qubaisi had his own crucially important patron that he needed to keep very happy. Accordingly, Vasco Investments would eventually send installment payments totaling roughly $166 million to the famed Bremen, Germany, shipbuilding firm of Lürssen, where engineers and craftsmen were putting the finishing touches on Sheikh Mansour's new, 482-foot superyacht, called the *Topaz*. With not just one but two helipads and eight large decks, the total price tag for the *Topaz*, when finally completed, was over $500 million—enough to make any Saudi crown prince very happy, one assumed!

By contrast, making a further down payment to ensure Prime Minister Najib's continued confidence and support had been relatively inexpensive for me. From the Aabar Ltd. account, I transferred about thirty million dollars into private bank accounts held by Najib with AmBank, Malaysia's largest banking group. In New York City, I closed a $33.5 million deal to purchase a sprawling condominium for Riza in midtown Manhattan overlooking Central Park and the Hudson River. I also arranged for about ten million in jewelry, handbags, and other gifts to be sent to First Lady Rosmah from one of Singapore's finest purveyors of world-class jewelry, designer handbags, and precious objets d'art. Last, key board members Casey Tang and attorney Jasmine Loo quietly pocketed the five million I wired to each of them in gratitude for their invaluable assistance in helping Tim Leissner gain the 1MDB advisory board's final approval of Goldman Sachs' rather pricey rollout of the twin $1.75 billion bond issues.

As for me, I now had sufficient working investment capital to pursue my own investment plans, at least for the time being. In fact, I was flush with cash! And at about this time, my focus had shifted.

Specifically, I wanted to make myself into a force to be reckoned with in Hollywood and, more broadly, the American entertainment industry worldwide. I now had the money I needed to make *The Wolf of Wall Street*, where I would eventually invest a total of about $238 million in what would become a blockbuster film, but I knew that was going to be just the beginning. By any standard, it was time to celebrate, and I began to orchestrate two of the most lavish and most outrageous parties I would ever throw in my life. One was to mark—with a big exclamation point—my thirty-first birthday; the other was to celebrate with my new friends in both the movie and music entertainment industries.

Chapter 11

In early 2012, while Tim Leissner and his team at Goldman were preparing 1MDB's first bond issue, together with my older brother Szen and my attorney sister May Lin, I formed a company called Jynwel Capital, chartered in Hong Kong. Jynwel's first order of business was to acquire a significant stake in EMI Music Publishing, whose chart-topping songwriter-performers included Alicia Keys, Usher, Pharrell Williams, Beyoncé, and Kanye West. In June, barely a month after 1MDB sold the first $1.75 in bonds, we succeeded.

In total, the acquisition of EMI was a $2.2 billion joint affair led by a stellar group of partner investors that included Sony Music Holdings; the Estate of Michael Jackson; the giant U.S. private equity firm Blackstone Group; the Abu Dhabi sovereign wealth fund of Mubadala, led by my old friend Al Mubarak; and—drumroll please—Jynwel Capital! Our stake was for only about a hundred million, but that was ample enough to enable me to become EMI's nonexecutive chairman for all of Asia and a vital member of the conglomerate's advisory board. Most exciting of all, it would enable me to move among the most fantastically popular pop stars in the world.

It was the beginning of my plan to build a media empire that would generate billions in profits in this remarkable digital, communications-saturated age of the twenty-first century, when, I'm sure you will agree, the worldwide appetite for online entertainment through music and film is utterly insatiable and growing astronomically.

You know this when you look around and see everybody walking around carrying their daily entertainment on their smart phones or on display screens in their cars and just about everywhere else. In turn, those massive profits would generate an enormous ROI (that is, return on investment) for 1MDB, and yes, I admit it, that would also help erase any inconvenient financial holes that were created when, let's just say, I may have "appropriated" those funds—though I had done that only as I endeavored to put 1MDB's capital to work as hard as it possibly could and in my effort to get the biggest bang for the buck, as the old expression goes.

So that was the business side of things, but I have to tell you, the EMI deal thrust me into some of the most exhilarating and scintillating experiences of my entire life, to find myself navigating among the world's most creative and cutting-edge music performers, particularly in the hip-hop genre that I have loved my whole life. At the same time, toward the end of 2012, the filming of *The Wolf of Wall Street* was ramping back up after an unfortunate delay caused when Hurricane Sandy slammed into New York City and the U.S. East Coast in late October. As with many of Hollywood's most audacious blockbusters, there would be a lot of gossipy, rumor-mill buzz going around about the film—this even though the film itself would not be released for another year. A number of still photographs had leaked out, as well as a couple of short, pirated clips that found their way onto social media. The word in the gossip columns was that DiCaprio was delivering some spectacular, Oscar-worthy performances on set, and, of course, all of the pundits and rumormongers were talking about the enormous amounts of money that Red Granite was allegedly pouring into the production of the film. That in turn, of course, attracted the attention of all kinds of Hollywood stars and directors and "starving" screenwriters with a script to pitch and even other producers and entrepreneur go-getters who also wanted to make blockbuster pictures—I mean, who doesn't, right?—but who simply didn't have access to the kind of capital that Red Granite had—through me, of course. And what that meant, suddenly, was that practically everyone in Hollywood wanted to come to my parties. It was perfect.

About a month after the EMI deal closed, we celebrated our success just off the French Riviera, aboard the 440-foot superyacht *Serene*. Of all of the great pleasure boats I have ever been on, I think the *Serene* is my favorite, though I have to say it's certainly hard to choose. You have to see this thing to believe it. This yacht was owned by Russian billionaire Yuri Shefler, whose holdings include Stolichnaya Vodka—better known as Stoli—and it was built to his specifications at a cost of $350 million. It had a sauna, a swimming pool that extended from the cozy interior onto an outside deck, a piano-bar lounge suitable for an intimate ensemble performance, and a spiral staircase crafted of Italian marble that connected the multiple levels of this floating palace. But the coolest thing of all was that, when at anchor, the *Serene* has these huge teakwood decks that open out over the water like something out of one of those sci-fi transformer movies—all the better for accompanying even more celebrity partygoers! I could go on and on about the boat, but you're probably much more interested in who was there—and yeah, the guest list was mind-blowing.

I paid Kanye West something like a half million dollars to perform for the gathering, and, naturally, of course, he brought along Kim Kardashian, who was just his girlfriend at the time. Anyway, the guests included—hold on to your seat—pop stars Rihanna and Chris Brown, Ludacris, Nicki Minaj, Busta Rhymes, and Swizz Beatz. Leonardo DiCaprio came out from Hollywood or New York or wherever he was—taking a short break from filming, I assumed—as did Kate Upton and my dear friend Paris Hilton, who was always up for a good yacht party! Naturally, Riza Aziz and Joey McFarland were there to represent Red Granite, bringing an entourage of the production company's creative staff with them. There were a couple of executives from EMI in attendance too, though I noticed they mostly stayed somewhat in the shadows; I don't believe they'd ever in their lives experienced a raucous party quite like this one! *Welcome to my world!* I thought.

And of course, Al Qubaisi wouldn't have missed this event for the world. Although, whenever he arrived, he always had me shaking my head and holding back a laugh, because he invariably showed up wearing a T-shirt emblazoned with some obscenely graphic image from an X-rated film or some hideous smut he found on an Internet porno website. To think that, in the days when I first met him, he would only appear wearing the formal, billowing robes complete with the Arab headdress called the *gutrah*, in the traditional garb of the Emirati—well, at least when he was in the Middle East. When he came to the West, it was a completely different story! Nobody appreciated more than Qubaisi the fact that I always made sure to fly in a dozen or so gorgeous models from the United States to mingle with the crowd and act as hosts for the party and . . . whatever else. It wasn't unusual for a fair number of them to be topless and nearly naked by about one or two a.m., by which time Qubaisi could usually be found hanging with two or three semiclad girls at a time while dispensing glass after glass of Cristal champagne from a magnum he seemed always to be carrying around with him at these events. Well, enough about the respected head of IPIC.

I very much enjoyed being in the company of all of these Hollywood folks and pop music artists. They were bright and funny and intelligent, even if they'd never set foot on a university campus and probably wouldn't know how to read a corporate balance sheet or an investment prospectus. Partying with them was exciting, exhilarating, and just crazy; you just never knew what outrageous thing they were going to do or say next. They were so utterly uninhibited. For the life of me, though, I never felt fully at ease. For all of my trying to let myself loose to be as free as these people were, I always felt deep down inside that never really fit it. I don't know, but if it's true that all the world's a stage, I always had a desperately hard time imagining myself as one of the players.

But there was a practical, business side to all of this. You see, all of that celebrity star power inexorably drew more and more Middle Eastern royals to these parties. Despite all the fantastic wealth and power they possessed, these guys could never gain access to the glitterati of the entertainment world the way I had done it. In effect, I was bringing the glitterati to them. With each successive event, more of them attended, but not only that. With each event, the *stature* of the attending royal guests moved up a notch. At that great party off the French Riviera, for example, two of the guests walking around the decks of the *Serene* and mingling cordially with the stars were a Dubai prince and a sheikh with connections to the ruling family of Qatar, that tiny but superwealthy country that juts out into the Persian Gulf just below Bahrain. Even as I avoided the limelight myself, it was essential that these people knew I was the one person responsible for staging these events—and for stuffing the guest list with movie and pop stars—because I knew that would open to the doors to more and even greater deals with the Middle Easterners.

Virtually all of the people who were on the *Serene* that night in July also came to my outrageous thirty-first birthday party in Las Vegas only about four months later, in November, and less than a month after Goldman Sachs completed the second 1MDB $1.75 bond issue—giving me and a select number of my guests, like Qubaisi and Husseiny and Leissner and Fat Eric, just to name a few, two great things to celebrate! Naturally, I wanted to do it up big.

For starters, I rented the magnificent Chairman Suites at the Palazzo. At $25,000 a night, the suites are the very best the Palazzo has to offer, featuring everything from a rooftop pool terrace with a sweeping view of the strip to a studio-quality karaoke room complete with a state-of-the-art sound system, plush leather sofas, and padded walls. But the Chairman Suites was just the beginning. More specifically, they were for the pre-party and the after-party attended only by my VIP guests, which as I said, included all of the above—that is to say, all of the folk who partied with me on the French Riviera in July—and then some! So DiCaprio came, but he also brought along actor Benicio Del Toro and Hollywood director Martin Scorsese, and the three of them wanted to talk to me about some up-and-coming film ideas. Can you imagine? They wanted to talk film ideas with *me*!

My god, I thought. *This is how far I've come in such an incredibly short time.* Here were some of the most influential heavyweights in the industry, and they wanted to discuss film ideas with me, a notion that

I dreamed of as a kid, yet never seriously imagined as even remotely possible. I thought back with sheer gratitude to that fateful day in Whistler, BC, when I made the acquaintance of Joey McFarland, and the several days later when I introduced Joey to Riza Aziz.

For a moment, it was all seashells and balloons, like I'd gone to heaven, and it was only much, much later on that it clicked in my head, literally like that proverbial light bulb, that what this magnificent triumvirate of DiCaprio, Del Toro, and Scorsese really wanted to talk with me about was the *financing* of their films. Ah and alas, the heartbreak of Hollywood.

Anyway, fantasy aside, people began to arrive at the Palazzo just as the scorching desert sun was setting, which is somewhere between five and six in Vegas in November, the night just beginning to cool the way deserts do. In walked Bradley Cooper and Zach Galifianakis, both of whom were in the middle of filming *The Hangover, Part III*. Pretty appropriate, don't you think? Pretty soon, the Chairman Suites were packed with very happy folks: Leissner was there. So were Al Husseiny and the ever-present Al Qubaisi, along with a couple of other notable Middle Eastern royals. Still other celebrities made brief appearances, including actors Robert De Niro and Tobey Maguire, as well as Michael Phelps, an Olympic Gold Medal winner several times over.

At about nine p.m., it was time to bring everybody to the main event, and I had made sure no one had any clue about where we were going. Most of them expected we were heading off into the desert for a fireworks display or something like that, and then presumably back to the Palazzo. Instead, the fleet of limos brought my inner circle of VIPs to an enormous tent-like structure made of steel pipe and Kevlar and plexiglas that soared high into the sky, big enough to fit three 747 jumbo jetliners within it. Constructed on vacant land on the outskirts of town and just within sight of the glaring bright lights of the Strip, I had arranged for this mind-boggling venue to be built—temporarily, mind you—just for the occasion of my thirty-first birthday party.

As one entered the structure, on one side there was a carnival-themed environment, complete with a carousel and clowns, a circus-style trampoline, a scary funhouse, and some side-show galleries, and all of that towered over by a working Ferris wheel. That'll give you an idea of just how tall this airplane hangar-sized structure was! The other side of the tent was all made up to look and feel like the most ultra-chic nightclub anybody's ever seen: a long, undulating bar stocked with the most premium liquors and wines from around the world and manned by two dozen bartenders, flanked by two cabaret-style stages with flashing strobe lights and hip-hop music playing over hidden speakers. Behind the bar and the stage stood a twenty-four-foot ice sculpture. And when the dozen or so limos filled with famous celebrities rolled up to the red-carpeted entrance of the venue, there were somewhere around 350 regular guests inside, dressed in party regalia, waiting in electric, finger-nail-biting anticipation of their arrival. It was, as far as I was concerned, an event every bit as exciting and glamorous as the red carpet parade at the Oscar ceremony!

The show was started off by Jamie Foxx on one of the bar-side stages and broadcast across several enormous flat-screen monitors strategically placed throughout the tented building. Shortly thereafter, Swizz Beatz brought down the house with a heart-pounding hip-hop performance that went on for over an hour—and for which I generously paid him $800,000. I thought it was well worth it. The party went on, fueled by such high-octane entertainment, until it concluded, maybe five or six hours later, when Britney Spears, wearing only a very skimpy gold-colored outfit, emerged from a giant fake birthday cake to the great delight of the crowd and commenced in leading the entire throng in singing "Happy Birthday" to me, as I stood there alone and a great glaring spotlight shone down directly upon me amid the surrounding darkness, as if I was the star of the show. As the singing continued, a small army of those sultry models in the short red dresses served thick slices of decadently rich, Belgian chocolate mousse cake to the nearly 400 guests who had packed the place. And while things more or less ended with the birthday cake climax for most of the regular guests, for my special VIP personalities, it was back to the Palazzo and the Chairman Suites to continue the party into the next morning—and into the next day and into the next evening and so it went, hour upon hour.

———

When I reflect back on those party days, I recall that I did genuinely enjoy them, or, at least, I think I did. Nowadays, I really want to believe that I did. But there are times when I find myself wondering about that. Seriously wondering. It's one thing—it's easy—to tell you about what these events were like—I mean, the things we did, the outlandish, crazy ideas I came up with and orchestrated to make those events so outrageous that nobody who came to even one of them would ever be able to forget what they saw and heard and felt for the rest of their lives. Like, at my thirty-first, I hired little people to dress and act as Oompa-Loompas, tearing around through the crowd of revelers, this while Cirque du Soleil performers strutted awkwardly about the main floor on twelve-foot tall stilts and female acrobats scantily dressed in lingerie swooped from multicolored trapeze rings and swings through the air and over the twisting heads of the crowd marveling at them. God, it's amazing nobody got killed at one of these things when I think about it! But the idea was to turn the whole event into a mind-blowing spectacle of sight and sound and of audacious wealth and utterly indulgent, hedonistic excess too. I think I achieved that. At my parties, you could get just about anything you could possibly want.

But it's a lot harder for me to try to explain what *my* experience of these extravaganzas was like or how they truly made me feel, deep down inside. Make no mistake, I was always very gratified to see how much other people seemed to enjoy themselves at these events. As I've explained, they served a vital business purpose in gaining entry into the elite and very closely guarded circle of the wealthiest financial power brokers in the world.

But what about me?

To this day, my thirty-first birthday party still ranks as legendary in the flamboyant fantasy folklore that surrounds Las Vegas, perhaps the most bizarrely extravagant event ever staged there. One other notable personality who was there was Robin Leach, the British entertainment reporter, gossip-page writer, bon vivant, world traveler, and TV broadcaster who had made a living out of emceeing his trademark *Lifestyles of the Rich and Famous* television shows and who, in so doing, had succeeded in making himself pretty rich and famous as well. Of the party, Leach would later write, "Everyone is used to extravagant parties in Las Vegas, but this was the *ultimate* party to exceed every other party."

Oh yes, I had specifically invited Leach to the event, and I wanted him to write about it in the most hyperbolically superlative terms that could come out of his pen or be typed into his laptop. Yet I felt compelled to include one very important stipulation in his invitation; namely, he could write anything he wanted about the party, but he was prohibited from naming the host. Part of that was simply prudent business, as I've pointed out before. It was important for me to remain anonymous in my innovative business dealings with people who themselves wanted no part of the limelight—or the gossip pages, for that matter. Middle Eastern royals, in particular, do not subscribe to the fabled adage of the Madison Avenue ad men that "there is no such thing as bad publicity." They much preferred to do everything behind closed doors.

But there was a far more personal and agonizing aspect to the felt need I harbored to remain out of sight, off in the shadows—the one who was there but wasn't there as well. It was a matter of dread.

So often, at those parties, I was afflicted with the strange, deathly disquieting sensation that I was out of body watching myself from some faraway vantage point, observing myself, like I was some sort of marionette, there trying to hold court amid the throngs of celebrities and dignitaries and just ordinary nameless people, there for the thrill of seeing their idols. Yet I sensed that I was also controlling the marionette me, like I was simultaneously both puppet and puppeteer, the one on high controlling my movements. What I was saying, what I was doing, who I was interacting with, as well as who I was introducing to whom, thinking about the deals I hoped would result from those introductions—I was also somehow observing all that, like an evil scientist observing a lab experiment from a safe vantage point, someplace where my presence would not taint or contaminate the results of the experiment. I would pull a string, and my arm would move; pull on a couple more strings, and I'd do a breakdance move. As the omniscient and omni-powerful puppeteer, I was in control of these things yet ever fearful that the puppet me would veer off script, would somehow take the power and control away from the real me, would do something absurd to draw attention to himself.

And ruin everything.

There is something I didn't tell you earlier, about my thirty-first birthday extravaganza. It was something that happened to me at the very end, when Britney popped out of that giant cake and led all the guests in singing "Happy Birthday" to me, me standing there alone in the spotlight.

That moment should have been the thrill of a lifetime. I should have been elated beyond the limits of human description and overcome with gratitude. But I wasn't. I felt instead like the leading player on the stage, horrified that he had forgotten his lines, desperately trying to remember them until he realizes to his even greater horror that no one is really listening to him in the first place. There, in the middle of a thousand people, many of them ultra-famous glitterati, I never felt so alone in my life.

And when the song was over and the applause had died down and that infernal, inescapable spotlight clicked off, the one person who, alone, had perhaps the best chance of anyone on Earth to truly understand me, to understand the depths—or should I say instead the shallows—of my soul, that person walked up and joined me on the now-darkened stage. Seet Li Lin grinned broadly as he clutched me firmly by the shoulders.

"Happy Birthday, man!" he declared, practically manhandling me in his enthusiastic delight.

I looked at him, dumbstruck, as if I had turned to stone. Seet must have seen the panic in my eyes, for his smile disappeared, and he looked at me the way that a doctor looks at a patient. "Whatsa matter, man?" he said, moving his head about like he was trying to peer past my skull and into my brain.

"I feel like a hollow man," I blurted.

Seet laughed, as if I had made a joke.

"What the fuck does that mean?" he asked, shaking his head. "You are such an enigma, you know that, Jho?" Seet declared. "You need to relax; it's your birthday, man! Lighten up! Have some fun. Look at all these people come to your party. Just amazing, man."

In an instant, simultaneously and paradoxically, this was both the last *and* the first place on Earth that I wanted to be. Don't ask me to try to explain it.

Fortunately, my moment of terror that night passed, and I was able to rejoin my VIP guests to continue the partying in the Chairman Suites. But I will never forget the anguish I experienced in that moment, and Seet and I never spoke about that moment again.

Look: As a physical human specimen, I am a small, round, pudgy man. My body is soft, like a child's plush toy. For a time, I tried to change that. I hired a physical trainer, and I paid him hundreds of thousands of dollars to travel with me practically everywhere I went around the world, an ever-present passenger on my jet, an Austro-Bavarian hulk of a human specimen whose own physique was like chiseled marble, a Freudian superego watching over me, making sure I behaved when it came to my diet and exercise. Let's just call him Lars. I exhorted Lars to turn my flabby muscles into ribbons of steal, to turn my puffy body into something resembling one of those Greek statues of sinewy warriors or ripped athletes or endowed gods or whatever they were. And he tried; he really tried. He took me to task again and again. But it was no use, and I'll admit that my addictive weakness for consuming buckets upon buckets of KFC—Kentucky Fried Chicken—certainly didn't help matters.

One time, when Lars discovered my stash of several boxes of Hostess Twinkies, he confronted me sternly.

"What's this?" he demanded, his exasperation evident in his stare.

I could only look at him with the shame I could feel blossoming across my face.

"Look, Lars," I whined, grasping desperately for the sympathy that I knew would simply never be forthcoming. "Let's face it: I could dine on nails and scrap metal and drink used motor oil, and it wouldn't make a damned iota of difference. It's my genetic heritage that's to blame," I pleaded.

"No, it's not," Lars gruffed in his Germanic accent. "You are *veak*, and you have no *villpower*."

I suppose he was right, but I cannot say that it didn't sting, and that was the end of Lars.

In my defense, the state of my own physique was barely even the half of it. Because I have a round, pudgy face to go with my round, pudgy body. With my almond Asian complexion, I would often come out of the steam room or the sauna and, wiping the condensation off the mirror, be struck by the dispiriting thought that my face, lightly glistening with sweat, looks a lot like a pie, freshly brown-baked from the oven, my eyes and mouth resembling the slits designed to allow the steam to escape. If I sound like I am cruelly or viciously stereotyping my own Chinese-Asian heritage, I caution you to remember that I am talking here about myself, about how I see myself. It has everything to do with me and nothing to do with anyone else, and it has nothing to do with my race. Are there not plenty of men across Asia whose countenances convey a sense of dignity and nobleness and strength and wisdom—and even wit and charm? I mean, were there ever any more striking figures across Asian history than Chiang-Kai Shek or, if you wish to look beyond China, whose looks commanded more respect and admiration—and inspiration—than Ho Chi Minh or Hirohito? I do not look like those men. Those men did not look like brown-baked pies steaming fresh from the oven when they step out of a hot sauna.

The truth is I look even less like the leading Western men in the Hollywood films that I love so much. Perhaps that was *why* I loved American movies so deeply and with such devotion. In Hollywood, you can be all of the things you can never be in real life. Hell, if I truly looked like anyone at all in those films, it would most likely be the evil villain or the evil villain's henchman. I am Odd Job in a James Bond flick. Bruce Lee the avenging hero, I am not.

And yet notwithstanding, it's curious even to me, but there were times in my career when I believe my unremarkable appearance was something of an advantage to me in my business dealings. People looked at me, and I think they came away with low expectations for what I could do, what I could achieve. I'm certain that Donald Trump felt that way when I first met him, at that breakfast with Ivanka. There's no doubt in my mind that so many of the bankers at Goldman and J.P. Morgan and Coutts, like Tim Leissner and all the others, felt that way about me, at least in the beginning. When I proposed to do really audacious things, to orchestrate complex business deals that no one else could have conceived, it was as though the business and investment types dismissed out of hand the prospect that I could, or would, actually pull them off, all of them thinking that I had a snowball's chance in hell of accomplishing them. It was as if all those haughty, self-important power brokers said, "Okay, go ahead. Knock yourself out."

The only thing was, I did just that. In a way, I knocked them out too. Because by the time they realized it, I was already on to the next major deal that was ten times bigger than the one they had just missed out on, or perhaps a deal they had indeed partnered on with me and had made their modest cut, but then they just couldn't keep up with me, couldn't keep up with the torrid pace of business I set that far exceeded that of anyone else I knew of. I left them in my dust.

Be that as it may, in love and romance, well, that was a different story.

There were all kinds of women in my life, although perhaps it may be overstating it to suggest they were truly "in my life." It might be more accurate to say that I crossed paths with all sorts of women. For a long time, I was obsessed with Paris Hilton and Britney Spears, but especially with Paris, all the way back to my days at Wharton, where Seet Li Lin and my other classmates teased me without mercy for watching Hilton's debut Hollywood film *House of Wax* about a dozen times, whenever I got bored with dorm life, which was pretty often. Later on, when, to my great delight, Paris came to so many of my events, and the paparazzi cameras caught the two of us nuzzling or embracing, the gossip columns made me out to be her new boyfriend, but our relationship was never going to progress to anything like that. Paris was just a girl who liked parties, and that was all there was to that. Besides, as the Hollywood rom-com cliché goes in so many movie trailers, Paris and I "came from different worlds." As for Britney, honestly, she was just too unstable for me, an adolescent in a voluptuous woman's body, and even though she and I were born barely a month apart, whenever I was with her, I had the unnerving feeling that there should have been a chaperone standing by to keep us apart.

At my parties and events, there was always a wide assortment of women to choose from. I'm sure that I'm not revealing any secrets when I tell you that hip-hop stars and movie icons have a way of attracting beautiful, highly desirable women wherever they go, like the proverbial moths to a flame. Particularly gorgeous were the showgirls and models I hired to adorn my extravaganzas. It's sort of horrible, but in the vernacular of the nightclubs and cabarets, some of these women were referred to as "ambient decorations." Pretty crass in this day and age.

Yet, strangely, I found that I really wasn't interested in these girls or even what they could do for me sexually, which would have been a lot, since I was paying them lavishly while also covering all of their expenses. It's kind of ironic. One time, as one of my parties was winding down, I asked an hourglass named Celina to stay with me in Vegas over the weekend. I offered to pay her ten thousand dollars and to take her shopping on the Strip, dinner at the best restaurants in town, and it wasn't at all like I wanted to spend the whole weekend in bed with her or anything like that. I just, well, I just wanted some companionship was all.

And you know what? She turned me down flat.

Still, there were some amorous relationships along the way,

although the only time I was truly knocked-off-my-feet smitten was over an all too brief span of months when I was with Elva Hsiao, the stunningly beautiful, petite Taiwanese pop star singer and musician. She was also smart, funny, and enormously talented. There were so many intriguing facets I admired about her that transcended her splendorous beauty, even as her loveliness was utterly impossible to overlook.

One night, after we'd been seeing each other in regular, secret rendezvous for many weeks, I escorted her in a chauffeured 1935 vintage Duesenberg SJ LaGrande Phaeton to the magnificent towers of the Dubai Atlantis Hotel. There, on the pristine white beach in front of the hotel, I showed her the candles I had arranged to be set up in the shape of a huge heart. There were over five hundred of them in the sand. Within the heart was a large dining table covered with an intricate Belgian lace tablecloth and adorned with fresh-cut American Beauty white roses (her favorite!), two place settings in Royal Doulton Carlyle, each with a Baccarat wine glass and champagne flute, and a chilled bottle of Roederer Cristal Rosé champagne off to one side. As we dined on the finest food that Dubai had to offer, a string quartet on a small platform just beyond the heart of candles softly played Mozart.

Then, at the exact moment I had planned, a helicopter suddenly appeared overhead, and two people parachuted to the beach, a man and a woman wearing silver jumpsuits, landing precisely where the gently undulating water meets the powdery white sand. They immediately clicked off their parachutes and then just as quickly zipped out of their jumpsuits to reveal the man was wearing an Armani tuxedo and bow tie, but the woman, unfathomably, managed to be wearing a short, elegant evening dress by Vera Wang. The two of them walked serenely up to the table, the man placing down a flat black box the size of a large billfold, the woman placing a much smaller box the size of a golf ball. They then returned to the place where they had landed, where, just as suddenly as they had arrived, two lifelines that had been lowered by the helicopter drew them swiftly back into the aircraft, and off they went toward the horizon. The quartet had also quietly vanished. We were alone.

"Open this one," I said, pointing to the larger flat box the tuxedoed man had placed on the table. Hsiao picked up the box and gingerly pushed back the lid to reveal a Blue Nile necklace holding an exquisite pink sapphire and diamond pendant. Her breath caught in her throat.

"Oh my, Jho!" she gasped. "It's stunning!"

I rose from the table and removed the necklace from the box, and, standing over her, I placed it around her neck, reaching around to clasp it in the back. She placed her hands on the pendant against her neck, the way women do, as if gazing into some unseen but imagined mirror, in subdued but obvious rapture. Then I stepped back slightly. I reached for the smaller box the miniskirted woman parachutist had left, and, holding it in both hands, I began to descend to one knee.

Abruptly, Hsiao put her right hand on mine.

"No, don't," she said. "Please don't, Jho." She moved both of her hands to her lap and looked down at them, like a penitent child.

I looked at her for a moment; then I sat down slowly, placing the small black box back on the embroidered tablecloth, and I waited. There followed what was perhaps the most excruciating moments of silence in my entire life, save for the sound of an almost imperceptible breeze across the water and onto the beach.

Finally, still looking down at her hands, Hsiao said, "I can't marry you, Jho," and with that she raised her head and looked at me directly. I could see the resolve in her eyes, and so I said nothing.

"I just know I couldn't live your lifestyle," she explained. Her voice was unnervingly firm, and this surprised me. "Knowing you has been wonderful," she continued. "I've enjoyed every minute. But I believe that you and I have very different goals in life. I just don't think it would ever work out between us."

I had no idea what to say at this point, but, as I tried to speak, she put two of her lovely fingers to my lips to silence them.

"Please don't," she implored again.

"I love you," she said, "but I don't love you enough to marry you."

She paused for a moment and then said, with discernible conviction in her voice, as if she was reading a prepared statement, "I love you enough to *not* marry you, because I don't think that's what will make you truly happy in your life. I don't know that I could even imagine what will make you happy, but I don't believe that marrying me will do that. I really don't. Not in the long run."

If, a moment earlier, I could not imagine what I should say, I now thought, rightly or wrongly, there really wasn't anything at all I could say that would change anything. I picked up the little box—symbolically perhaps, because, in reality, I had no other use for what it contained—and I slipped it into my pocket. Then I took her hand and kissed it. And I did not bother to queue the superyacht, floating out there on the gentle waves just offshore in the gathering night, to set off the fireworks that were meant to be the cinematic finale of a glorious evening that had cost me over a million dollars, including leasing the superyacht for the weekend that now would not happen.

As 2012 was drawing to a close, in late November, I attended yet another, very different birthday party in New York City that was much more intimate than the huge galas that I typically threw and by then had become famous for. This gathering was at a place called the Monkey Bar, in the Hotel Elysée, in midtown Manhattan, and the guest of honor was Martin Scorsese, on the occasion of his turning seventy. DiCaprio was there, of course; the director and his leading star had become constant companions during the filming of *The Wolf of Wall Street*, but Leonardo also introduced me to Daniel Day-Lewis, Harvey Keitel, and Steven Spielberg, among others.

At the highlight of the proceedings, many of the guests bestowed their birthday gifts on the great director, and many of those gifts were very special, but I like to think that mine was the most special of all: a Polish-language version of the movie poster for *Cabaret* starring Liza Minnelli. Martin would later send me a very personal, handwritten note profusely thanking me for the "very rare" poster and stating that it had "made my seventieth all the more special." I loved that note, but truth be told, the poster itself wasn't all that expensive—only a few hundred dollars with the frame—and it wasn't that hard to find.

What *was* really expensive—and also what one could only regard as the quintessential major find in the movie memorabilia world—was the birthday gift that Riza, Joey McFarland, and I had given to Leonardo DiCaprio, when, coincidently, he turned thirty-eight only a week or so earlier, on the eleventh of that same month of November. We had actually managed to find Marlon Brando's Oscar statuette for best actor in 1954's *On the Waterfront*—the very one that had gone missing from the late actor's Hollywood home only a few years earlier, under mysterious circumstances. We paid a well plugged-in New Jersey memorabilia dealer over $600,000 for the statuette, and we gave it to Leonardo (at yet another wild birthday party, of course) as a kind of symbolic gesture that we believed he was overdue to earn his own best actor award, and that of course, we would all be absolutely delighted if he did so for the performance he was currently putting into the filming of *The Wolf of Wall Street*.

This too, was money well spent. DiCaprio was appropriately moved by the gift, and even as the filming of *Wolf* was still underway, Riza and Joey were already intensely negotiating a development deal to produce a remake of the 1970s Steve McQueen hit movie *Papillion*, and they wanted Leo in the starring role. At the same time, the two Red Granite executives were also sitting in on casting calls with Scorsese for the director's next major film, *The Irishman*, starring Robert De Niro, hoping to play a significant role in the production of that film as well.

Between my own mega-birthday bash at the beginning of November followed by the birthday celebrations for DiCaprio and Scorsese and punctuated by numerous other boozy gatherings along the way, the end of 2012, in my memory, is something of a surreal blur, like it was one relentless nonstop party all hours of day and night. As Christmas approached, Joey McFarland arranged for a tin of Petrossian Special Reserve Ossetra Caviar to be sent to Scorsese and his wife's townhouse on the East Side of Manhattan, and, at yet another party convened at yet another New York City nightclub, this one called Marquee, he splurged on a $2,245 bottle of Cristal Rosé champagne as we all got together to celebrate the final wrap up of the filming of *The Wolf of Wall Street*.

As the sommelier almost solemnly uncorked the precious Cristal and filled our glasses, McFarland stood and raised his glass on high.

"A toast!" he declared, grinning ear to ear. "To *The Wolf of Wall Street*. May Red Granite's greatest film ever make a shitload of profits!" Joey paused, and someone at another table said, "Here, Here!" I still don't know who it was, but it wasn't one of our group. Then Joey spoke again, amending his original toast. "And maybe bring in a couple of Oscars too!" he said, winking at Leo.

And after we drank to promise of profits and Oscars, Leo DiCaprio himself spoke up. "I'd like to propose a toast," he announced, raising his champagne glass once again, "to Jho Low, the wizard of Wall Street, for helping make this moment possible." So the glasses were raised again, the champagne quickly downed by all.

It was one of those curiously agonizing, contradictory moments in my life, when I simultaneously relished the intense, warming glow of the spotlight and yet felt excruciatingly self-conscious scorched in its burning aura, as we all drank to me. It was unnerving, the bizarre feeling I had, although I cannot explain why.

Still, it had been a really terrific year, and I wanted to end it with a bang, a mind-blowing celebration that would top every other celebration I had ever conceived of before—the mother of all parties. So here's what I did.

At the end of December, I chartered a custom-outfitted Boeing 747-400—the kind that might be rented by Saudi princes or even used by government heads of state on round-the-clock overseas diplomatic missions. This thing cost me something like $20,000; that's *per hour* by the way! Then, with about forty-five guests that included DiCaprio and his *Wolf* costar Jonah Hill, Jamie Foxx, Swizz Beatz, and, of course, Joey McFarland and Al Qubaisi, along with a bevy of models dressed in the fabled little black dresses, we departed from

LAX bound for Sydney, Australia, where, for several days, we partied on the town and a couple of yachts—right up until the moment we counted down the seconds and rang in the New Year from a boat on the harbor with sumptuous food and popping the corks on dozens of bottles of Cristal champagne. The moment the New Year's fireworks display was over, we all piled into limos for the trip back to the airport, where we climbed aboard the 747 to fly back to Las Vegas to ring in the New Year in America all over again! To me, it was simply and sublimely a fitting end to a fabulous year, and at the time, I fully expected that 2013 was going to be an even better year, even if I could barely imagine what "an even better year" would actually look like.

However, it didn't exactly turn out that way. What I mean to say, actually, is that's when everything started to go south.

Chapter 12

Here's the thing. No matter how much money I funneled to the various accounts of Prime Minister Najib, it never seemed to be enough.

You have to understand that Malaysia's politics had been corrupt for quite a long time; you don't have one party in continuous, uninterrupted, virtually unchallenged control—for sixty years, in a so-called democratic state—without that dominant party winning election after election more by way of the cash box than through the ballot box. Even before Najib came to power, as early as 2006, there had gathered within the country an increasingly powerful reform movement in opposition to the UMNO. These were not some malcontented rabble in the streets; they called themselves *Bersih*, the Malay word for "clean," and the movement was populated by opposition politicians, lawyers, doctors, and other professionals—what you might call the "pillars of the community"—all whipped into a frenzy by some very clever and determined anticorruption activists.

In 2009, Najib had won the election as prime minister by doing what all UMNO party members had done for six decades—by spreading around lots and lots of cash. Yet the Bersih movement only got stronger and bolder and more vociferous during his first term, so much so that Najib faced perhaps the biggest challenge of his political career as the 2013 election cycle approached. I can tell you from my conversations with him that Najib was terrified about the very real possibility that he could become the forever ignominious guy responsible for ending the uninterrupted reign of power that the UMNO held over Malaysia for its entire existence since declaring independence.

It didn't have to be this way.

If Najib had just done what he told the people he was going to do. What he had told me in private conversation that he was going to do. If he had built the low-income housing that he had promised to build, or the new schools, or if he had delivered the job-skills-training programs throughout the country that he claimed would increase the wage-earning capabilities of average Malaysians, if he had created the industrial farming development of rural areas, like in Sarawak state, and through all of these initiatives improved the overall standard of living for all Malaysians. If he had done even a few of these things, Najib would not have been facing the electoral crisis that loomed in his nightmares like a specter from a horror novel as the 2013 election came closer and closer.

And all of these things, in case you are wondering, are the exact sorts of social programs and jobs and education initiatives and major infrastructure developments that, in a perfect world, shall we say, would be great candidates to be funded by a sovereign wealth fund like 1MDB for the benefit of the people. You see, I did have some of these things in mind with respect to the good that I believed 1MDB could achieve.

When I reflect on all this now, I can only conjecture that Najib had somehow lost the ability to understand how these ideas could have made him a rockstar PM so popular among the electorate that there would be no end in sight to his tenure. He could conceivably have made himself prime minister for life if he had a mind to—and he certainly did have a mind to! Perhaps he never even had the ability to fully understand this.

Instead, it seems that Najib believed that the surest route to popularity—in fact, the only route, in his mind—was through lots and lots of money. Perhaps he can't be completely blamed in a way.

After all, he'd risen to the pinnacle of political power in a nation where he'd probably never seen any elected public official do it any other way. This was political business as usual in Malaysia.

But you know, distributing money can be a tricky thing. You can funnel it to the political friends that you develop as you rise to power, with the implied notion that those friends-turned-cronies will, in due course, pass some of that money along to sway to your way of thinking the voters you need to win an election. Mostly, they will—as long as they get their cut and as long as the water keeps flowing from the mountain. But everyone gets greedy, and before you know it, those cronies are demanding more and more, or else they keep more of the money they were supposed to use to encourage people to vote the party line.

I remember one time, to my shock and horror, catching a glimpse of Najib at a campaign rally in Penang, handing wads of cash to a minor official—right out in the open, with the press milling around! In fact, I had to quickly step between the PM and a television crew before they noticed and might have filmed the transaction that was going down right in front of their cameras. We were in Penang, my hometown, trying to drum up support for the UMNO, because the Penang district had flipped to the opposition party in the previous election. That trip was a disaster, despite the fact that I had hired Busta Rhymes, Swizz Beatz, and some other rap stars to perform in concert, paying them a staggering amount of money for the service. I even hired Psy to perform his own concert, the South Korean pop star whose global hit song "Gangnam Style" had made him an overnight worldwide sensation.

As Psy was set to start, Prime Minister Najib himself got up on stage in a lame attempt to rev up the crowd—not his strongest suit. Sure, when he bellowed into the mike, "Are you ready for Psy?" the entire audience yelled, "*Yes!*" at the top of their lungs. But when he followed that with the question, "Are you ready to help me win Penang back to the UMNO?" it felt like the very foundations of the stadium reverberated with a resounding "*No!*" that sounded like the formidable rumblings of an earthquake. That response was an indication of the peril Najib's campaign was in at that moment, and it simply added to his panic. Najib was never very good at handling stress, and he was beginning to regularly make a fool of himself, as he had done at the Psy concert in Penang.

Of course, it did not help Najib's cause in Penang that 1MDB had bought up nearly a half billion dollars' worth of property in the province with the promise of building 10,000 units of affordable housing but, by the time of the campaign rally, had nothing to show for it beyond an array of weedy, rutted, garbage-strewn, vacant lots surrounded by broken-down chain-link fences with a half dozen rusting earthmovers sitting on the dirt inside the perimeter.

At the same time, the prime minister and his First Lady made no attempt at all to conceal the lavish lifestyle that became their trademark as soon as Najib came to power and which only became more decadent after the formation of 1MDB and the completion of the joint venture with PetroSaudi. The couple was constantly jetting around the world, to places like the Middle East or the United Kingdom or the south of France or America, staying in the most exclusive five-star hotels or on superyachts in the Mediterranean or the Persian Gulf or in the several mansions I had bought for the Razak family in New York City and Beverly Hills and elsewhere. It was difficult, even for Najib's PR staff and despite my repeated insistence, to toe the line that these homes had been acquired strictly to facilitate diplomatic travel, when Rosmah would bring so much luggage that the Razak entourage often required a second or third limo to haul all the stuff.

In public appearances and on many popular talk shows broadcast over Malaysian television, Rosmah seemed to make a point of wearing—I swear to god—as much of her most exquisite jewelry as she could without falling over from the sheer weight of it. Yes, it's true I had bought and given to her many of the most expensive necklaces and rings—and a tiara or two—but I had expected her to be a bit more discrete in wearing them. I had expected her to wear them to state dinners and official functions, for the honor and prestige of Malaysia as a proud and emerging member in the international community of nations. Not to go on local TV and flaunt them in the faces of everyday hardworking Malaysians who were struggling to put food on the table for their kids.

People in the press were starting to ask disturbing questions. Initially, the media were timid, asking, for example, why the prime minister and his wife were so often flying off to the Middle East or America or Europe on private jets instead of taking care of business at home in Malaysia. One headline read, "Is Najib Moonlighting as the Prime Minister of Los Angeles?" next to a cartoon caricature of Najib and Rosmah superimposed next to a pool at the newly rebuilt Beverly Hills Pyramid House, with champagne glasses in their hands.

But as the newspapers got bolder, the reportage became more vicious, particularly with respect to Rosmah, whom they seemed particularly to excoriate with glee. One such headline aimed at the First Lady read, "Where Does Rosmah Keep Her Jewelry? In Her Hermès Bags, of Course!" and yet another read, "Today's Quiz: What Weighs More, Rosmah or Her Jewelry?"

Meanwhile, the streets of Kuala Lumpur and other major Malaysian cities were weekly, it seemed, the scene of massive demonstrations by hundreds of thousands of yellow-shirted opposition protestors carrying signs and ugly caricatures of Najib and Rosmah. Worse, Najib's opponent in the 2013 election was Anwar Ibrahim. An eloquent and powerful speaker, Ibrahim had another remarkable talent; he was a consummate and persuasive coalition builder. To seriously challenge the incumbent Najib, Ibrahim had rallied together an astonishingly broad coalition of opposition parties and splinter groups—some of them factions that heretofore could barely even talk to each other—all committed to support Ibrahim under the banner of initiating sweeping governmental reform and removing Najib from power. And the first thing Ibrahim promised to do was to vigorously investigate the purpose and the financial state of the 1MDB fund.

And ominously, Ibrahim also promised to: Shut. It. Down.

Now, we are talking about something that would make me have night terrors, never mind nightmares, and never mind Najib's petty worries. I knew the numbers. Prior to the 2013 election, 1MDB was seven billion dollars in debt, and in its latest reported financial year, the fund showed a shocking net loss of thirty million dollars. With the PetroSaudi venture foundering and Project Wall Street going nowhere and the IPO of the proposed energy sector conglomerate still in flux, 1MDB had almost nothing to show for all of its investments. Fortunately, few other people knew these details, in part because I had leaned heavily on Shahrol Halmi and other board members to suppress the annual report, to make it really difficult for anyone to even get a copy of it, whether in print or online.

But the prime minister didn't seem to care about any of these serious financial concerns, or about the precarious state the 1MDB fund was in. All Najib wanted was more money for his campaign. And he wanted more fucking money than he ever wanted before. And he wanted it more quickly than ever before. He was in trouble, and he could feel the heat. And he decided to take action on his own.

Okay, by now, you know the drill—how these huge bond deals worked, I mean. Basically, just to run through it, 1MDB would zero in on some acquisition it wanted to make, like the phalanx of coal-fired energy assets across Southeast Asia owned by Ananda Krishnan and the Genting Group, or devise some massive urban development undertaking like Project Wall Street or the Iskandar Development Region. The fund would then begin to construct an enormous bond issue to acquire the investment funds they needed to underwrite the intended venture. By now, good old Goldman Sachs had become the go-to investment house to fully orchestrate the sale of the bonds to investors. Not only could this highly respected American investment firm be counted on to oversee all the details to create the bond issue, but it had pretty much become the routine that Goldman itself would buy up the whole damn bond issue, lock, stock, and barrel, as it had with the dual $1.75 billion Projects Virtus and Maximus. And if Goldman charged a usurious highway robber's fee for their service, well, 1MDB received the entire amount of the bond issues in cash in the nanoseconds it took to make the bank transfer between accounts. And, ho-hum, beyond once that happened, the advisory board of the Malaysian sovereign fund really didn't seem to care what Goldman took as a fee or, for that matter, what happened to the bond proceeds after that. But I did.

Of course I did. I cared very much.

That's why I had always made sure the funds were adequately layered through one or two (or more) offshore accounts and then through a couple of the most reputable and prestigious banks in the world—banks with hundreds of years of history surviving horrific wars and economy-destroying depressions, even apocalyptic regime changes in their countries of origin, banks that no respectable business investor or high-level executive would question before those monies made their way into the very liquid and highly accessible bank accounts that I had personally specially set up to receive them, and where they could do the most good to serve my future vision for 1MDB. So when nitpicky bank regulators and compliance departments saw these funds coming and going through all these accounts within the most respected and long-standing banking institutions since humanity stopped being savages counting beads and real banking was invented, they saw it all as business as usual, and they usually didn't pry into the specifics. I simply didn't need them screwing up my plans.

But it's also vitally important to understand that I went through all of these financial gymnastics to protect Prime Minister Najib, who, after all, was ultimately the one person who had total control over the money generated by or invested in the 1MDB fund. It's fair to say that the fund couldn't exist without him; nor of course, could my control over the fund. Initially, this worked fine. Najib didn't need to know the details, and he didn't ask. I took care of the financial arrangements, allowing Najib to attend to his duties as head of state (while, of course, knowing all along that I would make sure his political and campaign war chests were always brimmingly full). Finally, Shahrol and the other board members all knew that I was advising the prime minister regarding the activities of 1MDB and that they were obliged to do as I instructed because my instructions were, in essence, coming from Najib. This arm's-length-all-around arrangement was working well for everyone involved.

But as I said, facing a serious challenge to reelection, Najib needed money, and he needed it immediately. He began to panic—I mean, seriously panic. And he got really, really reckless beyond anything I could control anymore. So what does he do?

Najib goes to Davos, the famous Swiss ski resort, to attend the World Economic Forum that's held every year there. And while he's there, *he meets directly* with Goldman bankers, including a meeting with a vice chairman, Michael Evans, from their New York headquarters that was set up by Tim Leissner, and he proceeds to broker his own deal for another three-billion-dollar bond issue! He's freelancing! He does this on his own, without having me to run interference for him, and this is only about three months after Goldman had laid out the second $1.75 billion to purchase the Project Maximus bond issue! Just incredible!

Even though it's Davos, where both the physical and the electronic security is tight, and the very sparse information that gets released to the press or the public is also tightly controlled, often to the point of being virtually redacted, with most of the goings-on there kept completely secret, Najib is exposing himself. That is, in dealing directly with the Goldman guys, he is, for all appearances anyway, both displaying his knowledge about the inner workings of 1MDB and demonstrating, ostensibly, his direct control over the fund. Even though, between you and me, he didn't know half of what was going on—and didn't *want* to know, remember? Like I said, this might be Davos, and it might be a secret enclave of sorts, but people go home, and even the gods and wizards that rule the international business investment world—well, let's just say, everybody talks.

Still, on one hand, I had to admire Najib. Normally, this kind of deal entails reams of paperwork—proposals that describe the structuring, the expected yields, a summary of the potential investors—all stuff that I had to arrange to be put together for Projects Virtus and

Maximus so that Leissner could make his formal presentation to the 1MDB advisory board. But here, Najib was able, essentially, to put things in motion for another three-billion-dollar bond issue with virtually nothing more than a handshake at Davos, and almost instantly, Project Catalyze was born. Such is the power of being the prime minister, I guess.

On the other hand, he had accomplished this at tremendous risk to himself and to his position as prime minister. For one thing, in order to explain why he needed the funds very quickly, Najib told Leissner and Evans that his engineers and civic planners back home were putting the finishing touches on the proposed development of a new, state-of-the-art financial center in the heart of Kuala Lumpur that was to be named the Tun Razak Exchange, in honor of Najib's father. Then he further proceeded to explain that he was also in haste to seize immediately an opportunity through which Aabar, the Abu Dhabi wealth fund, had agreed to partner with 1MDB once again— putting in their own, matching three-billion-dollar investment into the project—to build this fantastic financial exchange complex. If he didn't act quickly, Najib said, the potential Aabar partnership deal was going to go away. I don't know where in the world Najib came up with that one; I certainly knew of no such commitment on the part of Aabar, either through Husseiny or Qubaisi, but Leissner and Evans apparently bought it.

But to add to all the drama, Najib went and stuck his neck out even further. In his position both as prime minister and as the head of the Finance Ministry, he signed a letter of support for the three-billion-dollar Project Catalyze bond issue, meaning a guarantee through which the government of Malaysia itself, no less, promised to repay the debt in the event of a default. In effect, Najib was literally betting his country on his own reelection, and he was now sailing on some really dangerous waters—god forbid—should he actually lose the election!

Whatever the case, in March 2013, Project Catalyze went through like clockwork, following pretty much the exact same blueprint as the previous bond issues. Goldman bought up the entire three-billion-dollar bond issue in one fell swoop, as before, when David Ryan (remember him, Goldman's president of Asia operations?) along with the Goldman lawyer working on the deal voiced concern over 1MDB's request that this huge amount be deposited into tiny BSI bank. Both were overridden—as before—by Goldman CEO Gary Cohn and Mark Schwartz, the Asia chairman that Cohn had installed in authority over Ryan for just this reason.

Oh, and by the way, Goldman's fee this time around was $300 million. Ho-hum.

Sure, that was fine for them, but now I had a real problem. With the May election looming so near, there was little or no time for me to arrange for the kinds of layered transactions that would protect Najib—and me too, if you want to know the truth—from the kind of regulatory and compliance exposure that such enormous and blatant money transfers are prone to if you don't take the proper steps. In fact, at three billion U.S. dollars, if it was processed as a single transaction, this bond deal would have been so impactful to the Malaysian economy that we needed to take steps, like breaking it into tranches, so as not to cause any visible ripples in the valuation of the ringgit—the currency of Malaysia. Just think about that. I was now dealing with transacting amounts of capital so huge that a single deal could conceivably rock the economy of an entire nation like a minor earthquake!

Actually, you want to know the god's honest truth? It still gives me chills down my spine just to remember what that was like! You want to talk about monetizing the state? Take that, Gary Cohn! Such a rush, you just can't imagine! But I digress again.

So the problem I had was trying to bury this glaringly huge transaction behind lots of smaller, more routine-looking money transfers that would not arouse the interest or the suspicions of nosy bank regulators and compliance people, as well as disguising Najib's involvement to the extent that was still possible under such urgent circumstances.

I knew I could count on the rest of my team of players to do exactly what they were supposed to do. On the advisory board at

1MDB, Executive Director Casey Tang and attorney Jasmine Loo would be ardent supporters helping push through swift approval of Project Catalyze. And by this point, Shahrol Halmi had pretty much fallen in lockstep, resigned to the idea that Najib and I were calling the shots and that he'd better do the prime minister's bidding or else. Of course, I could always rely on Yak Yew Chee—our trusted account executive at BSI Bank dutifully overseeing the pseudonym Aabar Ltd. accounts—to process the receipt of the three billion dollars from Goldman and to quietly arrange the subsequent set of transactions, all without wasting valuable time revealing any of these details to the attention of his superiors (who likely would have been on board with everything anyway) or unnecessarily consulting BSI's compliance department.

So, toward the end of March 2013, Goldman deposits the proceeds of the three-billion-dollar bond sale with BSI. Immediately, Yak transfers $1.2 billion to Tanore Finance Corporation, which was a British Virgin Islands-based company that I had set up together with Fat Eric and which Fat Eric controlled under my direction. From there, Eric must arrange for a total of $681 million to be deposited into a special account at AmBank, which you could regard as the closest thing to being Malaysia's major national bank, based in the capital of Kuala Lumpur.

I need to explain a little bit about this special AmBank account. I had personally opened this account, about two years earlier, in 2011, on behalf of Najib, working directly with AmBank's CEO, Cheah Tek Kuang. Eight or nine years before this, Cheah had been one of the first bankers willing to work with me, as well as to provide the substantial loans I needed, back when I was endeavoring to launch the Wynton Group in the Petronas Towers, when I returned to Malaysia after finishing Wharton. He had been very kind to me. AmBank loans had been critical to some of the smashing early deals that got Wynton Group off the ground, and I was happy to repay him in a way by giving him and AmBank the opportunity to be involved in potentially much larger investment business through Najib and the 1MDB fund.

The AmBank account, listed simply as AMPRIVATE BANKING—MR, was beneficially owned under the name of Najib Razak, and its existence was known only to me, Cheah, and, at most, two or three other AmBank executives. More specifically, it was initially marked as an account to be used for internal bank transfers only, which meant that the account itself would not be visible to the bank's own compliance staff. So this concerned me, because the capital deposits from Tanore were going to be a little different from the usual business for this particular type of account.

Look, the very worst thing that could have happened here would have been if any information about this massive transaction into a secretive account, nevertheless owned by Najib, somehow got leaked to the Malaysian opposition forces of Anwar Ibrahim or—god forbid—the press; the whole thing would have exploded in our faces like an atomic bomb, and Najib's reelection chances would be doomed. God knows where that would have left me!

So I took preemptive steps. For one thing, I fired off a Blackberry message to the banking manager at AmBank's Kuala Lumpur headquarters, warning her that "PM did not want his name, address, or identity card number" to appear on any of the coming transactions that would ultimately put $681 million into the AMPRIVATE BANKING—MR account. I asked her to be super vigilant, to keep her eyes and ears open. I instructed that access to the account, and any activity regarding it, must be carefully restricted and *tracked*. "If you suspect anyone might have looked at this activity or accessed any information about the account itself," I told her, "you must notify me immediately." Okay, so perhaps I was being a little paranoid about it. But I was also very uncomfortable about the very notion of all that money going directly from Tanore to the AmBank account, even if the plan was that it would be broken up into at least two tranches.

I instructed Fat Eric to first have Tanore set up an account with Falcon Bank, the one essentially "owned and operated" by my friends Al Qubaisi and Al Husseiny. Once that account was established, Tanore deposited the $681 million into the new Falcon account, and, from there, Qubaisi's people quietly and discretely transferred the money in two tranches to Najib's special AMPRIVATE BANKING—MR account at AmBank. Finally, as a means of trying to inject one further layer of protection between the source of the $681 million and its destination, more specifically with respect to the defined purpose of all that capital, the transfer was listed as a business loan from Tanore Finance Corporation to AMPRIVATE BANKING—MR, and the loan documents indicated that the recipient account belonged to a company owned not by the prime minister but, rather, by Malaysia's finance minister, though, of course, Najib was *both* the prime minister *and* the finance minister!

In the end, I suppose, it all went reasonably well, even if the whole thing was a nerve-racking ordeal for me. But it was all extremely reckless and dangerous and slipshod, and it caused me an enormous degree of anxiety and a lack of sleep as I tried to maneuver these huge amounts of capital under such urgent circumstances. What can I say? I had done everything I could think of. But as far as I was concerned, all of these transactions were just too damn transparent for my sense of security and comfort, and I agonized constantly over the possibility that the wrong people would get wind of what I was trying to accomplish with all this.

For now, at least, Najib had in his war chest the enormous sums of money he demanded, and I can tell you he proceeded to spend it—or, should I say, disperse it—like a madman. Hundreds of thousands of dollars flew in every direction across Malaysia, to the ruling party bosses and Najib's corrupt cronies, as well as to his family members and business associates. It was a virtual shitstorm of cash going everywhere and perhaps more openly than ever before, so that I feared anybody with a brain could see what was going on. It was like political graft on parade. You just had to be a friend of the UMNO and a supporter of Najib; that's all it took.

And even with all of that, Najib won the 2013 election only by the scarcest of margins—the skin of his teeth, as the expression goes. He failed to win major voting districts populated by sophisticated, educated urban voters who were simply disgusted by the money politics and the bullshit, his incumbent government coalition failing to win back Penang but also losing other metropolitan districts that went for the opposition for the first time in the nation's history. In fact, Najib actually lost the popular vote, gaining reelection only because of convoluted and ethically questionable electoral rules that reserve a minimum number of parliamentary seats for Malay-dominated rural districts, like the state of Sarawak, for instance. Questionable, because of the way those rules happen to have been written to benefit the UMNO, or so it seems. Najib, of course, easily carried those isolated areas, where, forgive me for saying so, but the ignorance and poverty of the indigenous people living in huts without plumbing made buying votes cheaper than purchasing a pack of cigarettes. Indeed, sometimes a free pack of cigarettes was itself enough to buy the vote of an indigenous man or woman.

None of this was particularly new to Malaysian political elections, but Najib's campaign in 2013 was notoriously sloppy—even chaotic—in the way he threw money around. It was as though the deals and payoffs that were usually arranged quietly behind closed doors, in the secretive back rooms of bars or perhaps a safe private residence, were suddenly being conducted in the street, for just about anybody to observe if they cared to pay attention. And the press cared to pay attention. Najib's obscene, ubiquitous campaign spending served to focus the media's attention on—well, on Najib's obscene and ubiquitous campaign spending; there's no other way to say it.

The journalists started to ask questions, both during and after the elections, but this too was nothing new. Back in 2009, Malaysia's English language weekly newspaper called the *Edge* had written a series of investigative articles that probed into 1MDB's joint venture with PetroSaudi while also raising questions about the abrupt resignation of the fund's first chairman, Mohammed Bakke Salleh. But when the newspaper could find no wrongdoing, they backed off and moved on to other news.

I knew that the glare of the journalistic spotlight was going to be much more intense this time around, in large part because of Najib's intemperate and alarmingly visible campaign spending but also because the multimillionaire owner of the *Edge* newspaper, Tong

Kooi Ong, was a close friend and ardent supporter of the opposition party candidate Anwar Ibrahim. Ong, as you might imagine, was not at all pleased with the election's outcome, a fact he made quite clear in several op-ed pieces that subsequently appeared in his newspaper in the days that followed. I expected some journalistic blowback from the press, but as before, but I wasn't really worried about it. After all, I'd done nothing wrong in directing 1MDB's international investments; as I've said all along, I'd simply been creative and innovative in ways that nobody else had thought of before. I also knew that my people on the advisory board, like Casey and Jasmine, knew exactly what to say, should they be approached by journalists at the *Edge* or affiliated with any other news organization. I was quite confident that, as with the earlier investigations regarding PetroSaudi and ex-chairman Bakke, these investigative journalists would find nothing amiss and would eventually be obliged to move on to other, much juicier stories.

As for me, my benefactor was still in place for another term, and with the latest Goldman-managed bond issue successfully executed, I had close to another one billion dollars to play with. I was exhausted and, I'll admit, a little depressed as a result, perhaps, of the unrelenting anxiety and stress I experienced during the campaign and the colossal mountains I had to move to deliver to Najib—in record time—the funds he need to win reelection. I needed something to raise my spirits, so I decided that the next thing I would do, I would buy myself some nice artwork. Oh, and I decided it was also high time I ordered my own superyacht.

Chapter 13

After Najib's reelection, I suppose I allowed things to go to my head. The money, I mean. There was just so much of it. I mean, just think about it for a moment.

In rough figures, there was more than $1.5 billion from the original 1MDB PetroSaudi venture, there was something like $1.4 billion from the first two energy sector bond issues handled so ably by Goldman, and now there was another $1.2 billion from the Goldman bond sale that we pushed through prior to the election in May 2013, and that was even after I had sent $681 million to Najib's private AmBank account to finance his successful reelection campaign. There was also another billion or so that I had similarly set aside from independent investors, such as the pension fund dedicated to Malaysia's civil servants known as SRC International. The funds were spread across dozens of discrete accounts and companies all around the world, and I could pretty much tap into any one of them at any time, in an instant, through a simple phone call or a text message. Most of the time, I was the only one who could do so. While my associates had a certain degree of access, especially Fat Eric, they usually needed me to pull the trigger on a deal or a transaction, because I knew how to get the banks to do what the banks were supposed to do. Fat Eric, in particular, I could trust to do nothing without first consulting with me. And yet no one—I mean no one—other than me knew about the vast number of the accounts that were out there in the network that I had created.

Tell you the truth, I was beginning to have trouble keeping track of it all myself. Tough to have such high-class problems, you're probably thinking, but it was.

I'm not sure I even realized it at first, but I was slowly, subconsciously, inexorably being consumed by an internally pervasive anxiety that I am at a loss for words to explain or describe. It was a kind of morbid loathing and paranoia that, at certain times, could be intense yet, at other times, might vanish like a ghost. Back then, I could never put my finger on what it was that troubled me. It wasn't the money itself; I loved spending all that money.

I think, maybe, it was my unrelenting compulsion to move on to the next deal. I should have been content. I should have been intent on working with what I had accomplished. I should have been focused on following through with my plans and objectives. Damn it! I should have been able to relax once in a while. Yet when the deal was over, so was the colossal, ethereal, indescribable high I got from it, and I needed the next one. I was an addict in need of my next fix, a Casanova who, after the conquest, no longer had any use for the conquered maiden but, rather, an unquenchable, all-consuming desire to pursue the next one. And for me the deals just could not come fast enough, never damn fast enough. You see, I had to *do* something with all that money, and there were always roadblocks in my way. Of course, that was always the challenge. Getting the deal done when nobody else in their right mind thought that I could or that the deal was even possible at all. Does that make sense? Am I making sense?

The month of May—that is, the month in which Najib was reelected—wasn't even over when I found myself in a private room at the New York offices of the famed British auction house Christie's, a private phone in my hand. I was bidding on a substantial piece of artwork, the 1982 masterpiece by Jean-Michel Basquiat called *Dustheads*. I say *substantial* for two reasons, the first being the piece is about seven square feet in size, so it's physically quite imposing. Second, Basquiat, if you don't know him, started out as a kid as a graffiti artist in New York City, where he led a troubled life of irrational, contradictory behavior fueled by drugs and alcohol, even as his work gained growing acclaim in the art world. He even collaborated with Andy Warhol for a time. He died in 1988 of an accidental heroin overdose, having reached only the age of twenty-seven, thus leaving behind a very limited number of works. *Dustheads* was his masterwork and the most sought-after Basquiat, and I had to have it. Unseen by the people gathered in the main gallery where the painting was prominently displayed, I watched intently the proceedings on an internal video feed, as did my unseen adversary, who could have been in the next room or quite conceivably somewhere halfway around the world. The bidding was intense, and I remember the sweat on my palm as I gripped the intercom phone tightly, squinting at the closed-circuit television monitor, my heart racing, my head throbbing.

The pressurized environment inside Christie's that afternoon was more than exhilarating; for me, it was downright narcotic, and, for me, it was the beginning of an artwork buying spree that lasted through the end of that year of 2013. With the help of Joey McFarland, who knew more about fine art than I did, I acquired works by Picasso and van Gogh, as well as by more contemporary artists like Roy Lichtenstein, Warhol, Rothko, Calder, and the bizarre contemporary works of Mark Ryden or those of pop artist Ed Ruscha. To be honest, I relied on Joey to tell me what was good or desirable. Or just easily marketable, should the need ever arise.

Like Najib, I too began to get sloppy about how I was paying for all of this artistic treasure. Most of it I bought directly through the Tanore account, taking little or no precaution to disguise the origin of the funds, not bothering to filter them through other accounts or institutions as I usually did, so as to not raise any scrutiny by any bankers, while also making them harder to trace should anyone get curious. Yet, even as I departed from my own strictly disciplined pattern of safely moving money through multiple venues for my own protection, there was a degree of paranoia creeping into the way that I conducted my affairs such that, while I freely accessed the funds in the Tanore account for my art acquisitions, I increasingly did so by using or signing under the name of Eric Tan—Fat Eric, that is. By December, in less than eight months, using the Tanore and several other accounts, I had acquired nearly $350 million worth of artwork.

You may be wondering, what did I do with all of that stuff? Did I display those masterpieces in any of the fantastic mansions or office suites I owned around the world, in Kuala Lumpur or London or New York or LA? I did not. Instead, I stashed everything in an ultra-secure warehouse in Switzerland known as the Geneva Freeport. You can think of this as a place for the uber-rich of the world to secretly park their most valuable possessions to avoid paying taxes on them. Plain and simple, it's a place for the wealthiest hoarders on Earth. These days, I don't know, but I kind of feel guilty about what I did with so much of that artwork, putting it where no one could actually see it.

I found out about the Geneva Freeport from Al Qubaisi, who stored dozens of his exotic cars there, including a Bugatti Veyron, a Lamborghini Huracán Evo, and a Pagani Huayra. I'd never even heard of that last carmaker brand before. Cars that Qubaisi never even drove, that just sat there in a giant climate-controlled parlor. The room was way too elegant to call it a garage.

Funny thing: I could see storing artwork there, which, of course, I did. But cars? One time I asked Al Qubaisi, "Don't you ever want to go there and drive those cars around?" You know what he said?

"I have people for that."

Awesome, I thought, shaking my head in disbelief, not knowing what else to say.

There's a tipping point somewhere where you're so filthy rich it's almost impossible to make yourself un-rich. You buy a Picasso for thirty million dollars. You're out the cash, but the painting is still worth thirty million dollars. In fact, it's worth even more. Having created a worldwide sensation in the news by plunking down such an unconscionable sum for a piece of canvas in a wooden frame, you could probably sell it for forty million dollars. These things have a way of self-inflating according to no known barometer of value—certainly no rational one. Or perhaps that barometer is simply avarice, plain old covetous greed.

That's the way it happened with the Basquiat. The bidding for *Dustheads* mounted with dizzying swiftness—$38 million, $38.5 million, $39 million, past $40 million—the bidding continued on fiercely in increments of a half million at a bid, although I twice tried to frighten off my unknown competitor with jump bids of one million. I was not going to be denied. I was the victor in the end. I acquired the painting for $43.5 million. That was probably eighteen million dollars more than its true market value at the time. But you see, in the art world, it was now worth what I paid for it, or so it seemed to me. It was worth even more than that should I decide to resell it. I would be the one that would dictate the price. Anyway, I didn't care. I won the bid, and that is what mattered to me.

Yet what had I won?

I would look at such timeless works of art and see the millions of dollars they cost as if the bills of currency were surreally woven into the very threads of the canvas or scattered among the billions of molecules in the dried paint forming the abstract images, myself oblivious to the creative vision, the emotion that came from somewhere deep inside the artist's psyche, perhaps from the roots of his very soul. My appreciation, such as it existed at all, atrophied, desiccated from my own ignorance. And when I reflect on it now, I realize to my own disheartening—even self-loathing—that I never seriously, honestly had any real appreciation for these works of the human experience and expression. Pearls before swine, as the expression goes. No, to me, they were conveniently portable wealth, easier to hide than bank accounts or offshore corporations, and a whole hell of a lot easier to transport—or sell quickly—than mansions or real estate. So, of course, as soon as I acquired them, I locked them in a vault. What else do you do with your treasure?

But even as I built my art collection, there were bigger issues to worry about, and they were coming from where everything started; they were coming from PetroSaudi, and it was going on as I had my hands full trying to secure the $681 million that Najib believed he needed to win reelection. It was a major distraction at that critical time.

I had tried to distance myself from the inner workings at Petro-Saudi ever since the whole fiasco in 2010, when the oil exploration company had failed to generate any sort of profit—profit that 1MDB as a heavily invested partner in the venture could then show on the books in its required annual report due in March of the year but that, by that time, was way overdue. That was when Patrick Mahony basically tried to blame the venture's initial failures on me, on my partying lifestyle. Whatever. That was also when we came up with the creative accounting solution of converting 1MDB's original one-billion-dollar investment in PetroSaudi to a $1.2 billion Islamic loan due in ten years, which, in turn, enabled the Malaysian fund to show a profit of $200 million for the year. Just one of those financial obstacles I had to clear, as I said before.

That was all well and good, except for the fact that, if the principals at PetroSaudi didn't get their asses in gear soon and do some genuine, substantial business that turned an actual—and significant—profit, all the Islamic loan conversion was doing was kicking the can down the road, which is to say, 1MDB would have to show profits in the succeeding years against their investment loan to PetroSaudi. Or to put it even more simply than that, PetroSaudi needed to *make some damn money*! But Mahony and Tarek Obaid did absolutely nothing, and Prince Turki, well, the good prince might be likened to Nero fiddling while Rome burned, so, of course, the problem of how to show a profit on 1MDB's books would inevitably come up again—every fiscal year, in fact. Remember that the internal 1MDB fund managers were also doing an abysmally god-awful job of making money themselves, such as in the still foundering, doomed-to-fail Project Wall Street right in their own home capital of Kuala Lumpur. So nobody was generating any substantial income for the Malaysian fund.

In any case, by June 2012, 1MDB's total investment in PetroSaudi had topped $1.8 billion, including the additional $500 million I had convinced Prime Minister Najib to commit to the joint venture, along with about a billion in other assorted funds invested through 1MDB by the SRC International pension fund and similar labor or insurance organizations based in Malaysia. So here once again, some very creative accounting gymnastics were required.

Listen: It gets pretty complicated at this point, and I don't want to waste your time. So I'll just hit the highlights here, okay? Suffice it to say you won't find this in your average university Accounting 101 textbook.

The first thing we did was to convert the 1MDB loan into shares of the PetroSaudi subsidiary—the one called PetroSaudi Oil Services—which owned the two drill ships that it had leased to the Venezuelan oil company I told you about. Then, a few months later, in September 2012, 1MDB sold its PetroSaudi Oil Services shares to another corporate investment entity I had set up in the Cayman Islands called the Bridge Global Fund. The price tag we put on the shares was $2.3 billion, allowing 1MDB to claim a profit of $500 million on the money the Malaysian fund had lent to PetroSaudi.

Only Bridge Global did not pay for the PetroSaudi shares with cash, because, of course, if you're following along here, Bridge Global didn't have any cash. It was just sort of a convenient fiction I came up with. Instead, Bridge Global gave 1MDB what it called *units* in the fund—2.3 billion units, to be exact. There was no money there, you see; these units were basically the emperor's new clothes, yet this transaction seemed to make everyone happy. Pretty ingenious, don't you think? At the time we created Bridge Global, I wasn't too worried about it; to me it was just another hole that I was going to need to fill somewhere down the road when I could get around to it. The only thing was, that hole was getting bigger and bigger all the time. And you know how it is: A lot of times, the bigger things get, the easier they are for a lot more people to actually start seeing them.

With Najib's reelection campaign needing to be maximally fired up the following spring of 2013, I much more urgently needed to focus all of my attention and energies on rushing through 1MDB's latest three billion dollars, Goldman-directed bond issue, and subsequently to acquire the funds from there that were needed to supersize Najib's war chest to the tune of $681 million. Did you get all that? You see, this was the kind of thing that would keep me up all night, usually hunched in front of the dim glow of my computer in the cramped quarters of my private jet at 32,000 feet, looking for the spectacularly lucrative deal that would solve these money-flow problems for 1MDB, even as I was winging off to my next business meeting somewhere on another continent.

Still, the fact that Najib had barely squeaked by to win reelection was also a source of serious concern and anxiety for me. The margin had been razor thin; we had come this close to catastrophe, should the election have been lost.

Hey, I couldn't control public opinion, but as embattled world leaders often do, especially nervous world leaders like the prime minister, I felt that Najib was looking to me, relying on me more as his devoted personal advisor than as a purely political or financial one; he was depending on me to make things right. After all, any public failure in connection with 1MDB would reflect badly on Najib and certainly would have been used against him by the opposition during the campaign, and Najib assumed I was the one who principally was directing the operations of 1MDB. Which was largely accurate. Needless to say, I absolutely did not want Najib to lose faith in me. The very idea was utterly unacceptable.

Fortunately, I well knew the easiest way to win back Najib's complete trust. It was through First Lady Rosmah, and her love for diamonds.

In my quest from time to time to procure the finest jewelry in the world—and the most meaningful, like the ring that, sadly, I had tried and failed to give to Elva Hsiao that fateful evening on the beach in Dubai—I had made the acquaintance of Lorraine Schwartz, the American Jeweler to the Stars. Lorraine had rocketed to fame after one of her uniquely designed pieces was worn by Halle Berry on the red carpet preceding the Academy Awards ceremony, becoming something of a celebrity herself among the glitterati of Hollywood.

In June, while the Razak family was still enjoying a postelection high (never minding how close a call it had been), I tasked Lorraine with finding a very specific item. I messaged her that I wanted a pink heart diamond of vivid quality or, if necessary, one that was no more than an angstrom unit short of vivid. I wanted it to be at least eighteen karats, and I wanted it to become the centerpiece of the most exquisite necklace that Lorraine, using all of her artistic genius, could create.

When Lorraine previewed the necklace for me, I was awestruck. Not since the time, as a schoolboy at Harrow, when I had gone to see the British Crown Jewels in the Tower of London, had I ever beheld such a magnificent piece of jewelry. The perfect pink heart diamond was the biggest such stone I'd ever seen and even more spectacular than I had requested—or even imagined possible.

"Lorraine, you've outdone yourself!" I breathed with excitement. I was literally short of breath.

She smiled lasciviously and flipped her wrist as she cooed, "Why, it's only twenty-two karats."

"'Only'?" I blurted out. "Are you kidding me?"

"Well," Lorraine pouted, "I found a bigger one, but it had a flaw, poor thing. And we can't have Malaysia's First Lady walking around wearing a flawed diamond, can we?"

Indeed not, I thought.

Nor did I stop there, because I wanted to turn this gift into a celebratory event all its own, one that would entertain, excite—even titillate, if you can imagine—Malaysia's First Lady, as Lorraine had so aptly referenced. So I chose an opportunity about a month later, in July, aboard the *Topaz*, Sheikh Mansour's superyacht, cruising serenely off the French Riviera, to bring Rosmah and some of her Malaysian friends together with Lorraine, whom I had directly flown out from the States just for this occasion. Al Husseiny was there as well and, of course, the prime minister himself, when the American jeweler unveiled from the folds of a small silken blanket the most stunningly gorgeous diamond I have ever seen in my life. Rosmah was awestruck, her breath catching in her throat as she gazed at it.

But even that wasn't all, because then we got down to work. Over copious glasses of Cristal champagne, we set about discussing the design of the necklace that would ultimately hold this twenty-two-karat pink diamond, and, of course, it would have to be no ordinary necklace; that was for sure. We decided unanimously on a substantial chain of twenty-four-karat gold studded with a continuous row of white diamonds. In the end, Rosmah was able to feel like she had actually had a hand in designing the exquisite $27.3 million necklace that Lorraine created using all of her talents, making it one of the most expensive single pieces of jewelry in the world. It was, as they say, fit for a queen, and when the finished piece was presented to her, Rosmah Mansor was beside herself with delight. And when Rosmah was happy, the prime minister was happy. And in case you're wondering, I paid for the necklace; or, if you want to get technical—Fat Eric paid for it from the Tanore account.

So, life goes on, right?

Najib got reelected. I'm not a politician; I figured he had paid off the right people (that's how it is done in Malaysia), and I had to be optimistic that, now, he had a whole brand new term to repair the damage that the opposition had done in accusing him of all that nasty corruption and such. Business as usual, I figured, even if my own nerves were a bit shattered from the whole protracted ordeal.

There was another problem that, for some time, had been quietly germinating at PetroSaudi. It was one that, for the longest time, I didn't know anything about, and by the time I learned of it, it was too late.

Through my confidants on the advisory board of 1MDB, like Jasmine Loo and Casey Tang, as well as through regular conversation with Mahony and Obaid at the oil company, I could oversee what was happening at the upper administrative level—the high-stakes financial dealings that needed to be closely managed, such that I was able to control the various investments and restructurings we needed to make, such as the conversion of 1MDB's investment into an Islamic loan and the creation of the Bridge Global Fund and that sort of thing.

However, I could not always see what was going on down with the operational aspects of things, the nuts and bolts part of the operation, if you will. You know—where the actual work of running the company business gets done. Think of it like I'm standing on the bridge of a massive ship, like one of those giant supertankers that carry millions of barrels of crude oil. Up there on the bridge, I have a bird's-eye 360-degree view of the whole horizon; I can see what's going on, and I can direct and navigate where I want the ship to go. But I can't see what's going on below decks, down in the engine room, where I have to rely on the people down there, the machine operators and technicians that need to carry out the orders from the bridge and perform the mechanical work that directs the ship through its proper course to the place I want it to go.

It's the same way with a corporation. I expected Mahony and Obaid to direct the ship of PetroSaudi to work vigorously at making the venture, at minimum, a functioning success turning a respectable profit. Had they the good fortune to discover and ultimately extract crude oil from the godforsaken regions in Europe and South America, where there was supposed to exist such world-shaking underground reserves (it *was* possible in theory, even in spite of the enormous risks and logistical challenges), well, then, so much the better. In that case, we would be talking windfall profits, and you already know how much I love windfall profits. And of course, I expected they needed to hire technical people to handle the day-to-day operations—competent, highly professional people they could trust—to keep critical information about the company business to the company, to keep everything absolutely confidential. Bottom line: I also expected the two principals of PetroSaudi to stay focused on doing their jobs, to diligently perform their leadership roles in guiding the company to make substantial profits. That's what great companies are supposed to do.

So shortly after the joint venture with 1MDB goes through, Obaid hires a friend and business associate of his, a fellow named Xavier Justo.

You have to try to picture this guy. Tall and lanky, about 6'5", with a shock of tousled blond hair, Justo is from San Jose, on the West Coast of the U.S., and he looks, when I first meet him, every bit like the California surfer dude you would think of if I said to you, "Think of a California surfer dude." It's ironic, in a way, but I often think that, had I met Justo under different circumstances, with his rugged Southern California good looks and his chiseled physique, I might have even introduced him to my Hollywood friends and set him off on a career as a heartthrob movie star, the next Paul Newman or Robert Redford. He looks that good, and there is a certain dreamy charisma in his personality.

But Justo is way more than just a pretty face. He's no dummy, earning both his undergraduate degree and his MBA, I was told, in five years at UCLA. And apparently, he was a good enough collegiate soccer player that, after bouncing around a number of professional teams among the typically haphazard league systems in the U.S., Justo was actually highly regarded enough as a midfielder to get a shot at playing in Europe. The team he tried out for was Manchester City—the team owned by Sheikh Mansour.

Without going through all of the complicated genealogical math, that was the connection through which Obaid and Justo became friends, and that led to Obaid hiring Justo to run the London office of PetroSaudi.

You see, Justo managed to earn a prized spot on the roster with Manchester City for about a season and a half, but he just wasn't able to measure up to the stratospheric level of play in the British Premier League. Nevertheless, he developed a love for England and the old city of London in particular, so he stuck around, landing a job with a British investment bank before striking out on his own by founding a financial services firm in the banking district known casually as the "City of London."

Justo also owned a significant share in a London nightclub with the not-so-original name the Premier Club, which did decent but not spectacular business. This was just another convenient connection, because when he was in London, Tarek Obaid liked to frequent the Premier Club.

When the initial joint venture between PetroSaudi and 1MDB went through, Justo naturally jumped to accept Obaid's offer to make him the managing director of PetroSaudi's London office at a very respectable salary of £400,000 but with the prospect of millions more in bonuses and performance incentives. In fact, Obaid offered Justo a couple million pounds in payment just for procuring and opening the London office.

One imagines that Justo, had he been reasonable, should have been very happy with that and that, therefore, this should have been the end of the Justo story. But it didn't turn out that way. Not at all. And actually, I blame Patrick Mahony and Obaid for what happened next at PetroSaudi. Which was nothing. I mean the company did absolutely nothing. To this day, I don't think that PetroSaudi at that time ever succeeded in sinking even one stinking exploratory oil well anywhere on the planet in search of the goldmine of oil reserves it had the development rights to.

Nobody could more easily observe this than Justo. He had virtually nothing to do. At first, one could imagine, this was fine with him, as it might be to any guy. You land a job at a great salary, there's no immediate pressure, so you are able to ease into things. You're given license to travel around the world a bit—first class—on the company's dime, so you do that for a while. Life is good, right? So at first, Justo is satisfied; he jets off, ostensibly on business, to tour the Middle East or to Kuala Lumpur and Singapore, sometimes to New York City. But Justo is an ambitious guy, a guy who wants to actually accomplish something. He's like me; he wants to conduct some real business, to be productive. For a time, he gets to work on the extensive arrangements involved in leasing PetroSaudi's two drill ships to the state-run oil company in Venezuela, requiring him to make numerous trips shuttling back and forth to Caracas and Maracaibo, but that's about it; he's just going through the motions, although it was Justo, by the way, who informed me what a couple of shitty, rusting hulks these "billion dollar" drill ships actually were, and, from what he told me, it's amazing they didn't sink to the bottom of the Atlantic on their way to South America.

So Justo is bored out of his mind and frustrated, and he is starting to get very upset about the state of affairs. But it gets worse.

When he complains to Obaid and Mahony about the situation, the two bosses of PetroSaudi are unmoved. Obaid is too busy renting private jets to fly between Europe and the Middle East, or renting superyachts on the Mediterranean off the southern coasts of Spain, France, and Italy. When he's not soaking up the sun on the French Riviera, Obaid and one or more of his girlfriends are jetting off on shopping junkets to New York or Beverly Hills and LA. Meanwhile, after having their first child, Mahony and his wife at this time settle into a £6.2 million townhouse they purchased in London's Ladbroke Square, overlooking the abundant greenery of a nearby park. Around the shopping districts of London, Mahony is flashing his Amex Black credit card, the exclusive, very-hard-to-get kind that is mostly used by mega-celebrities and billionaires and that you usually need the services of a private banker at, say, J.P. Morgan or Goldman Sachs to obtain.

In fact, most of Justo's time is taken up dealing with what you might call the grunt work for PetroSaudi's principals, like arranging jet travel and yacht rentals for Obaid or filling out the paperwork for Mahony's exclusive credit cards or watering the office plants—that sort of thing—the kinds of mundane things that a personal secretary might be required to do for the CEO of a major international company. Certainly not the duties of a respected managing director.

Yet neither of these two guys seems at all interested, as far as Justo can tell, in doing anything to attend to the business of running PetroSaudi. And this—*this*—is why PetroSaudi is making absolutely no money and why I am having to scramble to restructure—and restructure again—the oil exploration company's financial relationship with 1MDB. It's why Justo realizes that none of those bonuses and performance incentives are ever going to happen. To add insult to injury, the company falls way behind in his salary payments; the two million pounds he was promised to open the London office never materializes, and he even winds up having to cover some of his business travel expenses in connection with executing the drill ship leasing deal with Venezuela.

And Justo, perhaps rightly, seeing all of this decadent extravagance on the part of Obaid and Mahony while he's clearly getting the short end of the stick, Justo begins to feel like he's being used, and, more ominously, he begins to suspect that something's just not right about PetroSaudi. Honestly, who could blame him for his suspicions?

So, barely a year after he joined the company, back in the spring of 2011, Justo decides he's going to quit PetroSaudi, but he has no intention of going quietly. When, in April, he informs his friend Obaid of his intention to leave, Justo demands an immediate severance of 6.5 million British pounds. That's not as outrageous as it might sound, when you think about it, because much of that was money Justo felt he had been promised, like the two million pounds he was due for operationalizing the London office. If he wanted an extra couple million for his troubles and what he felt was his wasted time, well again, who could blame him for at least trying?

However, when Mahoney Calls Obaid up and relays this demand, Obaid flies into a rage. He's so angry that he declares he will never speak to Justo again. When Mahony tries to intercede as peacemaker, Obaid roars at him, "Tell that son of a bitch he can go to hell!"

Somehow, Mahony manages to calm his volatile partner down, at least momentarily.

"I'll handle it," Mahony reassures Obaid. "I'll meet with Justo and iron things out."

Mahony suggests what he feels is a reasonable figure; both of them know or believe that it's still too high, but Mahony thinks it will be enough to make Justo go away.

"This is fucking extortion!" Obaid yells into the phone. Still practically incandescent with anger, Obaid nevertheless finally agrees and immediately hangs up the line.

The meeting with Justo occurs privately in a back room of the Premier Club, where Mahony offers the soon-to-be-former employee a reduced severance of five million pounds. Justo grudgingly accepts the offer.

The matter could have been settled right there, if all of the parties had stuck to their word. But when push came to shove, Obaid later unilaterally reduced the amount to four million pounds. Now it was Justo who was livid, feeling that he'd been cheated out of £2.5 million. To make matters even worse, Obaid proceeded to go around openly bad-mouthing Justo to just about anybody who would listen, including Tim Leissner, calling Justo a loser and an ingrate who owed everything to PetroSaudi. This served no purpose other than to enrage Justo all the more.

So Justo devised a plan. Before he left the company, begrudgingly taking his "meager" severance with him, Justo took something else. He arranged with an unsuspecting PetroSaudi IT technician to obtain a copy of the company's computer servers—some 140 gigabytes of data, much of it highly confidential, and including nearly a half million emails, documents, and official papers—the very blueprint and corporate life-history of PetroSaudi, all in a big bunch of electronic computer files.

So I have to be very clear about this: I have no idea what Justo knew or suspected he knew about PetroSaudi and its dealings with 1MDB, whether or not he believed anything seriously illegal had been perpetrated. I'd be the first to acknowledge, as I already have, that I was never one to always do things by the book. I'm much too financially creative for that. But I insist that everything I did, from orchestrating the initial joint venture with PetroSaudi and beyond, I did with 1MDB's best interests in mind—as well as those of Prime Minister Najib, of course, and, I might add, I did them with Najib's blessings.

I learned from Mahony and Obaid about this blowup with Justo sort of after the fact, before anyone knew that he had taken the copy of the servers with him. But even without knowing that, I was nevertheless upset over the bad blood that had been created. You never want that sort of thing to emerge and fester, particularly at such a high level, across what amounts to the executive suite of the company. And you certainly don't want your key executives going around airing the company's dirty laundry publicly, as Obaid had done. When I did find out, I was pretty pissed at both Obaid and Mahony for their inept mishandling of this whole affair. With all the capital at their disposal, and—my god—with all they were lavishing on themselves, what was so hard about just writing Justo a check for £6.5 million and sending him packing—maybe even presenting him with a gift-wrapped, first-class one-way ticket back to America, for chrissakes, to LA perhaps. Maybe he could have gotten a job there doing TV commercials with that pretty face of his.

Of course, I didn't know it at the time, but from the moment he left PetroSaudi in about August 2011, and after the way Obaid and Mahony had mishandled the whole affair, Justo and his cache of extremely vital and highly sensitive company information was nothing but a quietly ticking time bomb waiting to explode.

Chapter 14

After all I had done for the Razak family, making Riza a moviemaking mogul in Hollywood, showering Rosmah with her beloved diamonds, and—most of all—helping get Najib reelected, I felt I deserved a little reward too.

Even before the votes were finally counted, I placed an order with the Dutch shipbuilding firm Oceanco to build a stunningly beautiful superyacht for myself. At three hundred feet in length and a cost of $250 million, it would be modest compared to the *Topaz* of Sheikh Mansour, but hell, I'm not greedy! Regardless, it would still rank as one of the most luxurious superyachts in the world—something that I could be proud of.

As I did with everything, I saw to every meticulous detail. I think I drove the Oceanco technicians fairly crazy, right down to referring them to experts at Tempur in choosing the most comfortable mattresses for the beds in the six staterooms and the mind-bending, Dali-esque melting lighting fixtures by British designer Tom Dixon.

My boat would have a helipad, a movie theater, a gymnasium and a sauna, a 2,000-bottle wine cellar, and enormous outdoor decks capable of accommodating dozens of my usual partygoers. It would also have a dazzling bar sophisticated enough to match the interior of any of my most favorite, intimate nightclubs in New York City. I wanted it to be perfect. When completed, my superyacht would have ultra-luxury overnight accommodations for up to twenty-eight guests; however, it would also have very comfortable quarters for thirty sailing crew and waitstaff. I wanted, you see, to make sure that there was enough support staff to see to every desire of my onboard guests and party attendees.

Some people at the time, even some of my closest associates and friends, questioned why I commissioned the building of a superyacht at such a hectic time, when I had so many other financial deals in the works. I think they could see how stressed I was becoming with all that was going on. Yet there were a number of solid reasons, some of them quite practical and at least one that I admit was not so practical.

First of all, as you have seen by now, I had established a particular style of enticing and gathering together the kinds of business partners I wanted. It was by throwing the most lavish and most spectacular parties anyone had ever experienced and luring to those events some of the wealthiest business and investment people in the world through the prospect of cavorting with celebrity music and movie pop stars, whether I paid for them to be there and perform or whether they just showed up, as they often did once the word got around. Because the word definitely got around that one really needed to experience one of my events to believe the hype that came to surround them.

Pretty shallow, some might think, but there's no denying how well it worked. Once the Burberry- and Brooks Brothers- and Hugo Boss–suited banker and investment types loosened their ties a bit, and once they met a movie star or two, or perhaps danced with one of the gorgeous models I employed precisely for these occasions, they were just a lot easier to do business with. Oh yeah, well, they may have been a little distracted in the moment, but like a narcotic that sublimely takes time to wear off, their ease about doing business would last long into the afterglow.

Accordingly, I couldn't just stop doing those events altogether. What would people think? I had embarked on a methodology, call it a business development plan if you want, and I had to stay the course, or people might think something had gone wrong. "When's the next party going to happen?" they would ask. "Are we doing San Tropez again next spring?" they would hound me. "Can't wait to see you in Vegas!"

I couldn't let them all down.

At the same time, I was concerned about all the publicity that was building around my events. Even celebrities talk, and even if they might publicly criticize the paparazzi or voice their outrage over salacious "unwanted" tabloid coverage, even the most famous celebrities know, deep down inside, that one needs to stay in the public eye or risk falling like a stone into the abyss of obscurity. In the entertainment business, it's always "What have you done lately?" or "What blockbuster are you working on now?" or "When is your next song coming out?"

In some ways, I didn't really care about any of this, particularly in the early days. As long as it was mainly the tabloids and the gossip columnists, as long as they were focused on the entertainment glitterati, that was fine. It served the purpose I mentioned earlier, of attracting the business and banking moguls I wanted to work with, and, in turn, the publicity from one event attracted even more celebrities to the next, which attracted even more business and banking people and so on and so on in a very productive cycle that suited my plans quite nicely, as long as the glare of the media lights and cameras were focused on the movie and pop music stars and not on me and my prospective business clients. For them, anonymity was essential, although it didn't help matters when some guys, like Al Qubaisi, so openly acted like asses at my parties. But that's another story we've already pretty much covered.

The problem was that some of my associates and business partners, not to mention my own business deals, were starting to receive increasing scrutiny from the more serious journalists who were researching and writing not about pop stars and movie actors but about international business investment and finance or politics. No longer were the photographers and journalists just a bunch of hacks from the *National Enquirer* or *People Magazine* or Page Six of the *New York Daily News* in the U.S. or the *Sun* and the *Daily Mirror* (and about a dozen other rags) in the UK, the sensation-seeking gossip columnists that I could just dismiss. They were increasingly the financial pages writers from the *Wall Street Journal* and the *New York Times* and the *Times* of London or *Forbes* magazine. They were political journalists from the independent *Edge* newspaper right in Malaysia itself, the only paper that, insidiously, Najib did not have any editorial control over whatsoever. They were asking a lot of questions, and this was all very decidedly bad for business.

In hindsight, I suppose I should have anticipated that the bigger the international deals got and the more players that became involved, the more likely it was that people would talk. Often, it was people whom you'd think would know better. On the business side of things, I got really angry when I learned about how Gary Cohn—the president and CEO of Goldman Sachs, no less—had bragged to a bunch of New York financial journalists attending a political charity gala in Manhattan about the enormous fees Goldman had been making selling (more accurately, that they were buying and upselling) the various bonds issues for Malaysia's 1MDB fund. Damned if Cohn's indiscretion didn't find its way into an extensive article published in early 2013 in the *Wall Street Journal* titled "Goldman Sees Huge Profit in Malaysian Capital Fund Bet."

Most of the executives on the advisory board of 1MDB read the *Wall Street Journal*—every single issue, from the front page to the classifieds. They were none too pleased. The article made them look like fools. Of course, some of them were; I'm talking about the ones who simply could not grasp my greater vision for the enormous future potential of the fund.

This was right about the time leading up to Najib's reelection, and it broke into the open for all to see the huge and atypical windfalls that Goldman was making with each successive bond issue—information that should have been so confidential that it makes your head spin to think how stupid Cohn was to reveal it to the press in the first place. It was just unfathomable to me why these otherwise very conservative and close-to-the-vest investment professionals couldn't seem to keep their damn mouths shut. But then, I had learned perhaps a little too late that the biggest, most unabashed egotists in the world are apparently drawn to Wall Street and so too, I learned the hard way, are the world's biggest braggarts. The two are essentially two sides of the same coin.

Politically, there's no doubt that Najib's dispersal of millions of ringgit during his reelection campaign ensured his reelection; that much was plain. However, the sheer recklessness and utter transparency of it also served to fuel the growing chorus of accusations of corruption leveled at him by the opposition, as well as garner even greater scrutiny of his political and personal affairs by the media. It's an open question whether, had he been more discrete, he might have avoided some of that scrutiny and staved off some of that bad press. By this point, however, probably not. What one is left to ponder then, was Najib's mysterious attitude toward all of this: He seemed certainly to care not at all. More and more, as the "donations" to his accounts poured in, Najib seemed to insidiously buy into the notion that he was doing nothing wrong, that this is how successful elections are won. More and more, he blamed the bad press and the questions about his leadership on his political enemies.

So as time went on, articles began regularly appearing in the *Edge*, and the *Straits Times*, out of Singapore, as well as other independent Southeast Asian newspapers basically asking where Najib had gotten all that money he had spent on the campaign while editorial opinion pieces in those papers repeatedly accused him of buying—or outright stealing—the election. Some journalists—most prominently, editor Ho Kay Tat of the *Edge*—upon reviewing the lackluster performance of the 1MDB fund, began to openly question, had all that campaign money somehow come from 1MDB? They had no direct proof, of course. I had covered the tracks of the financial transactions pretty well. You've got to love all those offshore banking havens where, unlike the executives at Goldman, they know how to keep things confidential—*they* being both the banks and the investment-friendly governments that run these havens and who very obligingly keep their mouths shut. Still, for Najib anyway, these insidious newspaper articles and editorial columns did nothing but stir up trouble among the citizens of Malaysia while also emboldening the opposition parties.

Then, a couple of months after the election, the first newspaper article talking specifically about me appeared in a national business weekly called *Focus Malaysia*. It was the cover story, and it was titled "Just Who Is Jho Low?" with the subtitle "And What Is His Connection to 1MDB?"

Though it certainly raised my blood pressure to see it, the article did little more than make a bunch of unsubstantiated claims about my connections to Abu Dhabi and the Middle East, about my purchase of a stake in EMI, and about my involvement with the Red Granite company's production of *The Wolf of Wall Street* while rather lamely trying to trump up some connection between those business dealings and whatever role I supposedly had in connection with 1MDB. Here, again, they had no proof, and the article failed rather miserably, as I saw it.

Regardless, the appearance of the *Focus Malaysia* cover story did nothing to soothe my nerves, I can tell you that. I had always gone to great pains, from the day I introduced Al Mubarak of the Mubadala fund to then–Deputy Prime Minister Najib when I pulled off the Iskandar development deal, right up to Najib's successful pursuit of a second term as PM, to be the prime mover to be sure but to remain in the background. Anonymity afforded creative latitude in my business dealings; it was the quality that, more than any other, would allow me to achieve greatness.

I didn't like any of this publicity nonsense. Not one bit. Which takes me back to getting my own private superyacht.

If you put all of this together, it ought to be pretty obvious how having my own boat solved a whole mess of problems. I could continue to host my signature parties and conduct my high-level business deals in a highly appropriate setting, given the luxurious amenities of the boat. I could do so anywhere in the world, out of reach of the paparazzi or nosy business and political writers—even beyond the reach of the legal authorities, when you think about it.

Read: complete anonymity.

Hell, I could party in international waters if I wanted. Not going to get any party crashers out there, surrounded by the sharks! Am I right?

The thing was, I was starting to worry about the law. Not that I had done anything illegal. I was beginning to worry about the prospect of having to explain my financial and investment work to authorities—you know, like banking authorities and government regulators—and to be called on to answer the questions the media was starting to ask. To have to explain all of this to people who I knew would not understand what I was doing, nor especially why I was doing it, well, that was just going to be impossible.

After all, genius is often misunderstood.

I needed time for my investments on behalf of 1MDB to really take off. When that happened, everybody would certainly understand. Everything would be cool after that. I'd be able to plug all of the financial holes I admit I created. But, in the meantime, in the case of an emergency, the yacht could be moved anywhere in the world at a moment's notice—with me on it. You didn't have to file a flight plan, and you didn't have to land, in most cases, at a public port like whenever I flew on my private jet. On a superyacht, you don't have to land at all, metaphorically speaking. Besides, once I had my own boat, I would finally be spared the humiliation of having to rent or lease them from other people, like the *Topaz* from Sheikh Mansour or a bunch of others from crummy agencies like Yachtzoo, as I had so often done in the past.

Okay, so this was that not-so-practical reason that I mentioned earlier, why I wanted my own boat—a despicably prideful reason, perhaps. I'll admit that, but it was what it was.

I have to tell you about the very first superyacht I ever rented, and I'm pretty certain it's going to shock you, because I was barely eighteen at the time. Technically speaking, I didn't so much rent the boat as borrow it for a couple of weeks.

It was in my hometown of Penang, in the summer of 1999, the summer after my graduation from Harrow and the last summer I would spend there before going off to Wharton, in the United States.

THE ART OF GREED

I had invited a number of my Harrow schoolmate friends to spend part of their summer in Malaysia, and to my surprise—and delight—they had agreed. But there was a bit of a problem. Let me explain.

Don't get me wrong; my father, Larry Low, had been successful in business and, among the general community of Chinese Malaysians, we were reasonably well off, certainly better than most. My father was educated; he had graduated from the London School of Economics and then earned his MBA from the University of California, Los Angeles. But the truth of the matter was that Larry never earned a great deal of money through his employment in the accounting departments of the string of companies he toiled for over his lifetime. Rather, he invested very shrewdly. He was also damn lucky, because he happened to do that investing at a time—in the 1990s—when Malaysia's stock market was taking off like a rocket. The economy was growing at five percent annually, sometimes higher, powered by an array of commodity exports—everything from palm oil, lumber, and other forest products to computer chips and electronic devices, not to mention crude oil and liquefied natural gas. Those were the hot export products at the time—still are. Yet ironically, my father snagged his biggest windfall through his investments in Malaysia's burgeoning garment industry—all that cheap labor making T-shirts and sneakers and baseball caps for the great unwashed of the world. When Larry pulled the trigger in selling his minority stake in one garment company alone—that being MWE, one of the largest clothing manufacturers in all of Southeast Asia—his payout was over fifteen million U.S. dollars.

By the way, my father was the one who introduced my brother, sister, and me to the distinct advantages of offshore finance and banking, so impressing my sister, in fact, that May Lin went on to become an attorney specializing in offshore investment vehicles and an enormous help to me in my investment endeavors. What is it that the most savvy investors say? "It's not the money you make; it's the money you keep."

So this was all well and good, and it enabled my father to send me to Harrow and to Wharton, where I could gain the educational pedigree I needed to achieve a bright and prosperous future, blah, blah, blah.

But the kids from Harrow who were coming to visit that summer in Penang, they all came from families that measured their wealth and stature in billions of dollars, not lousy millions. Frankly, I was ashamed, and I've already told you how much I hated what a backwater outpost in the middle of nowhere I always perceived Penang to be. *Just wait till they see this dump*, I thought and agonized.

So what was a boy to do?

Well, my father had a good friend—I'll call him Zack, although that's not his real name—who owned a superyacht that I'll call the *Star of the Orient*. She was only 160 feet long but luxurious in her own right. He kept the *Star of the Orient* moored at a government marina right there on Penang Island, just across the slight spit of blue water that separates the island from the main peninsular heart of the city. I begged Larry to ask his friend to let me borrow the *Orient* for a couple of weeks, just as long as my Harrow friends were in town. Somehow, my father seemed to understand, and that's what I did. Before my friends arrived, you know, well, I just went through that boat and—god help me—wherever there were photographs of Zack's children or of him and his family up on mantelpieces or on bedroom night tables, I swear that I went around and removed those pictures out of their frames, and I replaced them with photographs of my own family. For two weeks, for all appearances, the *Star of the Orient* belonged to my family, and my Harrow friends would never be the wiser. Zack even arranged for the elite sailing crew of the *Orient* to take us out to sea a time or two.

I can't say that I'm particularly proud of that now, when I reflect on it, as I sit stuck here in this locked-up mausoleum; you want to talk about being in the middle of nowhere? I realize now for how much of my existence I have been living a lie and from so early on in my life. The *Orient* was only the beginning. Contrary to what some people have said or written about me, I never told anyone at Harrow or Wharton that I was some sort of Malaysian prince, from a royal family, or any other bullshit like that. But once the rumors started,

I never did or said anything to stop them either, so that much is true. I'll tell you one thing: It was more often the case than not that people's crazy perceptions of me and what they believed about my background opened doors to opportunities I never would have had otherwise. Let's make no mistake about it: Whenever people let me through those doors, simply because of who they thought I was, I could get things done like nobody else. That's a fact too.

In the end, I make no excuses for my little *Star of the Orient* charade. All I can say for myself in those days is that I was very ambitious—that inner, all-consuming, intensely burning desire brand of ambitious—and I have stayed that way all of my life.

In my earlier remarks, I postulated that it's impossible for Westerners to fully grasp and wrap their minds around the way my culture embraces, dotes upon, and celebrates the firstborn son, how the eldest male child is abundantly favored over all of his lesser siblings, male and female. I may have taken my resentment a bit too far. I do very much remember, with stinging clarity, when my father's business associates would come to our house, how my father would beam with pride as he introduced Szen as his "number-one" son. There is no denying that, especially because when such formal introduction filtered down to me, I was often described as "Szen's baby brother" or "the baby of the family." Also seared in my memory are the times when Larry took my older brother to his place of work with him, and I was not permitted to go because I was "too young." This despite the fact that should have been obvious to all: that I, far more than Szen, desired to learn about business and enterprise, whereas Szen's attitude toward our father's professional life was ambivalent at best. He'd no doubt have preferred to go out and play in cricket matches with his friends.

One thing I have learned from living in many parts of the world is that these propensities, the distinctions that seem so unfairly accorded the eldest son, are also manifest, more subtly perhaps, in many Western societies, which is to say, more organically, without the ponderous weight of thousands of years of ancient culture. Western families dote on their firstborns simply because it's their first experience with child, just as it is with Asian families. Is such behavior understandable? Is it "natural" in an almost purely biological sense for a father to seem to have—or, more pointedly, to express to others—more effusive pride in his firstborn, even if he is *equally* proud of all of his children? Probably so. Probably, inevitably so.

Still, for reasons I can neither remember nor explain, I saw my father as taking this firstborn favoring thing too far, doting on my older brother Szen, showering him with attention, and I was deeply jealous. And I was hurt.

Somehow, I had to get some of my father's attention for me, or so I felt at the time. I wanted to please and impress him, and, to do that, I knew I wanted to succeed to a spectacular degree beyond anything any father would expect from a culturally inferior, third-in-line miscreant offspring. Even as a child, you see, I wanted to do things big.

When I first asked my father about borrowing Zack's yacht, he laughed at me.

"You can't be serious," he said.

But I was dead serious about it, and we argued for a long time until, I believe, my father was suddenly struck with a mortifying sense of just how hurtfully unequal I felt, measured head to toe and everything in between against my peers at Harrow; make that my classmates, because I in no way felt I qualified as a peer in that realm. Finally, perhaps reluctantly—and who knows, perhaps out of love—my father acquiesced.

"This is really important to you, isn't it?" he said, looking me soberly in the eyes.

I nodded.

"Okay," father sighed. "I'll see what I can do. But I want you to remember something. You have nothing to be ashamed of. You understand?"

"Yes, father," I replied, not expressing that, in my reality of those days, I would have begged to differ.

I guess you could say, if you wanted to play psychologist or psychoanalyst, that my earliest desires to achieve unparalleled success were culturally, even genetically driven by my heritage and the way my father treated me in the context of that heritage or by the way that *I thought* he treated me. It was my ultimate desire to please him—that whole Freudian subconscious resolution of the Oedipal complex, desperately seeking approval of the father bullshit. Only maybe it's not bullshit after all, because I can tell you there were times when I felt it to my core. You could say that my father made me the man I am. Oh good heavens!

He did, after all, get the yacht for me.

Sometimes I wonder if my father allowing me to pretend the yacht was ours was a way of giving me permission to create this false narrative, as if covering up my second-son status. I have also wondered if he regarded my older brother as not needing an invented persona, as being above such nonsense by virtue of his superior birthright. These days, whenever the ugly notion rears its head, that my father never gave me the attention I sought from him. He did, after all, pay for the party on the yacht, he did indulge me that much, and more, I am obliged to confess. I have to wonder: Had I asked too much? Had I wanted the one thing he could never give me—the status of the firstborn? That which was purely an accident of birth completely beyond my father's control?

Perhaps I might admit that, yes, I ordered my own superyacht to prove that I had succeeded beyond his or anybody else's wildest dreams. Owning my own superyacht felt symbolic of that massive achievement in my life and exceeded anything my father had ever done for me. And far exceeded anything his favored firstborn son had ever done.

In the end, however, I think what I needed most in those very hectic days following Najib's election was much more practical: a private sanctuary where I could put my mind at peace, if only for short stretches of time, so that I could then return to business with renewed vigor and a positive attitude. I thought, what could be better than an ultra-comfortable, ultra-private yacht as a kind of floating sanctuary, lulled by a gently rolling sea like the Mediterranean, for instance, or the South Pacific, as a place where I could escape all the petty, hand-wringing troubles of the people on the land?

So that's what I did. I ordered my own superyacht. And I decided that I would name it *Equanimity*, which means calmness and composure, even under stress.

Chapter 15

This is when the murders started.

In July 2013, less than three months after Najib was reelected prime minister, Hussain Najadi and his wife were murdered outside a Chinese temple in Kuala Lumpur. Actually, they weren't so much murdered as assassinated. Gunned down in broad daylight by a man clad head to toe in black, wearing a black hood over his head, a Ninja-looking guy with a Chinese-made Type 95 assault rifle, who fled the scene in a black, late-model Mercedes S-Class with darkly tinted windows, driven by an accomplice unseen behind the glass.

Najadi was the Bahraini chairman and CEO of the AIAK banking conglomerate that was originally formed as the Arab Malaysian Development Banking Group. He was also the founder and CEO of AmBank, where, coincidently, Prime Minister Najib happened to have most of his personal and business accounts. Most recently, AmBank was where the $681 million had been deposited earlier that spring by Tanore Finance Corporation, in the two separate tranches through Al Qubaisi's Falcon Bank, in Switzerland. The account from which Najib drew the funds he needed to finance his successful reelection campaign. That money.

As prominent and respected a figure as the AmBank CEO was in the larger business community of Malaysia, there was strikingly little that appeared in the mainstream newspapers or Malaysian

TV about this horrific killing, as shocking and abrupt as it was. Oh, it made the headlines, all right, the lead story that flashed across all the six p.m. nightly news TV broadcasts and the front pages of all of the major dailies across the countries of Southeast Asia the next morning. But the details were vexingly sketchy. The media reported that Najadi and his wife had been murdered, that the gunman had fled the scene in the big Mercedes, with a couple of the news outlets quoting an anonymous source, supposedly a high-ranking official within the police department, who suggested that the murderer had already managed to escape the country, although, again, the source provided no other details. That the murderer had gotten away just seemed incredible, given, shall I say, the general militancy of most Malaysian law enforcement.

But that was about all the newspapers said. No one seemed to even speculate as to *why* Najadi had been targeted; it was clearly a planned hit. They all just . . . reported it. Like a fact, like you would report the closing numbers for the trading day on the Hang Seng or the Nikkei Index, or the day's soccer results in the Euro conference or the UK Premier League. "In sports today, Manchester City have upset Liverpool one–nil." Like that. Strangely, within a few days, Najadi's murder seemed to have simply disappeared from the news, at least from the front page.

Anyway, for some reason, it all confounded and disturbed me. What had been the reason? I did not know Najadi well; probably my only connections with him were through faceless texts and emails, perhaps a murky video conference call or two in connection with the prime minister's business and investment dealings. But from what I did know of him, he had seemed a competent if unremarkable investment banker, very straightforward in his dealings with me or anyone else, as far as I could tell.

I resolved to talk to Prime Minister Najib about it as soon as I got the chance. Which I got, fortunately, pretty quickly, just a couple of weeks after Najadi's demise, on Sheikh Mansour's superyacht *Topaz*, when we gathered together off the French Riviera, in part to celebrate Najib's win in the election but especially to bestow on

First Lady Rosmah the gift of the fabulous pink diamond necklace procured and curated by Lorraine Schwartz.

One night after dinner, I managed to get Najib alone in one of the more subdued staterooms aboard the *Topaz*. Elegantly paneled in exotic Cypress wood all around, with several sets of built-in book shelves brimming with books and adorned with green-shaded brass lamps on a couple of mahogany end tables, the stateroom resembled a reading room in a London library. The single picture window that ran floor to ceiling was smaller than those in the party rooms, only about three feet wide, giving the room a more intimate, confidential feel, the kind of space where people talk in very low voices, judiciously voicing only thoughtful thoughts.

I always knew Najib to be a very quiet man, very reserved—unless, of course, one made him angry. But on this night, I remember, he seemed even more pensive than usual. I poured out a couple of generous glasses of Graham's forty-year-old tawny port from a crystal decanter that sat on the carved rosewood sideboard, and as I handed one of them to the prime minister, I decided this was as good a time as there was ever going to be to broach the subject of Najadi's tragic death.

When I asked Najib about it, I could swear that he seemed, at first, to smile thinly, until his smile morphed into a grimace. Najib looked down at his glass of port, swirling it in his hand, as if pondering his response before speaking it out loud.

"There are many things you don't know about Mr. Najadi," Najib said. His voice was grim, deeply serious. "Some things you don't need to know," the prime minister continued, looking me directly in the eyes. "But what I can tell you is that he was involved with some very bad people, some very corrupt individuals—gangland organizations—and not just in our country. You'd be shocked if I were to tell you. You see, Jho, just because one is the president of the most prestigious bank in Malaysia doesn't automatically make one an outstanding pillar of the community."

I think I was wide-eyed with these revelations—what the prime minister was suggesting. I said, "But to be murdered in cold blood like that? Right there in the street? And in the middle of the day!" I still hadn't quite been able to wrap my head around the whole affair.

Najib shrugged. "I suspect he crossed someone very powerful," he said. "Najadi could be very arrogant at times—bull-headed, you might say—and this time it seems to have gotten him in more trouble than he bargained for. I think it's just a shame they killed his wife too. There wasn't any reason for that."

"What do you mean?" I asked.

Najib looked at me abruptly, as if surprised by my question, his eyes widening slightly.

"Well," he said, emphatically, waving his free hand in the air, "it sounds like a botched hit, doesn't it? Why would anyone be so cruel as to target his wife as well? Certainly, she didn't do anything to deserve that."

"I don't know," I said, shaking my head. "Maybe she simply got caught in the crossfire," I speculated.

Najib pursed his lips together tightly and shrugged again. "Perhaps," he replied. "Still, even if there was some bad business going on, it's hard to imagine how anyone could do such a horrible thing to Najadi," the prime minister added. "Such a shame," he said, shaking his head in disgust.

Pausing to take a sip from his glass of port, Najib turned and stepped idly, in a manner of indifference, toward the picture window, where he bent forward slightly, squinting through the glass, as if trying to peer out into the Mediterranean darkness. What struck me at that instant was the realization that all he could see in the blackness of that night, in that moment, was his own reflection shimmering in the glass, pierced by tiny pinpricks of light from the nightclubs that were still open on the distant shore of San Tropez. He seemed uncomfortable about something.

Then, without turning to look at me directly and still peering into the darkness, Najib seemed to ask the window, "This man the police are looking for, the one named Koon Swee Kang, do you know him?" It was a curious question, and there was something odd about the way he said this, like he was probing for something, like maybe he had some bizarre notion I knew something about all of this. Or was he actually accusing me of knowing something, when the opposite was absolutely true?

I could only shudder. "I should say not!" I responded emphatically.

"Well," Najib said, finally turning and looking up, smiling thinly again. "He has connections to organized crime from Malaysia to Thailand, India, possibly China, and who knows, even further beyond that. He's a hit man, do you realize?"

"What? Seriously?"

"Oh sure," Najib said, shaking his head with conviction, his lips pressed tightly together as he once again swirled the aromatic amber liquid in his glass. "He's done this sort of thing before. Not in Malaysia, of course, but in those other countries? Oh, yes. And he's been caught, convicted, and put in prison before too, even gone to death row, but, somehow, he always manages to get himself back on the street."

"He escapes?" I asked.

"Of course," Najib replied casually. "They leave the door open for him. Either that or he buys his way out. He pays off the guards, and off he goes. Or, I should say, his organization pays off the guards on his behalf. After that, he travels freely across all of Asia, even though there's an Interpol Red Notice for his arrest, because his organization has enough Interpol agents on their payroll as well. There are some thugs, you do understand, who wear nice neat uniforms, right?

"But when we catch him, that's not going to happen, I can assure you. I'm going to see to it personally that, this time, he's executed before he can pull out his checkbook or before his gangland friends can save him. With my new administration, I'm simply not going to stand for this sort of organized criminal corruption in our country, with gang members just going around murdering people at will. The criminals have to be taught: You commit a murderous crime in Malaysia, you will be swiftly brought to justice. I assure you, Jho, we will apprehend Koon very soon. We believe he is hiding somewhere in Thailand at this very moment, and he will face the consequences for his despicable actions."

All of this might easily have been taken from a scripted page from one of Najib's campaign stump speeches—that is, until he continued, now off-script.

"That is, of course, unless the police kill him first. In which case, justice will be even swifter, and it will save the taxpayers a lot of money by avoiding a long trial." Najib smiled wryly as he said this.

As he spoke, I wondered how Najib knew all of this. None of the papers or the broadcast news media had reported the alleged murderer's name, and the seemingly clueless regular police apparently knew only that Najadi's assassin had somehow managed to escape Malaysia right through their fingers immediately after the murder.

Then I remembered that—of course—Najib had the considerable benefit of reconnaissance through his close, confidential coordination with the UTK, the Unit Tindakhas—the secret branch of the Royal Malaysia Police that was essentially Najib's private security detail. And, I thought, if Koon was unfortunate enough to be apprehended by the UTK rather than the regular police, he'd be enormously lucky to survive long enough thereafter to see justice rendered inside a Malaysian courtroom.

There was still the matter of who had hired Koon to assassinate Najadi and why.

"I don't know the answer to that question," Najib said. "But I'm determined to find out. I have my suspicions—" Suddenly, Najib became agitated.

"But you watch," the prime minister continued, his voice angry now. "My political enemies and the independent press will try to make a big deal out of this. They'll try to turn it into some fake news, some politically motivated thing, and try to claim that I had something to do with it. The press have hated me since I shocked them all by getting reelected—except for the papers I control, of course. Those papers will tell the true story, because, I'll just tell you this much, Najadi got himself mixed up in some dirty dealings with the mob, and I'm afraid he paid the price for it. I'll get to the bottom of—"

At that moment, Najib was interrupted by an abrupt knock on the door of the stateroom. We both watched as the door swung open fluidly, smooth as silk on its brass hinges, and the First Lady, Rosmah, meekly entered the room, resplendent in her array of jewelry, centerpieced by the massive twenty-two-karat pink diamond necklace that I had presented to her earlier that day.

"There you are, darling," Rosmah said to Najib, her face beaming with delight. She looked at both of us, glasses in hand, and she said, "What are you two plotting in here?"

"Nothing, my dear," Najib replied. "We were just having some port and discussing—"

"Not business or politics, I hope," Rosmah conveniently interjected. "Remember, my dear husband: This is supposed to be a celebration," she said, placing her hands flatly on her shoulders, conspicuously on either side of the necklace that hung heavily—but brilliantly—in the middle of her chest, as if anyone could have missed seeing the grandeur of the sparkling stone that seemed to emit its own light.

"No, of course not, my darling. We were just chatting," Najib said.

There was a pause during which no one spoke, as Najib stepped close to his wife and gently lifted the exquisite pink diamond in his hand to admire it.

"It's stunning beyond any manner of description," he said to her lovingly.

Then, looking at his Rolex, Najib said, "Well, it's very late. We should all probably turn in for the night." With that, Najib ceremoniously finished his glass of port, setting the empty glass down on the antique sideboard.

"Good night, Jho," he said, and with Rosmah on his arm, he turned and headed off, the two of them like a king and his queen, to their sumptuous suite on the most exclusively private deck of the *Topaz*.

As it turned out, Najib and I would never again discuss the circumstances surrounding Najadi's murder. In fact, thanks in large part to

Najib's powerful control over the editorial and news-reporting policies of Malaysia mainstream newspapers and online news outlets, the whole sad story of Najadi's demise might easily have just gone away altogether, were it not for a whole bunch of crazy circumstances.

Najib was right about one thing: The Malaysian papers he controlled did a good job of trumping up an assortment of serious questions about Najadi's business dealings and his alleged gangland entanglements. One tabloid even went so far as to suggest the seventy-five-year-old banker was having a torrid affair with a twenty-something lingerie model and aspiring actress, the former girlfriend of one of Malaysia's most notorious mobsters, who, in a fit of jealous rage, had ordered the hit on Najadi. You want to talk about fake news?

Anyway, toward the end of the year, in what appeared to be an unfathomable miscalculation, Koon, the supposedly diabolically cunning and infinitely clever alleged professional hit man, made the colossal mistake of trying to pass through the Kuala Lumpur airport on a stopover. And it was there, in a classic case of good news–bad news for Koon, he was immediately arrested and taken into custody by the regular Malaysian police, with the assistance of Interpol, rather than simply being picked up, taken to some filthy back alley in the city's slums, and summarily executed by Najib's always ruthlessly efficient UTK security forces.

The end result was that, under the dubious protection of Malaysian law enforcement authorities that were at least doing their level best to at least try to appear legitimate and even handed with respect to so-called due process and a fair trial and all of that, Koon would indeed have his day in court before a Malaysian judge and jury, where, about a year later, he was quickly convicted and sentenced to death by hanging.

Here, again, had that happened quickly—Koon's immediate execution, I mean—that too could have ended the whole matter for good, because a few months after the trial, the Malaysian law enforcement authorities announced that, with Koon's conviction in hand, they were no longer looking for any other suspects or alleged accomplices in Najadi's killing and that they had officially closed the case, which remains closed to this day. In fact, the only other person they arrested and charged with minor offenses was the luckless cab driver who had unwittingly driven Koon to the parking lot of the Chinese temple where the banker and his wife were gunned down. Truth was, as long as Najib would hold power, you could pretty much bet the legal authorities would use whatever excuse they could to avoid having to dig any more deeply into the matter than was needed to make it look like a real criminal investigation had taken place.

But listen: Koon is still alive! One might have quite reasonably expected Koon's erasure to have been delayed, somewhat, owing to the normal channels of often protracted legal appeals permitted—but, in reality, merely acted out—by the nevertheless corrupt Malaysian judicial system. Perhaps a few months, the appeals would take, before he would inevitably swing from a hemp rope. But the bizarreness of the murder and the characteristically inept prosecution's inability to establish a motive for the killing led to some not-so-normal political interventions and media outcries. The people and the independent press wanted answers, and some of those people were in high places or simply in influential positions. In fact, one of those people was or, should I say, *is* Hussain Najadi's own son, Pascal, a well-respected international banking consultant based in Moscow.

Since the day of his father's death, it seems, Pascal has waged a relentless campaign charging that Najadi was assassinated to silence his objections to the banking practices of 1MDB, going so far as to try to implicate the Razaks in ordering the hit—not just Najib but Rosmah, as a kind of coconspirator. Pascal has insisted to the press that "the convicted shooter is a key witness" and that "executing him would be a loss of the truth."

In any case, Koon still sits, even now, on death row in the squalid and infamous Sungai Buloh Prison, along with some 2,400 other inmates, awaiting his inevitable fate.

I'll tell you honestly: I thought Pascal was crazy. I thought his obsessive grief and anguish over his father's violent and untimely passing had driven him to certifiable insanity.

At least, that's what I thought at first.

Even if Najib was able to use his considerable autocratic influence to move the story of Najadi's murder off the front pages of the mainstream newspapers and then out of the local papers and news media altogether, he had no such power when it came to both the independent business and the financial media across Southeast Asia, nor with the world-class news and magazine publications across Europe and America that, for all intents and purposes, are international in their scope of readership.

Still, those news outlets didn't seem too concerned about the circumstances surrounding Najadi's murder. After all, what's the loss, in the brutal scheme of things, of one banker from a backwater state in Southeast Asia? No, they wanted to know what the hell was going on with the 1MDB fund. They wanted to know where the money was. Could anything be more important than that?

Pretty soon, the big, widely respected newspapers like the *New York Times* and the *Wall Street Journal* and the *London Times* and the *Guardian* began publishing story after story alleging that there was extensive financial reporting fraud going on at 1MDB. They accused the fund of overpaying for the power plants through the first two Goldman Sachs–managed bond issues and revealed what they claimed were shady dealings with Middle Eastern sovereign wealth funds. Locally, the *Edge* and the *Sarawak Report* began to criticize the glaringly huge disparity between the Malaysian fund's enormous debt, approaching ten billion dollars, and its minimal assets, which could be measured in mere millions—hence the fund's failure, according to them, to produce some measure of respectable profits from its meager investments.

In the early days, when I first established 1MDB with the help of Najib, it was relatively easy to keep the wealth fund's operations and financials under wraps. I could run things the way I wanted—and nobody would ask any annoying questions, even the executives who sat on the advisory board. Those that had misgivings, well, as I told you earlier, most of them simply resigned. I couldn't help it if some people simply had no innovative financial vision for a better future.

But as 1MDB's financial portfolio of investments expanded internationally and involved a greater number of worldwide financial professionals and banks and organizations and institutions, well, it just became harder and harder to prevent people from sticking their noses into the fund's operations. One financial writer with the *Wall Street Journal*—I don't remember exactly when this was—wrote that looking at 1MDB was like looking through a large picture windowpane that had heavily frosted over during a subzero night but was starting to come into clearer focus as the rising sun melted the obscuring frost.

What I objected to most about that was that these people just had no understanding of what I was trying to accomplish. It's one thing for the press and the politicians to demand more financial transparency, but it wasn't going to do them any good if they didn't understand what they were looking at. Do you understand? It's like, I could tell you that Einstein's breakthrough scientific theory of relativity is $E = mc^2$, but what the hell good does that do if you don't know what that means? In my view, too much so-called transparency would do more harm than good, because, well . . . it was dangerous because it could simply impede progress.

Most distressing to me, the questions and accusations, all the virulent commotion and the acrimony, weren't just coming from the financial press; no, the intensifying criticism of the 1MDB fund's alleged failures was coming increasingly from the prominent politicians of Malaysia. In some ways, this was Prime Minister Najib's own fault: His wanton recklessness so openly dispensing political payoffs and patronage money in the millions during the 2013 campaign meant that, now, even he could no longer stave off the scrutiny that began to gather around just exactly what was happening with 1MDB—a fund that, ultimately, Najib was directly in charge of and responsible for. The growing questions about whether some or all of that payoff money was coming from Malaysia's sovereign wealth fund.

Also very unhelpful was Rosmah's growing collection of ultra-expensive jewelry—more specifically, her abject refusal to make any attempt to be the least bit discrete about it. In numerous personal and diplomatic appearances, Rosmah chose instead to flaunt her fabulous jewels in the faces of the people. In one televised media appearance, she asked the program host, "Shouldn't the First Lady of our nation have and wear the very finest things as a way to show the rest of the world what a wonderful country Malaysia truly is?" On another TV talk show broadcast across the country, Rosmah complained about how it cost over $500 to have her hair dyed; that was more money than the average Malaysian earned in an entire month. So it was that Rosmah's own obscenely incorrigible behavior only added fuel to the public outcry over who exactly was paying for all of that golden glitz.

Politically, an enormous amount of pressure began to come from an amalgam of forces among Najib's political opposition. These were factional forces and splinter groups that heretofore spent so much time and energy squabbling among themselves that none of the competing factions had ever posed any serious threat to the ruling UMNO. Now, emboldened by their near-successful campaign to unseat the incumbent, these opposition forces were more unified than ever, increasingly becoming a foe too formidable for the UMNO party to ignore. Powerful opposition leaders like Tony Pua, who sat on the Public Accounts Committee of the Parliament—the direct committee charged with oversight of government spending—began to write letters to 1MDB's advisory board, the fund's auditors, and to the independent newspapers, alleging fraud and demanding a full, transparent disclosure of 1MDB's financial books. Long a thorn in the ruling party's side, it was bad enough that Pua was stirring up insurgency among the citizens of Malaysia. Now, he was also injecting fear into the hearts of the board members and among the fund's various international business and investment partners.

And while one would certainly expect criticisms and calls for transparency to come from virulent political opposition forces, the

THE ART OF GREED

most disturbing thing was that they were also suddenly coming from prominent and powerful people within Najib's own UMNO party. Spearheading a sinister groundswell of revolt within the UMNO was none other than Mahathir Mohamad, the former prime minister, who had served in the post from the early 1980s and brought the emerging nation through the beginning of the new millennium, until 2003. The author of over a dozen books on Southeast Asian politics, globalization, and Islam, Mahathir had remained quite active as a kind of patriarchal leader—and critic—of the UMNO, in particular, but, as well, of the leadership and the economic and political direction of the country of Malaysia as a whole. Mahathir, it seemed, was one of those rare charismatic politicians who somehow manage to become even more powerful and respected and influential—and even loved—after they leave office.

Claiming to have received leaked confidential information about the inner workings of 1MDB—a fact that, if true, infuriated me—Mahathir began to significantly turn up the volume of his criticism of what he called the "corrupt and inept mismanagement" while also making major accusations of massive misdirection of 1MDB funds. On his regular weekly blog, he posted some very incendiary statements—outlandish statements that I felt were just downright dangerous to the nation—like when he pontificated that the 1MDB fund's enormous debt risked toppling the country into a financial crisis like those seen in the past in Argentina and Venezuela and elsewhere.

Did he too not understand my plan and my goal of turning 1MDB into an international powerhouse like Abu Dhabi's IPIC fund?

As if feeling a renewed infusion of political power and still possessing enormous physical and intellectual vigor even at age eighty-nine, Mahathir also actually started to engage ominously in secretive backroom dealings and negotiations among the other influential party bosses—meetings intended to try to force Najib to resign and, potentially, to oust him altogether should he refuse to resign on his own. The crisis threatened to destroy the UMNO party literally from within. And while I really had no interest in party politics, or any desire to get involved in them, I absolutely needed Najib to stay in power if I was ever going to achieve the goals I had in mind for 1MDB. No one else was likely to give me the free rein that Najib had.

What became most worrisome for me was that, over time, most of the criticism from the press, financial experts, and the politicians became acutely focused on the $2.3 billion Cayman Islands account and strident calls to "repatriate" that money and put it toward in-country investments like infrastructure and jobs and housing investments that the critics claimed would better serve the people of Malaysia, as well as the nation as a whole. I, of course, had much bigger international plans for 1MDB, as I've repeated time and time again.

In a withering editorial published in the *Edge*, Ho Kay Tat demanded "on behalf of the people" or some such shit, that Najib reveal the name of the fund manager of the Cayman Islands account, while also calling on the prime minister to "bring the money home where it can do some good for the people." Shortly after Tat's editorial appeared in the *Edge*, some newspaper in Singapore published an article identifying Bridge Global as the fund manager. How they got this information, I had no idea, but I was furious about it. Still, rage wasn't going to solve the problem.

The upshot of all of this was simply this: Both Najib and I realized that 1MDB needed to do something really big to prove itself. And by *big*, I mean truly colossal; I'm talking about a major financial killing, yielding such enormous profits that it would shut all of the critics up, from top to bottom, once and for all. Don't forget the fact that, even as we were encountering all of these petty political difficulties, we were steadily moving toward the IPO of the energy sector power assets that 1MDB had acquired through the Goldman-directed bond issues. That IPO was expected to net 1MDB upward of five to six billion dollars, and even if that would not cover all of the debt the fund was currently carrying, it would go a long way toward righting the ship and setting things in the right direction.

This was why all of this scrutiny and criticism couldn't have come at a worse moment for 1MDB. Because just when we needed their utmost confidence, the rising tide of criticism of 1MDB started causing deep—and utterly unwarranted—concern among our financial partners—in particular, our auditors. I say *unwarranted*, because, I swear, I was bound and determined to bring this IPO to its successful consummation. But our partners, including our auditor, balked.

What had happened, in fact, was that KPMG abruptly resigned as the auditor for 1MDB, but the fund was able to quickly hire the firm of Deloitte Touche Tohmatsu to take over, sometime around March 2014. I wasn't all that happy that 1MDB was now with its third auditing firm, but I tried to keep my sense of humor about it, texting Fat Eric that "We seem to be running out of Big Four auditing firms!" But what can you say? Auditing firms for sovereign funds are a necessary evil, I suppose. Fortunately, Fat Eric was equally nonplussed about it. I laughed out loud when his text reply came back, "Maybe we need to start our own auditing firm."

But it was more serious than that, because even as they came on board, Deloitte expressed a lot of concerns about the Cayman Islands funds, sort of picking up where KPMG had left off. Things were coming to a head. Due to its enormous debt, 1MDB was bleeding interest at a rate of about seventy million dollars a month, and now Deloitte—which, having just landed this nice new client, should have been more eager to help 1MDB do business—was dragging its feet in approving and going along with the IPO.

In September, Mahathir Mohamad began releasing to the public much of the confidential, leaked information he claimed to have about the inner operations of 1MDB. But he wasn't the only one. Unfortunately, the same information had apparently fallen into the hands of a woman named Clare Rewcastle Brown, a journalist and the publisher of the *Sarawak Report*, who also began publishing this confidential information—and commenting on it editorially. Worst of all for me were a series of what should have been very private emails between the top management people at 1MDB and me and which Mahathir, Rewcastle Brown, and other journalists took as indicating that I was somehow involved in the critical investment decisions of the fund.

You have to keep in mind here that I held no official position within the management or even on the advisory board of 1MDB. I was merely an advisor, so all these accusations from the media were false, yet they would prove enormously damaging to the reputation—and a major hindrance to the immediate investment operations—of 1MDB in the near term.

Like, for example, Rewcastle Brown published an article titled "Jho Low's Spending and Malaysia's Development Money," in which she had the gall to write, "Malaysians are entitled to conclude that Low's record levels of spending in fabulous billionaire hotspots from San Tropez to Las Vegas has been paid for by them." It was inflammatory articles like this one that sparked so much panic at Deloitte that even our own auditing firm began to demand the repatriation of the $2.3 billion in the Cayman Islands account.

I could see that the energy assets IPO was in deep trouble. So could Prime Minister Najib. But, remarkable as it might sound for me to say this, I wasn't worried. I still believed I would succeed in getting the IPO done. And I had an even bigger deal in mind—one that would dwarf everything I had heretofore accomplished.

Chapter 16

China, in 2013, embarked on what has come to be known as the Belt and Road Initiative, which, if you were to read the Chinese Chamber of Commerce PR description (if there actually is a Chinese Chamber of Commerce, that is), it would probably say that Belt and Road is China's magnanimous, global infrastructure development strategy designed to invest in—and generously uplift the economies of—some seventy countries and organizations, particularly through vast modern road and rail transportation project to connect all of east Asia, Africa, and Europe within one vast vitally efficient commercial network. A modern-day Silk Road, if you will, though, of course, dwarfing in scope and scale the original Silk Road of the ancient Chinese Han Dynasty. The Silk Road on steroids—massive steroids.

Sounds like some fantasy economic dreamscape, doesn't it? You can just imagine, like, a high-resolution photograph taken from space at night, where you might actually be able to see this network of roads and rails pulsating with digital lights like neon tubes streaming across all of Asia, Eastern Europe, and Northern Africa, all connected, all seventy countries engaged in mutually beneficial investment and commerce, like something out of a Technicolor Walt Disney movie, where everybody lives happily ever after. And China is underwriting all of this out of the goodness of its heart, for the benefit and prosperity and improved living standards across the world and the advancement of all of humankind.

Nah, nothing subversively political going on here.

Of course, the Western world isn't buying that. Toward the end of his U.S. presidency, in a speech in 2016 touting the signing of the trade agreement known as the Trans-Pacific Partnership, Barack Obama warned his American people that the United States must continue to take a leadership role in the economic affairs in emerging regions like Southeast Asia. "Because, if we don't," the president said, "competitors who don't share our values, like China, will step in to fill that void."

Yet Obama's pronouncement was an enormous understatement. Anybody listening to that speech, whether they came from America or China, might have thought it just another reminder of the age-old struggle between communism and capitalism and might figure that, well, the beat goes on. But China's vision of Belt and Road is far more than a clash of competing sociopolitical ideologies. Never mind that most of the B&R projects are contracted and executed with or through Chinese state-owned companies, with workforce deployed from China, building materials manufactured and imported from China; sometimes even the food those Chinese workers consume over the many months or years of construction is prepared, packaged, and shipped to the job site from China. Meaning that the people living in those seventy countries do not benefit from greater employment opportunities or increased GDP within their own countries. Shit, if the Chinese ship their own food in, even the food vendors and restaurants get screwed! Maybe the people benefit from the anticipated upsurge in business and commerce after the project is completed, but even that remains an unknown quantity until it actually happens.

Here's the really sinister thing: Many of those seventy countries targeted to receive China's outwardly generous transportation improvement projects are—how shall I say it? How about *dirt poor*?

In other words, these quasi-third-world nations will likely never be able to even come close to paying off their financial obligations with respect to China's regional investment—the kinds of projects that can be measured in the twenties or thirties or even the hundreds of billions of dollars. Failure to repay those obligations means, ultimately, that China owns the finished project outright. It might be a brand new containerized seaport or a gleaming new rail hub or a state-of-the-art urban commuter system or a high-speed rail line, but China will own it. And control it, literally and economically.

Never mind political ideology; ownership is a concept any capitalist can certainly understand—even revere—and, apparently, so can a communist as well. Of course, the country in question will be weighed down by that enormous debt for many decades, perhaps indefinitely, while China gets a foothold to profitably operate, in a manner of speaking, on that country's native soil. Taken to its logical conclusion, China will basically own the ineffectual governments of these unfortunate countries, if not the countries themselves.

As I said before, I don't really care about politics either way. I only care about doing international business and investment deals—*big* international business and investment deals. I knew that one of the modern transportation projects that China had its greedy "economic imperialist" eyes on, that it very much wanted to appropriate under the auspices of its grander Belt and Road scheme, was a proposed forty billion dollar high-speed railway line that would run, it was hoped, the entire length of Malaysia, from its northern border with Thailand all the way to Singapore. Najib's government was already in negotiations with several international construction firms to build the project, but with that forty billion dollar price tag, the talks were currently stalled, and China wanted a piece. Actually, they wanted the whole pie.

As for financial debt, even substantial debt, well, I've never been afraid of it. Financial debt is just a tool; that's how I always looked at it. Financial debt was my friend; it enabled me to make all sorts of deals. If you look at it objectively, the bigger the debt, the bigger the deal I was able to make. It's amazing, isn't it? How debt can be your friend. How it can be the most powerful card you can play. At least, up to a point.

All I knew was, the Chinese had the wealth, the power, and, if Belt and Road was any indication, the genuine will to negotiate and take a stake in this proposed massive Malaysian railroad project that could lift 1MDB out of its doldrums and catapult the fund into the kind of international prominence and prestige—and prodigious wealth—that had been my sole vision from the very start. I also believed that, like me, China's massive state-run companies preferred to do things their own way, without allowing themselves to be too encumbered by the same sorts of restrictive rules and regulations that govern the operations of companies in Western-style capitalist democracies.

Most importantly, those state-run companies knew the value of operating under extreme confidentiality. China's B&R agreements with all these sovereign governments were not going to be subject to review by an independent advisory board or by a nongovernment international auditing firm; nor were the specifics of these regime-to-regime contracts likely to be revealed or aired or discussed by the press. Basically, if the project was approved by Beijing, the project was a go. I liked that a lot. Communism or not, it's certainly a way to get things done. The prospect of doing major business with China—just imagining what I might be able to achieve—was simply exhilarating.

I had barely taken possession of *Equanimity* when, only a few months later and feeling rather triumphant about it, I'll admit, I gave orders to my seasoned, handpicked captain and crew to set sail for Shanghai. If you see no other Asian world-class city in your lifetime, you must make it your goal to see Shanghai before you die. Standing on the waterside promenade known as the Bund, you have behind you rows of timeless, imposing, regal, meticulously architectured, historically significant, hundred-year-old buildings dating from the colonial era, while gazing out across the Huangpu River stands perhaps the most fantastically futuristic, almost utterly whimsical skyline on the planet: the city's twenty-first century Pudong district.

THE ART OF GREED

You know I'm a Hollywood movie buff, so allow me to tell you that Shanghai is so spectacular that it makes the Emerald City of Oz look like Penang. There was no mistake about it that Pudong is, after all, where they built Shanghai's Disneyworld resort!

The guest list of travelers on this voyage—one of *Equanimity*'s earliest yet most crucially auspicious, almost amounting to a state diplomatic mission—was very small but elite and very consequential in their effectual significance. It included me, of course, but more importantly, on board and staying in the best suite on the boat was Prime Minister Najib and his wife Rosmah, complete with about a dozen suitcases stuffed with her wardrobe and jewelry. Thank god it was a big boat.

Also a guest on this trip was Tim Leissner. Tim had asked if he could bring along some Asian model he was seeing. I had said yes, reluctantly, as long as he kept her out of sight when we met with the Chinese, I had instructed him. As a matter of fact, Leissner himself was pretty much just along for the ride. I'll explain in a moment. Thank god it was a big boat.

There was one other person who came along on this trip: Datuk Azlin Alias. Azlin was Prime Minister Najib's principal private secretary and confidant. I had previously met Azlin one or two times in connection to my regular, private meetings with Najib. He seemed an affable, diplomatic, and highly efficient administrator, capable of handling any task no matter how politically complex. Yet I was instinctively suspicious.

When I pressed Najib on the matter, he looked at me oddly, his head turned askew, and asked, "Do you not trust Datuk Azlin?"

I evaded the question by asking one in return. "The question is, Prime Minister, do you trust him?"

Najib seemed to shrug the question off. "I have found him to be intensely devoted and fiercely loyal to me and to serving our government, as well as our mission for a greater Malaysia."

In that moment, I could only acquiesce. Still, I quietly wondered whether Najib might be guilty of mistaking Azlin's undying loyalty to his homeland of Malaysia—which was clearly and abundantly evident even to me—for a more perverse loyalty to the prime minister he happened to serve. It was a question I could not ask: Najib had often expressed the unassailable belief that anyone supremely dedicated to the homeland of Malaysia must also be supremely loyal to him as the one chosen to lead the country to its greatest glory. In his mind, I feared, there was no separating the two.

Then, as if to provide an example of how greatly he trusted Azlin, Najib said, "I'll tell you something in strict confidence, Jho. Azlin was the only member of my inner circle courageous enough to directly suggest to me—privately, of course—that I order 1MDB to repatriate the money from the Cayman Islands account."

"What!" I gasped. If Najib's revelation was intended to shock me, he certainly succeeded, but for more reasons than he knew. One, in particular, that I've talked about before: the absolute conviction that I could not allow anyone to get between me and the prime minister, particularly when it came to advising the prime minister.

I looked at Najib wide-eyed and seriously alarmed when he told me this, but he stridently rebuffed me. "He was only looking out for me, Jho," Najib remonstrated. "And he was the only one with the guts to suggest something he knew I absolutely didn't want to hear. You see, Azlin felt that it would be good PR for my image if I brought some money home and spread it around a little bit. You know, start some domestic projects, create some jobs—to silence the critics, you understand."

I nodded, but I wasn't so sure.

On the other hand, Najib had trusted Azlin to open up a couple of business and personal accounts for him with AmBank in Kuala Lumpur, as well as another in Najib's own name with a major bank in Singapore. So Azlin must have known about the $681 million that had been transferred, first from Falcon Bank in Switzerland and then to Falcon Bank in Singapore and finally into Najib's AmBank accounts just months prior to his reelection, although I assumed that Azlin did not know where that money had actually come from. And, when I thought about it, Azlin had kept quiet about all of that. Anyway, he didn't ask any questions about any of it as far as I knew, just did his job. Perhaps Najib was right, and Azlin could indeed be trusted.

That's it. That's everybody who made the trip to Shanghai on *Equanimity*, a small but intimate group, you might say, on a big boat with plenty of room to roam.

Prominently missing from this tiny entourage, you might have noticed, were my Middle Eastern partners, Al Husseiny and Al Qubaisi. Frankly, Qubaisi's behavior of late had become a matter of some concern for me. Not his wild, unabashed borderline-obscene partying behavior that the tabloid newspaper photographers loved so much, at least not specifically. I really didn't care how people acted at my parties and gala events, as long as they were having a good time. But Qubaisi seemed increasingly determined to make a career choice out of it.

What I mean by that is, Qubaisi had poured over $100 million into the design and creation of an establishment he named the OMNI—a decadently outfitted nightclub inside the sprawling Caesar's Palace casino in Las Vegas. It was the most expensive nightclub ever built and was so huge it could accommodate over 3,500 party-mad revelers who were willing and apt to behave just as badly as Qubaisi had become famous for; it's Vegas, after all. You can see what my concern was: Qubaisi was morphing, right before my eyes, from respected high-level international investment strategist holding the strings to unlimited financial capital to glitzy, seamy nightclub entertainment impresario and denizen. And that's to say nothing of how the revelation of Qubaisi's vile new entrepreneurship venture would be received back home in Abu Dhabi or, for that matter, across all of the Islamic Middle East, where they had utter disdain for Western decadence. Still, one had to keep in mind that the Middle East was where the money was. I am a practical man, and I conjectured that it would only be a matter of time before my good friend Qubaisi would, like any other fool, soon be separated from his money. Once that happened, he would no longer be of any use to me.

There was a much more profound reason why neither of them was on board, and it had to do with the monumental diplomatic and political scale of the proposed deal. This was going to be a state-to-state partnership between China and Malaysia, crucially involving 1MDB but very much driven and directed by the prime minister as the country's head of state. Once successful, the deal would solve abundantly the financial problems that 1MDB was experiencing, and it also likely would become the signature achievement of Najib's second term—perhaps of his entire career as prime minister—silencing all of his critics and sticking it to the misguided and misinformed journalists in the press.

In other words, I wanted this partnership to help Malaysia's sovereign fund effectively break free of our dependence on the Middle Eastern sovereign funds whose support, admittedly, had been instrumental in getting us this far. Why? Because dealing with greedy sheikhs and self-absorbed Middle Eastern fund managers had gotten too messy. Guys like Qubaisi and Husseiny and a growing list of other hangers-on wanted way too much in the way of millions of dollars in paybacks for their help and cooperation, and the money drain was beginning to drag down my efforts to promote and build 1MDB into one of the world's biggest and most respected sovereign wealth funds. That's the real reason why neither Qubaisi or Husseiny was on the *Equanimity*.

As for Leissner, I wanted him there but at arm's length, just in case there might be a role in this deal for which I might need the services or the professed financial blessing that Leissner could provide—in other words, the formidable backing of Goldman Sachs, if only to impress the Chinese officials. Barring that, as far as I was concerned, Leissner could spend this entire trip drinking himself into oblivion at the sumptuous bar or banging his girlfriend in the hot tub in his private stateroom. Anything, as long as he didn't get in the way.

Let me tell you some things about this railway project. If you don't know anything about the jungle geography and the rugged topography of the Malay Peninsula or how difficult it would be to build a modern high-speed railway there, just think of the movie *Bridge on the River Kwai*, starring Sir Alec Guinness. Only it's more difficult than building the bridge on the River Kwai, because you can't build a modern high-speed railway out of bamboo and rubber trees you cut down in the neighboring forest along the line and tie together with liana vines. You've got to bring in massive quantities of steel and concrete and heavy excavating equipment and laborers and on and on. You've got to build temporary shelters along the rail route, bring in food and medical supplies for the workers, run communications and high-tension power lines. It's an almost inconceivably difficult, almost humanly impossible task on the order of a wonder of the twenty-first-century world magnitude.

The proposal itself was to run a high-speed rail link from the tiny state of Perlis, at Malaysia's northern tip, down to Johor, the urban center just above Singapore, at an estimated cost of some forty billion dollars. An overland journey between these two points can take as long as twelve hours; the rail link, once completed, would cut that travel time by half. From Perlis, the Chinese proposed extending the link to Bangkok, though, of course, they would need to negotiate with Thailand about that, thus none of our concern. For Najib, the proposed rail project represented a potential quantum leap into the twenty-first century, both technologically and diplomatically.

"You know, Jho," the prime minister said privately, his mood clearly pensive, his voice sounding very "ministerial," if you will. "I should like it very much, and I would be deeply honored, if the Johor station were to be named the Prime Minister Najib Razak International Rail Station."

He was referring to the massive terminal that was to be built in Johor, at the very end of the line—or the beginning of it, if one were headed north.

"I should think that entirely possible and most appropriate, Mr. Prime Minister," I replied, referring to him formally for effect. *And while we're at it*, I thought sarcastically but did not give it voice, *perhaps we can name you Prime Minister for Life*. For a fleeting moment, I was struck by my own sudden but deeply felt grinding cynicism toward the leader of my country, whom I was increasingly seeing as hapless, inept, and—dare I say it—as descending rapidly into a pit of self-aggrandizing corruption.

Of course, in case you haven't already guessed, there was no way on Earth that Malaysia was going to be able to repay the debt it would owe to China upon completion of the project—not if the price tag was sixty billion dollars, not if it was forty billion dollars, probably not if it was only twenty billion dollars—and certainly not within the twenty-year term that China would propose for repayment of the loan. It's almost laughable when you think about it: Twenty years is not a real lot of time when you're trying to pay back forty billion dollars! Anybody with an economics degree and a pocket calculator could have seen all of that. I saw it. I didn't care. It wasn't my business. Najib should have seen it as well, and he should have cared. After all, his political career was at stake. But either he didn't see it, or he too just didn't care. This is why I told you all that background stuff about the real goals of China's Belt and Road. China, as it always does, had its own agenda. Malaysia, economically speaking, would become for all intents and purposes, a new member state of the CCP and ultimately, enormously in debt to China. Apparently, that was okay with Najib, as long as it meant he would stay in power. And as long as his First Lady could keep buying herself outrageously expensive jewelry from everywhere around the world.

Look, I'm just stating this for the record, in case the legal authorities ever get a hold of this book. Just to add, the political blowback for all of this was simply not my problem. It was Najib's problem. I'm just a businessman, a facilitator of international deals, and in doing so, I have to work seamlessly with the powers that be. End of story. Except . . . well, I just tried not to think too much about the designs of the CCP.

———

As we motored slowly into Shanghai's enormous, sprawling port, with dusk approaching, the harbormaster directed the *Equanimity* to a restricted marina reserved for government and military vessels only and protected, much to my amazement, by military fortifications on either side of the waterway entrance, including some rather large guns. Once inside the marina, we tied up to the wooden and steel dock specified and ordered by the military official in charge of overseeing the marina. We would stay there for the night. By this time, it was getting late, and we enjoyed a nice dinner aboard the ship, after which Najib and I retired to one of *Equanimity*'s more private decks. There, we smoked cigars, engaging in some small talk as we gazed out at the shimmering lights of the city. We retired early; tomorrow was going to be a profoundly important day.

The mammoth China Trans-National Construction, Engineering, and Development Corporation (CTNCEDC) has its flagship headquarters in Beijing, and they most certainly have several satellite offices throughout Shanghai, so it was an enormous honor that they had agreed to meet with us on board *Equanimity* rather than insisting we travel to one of those Shanghai premises. This was, for all of Najib's intents and purposes, a political-diplomatic mission of sorts, one that, when successful, he could later tout to the people of Malaysia. Yet I still wanted to keep the facts and substance of the negotiations extremely confidential and well out of earshot of the financial newspapers like the *Wall Street Journal* and the *London Times*. *Equanimity* was about to serve its intended purpose in this regard, and my plan would turn out to work just beautifully.

At nine a.m. sharp the following morning, a huge black Lincoln Continental limousine pulled into the marina parking lot. The driver leaped out to hold open the suicide doors, from which emerged two men and a woman, the men impeccably suited, the rather attractive woman in a formal black dress hemmed smartly just below the knee. As they made their way on board, Najib greeted them effusively, bowing, shaking hands, smiling ridiculously, and introducing them to First Lady Rosmah and then to his principal executive secretary (as Najib phrased it), Datuk Azlin Alias. Standing deliberately a few paces back and out of the limelight as I always did, I could only smile as I allowed Najib to have his fumbling awkward moment.

How grand was it that, for once, someone else was pretending that *my* superyacht belonged to *them*!?

After cordial introductions all around, we escorted our guests to a unique conference room below deck, a space that I ordered built to my exact specifications. It had inch-thick, shatterproof, electrically powered windows that could be obscured with the touch of a switch, just like my old conference room in the Wynton Group Petronas Towers headquarters. All of the phone and data communications in or out were through dedicated lines, and the room was equipped with closed-circuit television capability with instantaneous, real-time worldwide access. Even the walls and doors were damped, so that it was impossible for anyone outside the room to hear anything said inside the room—even if it was shouted at the top of one's lungs. It was, if I may say so, a "leak-proof" conference room. You know, it's funny, but now, as I'm telling you this, I'm realizing how much that conference room was like the communications control safe room that I have right here in this compound.

Anyway, our prestigious guests were Zhang Haoyu, the CFO of CTNCEDC; Tan Yuchen, the company's COO; and Sun Jiahui, whom CFO Zhang Haoyu introduced as *his* "principal executive secretary," almost as if mimicking Najib's description of Azlin.

The proceedings were surprisingly short, even in my experience of such meetings, and despite the fact that I had learned from some of my business associates that the Chinese are generally inclined to cut to the chase, and do not like to dally over petty details and nuances. That suited me fine. The hard, nuts-and-bolts details of the massive railway project presumably would take months, even years for the expert construction engineers, planners, and designers to hammer out, a process that would likely continue to evolve even as the construction got underway. That, too, suited me fine. As with the PetroSaudi deal, I would not have to get my hands dirty with the construction details.

As the official Malaysian finance minister, in addition to being its prime minister, Najib could pretty much sign off on the spot, at least in principal, on an agreement whereby the Chinese would offer a low-interest loan to Malaysia in the tidy sum of forty billion dollars to underwrite the project, repayable, as I mentioned, over a twenty-year term. Good luck with that. Whatever. By the end of the meeting, the China–Malaysia Belt and Road railway project was, for all intents and purposes, a done deal.

Almost.

As the meeting was about to wrap up, Najib looked at his principal executive assistant and said, "Azlin, why don't you take Ms. Sun up to the forward promenade deck and show her the wonderful view of the city we have from up there?" Najib then turned, almost as an aside to CFO Zhang and COO Tan, and said, "I've arranged for some refreshments to be served up there, a little vintage champagne to celebrate our momentous agreement, if you can stay for a little while."

The two men nodded almost solemnly.

Turning again to Azlin, Najib said, "You go ahead. We'll join you shortly on the promenade. I just want to ask these two gentlemen a few questions in private."

Azlin nodded. "As you wish," he said, and proceeded to help Jiahui out of her chair. With this, I started to rise out of my chair as well, thinking Najib wanted to be alone with the two construction company executives.

"Oh, no, not you, Jho," Najib said, extending a flattened hand in a motion to stop. "I'd like you to be here as well," he continued, a thin, confident smile on his face. "Please sit."

I sat back down.

I could see the disdain on Azlin's face, the indignity of being excluded, but like a good soldier, he dutifully escorted Jiahui out of the conference room, the heavy composite door closing behind them with the firm click of the deadbolt latch.

There was a long, silent pause as Najib looked both of the construction company executives in the eyes, telegraphing, perhaps, that he had an important, provocative request he wished to make.

"These major transportation projects," Najib finally began, almost musing philosophically, raising his right hand and circling his fingers in the air, "I imagine that pinpointing the actual final costs, say, for this railway we're going to build across Malaysia, I imagine that estimating exactly what the final price tag is going to be, when all is said and done, that can be a pretty difficult thing to pinpoint, can it not?"

"Well," Haoyu said, "that's true, sometimes. But we have a pretty good track record of estimating these things, so I don't believe you need to worry too much over—"

"But don't you ever occasionally have significant cost overruns?" Najib interjected, cutting the man off midsentence. "I'm talking in the billions of dollars? You take this rail line; you're going to be cutting through some of the toughest jungle and over some of the most rugged, unforgiving terrain in the entire world. Might that not add—and significantly so—to the cost of successfully building the line, especially when you take into account the high design and construction specification standards we have set, I mean? We don't want to compromise on the latest technology, or the modernistic design we envision, you understand."

The two Chinese officials looked at each other, and then COO Yuchen averred, "We respect the fact that you want the rail line to be completely state-of-the-art, no compromises. That said, it must be recognized that there is always the possibility that the costs will escalate, depending on what we encounter on the ground. That's just a fact of this business—a risk, if I may respectfully say so, that one must assume for the sake of human and economic progress and for the benefit of your people. Sometimes, too, new industry innovations suddenly come along, like digital communications improvements, which are happening all the time, for example, even as construction is still underway, and deciding to incorporate those into the original plan can push the overall cost significantly higher. That's true as well, as I'm sure you can understand."

Najib smiled, folding the fingers of his hands together into a ball and placing them on the conference table in front of him.

"Gentlemen, here's what I'd like to arrange. I'd like you to increase the loan to Malaysia for the railway project to sixty billion dollars.

But—" Najib raised the index finger of his right hand for emphasis. The expression on his face was so serious as to appear ominous.

"But," he repeated, "when we announce our agreement on the project to the public and the press, we will, of course, state for the record that the projected cost of the railway is sixty billion dollars. However, China will provide forty billion dollars of that total as a loan directly to the official bank accounts of the government of Malaysia, which I will specify. The extra twenty billion dollars will be deposited, separately, into special, discrete bank accounts, in Malaysia and possibly elsewhere when necessary and appropriate, that I—as Malaysia's finance minister—will solely designate. These separate deposit transactions will and must be kept strictly confidential."

Najib paused again, pensively, as if formulating in his mind what he was about to say next.

"Think of that additional capital," Najib continued, "if you wish, as kind of an insurance policy against cost overruns that, I must tell you, gentlemen, I am almost certain you will encounter when you endeavor to pierce through our forests and our mountains, even with all your technology and expertise—which, by the way, I deeply respect and admire. And as well, just to be perfectly clear, again as finance minister, I will hereby stake the Malaysian government to repaying the sixty billion dollars in accordance with the same general parameters we have discussed and agreed upon with respect to the original estimated project cost of forty billion dollars, which is to say, over the same standard twenty-year term."

It was brilliant. The important thing was, looking with brutal, unvarnished, even somewhat cynical objectivity at the enormous task, anybody who'd believe that it would cost forty billion dollars to build an ultra-modern high-speed railway link through nearly 600 miles of some of the densest jungle in the world would almost certainly believe—just as easily—that it could actually take more like sixty billion dollars to do the job. I mean, who'd be to judge? So, in the scheme of things, what was the difference, really, except that pegging the estimated cost at sixty billion dollars would free up a whole lot of extra capital for other purposes.

The two construction company officials, sitting stone-faced, turned to look at one another, briefly seemed to be communicating wordlessly, as if mystically using eyes alone to collaborate telepathically in an immediate, impromptu side evaluation of Najib's new proposal. Finally, they smiled, and CFO Haoyu nodded and said to Najib, "We perfectly understand your concerns. What you suggest is actually not all that unusual, in our experience. You are quite prudent to try to plan for unforeseen circumstances, which may be inevitable. You are to be commended, in fact, for your foresight."

Haoyu then smiled broadly and said, "I believe this can be easily arranged, Mr. Prime Minister." And then there were smiles and handshakes all around.

For me, I was utterly pleased and extremely proud for Prime Minister Najib. He had done everything exactly as I had coached him.

Chapter 17

On the voyage from Shanghai back home to Kuala Lumpur, I felt like I was just a simmering cauldron of mixed, wildly volatile emotions—emotions that I struggled to try to keep under control, without a lot of success.

On one hand, I had just orchestrated a deal in principal with the Chinese that was bigger than anything else I had ever accomplished. I should have been simply euphoric, and, at moments, I was. The proposed high-speed rail line would be perhaps the largest single infrastructure project in Malaysia's history and would likely secure Najib's position as prime minister for life, if that's what he wanted. And he seemed to want that. Of course, there was absolutely no doubt whatsoever that that's precisely what First Lady Rosmah, the "queen of diamonds" wanted.

At the same time, 1MDB was moving inexorably toward the IPO of its power asset conglomerate, which, alone, would net on the order of five billion dollars or more—money that would be a huge win for the fund. I should have been utterly delighted about this major eventuality as well, but things were moving intolerably slow on that front. Everyone involved seemed to be dragging their feet and asking way too many questions, particularly about the Cayman Islands account. That included 1MDB's new auditors at Deloitte, which, almost as soon as they came on board, seemed to join the chorus of

Malaysian politicians and journalists and so-called financial investment experts calling for the repatriation of the $2.3 billion. I was very worried about all of this, because we did not have a lot of time.

Every year since its founding, 1MDB had struggled to avoid having to show a significant loss on the books when the fund was required to issue its annual financial report for the fiscal year each March. And each year, it had taken some creative financial gymnastics—usually orchestrated by me—to enable the fund to show a profit, however modest, but within the context of a believable annual report that would pass muster with the fund's auditors. This recurring, nagging, pain-in-the-neck annual problem did not go away just because we retained a new auditing firm.

By the end of 2014, 1MDB was losing nearly $900 million annually—in interest payments alone—on its massive and ever-increasing debt load. Deloitte did not know this. I had a chicken-and-egg problem. I urgently needed to bring in the five billion dollars from the IPO to show Deloitte a respectable profit (and make them forget all about the $2.3 billion "fund units" in the Cayman Islands), but I needed Deloitte to give its regulatory blessing to actually allow 1MDB to go ahead with the IPO. You can see my dilemma.

We didn't have a lot of time. I needed to get the IPO done immediately so that we could book the anticipated five billion dollars in profit for 1MDB that certainly would make everybody happy—the auditors, the press, even the politicians. I also needed to get it done quickly because, if I didn't, 1MDB was about to implode. There were already some key managers, like Lodin Kamaruddin, a close friend and confidante of Najib, who were so distressed by the fund's ballooning debt that they were beginning to talk—much to my horror—about selling off 1MDB's assets and shutting the sovereign fund down completely. I absolutely believed I could avoid that, if I could just get the damn IPO done.

And that's when Justo decided to pull the trigger.

Remember Justo?

It had been over three years since Justo had left PetroSaudi in 2011, and during that time, he had struggled to make a go of it as a nightclub impresario in the UK, primarily with his flagship Premier Club in London but also trying to branch out with similarly themed night spots in other major cities throughout England. Most of them had failed, and by the end of 2014, he'd had enough of trying to make it as a nightclub entertainment entrepreneur.

Over the preceding six months or so, Justo had been quietly negotiating the sale of the 140 gigabytes of information contained on the illegally stolen PetroSaudi file servers with Clare Rewcastle Brown of the *Sarawak Report*, never relinquishing his adamant demand for two million pounds in payment for the servers. By January 2015, Rewcastle Brown had found someone willing to pay Justo's fee. It was Tong Kooi Ong, the chairman of the Edge Media Group and owner of the group's flagship *Edge* newspaper in Malaysia—the newspaper whose chief editor, Ho Kay Tat, had, ever since Najib's razor-thin reelection victory, kept up a constant barrage of opinion editorials critical of Prime Minister Najib and his whole administration and making a lot of scurrilous accusations about the 1MDB sovereign wealth fund and its investments. Barely a month later, Rewcastle Brown published the bombshell article in the *Sarawak Report* that was titled "Heist of the Century." And that's when all hell broke loose.

But before we get into that, I need to tell you about what Rewcastle Brown revealed in her exposé article, which will help you to understand what was really going on here. First, you have to bear in mind the obvious fact that all of the information she received on the file servers came from the PetroSaudi corporation and, really, pertained only to the business activities of PetroSaudi. Perhaps the most glaring accounting "impropriety" that the servers revealed was the existence of the offshore Good Star account. I'll admit that probably didn't look good to anyone who didn't understand my purpose in creating the account, even among banking experts who are used to seeing these sorts of financial vehicles. I certainly wouldn't have expected the general public or Malaysian politicians to understand my strategy—you know, average people who are enormously challenged just trying to balance their checkbooks.

As well, by the time Justo finally got his price for the servers in early 2015, the data they contained was already three years old, so they obviously could not contain any information about 1MDB's involvement in the affairs and operations of PetroSaudi since way back in 2011. Remember what I told you earlier? I myself had spent essentially those same three years actively distancing myself and, to the extent that I had the power and influence to do so, 1MDB from PetroSaudi. That was back when I came to realize, to my disgust, that PetroSaudi was scandalously mismanaged, and the principals of the company not only knew absolutely nothing about the harrowing and risky business of oil exploration but were, in fact, only interested in enriching themselves in the first place.

Not surprisingly, what Rewcastle Brown did discover from the servers—and highlight in her exposé—was all of the shady things that Tarek Obaid and Patrick Mahony were engaged in, revealing the millions of dollars that they and Prince Turki had stolen from the till, which one could argue amounted to embezzlement on a grand scale and downright criminal corporate malfeasance with respect to running the company—or failing to do so altogether. Rather than working assiduously to find valuable oil reserves deep under the ground, Obaid and Mahony were effectively running PetroSaudi into it, if you'll pardon the play on words, while Prince Turki continued to fiddle and play aboard his superyacht.

Look, international investment ventures don't always work out. Financial risk comes with the territory, and one could make a reasonable argument that 1MDB's investment in PetroSaudi—first as a joint venture and, later, when the venture was converted into an Islamic loan—was an unfortunate gamble that just didn't work out; that's all—and not owing to anything that I or 1MDB had done wrong, other than to have invested in what turned out to be a corruptly and hopelessly mismanaged company.

But Rewcastle Brown's story, followed closely by a similar article written by Ho Kay Tat and published a week or two later in the *Edge*, in my opinion, just blew everything way out of proportion. I'm talking mainly about the political atmosphere throughout Malaysia and beyond, where Rewcastle Brown's revelations had severe, wide-ranging ramifications and consequences that—again, in my opinion—far exceeded what should have been the reasonable response to the whole situation. What I'm trying to say is that, if you looked at them closely, the facts of the PetroSaudi story and 1MDB's unfortunate involvement in it did not justify the hysterical uproar among the national politicians and the press that followed the publication of Rewcastle Brown's *Sarawak Report* article.

For starters, the revelations fomented a virtual major schism in the perpetually ruling UMNO party, where, after many months of working secretly behind the scenes to try to oust Prime Minister Najib from power, one faction led by former PM Mahathir Mohamad began openly and emphatically calling for Najib to resign. So did many journalists and editorial commentators in the independent press. Yet, for his part, Najib remained remarkably stoic and incredibly stalwart—both in vehemently denying any wrongdoing in connection with the operations of 1MDB and in proactively ordering an immediate and intensive internal government investigation into the allegations brought by a burgeoning series of newspaper and magazine articles that followed Rewcastle Brown's original exposé.

The official government investigation would be conducted by the National Audit Department of the Finance Ministry, a department charged with overseeing the general finances of the state but, of course, staffed with Najib loyalists largely under the control of the increasingly embattled prime minister. Yet there were other, subversive political factions and forces that were at work and over whom Najib had little or no control. One of those factions included the Public Accounts Committee of Parliament. The committee was headed by a UMNO party leader, but, under the chaotic circumstances, one couldn't be certain if that party leader was loyal to Najib or, god forbid, owed his allegiance to Mahathir.

So when the rumors started to surface, shockingly, that the Public Accounts Committee could be calling on me to testify before a hearing, Najib ordered me to leave the country immediately. As ominous as that seemed at the time, Najib was surprisingly calm about the whole thing.

"Just until the dust settles, Jho," he said, smiling and patting my shoulder confidently. I believed Najib was right. I believed the dust would indeed settle and things would return to normal. He had, after all, done the "presidential" thing, the thing of diplomatic leadership: He had ordered an official government investigation, and that investigation would get to the bottom of the controversy. Najib would see to that. His confidence bolstered mine.

Days later, from inside my private jet as I flew out of the country, I wrote to some of my more reliable friends in the Middle East, Europe, and the U.S. to reassure them about the situation. People like Al Mubarak of the Mubadala fund and Ambassador Otaiba and even Tim Leissner at Goldman. I wanted them to know that we—Najib and I—were effectively keeping the situation under control. Most of these emails read something like this: "Please be reassured that the wildly inaccurate *Sarawak Report* 'exposé' is a sensationalized sham filled with innuendo and baseless accusations. Malaysia's government has found absolutely no evidence of wrongdoing, and the authorities believe that the reports are based on fabricated PetroSaudi emails, most of which appear to have been criminally tampered with." In some of those emails, I also warned my partners and colleagues, "We expect the next several months to be filled with a lot of vitriolic noise, absurdly ridiculous and deliberate disinformation propagated by certain anarchistic, radical political quarters hostile to the Malaysian government and especially to its leader."

I even wrote to Al Qubaisi and Al Husseiny, even though those two gentlemen had no direct involvement with the whole original PetroSaudi–1MDB joint venture, having come into the picture later, and, I might add, even though I had already begun to lose my faith and trust in the IPIC and Aabar fund managers as reliable and serious investment partners. In hindsight, these two were hardly better than Obaid and Mahony when it came to enriching themselves while failing to meet their fiduciary responsibilities in the running of the enormous sovereign funds they were supposed to be managing. But, hell, I had worked too hard to build powerful partnerships with foreign governments and financial investment organizations, and I was damned if I was going to let a few renegade articles in a couple of two-bit newspapers like the *Edge* and the *Sarawak Report* destroy everything I had created and achieved.

But the ensuing fallout from the whole fiasco just wouldn't be contained. Ironic to say it, but it was over the days and months of the great COVID-19 pandemic that the reaction to the PetroSaudi revelations also spread like an insidious, unstoppable virus. Like so many countries that purport to be so, Malaysia has never really been a true (read: not corrupt) democracy; nor did Najib's power, as considerable as it was, quite amount to a full-blown autocracy, where he could do anything he wanted, or simply order subordinates to do what he wanted or flat out quash any opposition. Malaysia, for all its faults, did have—and still retains—some measure of the rule of law, meaning that there remained things Najib simply could not control.

Among the things that he could not control was when the regular Malaysian police raided AmBank and seized the prime minister's bank records and confiscated the computers and phones of the private, exclusive representative who had, from the very beginning, so loyally handled all of Najib's accounts or, somewhat later, when the principal and most fiercely independent, self-determining Malaysian law enforcement agencies were emboldened to work together to form a task force to investigate the 1MDB affair—not just the fund's connection to PetroSaudi, but to delve more deeply into the operations of the fund itself. The nature and composition of that task force was formidable; it included members of the National Banking Commission, the National Police Authority, the Malaysian Anti-Corruption Commission—organizations that rarely cooperated with one another. To top it all off, the task force was headed and directed by the office of the attorney general of

Malaysia, the country's top public and government prosecutor with far-reaching jurisdiction and power.

What they found shocked me to the core. I knew that Najib had been, let's just say, massively indiscrete in spewing political patronage cash all over the country during his reelection campaign. What I didn't know was how sloppy he had been with managing (if you could even call it "managing") his personal bank accounts, especially those in Malaysia's AmBank. It would eventually come out that what the police and the banking investigators found almost immediately was that, between 2011 and 2014, Najib had received into his *personal* AmBank accounts the equivalent of *over one billion U.S. dollars*! That didn't include official government accounts overseen and, for all practical purposes, owned by Najib—essentially, his political war chest—and it didn't include innumerable business and personal accounts the prime minister held at a half dozen or more other banks, not just in Malaysia, but across all of Southeast Asia. Oh, yeah, and Switzerland too.

I had repeatedly counseled Najib to keep the lion's share of his funds in more opaque offshore accounts—accounts that I had set up and that I mostly managed for him and where I could keep a watchful eye on things to protect his interests and investments. Anytime he needed cash, I could certainly get it for him, quietly and quickly, without fanfare, and he didn't have to be involved at all. That way, he wouldn't risk any exposure to his political enemies or detractors or nosy bank regulators. Despite all my warnings, apparently, Najib simply hadn't listened.

There's really no way of sugarcoating this. Keeping a billion dollars in his personal accounts at one major bank was, well, it was as dumb as it was unnecessary. I say this now, with no little measure of the benefit of hindsight, but even at this early juncture, I could sense that my good friend Prime Minister Najib was already in deep shit. The discovery of his AmBank holdings alone, in fact, were so earth-shakingly volatile to authorities that they initially withheld the information from the public for fear—literally—of plunging the entire nation into outright civil war! I mean, just think about that.

And you have to understand, this was just the very beginning of the investigation—essentially what should have been a harmless, run of the mill, limited internal investigation within the borders and the halls of government of Malaysia alone, ostensibly. That was until revelations like Najib's one-billion-dollar AmBank accounts induced the police and the banking authorities and the attorney general to start looking for connections outside of the country, starting just across the Johor Strait, in Singapore.

And they began looking into my accounts too.

Shortly after the story broke, the newspapers reported that Singapore's Suspicious Transaction Reporting Office alleged that a Singapore bank account under my name had received something like $500 million from Good Star over the course of a couple of years. My god, was I not entitled to be paid for all my hard work and due diligence on behalf of my elite clients? Were the Malaysian authorities now going to smear everyone connected to Najib and his greedy improprieties?

When I left the country at the behest of the prime minister, I had assumed that my self-imposed, voluntary exile would be short-lived, just until things would blow over, as Najib assured me they would. After all, corruption investigations come and go in countries like Malaysia, like they're just part of the landscape seen from a passing train. But when the authorities started sticking their noses into my accounts and business affairs, I realized that this was, in all likelihood, going to be a much more protracted expatriation, voluntary or not.

It wasn't really a problem. I had homes and real estate properties all around the world where I could stay anytime and for as long as I liked or needed. As much as I loved my home country of Malaysia, where after all most of my family resided, I strived to rationalize, for my own sanity, that, by this time, I had long been a broad-minded citizen of the world, more than narrowly aligned with any one nation. It wasn't that easy. For all I might criticize my homeland, I do love Malaysia.

Still, I decided that I needed to make some contingency plans. All of the fabulous homes I owned in LA and New York and London and so many other places—they were all great, but they were all a little too visible, if you know what I mean, should this Malaysian political scandal get any bigger.

As a fallback—and, of course, for travel and entertainment—I had *Equanimity*, and I just thanked my stars for having had the foresight to go build my own superyacht.

But I also resolved that I needed a much more secure land base, some place that was rock-solid safe, both politically, in terms of its location, and physically, in terms of its impenetrable construction, and well out of reach of the press and the paparazzi. Geographically remote but fully plugged-in to the digital electronic communications ether that connects the entire human world. And for that, I turned to my new friends at the upper executive echelons of the China Trans-National Construction, Engineering, and Development Corporation (CTNCEDC). I commissioned CTNCEDC to build this extensive compound from which I now sit comfortably, writing all this down and relating to you, as I certainly hope you understand by now, my side of the story. Because the truth needs to come out.

―――

Getting back to the PetroSaudi problem, all of these overblown accusations in the press were going to make the execution of the energy assets IPO all the more difficult to achieve. Investment bankers, for all their professed bravado in taking huge risks in pursuit of huge potential profits, can also run like frightened rabbits at the hint of trouble. Deloitte was no different, and as the newspapers every day were full of sensationalized articles—and a lot of misinformation—about 1MDB's alleged involvement in PetroSaudi's mismanagement, the firm started to balk, threatening to put a complete halt on the IPO altogether. In particular, in order to move forward, Deloitte began to step up its demands for a more transparent disclosure regarding the $2.3 billion Cayman Islands funds.

I turned to Tim Leissner to see if he could smooth things over with Goldman and get them to help push the IPO through. Tim assured me he could, but he acknowledged that it wasn't going to be so easy. To understand Goldman's reticence, I have to take you back about eight months, to the second quarter of 2014.

Back in New York, Goldman Sachs had been receiving its own firestorm of criticism from the American financial press—principally the *Wall Street Journal*—not to mention from their banking competitors, over the firm's huge profits emanating (in large part) from the excessive fees it had charged for its handling of the various bond issues for 1MDB. Make no mistake, Goldman still wanted to pursue a greater and greater role in financial development Southeast Asia, but, stung by the recent negative press at home and cognizant of the allegations made by Rewcastle Brown and the rest of the Southeast Asian press, they had become much more cautious about dealing directly with 1MDB. Thus, for a brief time, Goldman distanced themselves from the fund, being reluctant to openly get involved in any further lending. But they wouldn't stay away for very long. There was just way too much money at stake. I could bide my time with Goldman, because, you see, it's rather amazing how, when one major bank steps back from a risky investment opportunity, another major bank will cheerfully step forward to put their heads on the block.

That is how, in the meantime, I managed to fill the void by working out a deal with Deutsche Bank through which Deutsche would ultimately lend upward of $1.225 billion to 1MDB. It's somewhat complicated, but, in order to sweeten the original deals through which 1MDB successfully acquired the various energy assets—let's use Ananda Krishnan's international conglomeration of coal-fired power plants, known as Tanjong Energy Holdings, as an example—was to offer to the billionaire Ananda Krishnan himself the guarantee of the right to purchase a significant stake in the eventual IPO at a shamefully cheap price per share. Similar arrangements were made with most, if not all, of the owners of the other energy assets that 1MDB had acquired. You can understand how these bargain-basement price options offered to so many parties, once you added them all up, could seriously undercut 1MDB's profits emanating from the IPO. They'd practically be giving away the store.

Now, in advance of the IPO, 1MDB was scrambling to buy back those options. Yet even the buyback wasn't going to come cheap—never mind that 1MDB had little or no cash on hand—and that's where Deutsche Bank was happy to oblige, by agreeing to lend 1MDB the money it needed to buy back the options. The Deutsche bankers must have been licking their lips upon seeing the profits that Goldman had racked up working with the Malaysian Fund, because they were all too eager in providing several loans in succession, each loan larger than the one that preceded it. They were so eager in fact, to work with 1MDB, that the Deutsche bankers—and, presumably, their lawyers as well—were willing to accept the $2.3 billion Cayman Islands funds as collateral on the loans without a lot of fanfare, even when a number of other banks were starting to ask intrusive, rather annoying questions about the Bridge Global account. That was because Deutsche desperately wanted a piece of running the IPO when it would finally go down.

We started small, with 1MDB receiving a loan of only $250 million. But from there, the loans would quickly ramp up, as I mentioned earlier, to a total of over $1.225 billion. It was amazingly as if Deutsche subscribed to that old adage "In for a dime, in for a dollar." Only we weren't talking about just dimes and dollars here! Deutsche was all in, bigtime.

However, there was a problem here as well. As Goldman's financial advisor to 1MDB, it fell to Tim Leissner to explain to the advisory board why they so crucially needed to buy back the option rights from Krishnan and the others, and moreover, why they had to do so even at the inflated costs of hundreds of millions of dollars. Most of the board members already well knew of the secret charity payments that Tanjong and other Krishnan-owned companies had "donated" to 1MDB accounts controlled by Prime Minister Najib. And let's be plain: Most of these guys knew that this was how standard, off-the-shelf political–economic graft worked in Malaysia. Deliberate, government-sponsored overpayments for an industrial or business asset were rewarded in turn by the seller through a generous contribution to the UMNO, in this case more than most, directly to the accounts and pet initiatives of Prime Minister Najib himself.

However, this time, some of the board members were rather upset because they felt the numbers too abundantly favored Ananda Krishnan and his Tanjong Energy Group. They probably did, in the scheme of things. So it was that, in a very raucous meeting with the board in July 2014, Leissner faced a roomful of very angry directors who accusatively questioned whose side he and Goldman had been on in securing the deals for the purchase of the energy assets. One of the board members, the Malaysian textile manufacturing entrepreneur Ashvin Valiram, pointedly questioned Leissner, demanding to know, "Is Goldman acting for 1MDB or Tanjong?"

"Of course we're representing 1MDB," Tim responded weakly and explained rather unconvincingly that "Without the original deal with Tanjong, we wouldn't ever have gotten to the position to be able to undertake this important IPO in the first place." It was kind of a case of a desperate animal eating its own tail.

Just as an aside, Tim Leissner would later be absolutely furious when the management of 1MDB selected Deutsche Bank, and not Goldman, to run the IPO—in effect, rewarding Deutsche for stepping in with $1.225 billion loan to buy back the IPO options. He quickly came back to me, crying a river over the snub, whereupon I personally interceded with Shahrol Halmi and Lodin Kamaruddin, the fund's top managers, and convinced them to hire Goldman as a consulting advisor for the IPO. So, like I said, Goldman Sachs could not bring themselves to stay away for long, and they were quickly back in the fold, you might say.

With trouble in the local and international press and trouble among nervous partners like Deloitte and Goldman and upheaval on the 1MDB advisory board, I resolved that I needed a new plan to get this damn IPO finished and done once and for all. When suddenly one simply dropped in my lap.

Back in Abu Dhabi, the two Als were in big trouble.

What happened, directly stated, was that Al Qubaisi's flamboyant lifestyle and his all-too-public love for Western decadence had gotten the attention of Crown Prince Sheikh Mohammed bin Zayed Al Nahyan, none other than the principal ruler of Abu Dhabi and the brother of the much more playboy-ish Sheikh Mansour, for whom Qubaisi worked. The crown prince did not approve of Qubaisi's public persona, and he suspected there were other, more sinister problems in connection with Qubaisi's management of the IPIC fund. He ordered a secret investigation into Qubaisi, not just his handling of the IPIC but also Qubaisi's daily life and business dealings, and not even telling his own brother Sheikh Mansour about the inquiry. He did not like what he found.

Over the course of less than a year prior to the crown prince's investigation, Al Qubaisi had spent nearly a half billion dollars buying properties around the world, including a penthouse in New York City's Walker Towers for fifty-one million dollars, a couple of mansions in LA and Beverly Hills for a combined forty-six million dollars, and a rooftop luxury suite leased at the Bellagio Casino in Las Vegas for twenty-three million dollars. The latter residence he promptly stocked with 10,000 bottles of the best French champagne and vintage French and American wines obtainable. Over that time, he had also acquired a dozen or more of the world's most exotic and expensive cars, which he stored at the Geneva Freeport, as I told you about earlier. Qubaisi had recently launched the hundred-million-dollar Omni nightclub in Caesar's Palace, which one could easily regard as the very citadel of sinful decadence, a place that Faust himself would have gleefully applauded. Finally, the investigation uncovered millions of dollars that had been diverted from the IPIC fund to several offshore accounts ostensibly under various corporate entities or shell companies, but all apparently owned and controlled by Al Qubaisi.

To make matters worse, it seems that, just as Obaid and Mahony had so unwittingly engendered angry retribution from a disgruntled employee whom they had treated very badly—that being Justo, of course—so too had Al Qubaisi incurred the retaliatory wrath of an employee in whom he had entrusted a distinctly insider's view of all sorts of vital, sensitive information about his business dealings and then foolishly turned around and treated the man like shit. The guy's name was Jayquon Montiel, a French-Algerian, if I'm not mistaken, and he worked for Qubaisi for many years, mainly out of Qubaisi's offices in Paris but also often accompanying the IPIC chief on his travels around the world. You could think of Montiel as a kind of private secretary or right-hand man to Qubaisi, although he was really more of a glorified butler or bag carrier. A kind of worker drone, if you will. In another era and culture, Montiel probably would have served as the second if Al Qubaisi ever found himself engaged in a perilous dual involving loaded antique pistols or swords.

Anyway, Montiel's main duties were to schedule Qubaisi's appointments, make the necessary travel arrangements, reserve airplane tickets, hotel accommodations, car rentals, superyacht rentals—you know, that sort of domestic, logistical stuff. Eventually, he also came to act as a messenger or intermediary, passing notes and documents, sometimes cash and checks, between many of Qubaisi's associates, business partners, nefarious clients, and general ne'er-do-wells (in my humble opinion). Over the course of time, not surprisingly, Montiel became intimately aware of his boss's shady business dealings.

Oh. The "butler" also very often accompanied Qubaisi when he partied hard at nightclubs in Paris, London, and Las Vegas. And he brought along a small, easily concealable professional-grade Nikon camera.

Montiel was well paid for his concierge-like services, but he must have gotten jealous watching as his boss—and Al Husseiny too—socked away millions and millions of dollars in kickbacks or circuitously siphoned millions more dollars from IPIC and Aabar (both the real Aabar and the fake one!). Montiel wanted in, and, at one point, Qubaisi promised him a significant stake in a massive real estate development transaction in southern Spain. But at the last moment, he reneged on the deal. Then, in early 2015, for some unfathomable reason, Qubaisi abruptly fired his longtime assistant and erstwhile confidant. I don't know why; maybe Montiel kept badgering Qubaisi to let him in on the next deal or the one after that, and maybe Qubaisi just got sick of hearing it.

At the same time, Montiel had done exactly the same—or nearly exactly the same—as Justo had done during his tenure at PetroSaudi. He had secretly compiled an FBI-style dossier on Qubaisi's business dealings, as well as his boss's increasingly outlandish and profligate personal drinking and partying lifestyle, conducted in the garish spotlight of bars and nightclubs all around the world. Of which, of course, he had taken many dubious pictures of his boss in action, using his handy little Nikon. As a package, the dossier would have made a professional extortionist proud.

Ironically, in what I can only describe as a you-can't-make-this-stuff-up moment, Montiel leaked a portion of his stash of documents and photographs to the press—including Clare Rewcastle Brown—in April, almost exactly coincident to the *Sarawak Report* publishing her "Heist of the Century" travesty. The documents included Qubaisi's bank statements, which revealed even more information than Crown Prince Al Nahyan's investigation had found—for example, divulging the multiple châteaus and estates that Qubaisi had acquired in France and Italy. Other documents exposed the ongoing series of payments to the builders of Sheikh Mansour's superyacht *Topaz*, in increments of fifteen million dollars or more at a clip. One important piece of paper in that stash showed how a tiny company in Luxembourg owned by Qubaisi received at least one transfer of twenty million dollars from Good Star, in February 2013. That publicly linked Al Qubaisi to PetroSaudi and to 1MDB, nearly two years before Justo's release of internal information regarding the original joint venture. This was not good—not for Qubaisi, not for IPIC, not for 1MDB, and absolutely not for me either.

Then there were the photographs. Oh my god, the photographs! In the nightclubs! They showed Qubaisi dancing with topless women or making out with one or more of them on an overstuffed couch

THE ART OF GREED

or straddled on a chair or barstool; they showed him wearing the obscene T-shirts I was telling you about before, shirts with images like a buxom pair of naked female breasts or buttocks in a G-string or even, weirdly enough, disturbing phallic images. They showed him holding up magnums of $3,000-a-bottle Cristal champagne with sparklers attached to them, and there was one of Qubaisi drinking the bubbly wine right out of the bottle. Of course, about two weeks after publishing the "Heist" article, Rewcastle Brown published a whole new exposé in the *Sarawak Report* extensively detailing all of the information in the leaked documents she had received from Jayquon Montiel. She included in the article many of the photographs Jayquon had taken, in full living color. All in all, it must have made the crown prince sick to his stomach. Especially those pictures.

Al Qubaisi was summarily fired from IPIC on April 22, 2015. Al Husseiny was fired from Aabar about two and a half months later. Honestly, I was surprised that it took so long after dispatching Qubaisi for the crown prince to go ahead and fire Husseiny as well. But that's neither here nor there. Because either way, I saw my opportunity the instant the axe fell on Al Qubaisi.

Within forty-eight hours of hearing the news, I was on my private plane headed for Abu Dhabi. My former partner was essentially a dead man, headed to a long spell in prison, where Al Husseiny would shortly follow him. Already judged by the crown prince to have stolen millions from IPIC, Qubaisi was well positioned to take the fall for any other misappropriations that might be revealed in the documents leaked by Montiel or even possibly by Justo as well.

In Abu Dhabi, I was not permitted to meet directly with the crown prince; no foreigner ever is. But I managed to gain a meeting with the new head of IPIC, Abu Dhabi's energy minister, Suhail Al Mazroui, whom Crown Prince Al Nahyan had swiftly appointed to replace Qubaisi, at least in the interim. Al Mazroui, in turn, had cleaned house, firing the incumbents and appointing a whole new management team at the sovereign fund. Ahead of arriving in the capital of the UAE, I fired off a note to Ambassador Otaiba, who had been so helpful in accomplishing the original PetroSaudi–1MDB joint venture partnership, telling him how shocked and distressed I was to learn of Qubaisi's deception and corrupt dealings and of his outright theft of millions from IPIC—and possibly from Aabar as well.

"There's a rumor going around that I'm a buddy of Al Qubaisi," I wrote, "and that substantial money has gone missing. But that's an internal IPIC issue if some of the money 1MDB sent has not shown up in IPIC accounts as it should have. I suspect the crown prince's investigation of Al Qubaisi's dealings will likely discover whether funds have indeed gone missing and, more importantly, where they most likely have gone, as I'm sure we both suspect."

Even well before going into my meeting with Al Mazroui, I conjectured that the new management of IPIC had no doubt thoroughly and exhaustively reviewed their account financial statements, and I assumed they also no doubt found that they were missing, I'd say, about a couple of billion dollars they should have received as collateral for guaranteeing 1MDB bonds. Actually, IPIC was liable for something like $3.5 billion in bonds that 1MDB had sold but did not have the cash to repay—at least at the moment Qubaisi's transgressions had come to light.

But who's counting?

I also knew that Deutsche Bank had become almost hysterically alarmed by the rumors and allegations that were now flying around regarding the $2.3 billion in the Cayman Islands account, which they'd accepted almost without any discussion as collateral. So much so that Deutsche was demanding early repayment of the more than one billion dollars they had loaned 1MDB for the purpose of buying back the IPO options given to Krishnan and the other potential investors.

What was it that Rudyard Kipling said about keeping your head when all others around you are losing theirs? Well, I've always strived to do that.

I always go into my meetings extremely well informed and agilely well prepared for any eventuality, and this first-ever meeting with Al Mazroui was no exception. I had, you might call it, an offer the new IPIC head couldn't refuse.

I strongly recommended that IPIC pony up the one-billion-dollars-and-change that 1MDB needed to repay the loans from Deutsche Bank. In return, the Finance Ministry of Malaysia, headed, you'll remember, by Prime Minister Najib, would guarantee repayment of all monies owed to the Abu Dhabi fund by 1MDB in the combined form of cash and value assets. How the Malaysian government was actually going to come up with all that money was anyone's guess, but that was really beside the point. Al Mansoui really had no choice but to accept the deal without discussion or debate.

Here's why: Abu Dhabi absolutely did not want to see a public financial scandal implicating one of its most prestigious and globally respected sovereign wealth funds. After all, a few billion dollars were peanuts compared to the over seventy billion dollars the fund was worth, not to mention the economic power that represented among the many nations and multinational organizations and companies the IPIC fund did business with. Even more critically, Abu Dhabi's ruling family absolutely did not want a public scandal implicating one of its own family members. The Middle Eastern royal families fiercely protect their own, and in this case, that included the hapless Sheikh Mansour, under whose watch all of this had transpired and who, ultimately, as the guy in charge, was responsible for allowing Al Qubaisi to go rogue with the IPIC wealth fund's millions.

I got the strong, purely intuitive impression that the crown prince had come to believe—or convince himself—not only that Al Qubaisi was involved in the scheme but that, in nabbing him, they had very likely captured the ringleader, and they just weren't interested in looking beyond Qubaisi. Who knows? They might have concluded that Qubaisi had simply been irreparably corrupted by all the years living in the decadent, godless culture of the West. Regardless, it was clear that they just wanted to get past all this bad business and be done with it. Disgraced as he was, they would listen to nothing Qubaisi said in his own defense or to implicate others in his treachery. Which of course, was a very good thing for me.

I could never understand why guys like Obaid and Qubaisi, with all their wealth and success, could turn around and be so despicably miserly with their key executive managers or virtual private secretaries like Justo and Montiel (I'm talking about individuals with privileged, sensitive, insider information) only to have their unmitigated greed come back and bite them in the ass, ruining everything they might have achieved.

As for me, when I reflect on those days, I think I had the exact opposite problem. I was just too damned generous with all of my associates. What that extreme, over-the-top generosity only did, was make almost every single associate I did business with, or brought on board with one of my major investment ventures; it made them all want and even demand greater and greater amounts of money as the venture unfolded. And then they'd want twice or three times as much to participate in the next deal, and the one after that, and so on. It was never enough. Really, when you look at it objectively and more globally, I believe that my own generosity in trying to please everybody truly was the source of all of my problems. You might say that was my character flaw.

Chapter 18

If Suhail Al Mazroui wasn't too happy with the deal I'd made to have IPIC cover for 1MDB the over-one-billion-dollar loan that Deutsche Bank had called back early, neither was Prime Minister Najib. Najib did not like the fact that, somehow, suddenly, the Malaysian Finance Ministry was on the hook to guarantee repayment of that money, inconceivably, to one of Abu Dhabi's wealthiest sovereign funds. He didn't seem to grasp how such a thing could be.

Let me say this: For someone in his position, as the leader of a successfully emerging nation (Malaysia had experienced enormous economic growth over the previous twenty-five years), Najib had a rather myopic view of his country's economic status among the nations of the world. I think he saw the countries of the Middle East as intolerably rich and his own country of Malaysia as intolerably poor. Maybe that was because, with every election, he found himself obliged to spend so much time slogging around jungles and filthy backwater cities drumming up votes among the natives for UMNO candidates, including himself. He persisted, it seemed, to carry about constantly a kind of nationalistic inferiority complex.

Numerous times, I tried to point out to him that Malaysia has one of the strongest economies in the world, ranking about 36th or 37th among all nations in 2015, with a GDP of about $300 billion. That was only a few tics below the UAE, with its GDP of about 360 billion that same year, but also notably ahead of countries like

France, Australia, and South Korea. Yet I always thought—I still think—the country is capable of doing much more. This little bit of nasty business with Qubaisi's misappropriation of funds and having to guarantee repayments to IPIC in return for the fund anteing up the one-billion-dollar repayment that Deutsche Bank was demanding, was something of a distraction. If you looked at it the context of the entire scheme of things, it was all small change. On the other hand, it was big-time important for Malaysia. That is, I saw this little wrinkle as an opportunity for 1MDB to ingratiate itself with IPIC and with Abu Dhabi at large. We were guaranteeing funds to one of the wealthiest sovereign funds in the world, and *this* was the level I wanted to do business on—on the grand scale, for me and for Malaysia, and as I choose to see it, we were simply deepening the partnership of Malaysia with the Middle East.

Regardless of all that, suffice it to say that Najib was a whole hell of a lot happier when the money was flowing copiously in the opposite direction—from the Middle East to Malaysia, and believe me, he let me know it. I had never seen the prime minister so cross as when I met with him privately—offshore, in international waters, on *Equanimity*—only a few days after making the deal with Al Mazroui in Abu Dhabi. I had to try to be understanding. Najib was under an enormous amount of stress and political pressure at that moment, what with all the bad press and the imminent police and banking industry investigations. I had to give him some slack, to let him blow off steam if he needed. Fortunately, Najib remained determined to stay the course. So too, apparently, did First Lady Rosmah, who, as usual, accompanied the prime minister on this secretive trip to my yacht.

What had always worked in our relationship was that Najib pretty much gave me carte blanche to call the shots at 1MDB and to make financial decisions on behalf of not just the fund but also with particular emphasis on behalf of Najib himself and his political interests and ambitions. I had become something of a personal advisor as well, going back to the days when I attended the graduation of his and Rosmah's daughter from the Sevenoaks School, in Kent, in the UK, and thereafter helped her to gain admission to Georgetown University. I was happy to see that this working arrangement would not change; nevertheless, I had my work cut out for me.

"I expect you to straighten all this out and that you will do it very quickly," Najib said.

I assured the prime minister that I would, that the IPO would go forward and the proceeds from that deal would go a long way toward correcting the financial imbalances that were currently plaguing 1MDB.

"And don't forget," I added. "The ultra-modern high-speed rail line we are very shortly going to start building with the help of our Chinese partners is going to make Malaysia the envy of all of Southeast Asia." I did not need to remind Najib that it would also put twenty billion dollars in cash at his immediate disposal. For her part, the broadly smiling Rosmah gave me a big, perfume-infused hug.

"We know you can do this, Jho," she said. Of course, I had taken proactive measures to secure that "ringing" endorsement from the First Lady when I presented her with a $35,000, AAAA-quality-rated, white South Sea pearl necklace from Laguna Pearl Exchange the moment she first boarded the boat with about a thousand pounds of luggage for the weekend stay. Needless to say, that was all it took to restore and reinvigorate her undying faith in me. As I've said before, when Rosmah was happy, Najib was happy—a marriage made in Saks Fifth Avenue, you might say.

When the helicopter carrying Najib and Rosmah back to Kuala Lumpur lifted loudly off from *Equanimity*'s helipad, I was feeling reasonably comfortable about where things stood. Abu Dhabi's IPIC fund now had a vested interest in the success of 1MDB's impending energy assets IPO. Najib seemed girded and ready for battle with his political enemies at home and to take steps to counter the "fake news" coming from the rogue press. I thought, perhaps, things were beginning to stabilize once again. In fact, Najib, Rosmah, their family and friends, all had a very momentous and joyful event to celebrate: the marriage of their daughter in April 2015, to Daniyar Nazarbayev of Kazakhstan, who happened to be the nephew of that country's strongman president, Nursultan Nazarbayev. As I had her graduations from Sevenoaks and Georgetown, I was pleased to attend the lavish formal wedding in Kazakhstan and, later, the huge reception that Najib threw in the new couple's honor in the Pekan district, on the east coast of Malaysia, facing the South China Sea.

Both events were spectacular in their opulence and sheer scale. The wedding conducted at the famed Zenkov Cathedral, a wooden Ukrainian-baroque style structure in the city of Almaty, in southern Kazakhstan, resembled a coronation, as befitting the marriage of the nephew of a president to the daughter of a prime minister, and was followed by an elegant reception in the Grand Ballroom of the famed Hotel Royal Tulip. Not to be outdone, Najib hosted not one but three separate extravagant receptions across Malaysia. Just to give you an idea: At the one held in the glittering Kuala Lumpur City Centre, the floral arrangements alone were reported to cost three million ringgit, prompting vocal criticism in the press from Mahathir for this and other excesses. I managed to be among the over three hundred exclusively invited guests at the grandest reception of them all, held at a breathtaking private royal palace in Pekan, overlooking the ocean, although my attendance there was not without a measure of James Bond–style intrigue and drama. Remember, Najib had advised me to stay clear of Malaysia for a time, and were it not for Pekan's largely remote inaccessibility and for Najib's generous provision of a SWAT-team-caliber security detail, my presence among the distinguished guests would have been out of the question.

We moored *Equanimity* several miles off the coast of Pekan, where we were met by a speedboat under the command of an elite team of Najib's most trusted UTK royal guard. I remember thinking that these were really serious guys, with big AK-47-type automatic weapons—the kind of security personnel that wore mirrored sunglasses even in the dark and never smiled or laughed, even at the funniest joke or if someone farted. I got the distinct impression that if any one of them made the mistake of laughing at something funny, one of the other commandos would be obliged immediately to execute the guy with two bullets directly to the head.

Upon boarding the speedboat, I was struck by how no one spoke a word as we got underway and motored swiftly and silently to a private, well-guarded marina just north of Pekan town proper where I was whisked into the black Lincoln Continental limousine that would take me to the reception through an underground tunnel in the rear of the royal palace. I felt like an international spy, and my return to *Equanimity* at evening's end would go, like clockwork, exactly the same way. This was how I had to travel if I wanted to visit my home country of Malaysia.

At the reception, I spoke only briefly with Prime Minister Najib. This was, after all, a deeply personal, family-oriented affair and not the time or the place or the occasion for discussions of business or politics. Or at least that should have been the case.

At one point in the evening, probably around two a.m., I left the festivities in the main ballroom. I was searching for a door to the night outside; I was pretty fatigued, and I felt I needed some fresh, cooler air to revive me. On the way, as I passed by what I believe must have been a private conference room, and there, through the huge, ten-foot-tall oaken doors, I heard shouting. I heard a fist pounding on a table, loudly. I hesitated briefly by the doors. Two men on the other side were arguing. One of them I could clearly recognize was Najib. It took a while, but, eventually, I discerned that the other was Datuk Azlin Alias, who you'll no doubt remember was Najib's principal private secretary. I distinctly heard the words "1MDB" and "AmBank" and "six hundred and eighty-one million." I quickly moved away, down the hallway to a pair of ornate brass and stained-glass doors that opened onto a balcony overlooking the South China Sea, where I gulped the salty ocean air. And to this day, I wish I could unremember overhearing those two men arguing that night.

Because later that evening—or, should I say, in the gathering early morning glow of the reddening sunrise of the next morning—Azlin Alias boarded a state-owned AS365 Dauphin French-built helicopter for the short flight back to Kuala Lumpur. He was accompanied on the trip by four others, including Malaysia's minister of science, technology, and innovation, who had also once served as a special envoy to the United States. About ninety minutes into the flight, the helicopter exploded in flames over the jungles of Selangor on its approach to the capital. Azlin and everybody else on board were killed instantly.

When I heard the news, the first—truly disturbing—thing that crashed unbidden into my mind was the thought of Hussain Najadi, the assassinated AmBank president. The second and equally disturbing thing was the thought of Altantuya Shaariibuu. That's right, the Mongolian model whose body had been blown to bits in the jungle nearly a decade ago. Maybe my mind was jumping wildly and irrationally to conclusions; at that stressful time, I was prone to agonizing over all sorts of crazy, neurotic conspiratorial ideas. A lot of people that I knew and regularly did business with were on edge, and it was getting harder to know who you could trust.

Amid their usual air of dispassionate bureaucratic officialdom, the Malaysian authorities stated flatly that the investigation into the cause of the crash would take many months, perhaps a year or longer. That was largely because the debris from the fiery explosion was spread over a full square mile of dense rainforest, such that collecting evidence was going to be a monumental task.

That was in April. Barely a couple of months later, on a warm, sunny morning in June, Xavier Justo, the day's newspaper under his arm, was walking down a London street on his way to the Premier Club when he was set upon by at least six men, who, en masse, grabbed him from behind and forced him to his knees. Next, two of the men immediately threw a stiff black bag over his head and cinched it so tight at the neck that Justo gagged for breath while the others secured his hands behind his back using white plastic zip ties and larger black ones to tie his ankles and knees together. The six were disguised as British bobbies, though onlookers might have wondered why they looked so Asian in moustaches and beards, but then there was also the decidedly non-bobby-looking fact that several of them toted large semiautomatic weapons that they flashed openly to bystanders on the street, presumably to discourage anybody who might be thinking of becoming a hero. One of them shouted several times, "This is a police matter. Please stand clear!" No one interfered.

The abductors hustled Justo into a windowless, gleaming white Volvo transit van parked nearby, where they stuffed him into a huge canvas bag with a thick leather strap at the close. However, they hadn't quite calculated on Justo's six-foot-five frame, so when his feet and ankles protruded out of the bottom of the bag, they improvised by wrapping wads of duct tape around his lower legs in an almost laughable effort to seal the bag shut, such that Justo now looked like a gigantic version of one of those exploding party favors at children's birthday celebrations. As some of the men worked to secure the now-captive Justo, one of them calmly got behind the wheel and drove the Volvo to an international cargo terminal at Heathrow Airport, where they loaded their quarry onto a private airplane for the thirteen-hour flight to Kuala Lumpur. Once the plane was in the air, they let Justo out of the canvas bag, but it wasn't so merciful a gesture as it might have seemed. Because if they hadn't, he probably would have suffocated to death in there, and they needed him alive.

From Kuala Lumpur International Airport, still bound at the hands and ankles and with the taut tie-strings of the black bag chaffing at his neck, Justo was loaded into another transit van, this time a black Mercedes, and rushed to Sungai Buloh Prison, in Selangor. The same prison, you might recall, where Koon Swee Kang was being held for the murder of AmBank president Najadi and his wife. There, he was brought to a filthy, windowless six-by-six-foot prison cell that contained only a disturbingly darkly stained army-style cot and an open toilet, where he was finally released from his restraints. He was tossed onto the wet stone floor and left there, alone in the cell, without food or water, for some twenty-four hours before anybody came to explain what this was all about—although Justo presumably had a pretty good idea about what it was all about.

The first person to visit him was no less a figure than the superintendent of Sungai Buloh Prison himself, accompanied by two armed guards. Jangling a ring of keys—just like in the movies—one of the guards unlocked the cell door, and the superintendent entered.

"What the hell is going on here?" Justo yelled. "You've got no right to hold me here—wherever the hell this is. I'm an American citizen, you know. I have rights!"

The superintendent only smiled. "Please sit down," he said, gesturing toward the cot. As Justo slowly sat down on one end, the superintendent calmly sat down on the other.

"You Americans always amuse me," he said. "First, let me explain that you are in Sungai Buloh Prison, Mr. Justo, in Kuala Lumpur, and, right now, you are under the jurisdiction of the government of Malaysia. But please tell me. Do you think your American citizenship permits you to commit crimes against Malaysian companies?"

"Crimes? What crimes? What the hell are you talking about?"

"Oh, very serious crimes," the superintendent said. "We are talking about blackmail, Mr. Justo. And extortion, among other criminal offenses against the state."

"Extortion? What the fuck?"

"When you try to take money from a multinational company in return for not releasing confidential information you have stolen from that company, here in Malaysia, we call that extortion. If I'm not terribly mistaken, I think that's what they call it in the United States too, no?" The superintendent smiled, pausing for a moment, as if waiting for a response.

When Justo did not answer, the superintendent reached over and patted him gently on the knee. "Come, Mr. Justo," he said as he stood up. "As you might say in America, it is time for you to meet the press."

Justo followed his jailers up a flight of stone stairs to a waiting elevator, which transported them three floors higher to a glaringly lighted media room packed with news reporters, photographers, and television cameras. After so many hours in the darkness of his cell, Justo, still handcuffed, at first squinted and blinked reflexively, trying to see amid the intense light, as the guards sat him in an armless wooden chair. As his eyes began to adjust, he saw the table against one wall where his computers and cell phone sat, and that was the moment he realized that, as the six commandos were abducting him off the street, several others had been busy raiding his private office in the back of the Premier Club. They had confiscated all of the items that were now sitting as "evidence" on the long, low table in the media room, along with a couple of firearms that the police would allege were his.

After the superintendent detailed the charges against him and answered a few of the reporters' questions, Justo was led back to his cell, where a different visitor was already waiting for him—Paul Finnigan, a former British police detective who had recently left the force to set up his own private agency. After the guards left, Finnigan purported to be a "friendly" visitor of a sort, explaining to Justo that he was a police detective investigating the case. In reality, Finnigan had actually been hired by PetroSaudi. Regardless, Finnigan proposed a deal; if Justo would plead guilty to all charges, Finnigan promised him he would be out of prison and back in London by Christmas. The detective assured Justo that the principals of PetroSaudi would help him, as long as he was totally cooperative and did exactly as he would be told. As if to reinforce that assurance, a few days later, Patrick Mahony visited Justo in his jail cell and told him essentially the same thing.

Already deeply distressed by the ordeal he'd been put through, Justo apparently didn't even think about demanding to see an attorney, and he signed a twenty-two-page confession in which he apologized to PetroSaudi for stealing the information on the company's computer servers, and for first trying to use the stolen servers to blackmail PetroSaudi before then selling the information to Rewcastle Brown of the *Sarawak Report* and Ho Kay Tat of the *Edge* newspaper. In subsequent public statements published in the press, Justo made alternating and contradictory claims stating both that he had, in fact, tampered with the documents and emails and that Rewcastle Brown and Tat had secretly told him that *they* planned to alter the information contained in the computer server documentation. He also claimed that the journalist "buyers" of the servers had reneged on the deal, failing to pay him the two million he was promised for the servers. That of course was false, but no matter.

By this point, it really didn't matter what Justo said. The more contradictory his statements going forward, so much the better, because the real purpose of all of this was to discredit him as a liar and a cheat willing to do and say anything for money and thus to call into serious question the authenticity of the information allegedly on those servers—a classic disinformation campaign at the very heart of it.

Justo obligingly became the perfect dupe, which is to say, he took direction very well. He told the authorities exactly what Finnigan and Mahony told him to say, thinking that, by doing so, he was going to save his own skin. What he did instead was unwittingly provide the foundation for the UMNO party's accusations that the whole thing was a conspiracy against the prime minister concocted by Najib's "detestable" political opposition and facilitated by historically avowed hostile individuals among a renegade press.

So as Justo issued increasingly contradictory statements, the UMNO went to work, for example, by publishing articles in the *New Straits Times*—a popular and widely circulated Southeast Asian newspaper one hundred percent owned by the UMNO—citing unnamed reports from an obscure London-based cybersecurity firm—also hired by the UMNO—that it had supposedly analyzed the leaked data provided by Justo and found evidence that the documents and emails had been tampered with. It was all choreographed by the political opposition to stir up trouble for the prime minister, the papers claimed, and fomented by renegade journalists who were enemies of the state.

Prime Minister Najib did his part to foster that perception. Shortly after the *Edge* started publishing stories regarding Justo and the leaked documents, Najib himself ordered Ho Kay Tat and four of his editorial team picked up and detained under Malaysia's strict yet broadly interpretable Sedition Act; they were held in separate dank prison cells for several days before finally being released. It was purely an act of intimidation. Najib's administration also rushed through a new law that essentially eliminated the right of *habeas corpus* in matters related to potential terrorism or in connection with alleged crimes and conspiracy against the state. Now, Najib could order people held indefinitely by the authorities, for as long as he might want. And I'm afraid this was only the beginning.

I have, earlier in this story, disavowed any interest in politics, and I say that again here. You have probably presumed that the men who abducted Justo and brought him to a prison in Malaysia were some elite task force of the UTK, under the direction of the prime minister, and that the action was fundamentally politically motivated. But you'd be wrong. They were actually hired by me. That is, to be clear about it, they were hired by PetroSaudi, though under my direction. I hope you can understand why. I had to minimize this whole PetroSaudi connection with 1MDB. As I've said, we were on to bigger and better things, what with the energy assets IPO about to be launched, the massive Belt and Road railway project partnering with China, and who could know what great things would follow after that? The sky was the limit. I made sure that Justo was delivered to the Malaysian authorities so that he could be scapegoated, not unlike Qubaisi and Husseiny had collectively taken the fall in Abu Dhabi. I figured the UMNO and its operatives, including the newspapers and other media outlets the party controlled, would be able to discredit Justo as a fool and demonstrate that the information he provided was entirely bogus—an enormous, fraud-for-money scheme, almost laughable, were it not such an affront to the Malaysian people.

But then the stories accusing Najib of taking money directly from 1MDB began surfacing in international papers like the *Wall Street Journal* and *London Financial Times*. As prime minister, Najib possessed the power to shut down the *Edge* newspaper by ordering its publication license revoked—and with his new terrorism laws in place, he could have ordered Ho Kat Tat and others arrested and thrown in jail without trial, indefinitely. But there was nothing he could do to silence those big overseas financial newspapers.

And that's when he began to take things too far, politically, in his own country.

By the end of July, 2015, Malaysia's attorney general, Abdul Gani Patail, was putting the finishing touches on the serious criminal charges he was preparing to bring against the prime minister. The formal complaint charged Najib with allegedly receiving millions of dollars in payments from 1MDB, albeit through numerous convoluted channels and questionable entities, but nevertheless in direct violation of provisions under the Malaysian Anti-Corruption Commission Act of 2009, forbidding the payment or receipt of bribes and establishing a maximum prison sentence of up to twenty years for each offense. Confidentially, the attorney general dutifully disclosed his sobering plans to the chief of Malaysia's police, but it was not the sort of information that could be kept quiet for long. As soon as he learned of the attorney general's plans to bring charges against him; that's when Najib brought the autocratic hammer down hard.

First, on July 28, he fired Attorney General Patail, who, that morning, arrived at his office to find the doors padlocked and guarded by machine-gun-toting security officers of Najib's UTK royal guard. Patail was not even permitted to enter the office to retrieve his personal things, much less documents and other evidentiary exhibits related to his legal case against the prime minister. Next, Najib replaced the chief of Malaysia's Special Investigative Force, who had helped lead the probe into the prime minister's finances. The next thing you knew, the main police headquarters were on fire, dozens upon dozens of investigative documents and computer files going up in smoke and flames. Then Najib cleaned political house: He fired a half dozen of his cabinet ministers, including his own deputy prime minister, Muhyiddin Yassin, who, over the preceding months, had become more and more vocal in his criticism of the operations of 1MDB and just recently had gone so far as to call for a full and transparent investigation of the fund's finances and investments.

Some months earlier and no doubt as part of the continuing power struggle saga with his opposition nemesis, a federal court—the jurists privately urged on and pressured by Najib himself—had sentenced Anwar Ibrahim to five years in prison on trumped up charges of committing sodomy. Of course, Ibrahim had been number one on Najib's hit list ever since he had nearly defeated the prime minister in the 2013 election—in part on a frightening promise to shut down 1MDB and investigate the corrupt principals who ran it. Now, Najib was about to go even further toward quashing the opposition.

Ibrahim's imprisonment was roundly criticized by the United States and by human rights organizations around the world, while, at home, all of these repressive executive actions sparked massive protests in the streets of several cities across the country. On August 29, not even twenty-four hours after Najib had fired his attorney general, over one hundred thousand Malaysians flooded the streets and squares of Kuala Lumpur, marching in the streets while wearing those yellow T-shirts with the Bersih protest slogan on them—this in brazen defiance of an order issued in the days shortly after the election, by the Home Ministry, which declared that the shirts posed a serious threat to national security and banned the wearing of them under threat of arrest simply for doing so. A large majority of these demonstrators were young, educated, urban professionals—the people who represented the very lifeblood of the modern Malaysian economy and who were not so easily bought by political graft or patronage as the dirt poor tribal peoples living in the outlying jungle states like Sarawak and Terengganu.

The growing clamor in the cities and the streets threatened to bring the Malaysian economic engine to a grinding halt. Meanwhile, similar protest demonstrations were held by Malaysians and their supporters living in other countries around the world, from Southeast Asian countries to Europe and America, in political solidarity with the citizens back home. Leaders of other nations who had been friendly to Malaysia and Najib and who had wanted to partner with Malaysia's economic development—and, furthermore, who, in fact, saw Prime Minister Najib as a solitary beacon of democracy in Southeast Asia—including the United States, now began to back away.

What was Najib's response?

His resolve only stiffened. There's no doubt in my mind that Rosmah—as she had done so many times before in my presence—insisted to her husband that this crisis was yet another great test directly from Allah, this one being perhaps the greatest test of all. In point of fact, Rosmah never tried to hide her belief that she and Najib had been chosen by Allah as the first family of state to lead Malaysia into a glorious future. Almost certainly goaded by his wife, Najib directed his police forces to round up, arrest, and jail even more opposition leaders. A couple of weeks later, gangs of pro-government "demonstrators"—all wearing red shirts, apparently in some kind of bizarrely surreal response to the yellow of the Bersih—suddenly began showing up in the streets and knocking heads with the anti-government protestors and attacking their activist leaders. The red shirts were there, it was clear, solely to disrupt the antigovernment protests, and most of them had actually been paid in cash for their services by UMNO operatives!

There was sheer lawless chaos happening in the streets of the capital and other cities. I even feared that the prime minister was one step away from declaring martial law across the country.

You have to understand, this is when I became truly worried about Najib's increasingly iron-fisted grab for authoritarian, unilateral, unchecked power and, to say it honestly, his potentially dangerous descent into outright autocratic tyranny. He held a secret meeting with the key management executives of 1MDB. Among them was attorney Jasmine Loo, unquestionably the last remaining member whom I could implicitly trust to give me the straight dope on what was happening among the board members, as well as what was happening among Najib's rapidly fracturing inner circle. She was unflinchingly loyal to me. Loo was so frightened that she called me on a burner phone to clue me in to the meeting.

"The PM announced that he is launching a thorough, no-holds-barred investigation into the operations of the fund," she told me. "He's threatening to destroy any individual found to have leaked confidential information to the press or the police."

The truth was, Najib had no intention to initiate any formal, legitimate, open, financially substantive, by-the-books investigation of the fund; he was simply and singularly determined to ferret out any "traitorous" leakers or whistleblowers and get rid of them, one way or another.

"I fear that Najib has already started drawing up an 'enemies list,'" Loo had fretted in that same phone call, "and some key people we know may be on it."

I was certain of one thing. His bellicose speech to the board in that private meeting was just more intimidation, this time directed at people who had mostly been very loyal to him, who had mostly done what I had told them to do, acting as I was, on behalf of the prime minister.

I started to get scared; at various critical moments, I thought he might be about to lose his wits. I thought he might be capable of anything, and I had no idea what he was going to do next. Unpredictability is dangerous, and, in certain situations, it might be the most dangerous thing in the world, to my way of thinking. This, I believed, was one of those situations.

On one hand, I was sincerely concerned for my friend, for the national Malaysian leader for whom I had been both financial advisor and personal confidant for nearly seven years now, in some ways even his diplomatic entertainment director with some of the high-level gatherings—and very productive ones, if I may say so—that I had arranged and orchestrated to the smallest details. On the other hand, if Najib was about to go down in flames, in part because he couldn't withstand the political heat, I was absolutely determined that I was not going down with him. I thought again of the line from the poem, about keeping one's head when all around are losing theirs.

Would he turn on me? I simply didn't know. I couldn't predict. I had no control. And I don't like things I can't control.

To make matters worse, my strategic self-banishment from Malaysia made me feel increasingly removed from the gathering crisis and increasingly powerless to pressure the relevant players—intimidate them, if needs be—to take the precise actions and effect the specific maneuvers that I wanted them to take. My sheer remoteness from the center of the maelstrom also made it nearly impossible to choreograph the unfolding events to my satisfaction, as I had so often been able to do before my tight relationship with the prime minister had begun to unravel.

I'll admit this: At one point, I kind of lost my cool. I picked up the phone, and I called 1MDB executive director Lodin Kamaruddin, despite the significant risk that the line was being monitored and recorded, especially under the guise of Najib's no-holds-barred, so-called corruption investigation. I screamed at Lodin, "If you, or anyone else on the board—damn it, even if the prime minister himself—thinks that you people might get away by sacrificing me, I'll go nuclear on you all."

"Jho, take it easy," Lodin said, trying to calm me. But I would have none of it.

"I was acting on the instructions of the boss, and you damn well know that the board operated in lockstep with Najib's orders." Then I warned Lodin, "And I know where all the bodies are buried."

Still, all things considered, the difficulties imposed by distance notwithstanding, I thought it best to sequester myself on *Equanimity*, out of sight, out of harm's way, shuttling quietly among some pleasanter, anonymous seaside ports far away from the current turmoil in Malaysia. One place on land where I was reasonably safe was in Bangkok, primarily because the leadership of Thailand's government remained friendly with Najib. With the yacht as my safe haven, I even managed to sneak away to the Mediterranean, to the French Riviera, on a few pleasurable gambling junkets to Monaco and San Tropez, getaways that helped me enormously to take all of these troubles off my mind and gave me time to think. Shanghai was another place where I felt reasonably safe and protected. I thought that this would be a very good time to go and inspect the fine progress my Chinese construction company friends were making on my new and, by this time, nearly completed sanctuary compound in the peace and quiet of the dense rainforest—here, in the middle of nowhere, where I now write from.

Chapter 19

I don't like living in this compound.
True, I have described this place as having everything a guy could want—all the amenities you could conceive of for a residence. But it's also about as isolated a place as you can get on planet Earth, and I don't like isolation. At the same time, I like to keep my affairs, both personal and business, very private. It's something paradoxical about my nature that I'm not sure I can really explain in words. Why I'm that way, I mean.

But it is why I loved to orchestrate and host the most fantastic, outrageous parties imaginable, yet wished always to remain out of the spotlight, like when I allowed gossip and entertainment writers and reporters like Robin Leach to attend those events only on the provision that they could write about anything they wanted, but were strictly prohibited from talking about me—or even so much as printing my name in their salacious stories. It's also why, when I single-handedly put together the mechanics of some massive, multinational investment deal, I never wanted my name to appear as a signatory of the agreement documents or the bank records. I suppose I wanted it both ways: the glory of making the deal and the backroom anonymity. That, of course, is usually an extremely difficult mix to achieve, particularly in a digital age in which it seems that everything eventually winds up in full view on the Internet.

But it is the isolation that I abhor, which gives me a feeling of loathing that, I think, goes back to the way I felt as a child growing up in godforsaken Penang, where I felt isolated from the modern world. At least in Penang, there were streets lined with storefronts. There were places to go, like aging movie houses and parks, run down as they may have been in those days. And there was industry, of a sort, all sorts of people doing their work, from running the local shops to giving guided tours to the mainly Western tourists that seemed to wilt over time in the sweltering heat. It's paradoxical, how all of that routine pedestrian activity seems so pleasant to me now, almost bucolically free of stress. There were, in a phrase, interesting things to see and do amid the multicultural throngs of people, both local and foreign, even if they hadn't changed much in a hundred years. But here, inside this private compound, which I have come to see as the very definition of boring, I have little else to look at but these 143 walls.

Yes, I've actually counted them—several times—and yet I still can't figure out how the total can come to an odd number. Shouldn't every room have four walls? I must be missing a wall somewhere. Believe me when I tell you that you could see this compound as a stately pleasure dome, especially at first blush, but with time, you would likely come to see it, as I do now, as some sort of grim mausoleum. I might as well be dead here, lying in my solid-gold sarcophagus, hidden in some secret vault deep below. Well, perhaps I'm being a bit too morose, but living this way is sheer torture to me.

In the days when I still had *Equanimity* and earlier, when I still had my private jet, I could still travel rather freely around the world, even if there were some countries it would not have been prudent for me to set foot in, due to the growing series of investigations into 1MDB that were going on in places like the U.S., Switzerland, Singapore, Hong Kong, the UK, and so on. In due course, the initial revelations published in the Malaysian press led to further revelations published in the *NYT* and the *WSJ*, the *London Times*, and the *Guardian*, which, in turn, led to investigations in all of those other countries, led by legal authorities or banking regulatory authorities—or both.

Most damaging of all to my efforts to save 1MDB from total financial collapse, were the investigations by the U.S. Department of Justice and the Federal Bureau of Investigation, but all of these nationally driven investigations had the effect of shutting down my ability to work with the big international banks that had helped me get this far. In several cases, the authorities forced the banks to freeze the assets of the various entities and accounts that I had set up to coordinate my investment operations on behalf of 1MDB, on behalf of Prime Minister Najib, or on behalf of my own companies, like Wynton Group and Jynwel Capital. In some cases, the authorities initiated legal proceedings to try to seize some of those assets, claiming they belonged to some other entity or government.

This wasn't fair.

Freezing these assets only served to restrict my ability to transfer capital to different investment ventures around the world. If I was going to save 1MDB from bankruptcy, from defaulting on its loan obligations, I needed ready access to those funds, to be able to deploy them as effectively as possible. Because let's be perfectly honest: The complete failure of 1MDB would have caused much more damage to people and investment organizations and to certain governments than the relatively minor consequences of a few million dollars gone missing here and there. The authorities' overblown reaction, in my view, was a little like throwing a man in debtor's prison and expecting him to somehow miraculously repay his debts from behind bars. Freezing my assets only served to tie my financial hands behind my back.

I needed new sources of capital. Unfortunately, the blatant extravagances exhibited by both Al Qubaisi and Al Husseiny, which led to their abrupt removal as the heads of the IPIC and Aabar wealth funds, had also severely soured Abu Dhabi's attitude toward Malaysia as an investment partner. Understandably so, but I suppose even that's putting it mildly. Bottom line: The Abu Dhabi royals didn't want anything further to do with Malaysia, with Prime Minister Najib, or—most importantly—with me. This too was totally unfair.

I hadn't done anything wrong in connection with IPIC's decision to back the 1MDB bond issues. That had been their decision. My role had been to facilitate Middle Eastern investment in Malaysia; I was but an intermediary, as I had told the press, and it was Abu Dhabi's responsibility to perform their own due diligence. Regardless, I now had to look elsewhere for new capital resources.

While I certainly didn't approve of Qubaisi's personal excesses and his professional oversights, I have to say that I admired what he was able to achieve through his acquisition of Falcon Bank, the red-tape-cutting efficiency he was able to bring to bear with regard to money transfers, even large tranches like the ones Falcon had moved from Tanore to Najib's "special" accounts within AmBank so quickly in advance of the 2013 election. So I thought I would buy my own bank.

Did you know that there are some countries around the world where, if you are willing to make major financial investments, you can gain expedited citizenship—and a valid passport—in return for that investment? One such country is Cyprus, and at the time, that island nation in the middle of the Mediterranean seemed the ideal place for me to buy my bank.

The process of gaining the endorsements I needed and navigating the legal channels to Cypriot citizenship were surprisingly simple and relatively inexpensive. In return for a modest donation of 300,000 euros to the Church of Cyprus in September 2015, I gained the support and written endorsement of Archbishop Chrysostomos, who forwarded a highly favorable recommendation to the interior minister, Socratis Hasikos, asking him to fast-track my application for citizenship. In order to convince and reassure Cypriot government officials that I was indeed fully intent on doing business in their beautiful country, I purchased a hilltop villa that was still under construction, which only set me back about five million euros. In this property acquisition effort, I was helped enormously by the British firm of Oglethorpe & Partners, one of the top residence and citizenship planning firms in the world, for a fee of roughly thirteen percent of the purchase price, around €650,000 in total.

I want to say something about the many law firms I worked with in connection with my investment ventures. As I've already revealed in the writing, I regularly worked with executives from the most respected banks and financial multinationals in the world, from Goldman Sachs to J.P. Morgan, and from Coutts to Deutsche. In that world, I often encountered individuals who were reluctant, or who even outright refused to work with me and the grandly innovative investment scenarios I devised. I can only say, in the kindliest of terms, that because these individuals didn't have the future vision or the requisite courage to partner with me, they missed out on many very lucrative opportunities. Yet, funny thing, but I never had this problem with attorneys or law firms, who always seemed to be philosophically open to the realm of the possible, and to the idea that one could creatively use the legal system to "get things done," if you will.

Legally, of course.

Just like McCarter & Maxwell in the U.S., Oglethorpe & Partners was another case in point, in terms of steadfastly protecting attorney–client privilege. When questions later came up in the press regarding my business and personal interests in Cyprus, the firm categorically denied that they had a client relationship with me. If you think that's borderline dishonest, the fact is that a business law firm's client list is nobody else's business, and one of the first responsibilities of any firm in just about every business is protecting one's clients. Although their statements were also true; the firm was actually working through corporate entities that I had set up, but within which I held no official position as one of the principals. So when Oglethorpe also denied in the press that they had ever invoiced me for services rendered, or ever received any monies directly from me, they were again telling the truthful facts of the situation. One must truly love the respect for client confidentiality among lawyers!

I have never been one to put all my eggs in one basket, and I hate wasting time, so through my operatives, I investigated similar expedited-citizenship-for-investment opportunities simultaneously among a number of island countries, Cyprus in particular, because of its lax disclosure laws, but also Malta; the Comoros Islands, off the east coast of Africa; and Saint Kitts, in the Caribbean. If you're seeing a pattern there, well, I was looking for an island both literally and figuratively. In terms of targeting a bank to buy, I was looking for a host country that lay, shall I say, on the outlying periphery of the regulatory restrictions of the international banking world—a place ruled by a government under which I felt I could return to getting deals done and, ultimately, to get past this whole 1MDB fiasco. On the more literal or practical side, I was actually looking for island nations—real islands, geographically speaking—that I could conveniently travel to (or quickly depart from, if required) aboard *Equanimity*, considering that any other form of travel, particularly through international airports, was becoming exceedingly risky for me. I figured whichever of those island nations moved the fastest would win the lottery, which is to say, they would have me as a formally naturalized citizen, an aggressive and visionary investor, and, ultimately, a prominent banker, if everything went as planned. And Cyprus won the lottery. Now all I needed to do was find a bank to buy.

But then something happened that shocked all of Malaysia to its core. A high-ranking deputy prosecutor was brutally murdered in classic gangland style that very same month of September when I was bestowed citizenship status in Cyprus by the government there. The efforts to cover up the crime, if you could call them that, were pretty lame and stereotypically gangland style as well. That's always the thing with gangland-style murders. They're brutal and hideous and always at least obliquely visible, because they're usually meant to send a message. If you cover them up too well, you run the risk that your message doesn't get through.

Kevin Morais was a fifty-five-year-old Indian-Malaysian attorney who had risen through the ranks of the Malaysian attorney general's office to the position of deputy prosecutor, whereupon he had gotten assigned, perhaps somewhat unfortunately, as things turned out, to the government's Anti-Corruption Commission. It would later be revealed that Morais had been deeply angered over Najib's authoritarian crackdown on civil liberties in the wake of the publication of Rewcastle Brown's exposé, followed closely by Ho Kay Tat's accusatory articles in the *Edge*. In fact, there are some who believe that Morais was actually the person inside the attorney general's office who had deliberately leaked the information about the impending criminal charges to be brought against the prime minister that led to the firing of Attorney General Abdul Gani Patail. If Morais's intent was to fuel righteous outrage among the citizens of Malaysia, the move may have backfired, because the leaks only drove an enraged Najib to further ramp up his political crackdown, as well as to focus his wrath on the AG's office.

At the same time, Morais was also deeply worried about the corruption commission's hottest ongoing investigation into the affairs of 1MDB, which he believed Najib's crackdown was intent on quashing. Morais, after all, along with the now-deposed attorney general, had taken the leading role in drawing up the draft criminal charges against the prime minister. The prime minister whom Morais feared was now in war-like retaliation mode and would stop at nothing to hold on to power.

One morning, Deputy Prosecutor Morais gets into his modest little Malaysian-made Proton Perdana for his daily one-hour commute from his apartment in northern Kuala Lumpur to the Anti-Corruption Commission's offices in Putrajaya—the ultra-modern, splendidly preplanned city-from-the-ground-up that is the seat of the government—and of course, ironically, the location of the prime minister's regal office digs too.

Anyway, as he drives, the deputy prosecutor's car is followed by a black Mercedes transit van, not unlike, quite coincidentally, the one that spirited Justo from the Kuala Lumpur airport to Sungai Buloh Prison, in Selangor. You know what's coming: About twenty minutes into his last-ever-in-his-life drive to work, the transit van rams into the rear of Morais's car, forcing it off the road and sending it crashing into a ditch along the shoulder and up against a retaining wall on the other side of the ditch.

Now normally in all those Hollywood Mafia movies, this sort of thing is done in remote places, away from the everyday people and potential eyewitnesses—like somewhere in the middle of the winding labyrinth of dirt roads and watery channels that crisscross the New Jersey Meadowlands that sit quietly in the shadow of New York City—for example, in *The Godfather*. But there are few such remote stretches along the densely urbanized tract that runs thickly from Kuala Lumpur to Putrajaya and in virtually all directions beyond. Besides, as I said, these guys want to send a message. They want to make the front pages of the tabloids and the rest.

So they do this in broad daylight, in plain sight of other motorists and even some pedestrians, people who become eyewitnesses but who the thugs can be quite confident, due to the violent ferocity of the incident, will report to police that they saw absolutely nothing unusual on this particular morning's commute. Just another day on the way to work; nothing to see here.

Anyway, four men in black, police-looking uniforms jump out and grab a dazed Morais before he can even exit his crashed vehicle. They throw a black bag over his head and bundle him through the sliding side door of the Mercedes, slamming it shut as the van drives off, the tires squealing, gravel and dust spraying into the air.

When Morais failed to show up at his office, the inevitable alert was sounded almost immediately among his coworkers, who were already in a high state of anxiety and fear under the circumstances of the government crackdown to begin with. And while there were no eyewitnesses out there on the highway that morning who would talk to the police, like so many sprawling cosmopolitan cityscapes in the world these days, there were plenty of official roadside and privately owned security cameras that told in full-color digital video the full story of the car crash and the abduction and the speeding black Mercedes transit van taking away the deputy prosecutor.

A couple of weeks later, Morais's body was found in a remote swampy area of the Paya Indah Wetlands, located just a few miles east of Putrajaya and north of the airport. His corpse had been stuffed into a fifty-five-gallon oil drum that was subsequently filled with cement before it had been dumped into the swamp. When I read about that in the news reports, I thought, well, gee, perhaps the gangsters were watching those American Mafia movies after all. The coroner would rule that the likely cause of death was strangulation. Based on the video camera footage the police had obtained from the scene of the abduction, some of the perpetrators were arrested but, predictably, only low-level gangster-soldier types, henchmen with the IQ of a turnip, and none of the capos who would have ordered such a dastardly thing.

Naturally, Morais's murder struck terror into the hearts of the attorneys, administrators, and everyone else working in the attorney general's office, who were all now frightened for their very lives. Abdul Gani Patail had only just been fired from his job as the attorney general and replaced by a Najib loyalist. That sort of shake-up happened all the time in Malaysia, whenever the AG-du-jour might have gotten too close to some small, shady bit of treachery by the sitting PM or one of his other cabinet ministers. But this was a whole new escalation of terror.

If I've sounded cavalier in telling you this part of the story, let me be clear: It scared the shit out of me too. First a prominent bank president, then a trusted, inner-circle political advisor to the prime minister, now a powerful deputy prosecutor? Were all of these connected? Who the hell was doing this? Was anyone safe?

Was I safe?

By this time, I had known Najib Razak a long time, and for all that I knew about him, I couldn't conceive, whatsoever, of any notion that he could possibly be involved in any way in Morais's murder. Or in Najadi's assassination by the mob, for that matter. And Azlin's demise had been an unfortunate accident, hadn't it?

The Najib Razak I knew up until then was soft-spoken, always reserved, and—frankly—weak willed, often cowing to the bullheaded wishes and bizarre eccentricities of his domineering wife, Rosmah. Whenever I was in conversation with him, I often found myself thinking that, were it not for the deep financial pockets and the pervasive reach of political patronage and ubiquitous cronyism enjoyed by the UMNO that propped him up, Najib would never, on his own, have been able to hold on as prime minister for as long as he did, much less get elected to the post in the first place. In a word, he had zero charisma.

Here's the bottom line: Najib would never have had the balls, or the cunning and the financial creativity, to do the terrific deals I did on behalf of 1MDB to launch Malaysia's first sovereign wealth fund into the big time. He was far too meek, far too insecure and fearful. He couldn't dare to be outrageous the way I could. Oh, of course, I was always careful to feed his nonetheless oversized ego by giving him credit for my decisions or by feeding the myth that I was simply following his overarching financial and political game plan. But I thought, *He really needs me. He can't survive without me.* We had navigated through tough obstacles in the past. We could do it again.

Or so I thought.

So I did a daring thing. In December, as the year was drawing to a close, the prime minister was scheduled to attend a summit conference among the prominent leaders of a number of Southeast Asian nations, to be held in Hong Kong, to discuss international trade. I arranged a private meeting with Najib there, taking the not insignificant risk of arriving in port aboard my superyacht, *Equanimity*.

Actually, let me be honest: It was a carefully calculated risk and maybe not so dramatically daring as the Hollywood movie buff in me would like to think. Thanks to my new and expanding coterie of business associates among government-owned Chinese construction companies and investment-banking institutions and the growing influence and control exerted by the Chinese Communist Party over the city of Hong Kong, I was able to secure some modest but hopefully reliable measure of secret protection for me and my staff for the duration of our short, forty-eight-hour stay—just enough time to meet with Najib and then quietly depart the beautiful and historic port city. In fact, we met in the private Hong Kong offices of the Shanghai-based Redfield Group, a Chinese state-owned real estate and infrastructure conglomerate that would play a role in the sixty

THE ART OF GREED

billion dollar Malaysian high-speed rail project. After they completed work on my private Xanadu-like compound in the jungle, that is.

When Najib arrived at the secure, supposedly media-proof conference room in the Redfield Group's offices, I was already waiting for him. I knew him well enough to anticipate his standard gruff, imperious, belligerent, acrimonious, and demanding attitude, which I also knew to be nothing more than the thin veneer of self-righteous superiority that the prime minister tried desperately to hide behind whenever he felt threatened. It was all a lion's façade, and once he felt he had made his fierce impression, he would settle down, become once again the demure fellow he was. Only this time was different. This time, I hadn't counted on his quiet manner of vindictive rage—the rage, I soon surmised, of an evolving dictatorial autocrat. Markedly, it was one of the few private meetings I ever had with Najib at which Rosmah was not present.

"You've taken some significant risk in coming here today," Najib said. His demeanor was stern, like a man prepared for a fight and wanting to deliver the first blow.

"I've taken precautions," I replied, straining to sound nonchalant despite my anxiety.

Najib smiled thinly. "Not any risk from the Chinese," he said. "I'm talking about from me. You realize I could have you taken into custody right here, right now. My security detail could have you back in Malaysia and in front of a judge so fast it would make your head spin."

"You would do that here, in Hong Kong?" I shot back defiantly. "Wouldn't that be rather messy—politically, I mean—should it make the newspapers and the TV screens? 'Malaysian Prime Minister Abducts Citizen-Financier from China.'"

As I said the last part, I ran my hand in the shape of a bracket horizontally in the air, as if scanning across a newspaper headline, or a TV news screen crawl.

Najib only smirked, shaking his head as if in disdain. "We're a long way from Beijing, Jho. And *your* friends, well, most of them are all the way up in Shanghai. They can't protect you here. China hasn't taken over full control of this city—not yet anyway. And who do you think in authority, here in Hong Kong right now, is going to have the nerve to stop a sitting prime minister from personally arresting a national fugitive and repatriating him to face justice in his own country? You'd be talking about an international diplomatic incident. And you of all people know how much international financial city centers like Hong Kong hate international diplomatic incidents, especially in their own back yards."

Najib paused, and then he said, "Far from being 'messy,' I could look like a hero back home." And running his hand through the air to mimic—or, should I say, to mock—my headline-reading gesture, he said in the style of a TV announcer, "'Prime Minister Singlehandedly Nabs 1MDB Perpetrator.' How do you like that headline?" he inquired, now smiling broadly, almost leeringly, as he leaned his face toward me. But he did not stop there.

"And by the way, you do know you are wanted in Singapore for questioning about your business dealings, don't you, Jho?"

I nodded.

"And then, of course, there's the United States. I understand their Justice Department is really quite anxious to talk to you as well, probably even more than Singapore is. And then there's the banking authorities in Switzerland; they'd also like a word with you. Can you imagine the international political capital I would gain if I turned you over to the American authorities right now? It staggers the imagination."

There was nothing I could say that would represent an adequate response to this barrage of words, but I also knew from years of working with him that the prudent thing to do was to let little Najib have his moment, this tantrum as it was. I looked at him in silence, feigned solemnity in a manner of due respect that signaled, I hoped, that I would wait for as long as he wished to continue. Until he was finished and satisfied with himself, buoyed with his own superficial bluster.

And that's when he blinked, figuratively speaking. His body seemed to deflate, and I could see how exhausted and stressed he was.

"Look, Jho," Najib said, his voice now a bit less stern, calmer.

"You have been very good to my family. My stepson, my wife's son, is a successful Hollywood producer thanks to you. And you've been especially kind to my lovely wife, Rosmah, although, right now, she's very upset with you too, by the way."

"She didn't come with you this time, on this trip to Hong Kong?" I asked, trying to deflect the serious course the conversation had taken to that point.

"Oh, she's here. She's back at the hotel." Najib looked toward the ceiling abruptly and then continued, "As a matter of fact, she's probably out shopping by now. She decided not to come to this meeting, Jho. That's how upset she is. But she still has faith in you; we both do. We know you can fix this whole mess."

"What about the Anti-Corruption Commission indictment?" I asked.

I had barely gotten the words out of my mouth before Najib flared into a rage, rising from his chair like a rocket and banging his fist down so hard on the antique wooden conference table that I think he may have put a crack in the mahogany top from literally from one end to the other.

"I'll deal with the Anti-Corruption Commission!" he shouted. Then he paused, leaning his weight on his fist as if he were trying to push it through the tabletop, and then, collecting himself, seethed, "Listen to me, Jho. I assure you. There are not going to be any indictments. Period. I've already taken aggressive steps to make absolutely sure that never happens. I've already moved to clean house in the AG's office, and anybody there would be an absolute fool to oppose me now, do you understand?"

I nodded.

"Good. You let me worry about taking care of things in the government. I know how to handle those people, and I know how to respond to my political enemies. You've got your own housecleaning to do. I expect you to straighten out this whole mess with 1MDB, and I know you can do it. So does Rosmah. We continue to have every confidence in you. But you must act fast. I don't care where you get the money, but you've got to fix the books of the fund. We've got to get the accounts balanced and show a goddamn profit. Can you do that quickly?"

"Of course," I said.

"Good. Then we are through here," Najib said. He rose once again from his chair, reached across the table to shake hands. Then the prime minister turned, walked briskly to the door, opened it, and disappeared on the other side as it shut behind him. Now alone, I felt a chill running through my spine, and I remember thinking that, all things considered, there were, after all, certain unequivocally unique advantages to living in this remote little jungle compound.

Chapter 20

There was only one way for me to get back once again into the good graces of Prime Minister Najib, and that was to fix the financial problems of Malaysia's 1MDB sovereign wealth fund. There were wild estimates floating around, disseminated by the independent press and especially by Najib's radical political opposition, from Mahathir Mohamad and Anwar Ibrahim on down, about the extent of debt at the fund. One of those estimates put the figure at nearly thirteen billion dollars.

For what it's worth, I would have vehemently disputed such absurd figures on their face as nothing more than political propaganda intended to undermine Najib and the UMNO party. Looking at the situation more objectively—and more optimistically, as I tend to be an eternal optimist—the IPO of the energy assets conglomerate would earn the fund at least five billion dollars in a single stroke, if the investment banks handling the deal would just stop dragging their feet and pull the trigger on the deal. Beyond that, there was still a long way to go toward erasing 1MDB's debt, but I now saw enormous opportunities with Malaysia's newly emerging financial investment relationship with China. To me, these were funds in flux, not debt. They were negative capital I was putting to work to make positive capital, if you understand what I mean.

Anyone could see that China was interested in expanding and enhancing its sphere of influence across Southeast Asia, not to mention across the entire subcontinent of Asia to Africa—and even beyond, to South America. It's even truer now than it was then. This is really what Belt and Road was all about from the very beginning. B&R is not some all-altruistic, beneficent program designed to uplift the living standard of the nations of the world; it's a program to make a lot of poorer nations financially beholden to China, in the form of the enormous debt these countries will incur in return for the infrastructure development that China will provide.

No, I certainly am not a politician, and so I cared nothing about this continuing postwar clash between Eastern and Western political ideologies dating back to the formation of the People's Republic of China, in 1949. It was all political bullshit to me. In fact, I think all politics is basically bullshit, and the problem with it is how often all that political bullshit insidiously gets in the way of people and corporations doing business and investment. I am a pragmatist when it comes to doing business. If I saw that the major American and European multinationals like Goldman and J.P. Morgan and Deloitte and Deutsche were now reluctant to do business with Malaysia and with me—freezing my assets, questioning my investment initiatives and decisions, and all of that—I also quickly surmised that Chinese state-owned construction and development businesses, and state-run investment banking firms as well, appeared more than willing to step in—and to do so big time.

Building partnerships with Chinese firms would also effectively fill the economic void of capital investment that was no longer going to come from Abu Dhabi and its massive sovereign wealth funds, burned as they were by the corruption and embezzlement perpetrated by Al Qubaisi and Al Husseiny, which the royals mistakenly linked to 1MDB. Furthermore, having loaned billions of dollars to bail out the 1MDB fund in their efforts to cover up their own internal scandal, the new management heads of IPIC were demanding rapid repayment of those loans as well. Chinese capital investment was just the ticket to fill 1MDB's current shortfall of incoming funds.

Working behind the scenes as I so much prefer to do, I began—with tacit, unpublicized, silent support from Prime Minister

Najib—to negotiate deals with a number of Chinese state-owned companies. These companies would buy up many of the assets held by 1MDB, such as portions of real estate the fund owned in Kuala Lumpur and elsewhere across the country, as well as major utility holdings and office buildings the fund owned in Malaysia, Singapore, Thailand, and elsewhere abroad. The sale of these properties and corporate entities, if successful, could net the 1MDB as much as another four to five billion dollars, and thus combined with the impending IPO, would go a very long way toward righting the ship, putting 1MDB back onto a solid financial foundation and getting it headed, hopefully, toward substantial profitability in the very near future.

This plan started to work. As the asset acquisitions began to happen, Najib was able to go on the offensive in the media, to claim that he, personally, had taken steps to correct the problems at 1MDB, not only to put the fund back on the road to solvency but to fulfill its fundamental mission to directly benefit the people of Malaysia. Meanwhile, the prime minister continued to tighten his autocratic grip on power, ratcheting up his efforts to intimidate and disrupt his opposition. When the National Audit Department—the one under the control of the Finance Ministry headed by Najib himself—completed its so-called independent internal investigation into the workings of 1MDB, Najib ordered the department's report classified—and sealed—under what was called the Official Secrets Act.

The Secrets Act was a recent, unilateral creation through executive order of the prime minister, and when a prominent opposition leader in league with a couple of radical Bersih protesters managed to get a hold of a copy of the report—and started to release details of the Audit Department's ominous findings—the three were immediately arrested and imprisoned without trial, branded by the UMNO as domestic terrorists intent on overthrowing the government and tossing the nation into political chaos. They were worse than simple terrorists, Najib proclaimed; they were anarchists.

As for me, I was simply delighted with the prospect of having a whole new, seemingly unlimited source of capital to work with, this infusion of investment capital coming from all these Chinese companies, hopefully minus some of the pain-in-the-ass, red-tape regulatory scrutiny of the bureaucratic Western investment banks. I hoped to have, let's just call it, even greater creative investment freedom.

This of course was just the beginning. Because, while it might take as long as two years to get things rolling, if you'll forgive the pun, the sixty-billion-dollar high-speed railway project promised to catapult 1MDB from the minor leagues into the realm of the wealthiest and most prestigious sovereign wealth funds in the world—the achievement that had been my goal for the Malaysian sovereign wealth fund from the moment I convinced Prime Minister Najib to found it.

But then the whole thing got blown to shit. In late July 2016, the attorney general of the United States announced the largest seizure action of private assets ever brought by the U.S. Department of Justice. Most of it was my stuff, but the seizures also severely impacted people who were my good friends and important business associates. Just to name a few properties, the DoJ had moved to take several of my mansions (funny thing—only the ones they knew about!) in Los Angeles (the completely reimagined Pyramid House, the Beverly Hills mansion and compound), in New York City (the Park Laurel Townhouse, the Walker Tower Penthouse, the Warner Building townhouse), and in London (don't ask me how they were able to take property located in a separate sovereign country, but they took my sublimely beautiful townhouses in both the Mayfair and Chelsea districts). They took several of my valuable paintings—priceless works by the likes of Monet and Van Gogh and Picasso and Warhol and Lichtenstein, worth hundreds of millions of dollars collectively. They even took my Bombardier Global 5000 private jet. Although that, I didn't mind so much. I wasn't really using it much anymore anyway.

They outrageously took the historic L'Ermitage hotel, in Beverly Hills. L'Ermitage, at this time, it's worth noting, had become fabulously more successful than at any other time in its history. The place was making profits hand over fist, thanks in large part to the improvements—both in the physical plant and in the brand image—that I had orchestrated. Maybe that's why the DoJ listed the L'Ermitage entity first in their seizure filing, and listed the hotel business and the property it sat on separately, as if to reinforce the claim! They apparently didn't want to leave any scraps for the mice. So this one really hurt.

Yet the claim that hurt even more: They took my entire stake in EMI Music. I've already expressed how passionate I am about music, particularly about how rap and hip-hop are like the very lifeblood running through my veins and mind. It was as though the DoJ had ripped out my very soul. Destroying my beloved connection with EMI would only serve to damage my personal relationships with people like Swizz Beatz and Kanye West and Pharrell Williams and Jaime Foxx and Lil John and even Alicia Keys. It wasn't right.

Incorrigibly, the U.S. authorities went after many things that would hurt my friends and destroy the close relationships I had worked so hard to build. Like, they appropriated the future profits of Riza Aziz's and Joey McFarland's Red Granite Pictures—without identifying, incredulously, a specific dollar amount or project time frame they intended—essentially, to keep garnishing those profits indefinitely.

In the wake of the DoJ's indictment, all the ensuing bad publicity generated by the reporting in the *Wall Street Journal*, the *New York Times*, and the *LA Times*—not to mention *Variety* and the other Hollywood rags—would very quickly have extremely serious consequences affecting the future success of Red Granite. In point of fact, their golden asset, Leonardo DiCaprio, abruptly turned down the lead role in Red Granite's next big blockbuster, the remake of *Papillon*, the role made forever famous by the iconic performance of Steve McQueen. The very second that Charlie Hunnam (who the hell is he?) signed up for the role, the remake went from potential blockbuster to not having a snowball's chance in hell of making a profit. To make matters worse, director Martin Scorsese broke off negotiations with Red Granite in connection with his film *The Irishman*, which would feature an all-star cast led by Robert De Niro, Al Pacino, and Joe Pesci. Scorsese would eventually sign with a consortium of production companies led by TriBeCa Productions, in New York City. Adding insult to injury, Leonardo returned to the Academy the 1957 Marlon Brando Oscar statuette I had given to him as a birthday gift, as well as turning over—on demand by the DoJ—the several paintings by Picasso and Basquiat I had gifted to him. I thought this was utterly reprehensible on the part of the U.S. Justice Department—and unnecessary.

I guess it seemed like I was never again going to see my name rolling in the closing credits of a major motion picture the way I did, however understatedly, in *The Wolf of Wall Street*.

What was even more incredible was the conga line of different people that the DoJ named in their indictment. Just look at the list! It included Riza Aziz and Khadem Al Qubaisi and Mohamed Al Husseiny. It included Tim Leissner—identified in the initial document filing as "Goldman Managing Director"—and the filing was later amended to include Tarek Obaid and Patrick Mahony, whom it identified as "PetroSaudi Officer." But that wasn't the half of it. The only thing more outrageous than the indictment naming, of all people, Prime Minister Najib (identified as "Malaysian Official 1") and, in the later amendments, First Lady Rosmah ("wife of Malaysian Official 1") is that it also named me—by name, that is. Me, who never before in my life had I ever been a party to a lawsuit of any kind, as a plaintiff or as a defendant. Previously, I'd never gotten so much as a speeding ticket.

Maybe some people in this situation would have been mortified. I was outraged. This was a U.S. government–sponsored witch hunt. You're wondering why I say that, aren't you. Well, I'll tell you. Look at all those people indicted. In reality, they have little or no connection to each other; they're from all over the lot. I saw this as a case of the DoJ throwing a whole bunch of shit at the wall and hoping something sticks, as the expression goes. From there, they hoped to spin this civil suit into a criminal one. I know how they operate. And I thought it was disgraceful and irresponsible. Even the way the DoJ publicly presented this huge asset seizure legal action was optically

THE ART OF GREED

sleazy, sensational, and unprofessional. For maximum tabloid-style publicity, they had named the lawsuit *United States v. The Wolf of Wall Street*, and Attorney General Loretta Lynch personally made the announcement from a podium at the District Court for the Central District of California—from Hollywood itself, that is to say. How theatrically vulgar.

The ramifications were swift, for me and many others who were affected. Within a few months, my efforts to buy the bank in Cyprus were denied. The government of Saint Kitts revoked my passport and summarily rejected the foreign investor citizenship application I had filed there, similarly ruining my plans to buy another bank on that Caribbean island. And among even more of the bank accounts I held around the world, the assets were frozen by the U.S. government.

On a wider scale, Deutsche Bank put an immediate, strict hold on the IPO, which would ultimately represent a devastating blow to the future fortunes of 1MDB. Then, like falling dominoes, many of the Chinese state-owned companies that had been so anxious to purchase the premium assets of 1MDB began to back away from the negotiating table or to abruptly break off discussions entirely and walk away from the deals. Worst of all, the CCP began to pull back on plans for the Malaysian high-speed railway Belt and Road project. This was nothing short of catastrophic to my future plans—my plans for Malaysia, for Najib, for 1MDB, for me . . . for everyone.

Even with all of this, it wasn't as though my world had completely collapsed. It was more like everything was just on some twilight-zone hold. With billions of assets frozen and mega-business negotiations halted in midstream, the world felt like a stop-action shot in a movie thriller—a freeze-frame, if you can picture it. The major problem was, though, things couldn't stay that way for long. Time doesn't wait for anyone, and even I can only hang in midair for so long. All I had to do was figure out how to get things moving again. I'd been in some really tight spots before, and always found a way.

For the next several months, for obvious reasons, I was obliged to spend most of my time on board *Equanimity*, keeping moving on the open ocean waters endlessly shuttling between my working offices in Shanghai and Bangkok. I was constantly on the phone or the Internet, usually both simultaneously, like, twenty-four seven, desperately trying to straighten out this colossal mess that, frankly speaking, was far greater and far more complex than any petty scandal stories that Clare Rewcastle Brown and her yellow-journalist comrade Ho Kay Tat could conjure up and spit out in their respective rogue newspapers.

Then, one evening just after dinnertime aboard *Equanimity*, I got a frantic call from Fat Eric. We happened to be just about leaving the Gulf of Thailand, cruising below the southernmost reaches of Vietnam and about to enter the South China Sea on our way to Shanghai. Fat Eric was one of those individuals who was always calm and cool under any sort of pressure, a fearless beacon of confidence and self-assurance. I'd never in my life heard him so frantic, so obviously frightened, as he was on this call.

"Jho, we've been raided!" Fat Eric huffed into the phone, his breathing like that of a man having a heart attack.

"What?" I exclaimed. I couldn't imagine what he meant. "Raided?"

"The offices," Eric said. "The Wynton offices. A bunch of guys came in. They ransacked the place!"

"What the hell are you talking about? What the hell happened?"

"A few hours ago, I got a strange call. The guy's voice was all screwed up. You know, like it was scrambled or electronically altered? Anyway, the caller said that a bunch of guys from the Anti-Corruption Commission were on their way to the Petronas Towers, that they were going to break into Wynton's offices and confiscate all of our files, our computers—everything. And then he just hung up before I could even say anything. At first, I thought it was some sort of crank call.

"But then I got worried. So I rushed over there, and, just as a precaution, I copied all of the 1MDB account files onto a portable hard drive. Then I grabbed all of the file folders that I could fit into two briefcases—you know, the hardcopy paperwork, the signed contract originals, all that critical shit. I shoved them into my briefcases—two of them—and just as I did that, there was a lot of yelling and banging out in the hall, and they started breaking down the front door. They had axes, for chrissakes!"

"Eric!" I shouted into the phone, but, apparently too panicked to hear me, he continued to barrel hysterically headlong into the details of the break-in.

"So I set the mainframe computer to erase all the files. Oh my god, all of that vital information, Jho! I feel sick! But I didn't know what else to do! I told it to erase, and then I ran out the back service entrance. I heard all this breaking glass and—my god—I don't know if the mainframe had enough time to erase everything or if they were able to stop it from erasing. I have no idea how much information they might have got off of there."

"Hold on, Eric!" I shouted into the phone once again. "Don't say anything more. This phone connection might not be secure. Somebody could be monitoring the line. They could be listening to this conversation—"

"Who the fuck are you talking about? And why would anybody want to bust up our offices?" he cried.

"I don't know, Eric. Right now, I just don't know. All I know is we've got to be really careful about all of this. Don't say another word."

"What do you want me to do?" Eric said pleadingly.

I thought for a brief moment.

"Listen," I said, "how quickly can you get to Bangkok?"

"I've already booked a flight out of KL. It leaves in about five hours. I'll be in Bangkok in seven, eight hours maybe."

"Good man," I replied. "Well done." This time, it was me trying to be the calm and cool one in the conversation, to help Fat Eric keep his head, even as my heart was pounding like a jackhammer.

"I'm on the boat," I said. "We're about, oh, seven hours out from the Bangkok marina. I'm instructing the captain to reverse course and get me back there ASAP. You know where to meet me. You got it?"

"You bet," Fat Eric said.

"And Eric," I said sternly. "Don't talk about this to anyone—not a soul, you understand? Not until you and I have a chance to discuss where we go from here."

"Absolutely," Eric said, and then he hung up the phone.

When *Equanimity* at last cruised into the exclusive, private, luxury marina where I kept it berthed whenever I was in Bangkok, it was still dark, about four in the morning. One of my stretch limousines was already idling on the pier, the driver ready to shuttle me to my office on the nineteenth floor of the China Resources Tower, a modern skyscraper in the Pathum Wan district of Thailand's ancient capital city. When I arrived at the building, Fat Eric was already there, in the lobby, waiting anxiously for me, closely guarding the two bulging leather briefcases he had hauled with him from Kuala Lumpur, stuffed with documents and files.

"Come," I said, gesturing toward the bank of elevators. "Let's go upstairs." We rode the elevator silently up to the nineteenth floor, neither of us speaking a word, finally arriving at the floor and making our way to the office and then to a small, private conference room within with a panoramic view of the city, just as the first pastel glimmers of dawn were painting the eastern sky.

"So tell me what happened," I said to Eric.

"Well, it's like I told you on the phone. These guys came in. They ransacked the office. I have no idea who they were or what they were after. I have no idea what they took. They left the place a freaking mess, so it's impossible to say at this point what's missing."

"Did you get a good look at them?"

"No, Jho. I'm sorry, but I didn't. Barely a glimpse as I was running out the back door. Honestly, I got out of there as quickly as I could. I thought they might arrest me—that is, if they were the law. And if they were robbers or thieves or god knows what else, I thought they might kill me."

"That's fine. I understand, and that's okay. I'm glad you're okay, and I'm really grateful you were able to gather all this stuff and get it out of there," I said, patting one of the briefcases that Eric had placed on a corner of the conference table.

"What's going on, Jho?" Eric pleaded. "Who the hell were those guys?"

"I'm not sure at this point, but there's a lot of crazy shit going on in Malaysia right now. Between Najib's crackdown and the leftist radicals among his opposition, it's hard enough to know who your friends are, much less who your enemies are, and I'm talking about your real enemies. So much chaos going on. The violence. I'm afraid things are just getting more dangerous, seemingly by the day. It's like we're heading toward civil war, or something as crazy as that."

"The warning call I got, the caller said they were from the Anti-Corruption Commission."

"Possible," I said, "but I'm really not so sure about that. Could be anybody, really. Don't forget: With the government factions all fighting among themselves, the criminals feel like they can do whatever they want. That's the reason why organized crime is on the rise throughout Malaysia, especially ever since all the bad business with the murder of that deputy prosecutor."

Fat Eric nodded ominously.

"And they're taking sides in the political wars," I continued. "They'll do the dirty work for whoever pays them the most. You want somebody out of the picture? There's a gangster for that."

"So you think the mob might be involved in this?"

"I think they probably did the raid on our offices. The critical question is, *Who were they working for?* As I said, that could be anybody."

The truth of the matter was I didn't know—didn't have any statistics to prove—whether mob activity was on the rise throughout the country or not. Probably it was just business as usual, such that criminal activity was simply as healthy and robust as it had always been, like it was part of the general Malaysian economy. I only knew that the gangsters had gotten more brazen in recent years, which I attributed to the political strife and the antigovernment feelings the political infighting had recently generated. They just figured they could get away with more was all.

The thing you must understand about gangland Malaysia is that you need a scorecard to figure out which mobster factions are working for which political factions—or vice versa. That is, it's not simply a matter of who the good guys are—presumably the "law and order" government—and who the bad guys are—presumably the gangsters. It doesn't work that way. In practical terms, the gangsters might actually be working in harmony, at least for a time, with legitimate law enforcement in some situations, even though that was usually as a means of working *against* their gangland adversaries—a marriage of pragmatic convenience, you might say. And of course, this temporary harmony could shift and reverse itself very quickly, blown by the erratic winds of political volatility—specifically, who was in power at any given moment.

I sat silent for a moment, thinking about all of this, about what had happened at the Wynton offices and what it all could mean. Then I said, "Eric, how did you get here? I mean, from the airport?"

"God's honest truth?" Eric said in the form of a question. "I took a cab. Yeah, a regular cab. I figured the least conspicuous way, the most ordinary way, the better. Not to be noticed. Not even an Uber; they're traceable, you know. And I paid the cabby in cash."

"Good thinking. Here's what I want you to do. My limo is waiting downstairs to take me back to the marina. It's in the private parking lot reserved for the execs who have offices here. I want you to go down there and tell the driver we have a change of plans. He's to take you back to the airport. When you arrive back in KL, just go home, and lay low until you hear from me."

"What are you going to do?"

"I have a dedicated, secure line from this office direct to the prime minister—tamperproof, bugproof, all of that. I'm going to try to see if I can't get through to Najib to see if he knows what the hell this was all about. I'll stick around here for a bit while I try to contact him and see if he can help. I'll just have another limo sent up here later on to take me back to *Equanimity*."

"As you wish," Eric said as he stood up to leave.

Fat Eric and I walked back into the hallway. As the elevator doors were closing on him, I reminded Eric not to discuss what had happened at our offices back home or our conversation that morning with anyone. He was to deny even that he had met with me, should anyone ask that particular question. After he left, I went back to the office, where I opened one of the briefcases, took out some of the folders, and began, somewhat absentmindedly, thumbing through the contents. As I did so, I reached to pick up the handset for the dedicated direct phone line to the office of the prime minister.

Suddenly, there was an enormous, ear-splitting explosion outside, somewhere down on the street, followed by the sound of car alarms going off everywhere, the tinkling sound of shattering glass falling from buildings and crashing into the street. I dropped the phone on the blotter pad on the desk and ran to the window.

As luck would have it, I had a clear view of the executive parking lot directly below. There was my limousine, engulfed in flames, sparks flying, black smoke billowing. Odd as this may sound, the first thing that immediately struck me was that the car hadn't been blown to pieces in the spectacular fashion that you always see in the movies, shards of car parts rocketing through the air, balls of fire billowing upward like nuclear clouds, the entire vehicle blown to unidentifiable bits and obliterated. Rather, the body of the limo—the frame, I guess—and most of the doors too, remained in one piece, the flames shooting in profusion out of all of the windows, the engine compartment—even from out of the trunk, which the force of the blast had blown wide open.

I would learn later that, in real life—that is, in real *mobster* life—this was due to a professional technique in which the goal, rather than to achieve some cinematically spectacular, Oscar-worthy special effects in pyrotechnics—entertainment value for the Hollywood big screen—is to ensure in workmanlike fashion that the occupants within the vehicle absolutely are not permitted to survive the event.

The nanosecond the driver turned the key in the ignition, both he and Fat Eric were instantly incinerated beyond recognition. The second thing that struck me—almost in passing, strangely enough—was that I was supposed to be in the back seat of what, heretofore, had been a perfectly fine and luxurious automobile. One of those weird moments when you feel like you're floating high above, looking down on yourself from some point in space, like, from, say, nineteen stories up in the air. And yet, somewhere in the maelstrom of emotions that swept over me in that instant, I felt an enormous sense of remorse, when, oddly, it occurred to me that I didn't even know the driver's name or whether he had a family or not.

Collecting myself from the shock, I rushed back to my desk and picked up the handset to resume dialing the call to Najib that I believed was now more urgent than ever. But then I stopped abruptly, looking at the handset in disbelief.

The line was dead.

I stood there, phone in hand, looking dumbly at the now-useless device for several moments, incredulous, trying to process this disturbing development. Then, feeling I had no time to lose, I quickly gathered up all of the documents I had taken out of the briefcases and hastily slid them back in, making sure the portable hard drive was among them. I ran out into the hall, where I took the service maintenance elevator down to the basement, the underground garage there. Climbing a flight of concrete stairs and emerging at street level, donning a set of dark sunglasses against the bright early morning light, I did precisely what Fat Eric had done on his final earthly trip, the inconspicuous one he had taken from the airport to the China Resources Tower: I hailed a regular street cab to take me to the marina, where I quickly boarded *Equanimity* and got the hell out of Bangkok.

Chapter 21

As I boarded *Equanimity* in Bangkok Harbor, I instructed the captain to sail for Beijing, the plan being to then travel from Beijing to this compound and try to regroup. There was a lot to think about on the trip.

My efforts to contact Najib continued to be unsuccessful, yet I knew he was facing his own handful of crises back home. After all, he had been named in the DoJ lawsuit too—well, not named exactly, but no one familiar with the situation would have wondered about the exact identity of "Malaysian Official 1." I conjectured that Najib was just extremely busy fighting off the allegations in the suit, and, while it took a little soul-searching, I also rationalized that I was the last person Najib wanted to talk to right now. We were both being watched, and any contact between us that might be detected by our mutual enemies, or even some nonmutual enemies, could be detrimental to both of us. Staying out of any obvious contact was the best for both of us.

In the days after departing Bangkok so abruptly, I scoured the Thai newspapers and news outlet websites looking for any stories about the extraordinary disaster that had happened in the parking lot right outside my building, which had killed both Fat Eric and my driver. Despite its military leadership, Thailand's news media enjoys a surprising degree of journalistic freedom of speech, with little or no oversight or censorship by the government like in Malaysia. I had hoped the papers might provide some clue as to who was responsible for blowing up my limousine and, presumably, trying to kill me, of all people.

Yet there was virtually nothing in the newspapers or online. I found only a brief wire story, maybe three column inches max, that was repeated, rather frustratingly, almost verbatim in the back sections of several papers, as wire stories often are, which told of an automobile explosion in front of the China Resources Tower, in which two people were believed to have been killed. The articles disclosed the name of the driver—it was kind of a stake through my heart to only in this way be reminded of his name—but described the other victim and an "unidentified male" and gave no further details about the incident, other than to say that the cause of the explosion was "under investigation," according to police.

Given, as I said earlier, the freedom of the press in Thailand, I could only assume the newspapers printed all of the pertinent information that had been provided to them by police regarding the incident and that they knew nothing more beyond what they had reported. Of course, that certainly did not mean that the Bangkok police told the journalists everything *they* knew about it. Whatever the case, the news stories told me nothing beyond what I already knew; my good friend and business partner was dead by car explosion, and I was at a loss to understand who had done this and why.

For a time, however brief, I found myself unsure of what course I should take going forward—an unusual state of being for me, because I do not like to stand still. Even under hectic circumstances, I am almost always able to seize my next course or opportunity to pivot. I stayed up late at night, listening to rap music in my bedroom suite, trying to read the evolving situation with 1MDB, with Najib, and with the investigations by the United States and others. During the days, I must have read a dozen papers from all around the world, the online editions, essentially doing reconnaissance on anything that was happening that could have an impact on the fund. Or on me.

Then, as the end-of-year holidays approached, a totally unexpected opportunity dropped right into my lap, thanks to a startling event that occurred in early November in the United States: To the world's shock, Donald J. Trump was elected president. My old friend. And suddenly I had a new plan. As convoluted and complex as the international intricacies of my financial network were when you looked at them on a global scale, the basic problem for me was relatively simple. With most of my own monies, and with the capital asset accounts I controlled in numerous countries around the world all frozen by order of the U.S. DoJ, the most direct solution was to find a way to get the United States to drop its investigation of 1MDB entirely. Once I could make that happen, all of the other nations from Singapore to Switzerland would subsequently drop their investigations, the halt on my use of these billions of dollars of assets across dozens of international banks would be summarily lifted, and I would be allowed to get back to work. That's how I figured it. Simple, right?

From the moment Donald Trump took the oath of office on January 20, 2017, he signaled that he was going to become one of America's most unorthodox presidents across its 240-year history. In hindsight, one need only remember how, less than halfway through his four-year term, President Trump threw out the ridiculously arcane diplomatic playbook with respect to North Korea—tossing away the bureaucratic rulebook like last week's newspaper—and met with Chairman Kim Jong Un directly, face to face, against the advice of all of his so-called diplomatic advisors—and many of his allies in Europe and Asia as well.

I remembered the sage advice he gave me that first time I met him, in that nondescript Philadelphia coffee shop on the Wharton campus, sitting across from me and his daughter Ivanka, when he said, "If you're going to do something, you should try to do it big—as big as you possibly can." Even more importantly, when he said, "Don't let the bullshitters get in your way." He had certainly done it big, all these years later, in the way that he ran his own presidential campaign strictly his own way, even doing things that were counter to what his party bosses had advised. And he won. Now, the party bosses feared *him*, and *they* were now obliged to do everything Trump told *them* to do.

For all of these reasons, I knew that President Trump could and would put an end to this whole 1MDB investigation mess—if he was approached in the right way. I believed I knew exactly how to do that, and I set about creating a plan to reach out to the new president. By the way, I very soon had another big reason for being optimistic, because just days into his presidency, Trump appointed Gary Cohn to a seat on his National Economic Council. Yes, the very same Gary Cohn who, as president of Goldman Sachs, had been one of the biggest supporters of the firm's business with 1MDB! Certainly, Cohn would be in favor of calling off the dogs at the DoJ and the FBI!

As soon as Trump had won the election and even before he stepped up to the podium on the steps of the Capitol to take the oath, I sought to identify and hire his biggest supporters. They weren't hard to find (isn't that always the case when you win?), and I ultimately retained the services of two top Washington, DC, insider lobbyists: Elliott Broidy and Nickie Lum Davis. Broidy was a long-time, powerful and prodigious Republican Party fundraiser, as well as the owner of a major U.S. defense contracting firm. Oh, and a good friend of Donald Trump—so good a friend, in fact, that Broidy quickly became one of Trump's first major supporters from the moment Trump announced his candidacy, pledging millions of dollars in donations to the Trump campaign at a time when most of the elite Republican donor-powerbrokers were skeptical at best of Trump's chances and when most of the U.S. voters would have thought Trump's presidential bid was some sort of joke emanating from the theater of American political humor. Nickie Lum Davis was a smart, savvy, and politically powerful businesswoman, with Asian roots, based in Honolulu, Hawaii. She too had become a major Republican fundraiser, and an extremely sexy one at that, the kind of woman Donald Trump might try to grab by the ass, or elsewhere, when Melania wasn't looking.

Hey, don't despise me for that despicable remark—the hunter has always got to know his prey, you understand? Otherwise, you don't succeed.

THE ART OF GREED

As I said, both Broidy and Lum Davis were Trump loyalists from the very beginning, and they had been tremendously successful working as fundraisers over the course of the presidential campaign. I knew that they were both close to the new president, endeared in his heart, and I hoped they had his ear. The idea was I wanted my two American operatives to vigorously lobby President Trump to order the Justice Department to stand down or, better, to altogether drop its investigation into the operations of the 1MDB fund—and by extension, of course, to drop any part of that investigation having to do with me. I paid Broidy and Lum Davis something on the order of about fifteen million dollars, all told, some of which they used to engage the help of George Higginbotham, a powerful senior congressional affairs specialist who was actually working for the Department of Justice and therefore had access to all of the inside information regarding the investigation, including its major flaws and weaknesses. If anyone could create a rational argument to present to President Trump for why the DoJ's Malaysia investigation should be dropped, I believed Higginbotham could. So this part of the plan was set. I say *this part* because I had another really brilliant idea to get things back on the fast track.

There was simply no time to lose. I knew that, assuming my American operatives were ultimately successful in convincing the president to put an end to the DoJ investigation, I nevertheless had no idea how long that would take, and at the same time, I knew I had to move fast to save 1MDB from complete disaster. The situation was getting worse by the hour as the fund accrued millions more daily in unpaid interest on its loans; in short, 1MDB was now a runaway train barreling down the tracks to default and utter collapse.

But I knew a way to save it, and it very pivotally involved the Chinese government. Because I knew how ardently the CCP wanted to get their hands on a particular Chinese dissident presently living in the United States, presumably residing in New York City or Washington, DC, perhaps splitting his time between both of those financially and politically important cities.

Guo Wengui is an enormously successful businessman, originally from Shandong Province, and the principal owner of a massive multinational conglomerate known as Beijing Zenith Holdings. While making himself into one of the richest men in China, Guo became increasingly critical of the CCP and its restrictive policies toward business and industry—including China's growing stranglehold on once-democratic Hong Kong—to the point that Guo found himself obliged to flee his homeland and go into self-exile or face arrest and likely indefinite imprisonment by the Chinese government. Not surprisingly, Guo chose to go to the United States, where his increasing and outspoken political activism against the Communist regime in Beijing—and his influential proximity to the top policymaking leaders in the upper echelons of the U.S. government—had simply infuriated the CCP, which would like nothing better than to take Guo into their custody.

My thinking was, if I could help the Chinese succeed in bringing Guo to justice in his homeland—if I could play even an indirect role in getting that done but one that was highly visible—I believed that would curry enough favor and goodwill such that China would agree to reengage its partnership with Malaysia and with 1MDB under my direction, especially once the U.S. Department of Justice investigation was halted. I was convinced that the CCP was so determined and anxious to collar Guo (and shut him up, basically) that, once that was achieved, the original group of Chinese companies that planned on buying up some of the more prime assets of 1MDB would be permitted by their government to happily restart those negotiations in earnest. I further believed that, with all of the U.S. investigatory meddling out of the way, the Chinese construction and development corporation would be eager to fast-track the preparations to start work on the massive Malaysian high-speed railway Belt and Road project.

I'll admit I wanted them to do that by first sending the previously agreed-upon tranche of twenty billion dollars to Prime Minister Najib's special accounts within 1MDB as soon as fucking possible! I was pretty certain that receiving the initial loan would make Najib and Rosmah like me again.

But seriously, I also knew the infusion of twenty billion dollars into the fund's coffers would be more than enough to kill off any other unwarranted and meddlesome investigations into 1MDB by any other entities, be they foreign governments or international banking regulatory authorities. After that, Najib and my other partners—we could all get back to business as usual.

I immediately got to work behind the scenes, in conjunction with my important business associates in China, while also notifying Broidy and Lum Davis in America to diplomatically and as compellingly as possible press the crucial case for Guo's deportation directly with President Trump. I believed that, by working both sides, I could get the deal done and—just imagine this—make both the capitalists and the communists happy!

Accordingly, in April 2017—three months after Trump became president—the Chinese government filed a formal demand with Interpol for the immediate apprehension, arrest, and repatriation of Guo Wengui to face corruption charges in China. Three months later, in June, the Chinese government sent a formal letter directly to President Trump officially requesting that the president deport Guo Wengui back to China. The letter, by the way, was hand delivered to Trump by casino entrepreneur Steve Wynn, perhaps the leading pioneer of the casino industry and a god-like icon of the Vegas gaming scene that I had loved so much back in the day.

Thus the wheels were set into motion. If I could pull all of this off, I could jump-start or jump-*re*start, if you will, 1MDB right back into business. Not only would I end the DoJ investigation for good, but I'd acquire a power infusion of twenty billion dollars in Chinese capital for 1MDB that would enable the fund to do investment ventures on a higher plane than it had ever been able to do before.

You know, it just occurs to me: I've said repeatedly that I'm not a politician. But when I look at the brilliance of this plan—this enormous, international win–win–win plan—maybe I really should have gone into politics. Imagine what I could have accomplished for the benefit of the nations of the world!

Now, I have to acknowledge that, at the time when Donald Trump was assuming the presidency in the U.S., it was hard to gauge the status of my relationship with Prime Minister Najib back in Malaysia. I would have preferred to describe our relationship as, well, seriously strained, let's just say. I couldn't tell you how Najib felt about it, because he categorically refused to return my phone calls or respond to any other efforts I made to reach out to him, like instructing his royal guard to turn away covert couriers I had sent to Kuala Lumpur on a couple of secret contact missions. It's hard to recall exactly, but I don't believe I had spoken directly with Najib since the previous July, when the U.S. DoJ publicly announced its investigation.

In the press, however, Najib started openly blaming me for the financial crisis within 1MDB, claiming that he had "no knowledge" of the "excessive control" I had wielded over the day-to-day operations of the fund; nor, he claimed, had he been fully and properly informed by me or anyone else about the significant major deals that I had directed on behalf of the fund. This was utter nonsense, because, as I've insisted all along, Najib was fully briefed on each and every financial megadeal or investment opportunity that I had worked so enormously hard to create, and it was Najib who, in every case, gave final, authoritative approval to consummating the deals. The idea that Najib would throw me under the bus this way was, to say the least, terribly disappointing to me.

In retaliation and in a moment of weakness and frustration, I admit I may have said some bad things to a nagging reporter, one of those annoyingly sleazy bastards who always announced himself by last name only. He had a habit of barging right up into your personal space and practically shouting in your face, "Braddock from the *Star*," which was appropriate, because the *Star* was and remains Malaysia's number-one sensationalist tabloid rag. And he smelled bad too.

During these difficult days, I was extremely careful about keeping my travel under wraps, mostly aboard *Equanimity* and, when necessary, entering and departing Southeast Asian nations through out-of-the-way ports where customs was exceeding lax. Anyway, Braddock had an uncanny knack for discovering where I was going. There he'd be, standing on the dock with recorder in hand, ready to badger me again to try to get an exclusive. The only solace I could take from this was the delicious confidence that Braddock was too stupid to realize that, if he were only to alert the authorities of my next port of call and thus turn me in, then he'd *really* have a truly fantastic exclusive as the only reporter on the scene of my arrest. Such an imbecile.

On the occasion in question, as I made my way down the pier and toward our inevitable confrontation once again, I glared at him and sneered, "Whatta you want, Braddock?"

Braddock smiled his greasy smile. "Nice to see you too, Jho. I just want to know how you ran 1MDB into the ground and what you did with the billions of ringgit you stole. Didja buy that boat with some of it?" He nodded his head toward *Equanimity*. "That's what the prime minister is saying."

And that's when I said it. I blurted, "Why don't you go ask Najib Razak about his wife's vast exotic jewelry collection—or maybe you should ask Rosmah herself how she and her corrupt husband paid for all that glitter. Ask them about her twenty-two-karat pink diamond necklace."

I regretted saying it the moment the words left my lips. Because I knew it would accomplish nothing and because, as I anticipated, sure as shit, my statement was published in the next day's morning edition of the *Star*.

Anyone who was familiar with the situation and the strain it put on our relationship would probably have thought this would have been the end of things between Najib and me, including our friendship—as well as the unique friendly relationship that had developed between me and Rosmah. Yet, as they had so often during our long association together, going all the way back to the days when I launched Najib's stepson Riza into Hollywood moviemaking and helped Najib and Rosmah's daughter gain a scholarship to

Georgetown University, our mutual goals serendipitously dovetailed once again at a critical time. Even though, in this case, Najib and I might not be deliberately working in direct, coordinated, communicative collaboration with one another, as we had so many times before, we were, in fact and for all practical purposes, working toward the exact same goals, albeit somewhat independently.

Look, more than anything else in the world, Najib wanted to be the man in power over Malaysia. He had needed me to get reelected in 2013, and he had needed me ever since to advise him on the complex management of the fund, as well as to make sure that the political "donations" from our foreign investment partners kept flowing into his political war chest accounts. It's just the plain fact of Malaysian politics that money had gotten Najib elected prime minister, as it does all prime ministers. It had gotten him reelected once so far, and now, in order to continue his reign, he needed to rely on, let's just call it, the financial power and prowess of a robustly healthy, profit-generating, and abundantly cash-laden 1MDB sovereign wealth fund. For reasons that ought to be fairly obvious by now.

But the fund was in trouble. I preferred to think the fund was just "ill," in large part due to these invasive investigations in the U.S. and elsewhere that were preventing 1MDB from engaging in the kind of business, directed by me, that would make it healthy and robust, and an international economic force once again. The outside investigations were like a devastating virus, like COVID-19, preventing the fund from being able to work properly, essentially forcing the fund into quarantine. Being at the center of the viral outbreak, if you will, Najib could not restore 1MDB to full health on his own. Once again, he desperately needed my help, whether he would have admitted it or not.

So you see, that part I mentioned earlier about Najib's and my goals dovetailing together, regardless of what the prime minister thought about me at the time—Najib, too, had, at the top of his political agenda, the primary and immediate goal of getting the U.S. to end the DoJ's highly unwelcome probe into what Najib insisted publicly was strictly a Malaysian affair, one that Malaysia alone would deal with and correct as was needed. In fact, Najib further insisted that the U.S. probe was strictly illegal, and as the country's leader, he had the requisite political stature to insinuate in the international press that the DoJ investigation was akin to a hostile invasion by another nation—not a military one *per se* but nevertheless an act of aggression that grossly violated the sovereignty of the independent nation of Malaysia. The U.S. government—Najib pleaded and cajoled in the courts of domestic and international opinion—had no business sticking its nose into the strictly sovereign affairs of another country, be they financial issues or otherwise.

I felt so strongly about how Najib and I should work together on this that I took a chance. I went out and purchased a burner phone. Holding my breath, I called the private line that had once linked me directly to Najib's cell phone, hoping to god it was still live.

To my utter shock, it was, and when my call went to voicemail, I explained as succinctly and as quickly and as thoroughly as I could how we could work together to quash the DoJ investigation—he from the top as the prime minister at the highest diplomatic level of government speaking one-on-one with the U.S. president and me from the ground level, working diligently through my important contacts in the U.S. State Department. On I went, hoping that I was making myself—and my best intentions—clear and coherent, until the digital recording device on Najib's end shut itself down.

About an hour later, I received back a text from Prime Minister Najib. It read simply: "You're mad."

When I persisted by trying to call once again, the line was dead—this time, I assumed, for good.

In September 2017, barely eight months after Trump took office, Najib, accompanied by Rosmah and his entire entourage, set off on a diplomatic mission to Washington for official face-to-face talks—at the White House, no less—to curry favor with the new president. Despite whatever animosity might have existed between us or not, I was proud of him; this was the first time he had organized a political junket on this scale and magnitude without my guiding help!

In fact, they even stayed at the Trump International Hotel, just two city blocks away from the president's residence. A very smart and savvy move: There is nothing in the world that Mr. Trump likes better than to see his most exclusive penthouse suites filled with wealthy dignitaries and his sprawling luxury hotel empire making tons and tons of money off the rich and famous. It's exactly what I would have instructed the prime minister to do, and I'm quite sure the president was already taking a strong liking to the prime minister the moment he and Rosmah, escorted by their legion of support people, regally checked in under tight security at his grand hotel.

In subsequent formal state meetings with President Trump, Najib made subtle but enticing overtures suggesting that Malaysia wanted to buy military hardware—jet engines from General Electric, fighter jets from Boeing, naval ships and submarines from Huntington Ingalls—military purchases that would amount to billions of dollars that, I'm sure, would have had Donald Trump just licking his lips. (Come to think of it, it probably made armaments dealer and presidential confidante Elliott Broidy pretty happy too!) Najib promised that all of this military firepower would be used to enable Malaysia to stand firm, as an ally of the United States and the West, against Chinese incursionary behavior throughout the region of Southeast Asia, including China's efforts to control the waters of the South China Sea. Finally, for President Trump, standing firm with Najib and Malaysia against China would also be very good politically among his base of conservative supporters, and, even if he might simultaneously cooperate with China by deporting Guo Wengui into their hands, if you know Trump and his art-of-the-deal passion, nothing would be more delicious to him than dealing duplicitously with a communist government that, in fact, Trump despises (as do those conservative supporters). As long as Trump thought he was winning in the end, of course.

You see, in a weird way, Najib and I were essentially working as if in choreographed concert—almost in spite of ourselves! And everything looked like it was all coming together once again.

Until Prime Minister Najib Razak screwed the whole thing up— this time, for good. Or should I say ex-Prime Minister Najib Razak.

Incredibly, Najib lost the May 2018 election to ninety-two-year-old Mahathir Mohamad, and in so doing, he became the first and only UMNO candidate to lose a prime ministerial election in the entire sixty-year history of the country's existence.

From there, events in Malaysia and in the United States simply spiraled out of control. As soon as the election results were officially certified, Najib and Rosmah attempted to flee the country. They were stopped at the airport by a huge crowd of thousands of angry citizens who had gotten wind of their planned departure. The mob chanted, "Arrest them! Arrest them!" and that's exactly what the Malaysian police did as soon as they arrived on the scene. In the government seat of Putrajaya, no sooner had Mahathir been sworn in than he immediately took control over 1MDB, ordered the reopening of the Anti-Corruption Commission's investigation, and cleaned house among the board of advisors, removing all of the executives who had loyally taken without equivocation their orders from Najib (through my direction, of course).

Shortly after his detainment at the airport, Malaysian authorities raided the several Kuala Lumpur residences of now former Prime Minister Najib and First Lady Rosmah, removing some $275 million worth of merchandise, including 12,000 pieces of jewelry, 567 designer handbags, and 423 watches. They also recovered nearly thirty million dollars total in cash, in several denominations, that was stored by the first couple in each their own separate his and hers steel safes. In addition, investigatory documents compiled by the Anti-Corruption Commission that had been suppressed by the Najib regime but which were now made public by Mahathir's new government coalition, revealed that Najib had over a billion dollars in his private accounts with AmBank and several other banks both within Malaysia and offshore. Less than two months later, on July 3, Najib was indicted on one charge of abuse of power and three counts of criminal breach of trust. Over the next several months, the number of charges brought against him would mount to a total of forty-two.

I was astonished, and, frankly, I was angered. I knew—of

course, I knew—that Najib used the massive donations he received from our partners in the Middle East, principally the UAE and Saudi Arabia, among others, to fund his reelection campaigns and ensure support among his constituents for his governmental agenda between elections. I also should not have been surprised that he'd buy a bauble or two from time to time to keep Rosmah happy. But honestly, I never thought he'd basically lock up and hoard hundreds of millions of dollars, essentially in cash, in places where that money was basically sitting there doing nothing. As I've said earlier, if there's one thing I hate, it's capital that isn't working to produce even greater capital. That's the whole point, isn't it? For Najib to just sit on all that money, well . . . it just kind of goes against my religion!

Anyway, if we fast-forward to July 30, 2020, that's the day Najib was convicted on seven counts of abuse of power, criminal abuse of trust, and money laundering, and the other thirty-five charges are still pending! For the seven convictions alone, the former prime minister has been sentenced to twelve years in prison, but Najib is currently walking free while his attorneys are appealing his convictions in the courts.

On the other side of the world, in the United States, the Justice Department continued to press on with its investigation into 1MDB. While he was still in office, Trump allowed the investigation to continue, perhaps in part because Najib's defeat in Malaysia meant that Trump could no longer expect Najib to fulfill his promise to buy billions of dollars' worth of U.S. military hardware; nor, more crucially, could he expect the new government in Malaysia—and I mean brand new, the first non-UMNO-led government in the country's history—to stand as a staunch ally with the U.S. against the ever-increasing incursionary activities of Communist China in the greater region of Southeast Asia—the way Najib had also promised he would.

I couldn't blame the president; with no previous track record of domestic governance or definitive, expressly stated foreign policy agenda, there was absolutely no one on Earth who could predict which directions Mahathir's new government would go or how it would politically align itself with other nations in the region or around the world. I had to assume Trump was taking a wait-and-see approach with respect to whether Mahathir would be as cooperative to the U.S. as Najib had been.

Finally, President Trump had also decided not to deport Guo Wengui back to China and into the hands of the authorities there. The word I got—which, frankly (and unfortunately for me), made perfect sense from what I already very well knew about Mr. Trump—was that he flatly refused to give up the political dissident the CCP so desperately wanted without getting something big in return. Trump insisted on getting something of real value from the Chinese that was at least as substantially important to the interests of the U.S. as Guo's repatriation was to the CCP. Knowing Trump and what makes him tick, what probably would have made him the happiest would be to get a whole boatload of cash in return for Guo. And, as a kind of postscript, the new American administration under President Joe Biden seems to have no interest at all in deporting Guo.

In what seemed like an instant, after all my years of hard work, everything had gone to hell. Or had it? I refused to believe that, and I decided to take a new tact.

Only a few days after Mahathir surprised everyone by winning the 2018 election, I contacted the new Malaysian government to offer my assistance in their efforts to get back as much of the misappropriated 1MDB assets as might be possible. I also reached out to negotiate through channels with the U.S. to offer to help identify and return properties and objects which the DoJ seemed to insist had been paid for with some of those misappropriated 1MDB funds. Or so they claimed. Okay, so whatever.

The thing is, I believe I could effectively help the authorities in Southeast Asia and the U.S. get the best deals on all of those properties so that 1MDB gets as much money as it possibly can back into its accounts. You take the superyacht *Equanimity*, for example, which, by the way, was seized in Indonesian waters by the American authorities in October 2018. The U.S. then turned my boat over to the Malaysian government, which moored it in Johor and then moved to liquidate the asset by offering it for sale in Southeast Asia. This was a terrible mistake, because Malaysia could have gotten a much higher price for *Equanimity* simply by sailing it up to the Mediterranean and offering it for sale among the rich and famous people who party along the French or the Italian Rivieras. They'd have gotten tons more money for it there! This is the kind of savvy expertise I can provide!

If you want to know a really sweet irony, according to the latest I've heard, it turns out that the Malaysian authorities wound up selling *Equanimity* to the Genting Group, the giant Malaysia-based mostly casino and plantation conglomerate. Genting Group, you might recall, had profited extremely handsomely through its multibillion-dollar sale of the other side of its business holdings—their network of Southeast Asian power assets to 1MDB—assets that were supposed to be a major part of the now-failed IPO. I understand that Genting acquired *Equanimity* from Malaysia for a song! I can tell you I certainly would not have allowed that to happen!

The point is, I could really help the Malaysian and U.S. authorities gain the biggest return for the benefit of restoring the greatest amount of funds to Malaysia's 1MDB. I really know these things better than anyone else, and I know how to create the best deals! I can guarantee I'd do a much better job of getting the highest price, say, for the residential and hotel properties in New York and Los Angeles, if the powers that be in the U.S. would only let me help them.

Naturally, in return for my efforts, I'd want Malaysia and Singapore to drop the Interpol Red Notice that each has put out on me and the U.S. DoJ to drop its absurd and outrageous warrant for my arrest on trumped-up charges of bribery and money laundering. I think that's only fair. Some people in the press had viciously attacked me by saying that my offer to cooperate and to help the authorities restore assets to 1MDB is a desperate effort to bargain for my freedom, but that's unfair. If the authorities say that these properties were acquired and paid for with misappropriated funds, well, I agree that those funds should rightfully be returned to 1MDB. By the same token, I don't think anybody would want to be confined, like in exile as I am, thanks to carrying around an Interpol Red Notice that prevents me from traveling anyplace else.

What I had hoped was that, by cooperating and working assiduously to help the Malaysian government regain the funds that had been misappropriated, I would be able to show Prime Minister Mahathir how he and I—together—could restore the economic integrity of 1MDB, where Najib had clearly failed due to his own personal shortcomings. And frankly, due to his and Rosmah's ravenous greed.

Unfortunately, not even the leaders of my own sovereign country of Malaysia have seen fit to cooperate with me in this way. Nor has the U.S. Or anyone else.

Why is this so?

I firmly believe it is because the personal and political accusations against me amount to the quintessence of fake news, and it is patently obvious that, at this point, given the hyperbole and sensationalism that surrounds me now, it is no longer possible for anyone to get the real truth from the international press, and that goes as much for the most respected news outlets of the world as it does for the tabloids and the gossip rags, with their malevolently catchy headlines and salacious photographs. It also goes for governments and political leaders around the globe who happily participated in these innovative financial dealings and benefited handsomely from them. For all these reasons, I suspect it is no longer possible for me to get a fair hearing anywhere in the developed world—anywhere, that is, where international finance is of critical concern to the people of the world. Which is everywhere in the world, the way I see it.

Some time ago, I issued to the press the public statement that "I will not submit to any jurisdiction where guilt has been predetermined by politics and where there is no independent legal process." But this begs the question: Is there such a jurisdiction left anywhere in the world? I don't think so. Certainly not for me. Even the charges brought against me in the United States are founded superficially in the reprehensible lies and false allegations concocted and widely propagated by the corrupt leaders of the government of Malaysia. Government-sponsored fake news. Regardless, I stand by my statement.

Chapter 22

So here I am.

I sit in a castle built to my own specifications, not unlike the medieval castles of old, except that the defensive ramparts and walls are made of electronic wizardry and silicon and rare earths instead of stone and mortar and moats. I'm surrounded by the most sophisticated communications and surveillance security capabilities ever created by the mind of man, yet, ironically, I am as isolated as if I were alone on the International Space Station, floating 250 miles above the Earth.

Despite my state-of-the-art communications capabilities and, admittedly, for reasons largely unrelated to technology *per se*, I have lost touch with almost all of the business associates who, over the years, had become my closest friends and operatives. I'm led to believe that Seet Li Lin left Malaysia and went to the United States, where he works in the financial industry, on Wall Street, in New York City. While I also understand that Seet's business often takes him to Southeast Asia, the media reports claiming that I have been seen with Seet in Macau are totally fake. If you don't believe me, ask those tabloid journalists to produce a picture, an actual undoctored, unphotoshopped photograph of me and Seet together. They won't be able to.

Jasmine Loo, 1MDB's former chief counsel, left for Thailand and went into quiet private practice there. Or at least she tried. Because it's been all over the papers that she has recently surrendered to the Malaysian authorities. I should be hopeful that Jasmine's testimony can begin to set the record straight regarding our efforts to restore the financial integrity and economic power of 1MDB, but I'm not very optimistic about that. In truth, I have no doubt that the legal, prosecutorial deck is as stacked against her as it is me.

Yak Yew Chee is just one of perhaps a dozen former banking and business associates who, somehow, have simply disappeared, some of them under mysterious circumstances. Maybe, like me, they've simply been forced to go into hiding. I just don't know. Riza Aziz, Najib's stepson, continues to run Red Granite Pictures out of West Hollywood, California. Of course, my closest confidante and friend, Fat Eric, is dead.

For a time, Tarek Obaid and Patrick Mahony apparently attempted to refocus their "entrepreneurial" efforts on turning PetroSaudi into a bona fide profitable oil exploration and extraction firm. Neither of them are, by any stretch of the imagination, true, industry-savvy Big Oil men, and, therefore, their chances for success are slim at best, particularly when you consider that they no longer have the financial backing of 1MDB—or, for that matter, of any of the Middle Eastern wealth funds. Presently, they are both under investigation for bank fraud and facing potential charges in Switzerland, but it seems unlikely that indictments will ever be handed down. Beyond them, and to the best of my knowledge, however, none of my other friends and business associates have ever been criminally indicted in connection to 1MDB.

Speaking of the Middle East, hard on the heels of the release of the DoJ report at the start of its investigation and with all the swiftness and decisiveness that Middle Eastern governments are famous for, Al Qubaisi and Al Husseiny—who had previously only been fired and removed from their posts as the heads of IPIC and Aabar, respectively—were both arrested, tried, convicted, and sentenced to long prison terms of something like ten to fifteen years for each of them. You must understand that, on one hand, Middle Eastern governments like the one in Abu Dhabi turn on the whim of the ruling royal families, and there is generally little or no, so-called democratic due process, particularly if one upsets the crown prince. And let's not overlook the fact that Qubaisi and Husseiny were convicted of crimes within the UAE against IPIC and Aabar; they were *not* convicted of crimes by Malaysia directly in connection with 1MDB. Again, among all of these and many other players, no one has been accused or indicted for alleged criminality in connection with the management of 1MDB—except me.

Tim Leissner is a case in point. Leissner was initially banned from working in Singapore's financial industry for a period of ten years, and then, when more of the facts about his direct involvement were revealed, he was banned for life. In America, the U.S. Financial Industry Regulatory Authority cut right to the chase and banned him from the American securities industry for life. Leissner agreed to forfeit nearly forty-four million dollars to the DoJ on behalf of 1MDB in return for avoiding prosecution. And let's be fair: Leissner's forty-four million dollars is chicken feed compared to the $700 million that I have already willingly restored to the DoJ as a matter of good faith in trying to help them clean up this whole unfortunate mess.

Then there's all the big banks and multinationals that remain, to this day, under the microscope of the DoJ 1MDB probe. Deloitte and KPMG have each already paid fines of eighty million dollars to the government of Malaysia; AmBank has paid a fine of $700 million. Falcon Bank was forced to shut down altogether, a fate it truly deserved for the corrupt way that Al Qubaisi ran it. But behind them is a virtual conga line of more than twenty other financial institutions based in different countries all around the world that remain under scrutiny and which will soon very likely face similarly massive fines as a result of the ongoing DoJ investigation. They include such prestigious names as J.P. Morgan and Credit Suisse Singapore and Deutsche Bank Singapore and Malaysia.

And then there's the granddaddy of them all: Thus far, Goldman Sachs has paid out a mind-blowing five billion dollars in fines and settlements with the U.S. Department of Justice. As for Gary Cohn, the president of Goldman who had endorsed and eagerly pursued aggressive business dealings with 1MDB, Cohn moved on from the bank to accept an appointment to President Trump's National Economic Council.

Here's the thing: All of these fines and settlements assessed against the major financial institutions of the world—and, no doubt, the ones to come—have all been paid with no admission of any wrongdoing. Things may have gotten screwed up with the operations of 1MDB, but I could never have accomplished all that I did manage to accomplish—which you have to agree was pretty phenomenal—without the help and cooperation of all of these storied and internationally respected institutions and the dozens of executives that ran them.

Let's also not forget all the international and domestic bank regulatory agencies and internal corporate compliance departments that approved—or at least, let through—so many of my innovative investment ventures. Oh yes, I freely admit that I tried as much as possible to avoid them, and urged my business partners as well to always try to work around the regulators, but that was only in the interests of *getting things done*. It was simply a matter of cutting the bureaucratic red tape that everyone in business, or who must deal with government entities, simply despises. Nor could the regulators and compliance officers be avoided entirely. In fact, if you look at the record, every deal I crafted and orchestrated had to be signed off on, in one way or another, by bank regulators and corporate compliance departments—or by Prime Minister Najib himself.

My point is, in all of these 1MDB investigations, from the U.S. to Switzerland to Singapore to Malaysia, you'll also find no one accusing the regulators of serious wrongdoing—negligence, perhaps even gross negligence—but no criminally indictable wrongdoing. Last, don't forget that all of those tax havens, like Panama and the Cayman Islands and the Seychelles—or even the Geneva Freeport so favored by Al Qubaisi—they are all, to this day, in full operation and doing just fine. There are no legal authorities that I know of who are accusing them of any wrongdoing either.

Where is the justice in all of this?

A number that gets kicked around a lot these days in the aftermath, in both the financial press and the sensationalist tabloids, is the accusation that $4.5 billion was "stolen" from 1MDB, but that is so false. In fact, in November 2018, none other than *Forbes* magazine, the world-respected American financial magazine that has been published for over a hundred years, since 1917, got it right when they plainly stated that the capital in the 1MDB fund—using *Forbes*'s own words now—was "incorrectly managed." I couldn't agree more. If all of these banks and investment institutions and their executives had done the right thing, none of them would be in the predicament that they all are presently in, facing prosecution and punishment for their financial indiscretions. All as a result of their colossal mismanagement of the business they conducted with the Malaysian sovereign fund, not to mention with me and all of my associates at Wynton Group and Jynwel Capital and elsewhere.

When you've gotten through all of those financial industry players, that leaves only one other group to consider the role they played. Who, you ask? Why, the lawyers, of course.

Ha! The lawyers? Well, you know how it is with lawyers; they are always the ones who come through utterly unscathed and squeaky clean. After all, everybody knows that you need the lawyers to write up the court settlements that must include that important absolving legalese language that indicates "no admission of wrongdoing." And then the lawyers generally get to keep their usurious fees!

After many months during which nothing seemed to be happening, I took the chance of reaching out to a still-influential individual who managed to hang on to her position within the new, post-UMNO Malaysian regime. It goes without saying that I cannot identify this person, other than to say that she was something of a friend and, let's just say, sympathetic to me and my cause. I'll call her Faith, because I actually called her on the phone and I tried to convince her, in good faith, that I very much wanted to negotiate my return to my homeland as a citizen in good standing so that I can correct the many things that have gone wrong with the 1MDB wealth fund.

"I'm the only person who can fix things and make it right," I implored.

Faith responded, "From what I'm hearing, Jho, if you are really serious about wanting to return to Malaysia, the government will accept nothing less than your surrender on arrival for immediate arrest and incarceration and, from there, to stand for prosecution in the courts. They're adamant about it, Jho."

"But why?" I retorted.

"My god, Jho," Faith sighed. "They're prosecuting the prime minister! Do you think they'd do anything less to you?"

I refused to accept this. "What about a reprieve, or a pardon?" I pressured. "Some arrangement where I could come back and be permitted to restore 1MDB to the stature it had before all of this bad business with Najib? For the benefit of all of Malaysia."

"I've looked at the statutes, Jho, and I'm afraid that no legal mechanism exists anyplace in Malaysia law for the granting of a reprieve. It just doesn't exist."

It's a damn shame. It should be clear from what I've just explained to you that, in the United States and Europe, precisely this sort of mechanism gets applied all the time, as far as I can see. It's no big deal. So why me?

―――

From time to time, we have a security alert here. Alarms go off, sirens whine, red lights flash in the major corridors, and my own personal amber alert rings into my cell phones—all half dozen of them at once—as an urgent text message. It means we have had a breach somewhere on the perimeter of the compound, and a small but well-armed contingent of my personal security guards fans out along the walls and razor-wire fences looking for potential intruders. Honestly, when this happens, it looks deplorably like a paramilitary force in some dictatorial banana republic double-timing out to protect the self-appointed, all powerful, and ruthless monarch. We go on lockdown, steel doors automatically shut, secret infrared-detecting cameras turn on, looking for warm bodies. It's a deplorable way to live.

The perpetrators of these breaches are almost always some large jungle animal out there, run amok of one of the sensors in some perimeter fence, or a large tree branch that has fallen and crushed a wall. One time, amusingly enough, it was one of my security team who hit the gas instead of the brake and crashed a heavily armed Hummer through a little-used security gate at the rear of the compound. Yet these alarms, I have lately noticed, seem to be going off more frequently, and I am beginning to become suspicious of the eerily grinning, almost gratuitous reassurances of my mostly Chinese security team (Did I mention before they are mostly Chinese? Perhaps I didn't.) oh-so-cavalierly telling me that it was "just an animal caught in the fence" or "a tree has fallen across a power line." Why do I feel like they are flipping me off behind my back?

After all, the people who blew up my limousine are still out there, even though I have no idea who they were or why they did what they did, much less who put them up to it. Could some of these recent security alerts be renegade assassins at the gate? I don't know, and what's more troubling is that I no longer trust what the guards are telling me, that they're all harmless false alarms. I cannot fathom what anyone would gain by killing me, except, I suppose, some measure of revenge for some slight they might feel I had done to them. Sometimes it keeps me up at night, thinking about things like that.

In Malaysia, Prime Minister Mahathir's fragile, reformist government coalition fell apart in February 2020, after less than two years in office. Say what you want about the integrity—or lack of it, if you prefer—of the UMNO; the party may thrive on money and loyalist patronage, but it knows how to govern a country—and how to stay in power. Or, at least, it used to know. There is so much I could do for them, but it doesn't look like I'll be able to go back there any time soon.

Over in America, the Department of Justice investigation agonizingly plods on, and probably will do so for many years to come. Most recently, in May 2023, they convicted and sent to prison a couple of Goldman Sachs executives, but as is so pathetically typical in these cases, the people who were convicted were middle-management types, while the C-suite execs continue to run free.

On the other hand, if the DoJ gets frustrated enough with their foundering investigation of 1MDB, who knows but that they may press the State Department to agree to extradite the fugitive Guo Wengui back to China in return for sending *me* to the United States. It could happen. It's no secret that the DoJ—and the FBI, for that matter—would really like to talk with me about a few things. Such an exchange, me for Guo, has been suggested repeatedly in editorial opinion pieces published in several of the most important newspaper in the States, like the *NYT*, the *WSJ*, and the *WPO*—the same ones that contributed so viciously to bringing down the Malaysian financial empire I was trying to build and that, I assure you, I would have succeeded in building if people would have just cooperated. None of these American papers appear to be willing, once and for all, to let the whole damn thing alone so that everyone can move on.

And then there is China, within whose geographical jurisdiction I am currently permitted to reside without interference, in relative safety, and without any threat of legal jeopardy from the state, at least for the time being. However, the Chinese Communist Party, the Chinese government, is not a government whose political actions may be described as "predictable" in any sense of the word. They do what they want, when they want. Nevertheless, one often can ascribe a certain perceptible component of objective, core *utility* that seems, at the very least, to be a common, driving, connective theme in the decisions they make and the directives they issue, both domestically and internationally. Meaning I think, that right now, at least, I am relatively safe, as long as the CCP thinks that it might still have some practical or political use for me, even if, at this particular moment, they haven't decided what that use might be. God forbid that use should become trading me to the U.S. DoJ in return for Guo Wengui! It's almost funny, but it's entirely conceivable they could, quite cavalierly, just grow weary of me, decide that I'm useless to them, and throw me the hell out of the country (if and when I run out of money, that is).

So, as if the present state of my mind-numbing isolation wasn't enough, I live, also, precariously on a knife edge. There is no way of knowing how long my circumstances will stay as they are now. The only thing I do know is that they will not stay this way indefinitely; something, somewhere, will eventually change everything, whether for the better or for the worse, for me. I'll just have to deal with it; that's all.

But you know, sometimes when I'm sitting up at night, late and alone, I turn off the television, I log off my computer, and I mute my phones, whichever ones I happen to have with me, and I muse about what could have been, if only—

You might think of it this way: I was like the master architect and general contractor for the building of a huge, magnificent family mansion. In order to accomplish that task, I would have to hire all sorts of specialized professional subcontractors, from carpenters and plumbers and electricians and masons to interior designers and artisan painters and so on, each an expert in their particular craft. I would have wanted each of these craftspeople to do their part in the project without worrying about—or even asking about—what the other craftspeople were doing. Yes, of course, everything had to be properly organized and intricately coordinated for the project to be successful. But coordinating everything was my job, not theirs. If I could mix metaphors here a little bit (with your forgiveness), there's that old expression that too many chefs in the kitchen spoil the broth. Well, I found that I could get things done a lot faster if I was the only person in the kitchen holding the stirring spoon in my hand.

Or I was the maestro on the podium with the baton in my hand, directing the world-class symphony in which each member of the orchestra need only play their own instrument to perfection. Only I would ensure that it all came harmonically together with perfection; no one else needed to know the particulars of precisely how I was going to achieve that perfection, for the extreme benefit of every player involved, as well as the pleasure of the listening audience.

Better in fact that they shouldn't know, so that they may concentrate solely on executing their own part in my plan.

Or other times, other nights, I think of myself as the writer and master choreographer of a vast and elegant European-style ballet, in which all of the performers must move in precise unison and harmony to create a breathtaking display of dance in its most sublime form. If only one player moves out of step, the entire effect is ruined, but if every one of them dances their part flawlessly and integrally, everything coalesces, everything moves as one intricately coordinated creation. The effect is a vision of pure, celestial rapture. The problem for me and for 1MDB was that too many of my players simply blew their parts.

And you know, the more I think about it, the more I absolutely believe that, if all of these people hadn't had so much greed, they'd all be a lot richer today.

Afterword

The incredible saga of the 1 Malaysia Development Berhad scandal, commonly referred to simply as 1MDB, is by no means over. It is widely believed that Jho Low continues to reside in China; the Chinese Communist Party displays no compulsion to turn him over to Western authorities. Most recently, Al Jazeera and other news organizations[1] have reported that Jho has been seen in Macau, freely walking the streets and dining in exclusive restaurants in the company of several of his long-time associates. Meanwhile, former Malaysian Prime Minister Najib and First Lady Rosmah are likely to be embroiled in court proceedings for many years to come. Criminal and civil investigations into the scandal and efforts to recover billions of dollars of stolen money are ongoing in several nations, including Malaysia, the United Kingdom, Switzerland, and the United States. Yet Jho Low's sphere of influence—as well as his circle of security—may be beginning to crumble. Recently, Jasmine Loo, the former director and legal counsel of 1MDB, surrendered

---

1   Mary Ann Jolley, "1MDB Fugitive Jho Low Placed in Macau as Associates in Spotlight," *Al Jazeera*, May 30, 2023, https://www.aljazeera.com/economy/2023/5/30/1mdb-fugitive-jho-low-hiding-in-macau-malaysian-authorities-say.

to Malaysian police authorities.[2] Others involved in the scandal are likely to follow.

One thing is clear: The final chapter of Jho Low's story is yet to be written, and the full, outrageous truth about the operations of 1MDB has yet to be revealed.

—*H. P. Brunner*

---

2   Austin Camoens, "Ex-1MDB Lawyer Jasmine Loo Arrested after Turning Herself In, Says IGP," *The Star*, July 13, 2023, https://www.thestar.com.my/news/nation/2023/07/13/ex-1mdb-lawyer-jasmine-loo-arrested-after-turning-herself-in-says-igp.

About the Author

Photography by E-J Lim

An international banker for more than forty-five years, Hans Peter Brunner began his career with Credit Suisse (CS), where he worked for twenty-seven years, eventually specializing in private banking.

Brunner was the first Swiss banker in China, opening CS's representative office in Beijing in 1985. Three years later, he was promoted to head of North Asia, overseeing people working in offices in South Korea, Beijing, and Hong Kong. Under Brunner's leadership, the North Asian region became one of the most profitable areas of CS.

Later, Brunner left CS to become chief operating officer of the Asian region of Coutts International, based in Singapore. By 2000, he had risen to CEO, based in Zurich.

In 2010, Brunner became head of BSI Bank's Singapore-based Asia operations, building it from virtually the ground up into a highly profitable operation with more than two hundred employees, many of whom had followed him from Coutts to BSI.

His awards include being voted Outstanding Private Banker, Asia Pacific, by *Private Banker International* in 2008 and Asian Private Banker of the Year 2010 by *Asian Private Banker* in 2011.

A Swiss citizen, Brunner resides in Singapore with his wife of thirty-eight years. They have two sons.